Dead Men's Bones

A Detective Inspector McLean Mystery

JAMES OSWALD

PENGUIN BOOKS

PENGUIN BOOKS

UK | USA | Canada | Ireland | Australia
India | New Zealand | South Africa

Penguin Books is part of the Penguin Random House group of companies
whose addresses can be found at global.penguinrandomhouse.com.

Penguin
Random House
UK

First published in Penguin Books 2014

001

Copyright © James Oswald 2014
All rights reserved

The moral right of the author has been asserted

Set in 12.75/15 pt Garamond MT Std
Typeset by Jouve (UK), Milton Keynes
Printed in Great Britain by Clays Ltd, St Ives plc

ISBN: 978-1-405-3127-4

www.greenpenguin.co.uk

MIX
Paper from
responsible sources
FSC® C018179

Penguin Random House is committed to a
sustainable future for our business, our readers
and our planet. This book is made from Forest
Stewardship Council® certified paper.

This one's for the Bobs – Duncan, Elspeth, Fingal, Hector and Magnus. Thanks for all the Ham Nights and beer.

I

The pain is everywhere.

It pulses through his head as if there's a hole in his skull and someone is squeezing his brain in time to his heartbeat. It shoots through his veins like acid, burning him from the inside. It grinds in his joints even though he is motionless. It smothers him like a blanket made of fire.

He doesn't know where he is. There is only the darkness surrounding him and the echoing roar in his ears and the all-consuming agony. Is he back in Afghanistan? Has he gone the way of Bodie and Jugs? Trodden on one of those towelhead IEDs? No. That was then. He did his tour, survived. For all the good it did him.

He remembers the city, the secret life of the street people. His people. He'd been safe there, for a while. He'd steadied himself, built a life of sorts. Something he could understand, fighting for survival, hustling for the next hit of booze.

Calm. Try to be calm. Let the training kick in. He's been in worse situations than this, surely. Just needs to get his shit together. Easier said than done with the pounding in his head, the itching all over his skin, the sandpaper in his hips and knees and shoulders.

Slowly the panic subsides, leaving just the pain. He can cope with that. Focus beyond it. Try to work out what's going on. He flexes his hands, grunts as the pain lances up his arms. The noise is a reassurance, something he can understand, and he feels the restraint on his left wrist give a little. Concentrate on that. Use that. Ignore the agony sapping his energy. He works at the strap like a terrier with a rat. Tenacious, stubborn, fixated.

When it gives it's as if someone's put a bullet through his brain. The darkness explodes in a kaleidoscope of colours, swirling and flashing even as he can feel himself going under. He grits his teeth; chokes out a short, sharp bark. Half triumph, half defeat. Lets his freed hand fall down by his side as he gathers his strength for the next battle.

The head strap first. Sweat-slick fingers struggle with a buckle pulled too tight. It seems to take hours before it finally clicks loose. He'd hoped the release of pressure would ease the pounding in his head, but if anything it worsens. Touching his forehead, the skin is rough and puckered, the point of contact exploding in fire.

He has known agony before. Training for Special Forces they did things to your body most people wouldn't believe. This is far, far worse. It's only the straps tied tight around his ankles that keep him from falling when he tries to sit up. The effort of untying them almost kills him. There is nothing he can do to stop himself slithering to the floor. At least it's cold, soothing the parts of his skin that come into contact. He hugs it like a child hugs its mother, desperately clinging to that tiny relief.

It is only transient, the cooling touch inflaming his skin to new levels of torture. As if the stone has become sandpaper, rasped across flesh already raw. Salt and lime rubbed into the wounds.

He staggers to his feet. Steadies himself on the gurney. There is light here. Real light, not the fireworks that have filled his vision since he first tried to move. Soft and low, it barely illuminates the room. Still, what he sees is enough to bring the panic bubbling back up his throat like vomit.

It is a torture chamber. He is surrounded by a collection of apparatus designed only to inflict pain. Needles on long mechanical arms, boxes with wires looped around them, crocodile clips lined up on chrome rails. Bottles of coloured fluids, poisons, acids.

He pushes away from them, recoiling in horror, and as he does so he glimpses movement across the room. Glass, a mirror, an unfamiliar figure echoing his own ungainly movements. It's too dark to see clearly, but he staggers towards it anyway. Closer and closer, not quite able to say what is wrong with the image he is seeing.

And then it is there. Glaring out at him in the half-light. The face. His face. But the face of a demon. Wild eyes staring. Black swirls curling over cheeks and nose, forehead and shaven pate. He looks down at his arms and sees the patterns writhe and snake across his body. They are in him: alien, spectral creatures under his skin, devouring him.

The panic hits full on. Adrenalin sweeps everything else away. There is only running. He crashes through doors, down empty corridors, oblivious to anything but the fear. There is no direction to his flight, no plan beyond getaway.

And then he is outside. White snow blizzarding out of a night sky. He hardly notices his nakedness as he runs

3

from the building. Barely feels the icy cold on his feet or the ripping of low branches against his battered skin. His terror is so complete that he doesn't even notice when the land runs out. Arms and legs pumping as momentum carries him off the cliff and down and down.

2

'Jesus wept, but it's cold.'

Detective Inspector Tony McLean stamped his feet in the ankle-deep snow, trying desperately to get the circulation going. He stuck his red-raw hands under his armpits in search of warmth, all too aware that he'd come out without really thinking through where he was going. Roslin Glen was a wonderful spot in the summer, the River North Esk burbling through a narrow gorge cut deep into the sandstone. It widened out here, where the road to Rosehall and Dalkeith switched up the hillside, and was normally a sheltered suntrap. Not today though. Today the wind was funnelling up the river, swirling the snow in eddies that stung against any exposed skin.

'Should've brought a coat with you, sir. Gets a bit parky here at times.' Detective Sergeant Laird, Grumpy Bob to friend and foe alike, looked like someone's grandad at Christmas. He was wrapped in a quilted jacket, heavy gloves on his hands and a bright yellow knitted bobble hat keeping his balding head warm. The cold wind had turned his cheeks and the tip of his nose red. Well, it was either that or a lifetime of drink. Or both.

'You any idea where we're supposed to be going?' McLean swivelled on his feet, taking in the entirety of the car park. There were a couple of squad cars, a Scene Examination Branch Transit van and a rusty old Peugeot estate car parked close by, but no sign of any people. This time of year, and with the snow still falling out of a sky the colour of an old bruise, it was hardly surprising. You'd have to be a hardy dog walker to chance not getting lost.

'River's this way, I think.' Grumpy Bob motioned past the nearest car. A path of sorts had been bashed through the snow, though it was being filled in again. Looking up, you should have been able to see the castle on its rocky promontory. Possibly even the chapel, if memory served. No chance of that today, though. McLean started to trudge along the track, but as he passed close to the SEB van, its side door slid open, releasing a blast of warmth, the unmistakable aroma of real coffee and Detective Constable Stuart MacBride.

'You're here, sir.'

'That much would appear to be obvious, Constable.' McLean peered past him into the van, and saw a couple of scene-of-crime officers huddling around what looked like a portable gas heater, something Health and Safety would no doubt frown upon if anyone brought it to their attention.

'Don't suppose you've got a spare jacket in there or anything?'

It might have been fluorescent yellow with 'Strathclyde Water' written across it in large blue letters, but it was warm. McLean hugged his newly acquired jacket close as he followed MacBride and Grumpy Bob down a narrow footpath away from the car park and deeper into the glen. The trees growing either side linked overhead to form a tunnel of sorts. They shielded him from the worst of the wind, but threatened to dump snow on the unwary at any moment.

'What are we looking at, Constable?' McLean asked, as the path opened up across a small grass field of miserable sheep.

'Dead body in the river, sir. Must've fallen in somewhere upstream. There's been a lot of water running through lately. Swept it down until it hit the rocks just a ways up ahead.'

They clambered over a broken stile and into a more forested area. Here the snow had hardly settled on the ground but was just a thin dusting, sufficient to make the going slippery. The steep slope down to the water's edge didn't help either. Somehow McLean managed to make it without falling over, stepping on to a flat rock that protruded out into the water. A few paces away, a couple of uniform officers were huddled into their own bright jackets, breath steaming in the Baltic air.

'Down there?' McLean indicated the river where it cut a narrow channel between the flat rocks. He could hear the water echoing below. The nearest uniform nodded. A couple of SOC officers were busy setting up some kind of pulley system and framework over the channel. They both wore heavy-duty wet weather gear and the kind of helmets favoured by kayakers and potholers. No doubt they'd drawn the short straw when it was decided who was going to recover the body.

'Who found it?' McLean asked the constable as he inched closer to the edge, wary of ending up headfirst in the North Esk.

'Local from the village. Walks his dogs here every day. Bloody nutter if you ask me.' The uniform officer looked slightly sheepish, before adding 'Sir.'

McLean said nothing, just peered down into the gully. The whole of the glen had been cut from the sandstone over millennia. In places the cliffs were well over a hundred foot high. Here, the river had met harder rock, and ancient spates had pushed vast boulders up against one another to form a barrier. The narrow channel into which he was looking was just one of many routes the water took around and through this obstacle before carrying on its journey to the Firth of Forth. There was all manner of detritus deposited: fallen trees; plastic carrier bags; even the occasional shopping trolley. And now the naked body of a man.

It was difficult to see in the half-light, but McLean was fairly sure it was a man's body. The water hadn't been kind, tumbling it over, bending arms and legs in ways they were never meant to go. The head wasn't visible at all, wedged hard into a jumble of rocks. He shivered from something other than cold as he contemplated the possibility that it might be missing entirely. It wouldn't be the first time someone had tried to make their job more difficult that way, and it was never pleasant.

What struck him first about the body though was its colour. Not unusual to see a black man in a city the size of Edinburgh, of course, but there was something not quite right about the colour of this man's skin. Or maybe it was the texture.

'You ready for us to bring it up?'

McLean looked up into the face of one of the SOC

officers, much closer than he'd been expecting. The constant roar of the water made it almost impossible to hear people moving about.

'Can't do anything useful with it down there. Yes. Bring it up.'

He stood back and waited while they lowered a small stretcher into the gap. One of the SOC officers played out a rope tied securely to a nearby boulder, while his colleague climbed carefully down to the water. After an age, in which McLean's feet began to lose all feeling, the SOC officer clambered back out again and gave the thumbs up. The two together then hauled the stretcher back, swinging it over, before placing it carefully down on the flat rock surface.

'Bugger had his head jammed right into a crack. Pain in the arse getting him out of there.' The SOC officer was busy coiling up ropes while his colleague dismantled the frame and pulley. They had the look about them of men who wanted to get back to the Transit van and its nice little gas heater. McLean couldn't really blame them.

He crouched down beside the body, still twisted and broken from its time in the river. He couldn't see the man's face without touching the body, but it was very definitely a man. That much was shrivelled and small but evident nonetheless. What was also evident was that the man wasn't, in fact, black. There were a few traces of pale white skin visible on his body, but they were very few.

The rest was covered from head to foot, arms, hands, fingers, and yes, even his penis, in a dark swirl of tattoos.

3

'. . . getting reports of a shooting incident at a farmhouse in north-east Fife. A man thought to be Mr Andrew Weatherly shot and killed his wife and two daughters before turning the gun on himself. We cannot at this time confirm that the man in question was indeed the MSP for Fife West . . .'

McLean thumbed the button on the steering wheel that changed the channel on the radio, searching for some soothing music. He had enough troubles of his own without listening to the woes of other forces. Except of course they were all one big happy family now, Police Scotland. Or Greater Strathclyde, as the wags had it. Not far from the truth, either.

A gap appeared in the traffic ahead and he accelerated, enjoying the surge of power that took him forward a good fifty yards before he had to brake and slow again. Commuting was hell, and not for the first time he missed his old flat in Newington. Being able to walk to work had its benefits, even in this cold and snowy weather. Easier to think to the rhythm of feet on pavement than this stop-start slow-moving car park.

At least the car was working fine, and he didn't have to worry about it dissolving in the salt spread on the roads. His old Alfa was away being restored, and he couldn't help thinking its indisposition had been a blessing in disguise.

He was just about to take a side street, hopeful that it might cut the journey time by a couple of seconds, when his phone rang, loud through the stereo speakers. A less welcome benefit of the modern car; he tapped the button on the dashboard that activated the hands-free.

'McLean.'

'Where the hell are you?'

Good morning to you too, Detective Superintendent Duguid, sir. McLean glanced at the clock in front of him, orange digits showing that there were still twenty minutes to go before eight o'clock.

'Currently, sir? I'm in my car in a traffic jam on Lothian Road. Where are you?'

'Don't get cheeky with me, McLean. You were meant to be at the morning briefing here, half seven.'

That was the first he'd heard of it. He'd been taken off active duty after the incident in his attic, ostensibly while his broken leg healed, but also until he'd completed a seemingly endless series of counselling sessions with his favourite hack psychiatrist, Professor Matt Hilton. The visit out to Roslin Glen the day before had been his first proper case in months. 'Morning briefing, sir? What morning briefing?'

A short pause, as if the superintendent were thinking deep thoughts. 'Ah, right. You're not on that team now, are you?'

Duguid's brief stint in charge of the running of the whole station had been mercifully cut short by the creation of Police Scotland. That was probably the only positive thing anyone in plain clothes could come up with about the whole sorry affair, though. With CID having now become the Specialist Crime Division and being split into a bewildering number of teams, each specializing in some different facet of the Scottish criminal mind, it was a full-time job just working out where you were meant to be from day to day.

'Never mind.' No apology for his mistake, but then that was never Duguid's style. 'Just come and find me as soon as you get here, OK? I've a job for you.'

The line went dead, the superintendent's voice replaced with a slow fade-up of the radio, playing some chirpy modern pop song McLean didn't recognize. He stared ahead for a moment before realizing that the car in front had begun to pull away. Dipped the clutch and dropped a gear, gunning the engine to catch up. He'd been looking forward to making a start on the investigation into the body found in Roslin Glen. As was so often the case, it looked like life had other plans.

'I know it's a bloody disaster. Couldn't be worse timing either. And it's not as if we haven't got enough on our plates here.'

Detective Superintendent Charles Duguid had somehow managed to keep hold of the big office on the third floor in the upheavals following the creation of Police Scotland. In theory he was meant to be in charge of Divisional Crime and Public Protection for what had once been Lothian and Borders, so it made a certain kind of sense. McLean still wished its former occupant had come back to take up the new post. Alas, wishes had a habit of going unanswered in these parts.

In a small nod to his predecessor, or perhaps because

he had a pathological need to know what was going on, Duguid had taken to leaving his office door open some of the time. McLean stood outside, half-listening to the phone conversation, trying to judge when it would be best to interrupt.

'You know what this is all about?' he asked of the secretary sitting at the desk just outside the office door.

'Something to do with that MSP shooting his family, I think. Horrible, horrible case.' She shook her head and went back to whatever she had been typing at her screen.

'Well, don't just stand there chatting up the secretaries, McLean. Get in here. And shut the door behind you.' Duguid stood just inside the doorway, impatient as ever. He had his phone in one hand and raised it back to his ear as McLean did as he was told.

'No. He's here now. I'll get it sorted, don't you worry about that, sir.'

McLean raised an eyebrow, not really expecting Duguid to explain himself. He wasn't disappointed; the superintendent rang off and dropped the phone on to his desk, slumping into the large leather seat with its back to the window before finally looking at him.

'How's the leg?'

McLean shifted his weight slightly. His hip still ached where he'd broken the bone several months earlier, but it was mending. The cold weather didn't help, though.

'Better, thank you. Still seeing the physio once a week, but it's not a problem.'

Duguid's eyes narrowed. He pulled a sheet of paper towards him, didn't look at it.

'Your initial psych evaluation says you're fit for work.' Almost as if the fact were a personal insult to him.

'I'm glad to hear it, sir. I've been back at work long enough.'

'Don't get all sarky with me, McLean. You heard about Andrew Weatherly, I take it?'

'The MSP? There was something on the radio this morning, but I didn't think it had been confirmed—'

'Oh, it's him right enough. Stupid wee bugger.' Duguid rubbed at his face with prehensile fingers, long and thin and with seemingly far too many joints. 'Looks like he's shot his wife and kids, then turned the gun on himself. Why the fuck would anyone do that?'

'I've really no idea, sir. Was he under a lot of stress?'

Duguid looked up at him like he was mad. 'What am I, his therapist? How the fuck should I know?'

McLean didn't answer. It was always best just to stand there and let whatever Duguid had to say roll over you. Deal with the fallout later.

'He was very well connected, was our Mr Weatherly. Sat on the Police Liaison Committee for one thing. His fingerprints are all over our beloved Police Scotland, too, so you can imagine how well this is all going down with our overlords. They want it tidied away as quickly as possible.'

'Is it not Fife's investigation? It happened on their patch.'

Duguid gave him a contemptuous glare. 'There's no "patches" any more. We're all one big fucking happy family, remember?'

McLean flexed his feet, tried not to bounce up and

down impatiently. Of course he knew about the new structures, but the old regions still existed within the Specialist Crime Division. There was no need for someone to go up to Fife and upset the locals, surely.

Duguid did the finger thing again, then slumped back in his chair. It squeaked alarmingly, tilting back as if it was going to tumble him to the floor.

'Look. Fife are on scene right now. Yes, it's their patch as you put it. But Weatherly's an MSP. He has a house here in Edinburgh, his business is based here. So whether Fife like it or not, we're involved.'

'What do you want me to do?'

'I'd have thought that was obvious, McLean. Do what you always do. Dig deeper than is really necessary. Complicate things.'

McLean frowned. This wasn't what he expected to be told. Not by Duguid.

'But I thought you said HQ—'

Duguid leaned forward, placed his elbows on the desk in front of him. 'Oh, this goes higher than HQ, McLean. Right up to the top. They want it tidied up nice and quickly. Tidied away like it never happened. Well, fuck that. An innocent woman and two young girls are dead. I don't care if their murderer killed himself. I want to know why he did it, and if that means putting a few noses out of joint, then so be it.'

The CID room was its usual hive of inactivity when McLean pushed his way through the door half an hour later. His brain was still reeling from the conversation with the superintendent; the sheer neck of the man never ceased to amaze. There was the small matter of who would take the blame when it all went to buggery, too. As it inevitably would. Not the first time he'd been set up for a fall; probably not the last.

'Morning, sir.' The voice that piped up from behind the opened door was fresh and eager, much like the chubby, scrubbed pink face that went with it. Detective Constable Stuart MacBride looked up from his desk.

'Morning, Constable. You the only one in?'

'Briefing in the main incident room, sir. DCI Brooks is bringing all the DIs and sergeants up to speed on current investigations.' Even as he said it, the constable's face furrowed into a frown that probably matched McLean's own.

'I must have missed the memo.' Still, it would explain Duguid's earlier confusion. 'Never mind, I've better things to spend my time on than listening to Brooks prattle on. You get anywhere with our mysterious tattooed man yet?'

MacBride shuffled briefly among the ordered folders on his desk, coming up with one that looked distressingly empty. At least it had the official code stencilled on the outside.

'Nothing yet. Body's at the mortuary waiting for a PM. I've had a word with Missing Persons. No one fitting the description. Can't really do much more until we know if it's suspicious or not.'

'He was naked, Constable. That seems pretty suspicious to me. If he'd just fallen in upstream, I'd have expected at least a few clothes.'

'He might've taken them off, sir. Isn't that what people

do sometimes, when they get really cold? The brain goes all weird and they think they're overheating. Think I read something somewhere . . .'

'Hypothermia madness. Yes, I suppose it could have been.' McLean shook his head. 'Well, we'll find out soon enough. You got a time for the PM yet?'

'No sir. I can call and find out.' MacBride reached for his phone.

'It can wait. I've another errand to attend to first. Is Ritchie about?'

'In Brooks's briefing along with everyone else. Anything I can help with?' The look of hope on the young constable's face was a sight to behold. Like a puppy desperate to be chosen from the basket. McLean could hardly bring himself to disappoint him.

'I need her special skills,' he said, searching for a diplomatic way of saying he'd rather not spend a couple of hours stuck in the car with MacBride when there was less eager company to be had. 'And she's friends with some of CID in Fife Constabulary, which might come in useful.'

'Fife?' MacBride's expression went from momentary confusion to wide-eyed understanding. 'Oh.'

'Yes. Oh. Duguid wants me to look into that bloody mess. If you've any sense you'll keep your head down here.'

4

In the end it would probably have been just as easy taking MacBride. Detective Sergeant Ritchie was clearly grateful when McLean dragged her from the useless morning briefing, but she looked tired and said very little as they drove across the city towards the bridge.

'Brooks really that bad to work for?' he tried, as they slowed to a crawl through the endless road works at the north end, where the new crossing landed in Fife.

'You have no idea.' Ritchie shook her head.

'Well, you're back on my team now. Might come to regret that, mind.' McLean dropped a gear and revved the engine, surging forward as the traffic finally freed up on the approach to Halbeath. There was a simple pleasure to be had in being pressed back into the seat by the power of the big V6. It sounded good, too, even if it was almost as inappropriate for his line of work as the classic that was being expensively rebuilt in a specialist workshop down in England. And quite literally a pain to get in and out of with his leg only recently out of its stookie.

Snow piled at the side of the road, grey with salt and grime; they sped past in silence. It was a long time since last he'd been out this way, but nothing much seemed to have changed. A few more modern warehouses on the outskirts of Kinross, perhaps, but what little money leached out of the capital evaporated the further north you went into the old Kingdom. Past Auchtermuchty and even the potholes felt like they'd been growing for decades.

McLean had printed out directions, but even so it took a couple of wrong turns and the helpful advice from a ruddy-faced farmer for them to finally find the place. Andrew Weatherly had not started life wealthy, if the sparse history of the man were true and not some media-spun fabrication, but he'd embraced the life of the country gentleman with great enthusiasm. His Fife residence was a large mansion, set far from the main road in a natural hollow at the end of a gentle valley. Rising up above it to the west, the largest hill in the area was swathed in deep snow, dark conifers marking out its flanks in angular blocks. It was undeniably a beautiful spot, a fact made harrowing by the terrible events that had taken place there.

A pair of uniform constables flagged him down before he could turn off the main road on to the drive. It was impossible to miss the journalists' cars parked all around; the outside broadcast vans and television crews. McLean's warrant card saw him through with nothing more than a raised eyebrow, but as he reached the end of the driveway, where it opened up to the front of the house, he was stopped again, this time by blue and white police tape.

'No point pissing them off any more than we have already.' He parked as close to the edge of the drive as he dared. Out of the warm car, the winter air hit like a slap to the face, a chill wind whistling down from the hill and going straight through him. McLean reached back into the car, dragged out his heavy woollen overcoat and pulled it on as another uniform approached.

'You the DI from Edinburgh, aye?'

McLean nodded, showed his warrant card again. Ritchie had climbed out of the car and was checking out the scene as she pulled on a pair of black leather gloves.

'SIO's over in the tent.' The officer nodded in the direction of a squat white construction a few yards away from the front door. McLean was about to head towards it, but a hand on his arm restrained him.

'I'll let him know you're here. Wouldn't want to muck up things for the forensics boys.'

McLean held the uniform's gaze for perhaps a little longer than was polite. He was an older man, a sergeant. Perhaps the same age as Grumpy Bob. Maybe it would have been wiser to have brought him along; there weren't many serving officers in the central region that Grumpy Bob didn't know at least in passing.

'You're right,' he said eventually. 'No point us getting in the way. Just give us a shout when you're ready.'

The old sergeant nodded, and wandered off at a leisurely stroll before disappearing into the tent.

'A bit bloody rude, wasn't he?'

McLean turned to see Ritchie leaning on the roof of the car, a scowl plastered over her freckled face. The effects of the cold wind didn't sit well with her short-cropped red hair.

'I seem to remember you being less than welcoming when I turned up at Donald Anderson's burial. No one likes another force sticking their nose in.'

'Isn't that what Police Scotland's meant to be all about, though? No more petty rivalries between regions. All in it together and all the other motivational bollocks I spent half of last year trying to understand.'

'Give it time. And try not to take it too personally.' McLean gave her what he thought was a friendly smile, got a weary one back in return. Then Ritchie's gaze shifted to something behind him, and she pushed herself upright as if coming to attention.

'Detective Inspector Tony McLean. Didn't think I'd be seeing you in these parts any time soon.'

McLean turned, recognizing the voice but taking a moment to place it. A tall, thin man approached, flanked by the uniform sergeant and a white-boiler-suit-clad crime scene photographer. He was wearing a white boiler suit as well, but had undone the top half, tying the arms around his waist in a loose knot.

'Jack?' McLean couldn't hide the question in his voice, even though he knew it must have sounded strange. He should have realized that a high-profile case in Fife would have had a high-ranking senior investigating officer. Detective Superintendent Jack Tennant was certainly that. And of all the people McLean could have hoped to find in charge, this was certainly his preferred option.

'I've not changed that much, have I?' The superintendent ran a hand over his forehead, chasing his receding hairline. It had been like that when McLean had first met him, must be nearly eighteen years ago. His face was a bit more lined now, thin, maybe unhealthily so. But he was undeniably the same man who'd taken a young constable on the fast track and taught him how to be a detective.

'Sorry,' McLean said. 'Just didn't expect to see you out here. I thought you were desk-bound these days.'

'You make it sound like a painful disease, Tony. Which I suppose it is, in a way. You know as well as I do that a case like this . . .' Tennant waved an arm in the general direction of the house. '. . . is way too important to be left to the people who know what they're doing.'

'I guess that's why they sent me out to get in the way then.'

Tennant cocked his head to one side at the remark, then turned his attention to Ritchie. 'And who is your new sidekick? Grumpy Bob getting too old?'

'Detective Sergeant Kirsty Ritchie, this is Detective Superintendent Jack Tennant. It is still just superintendent, isn't it?'

'Ritchie. You were in Aberdeen before, weren't you. Worked with DCI Reid.' Tennant talked in statements, not questions, as if he were reading a résumé from inside his head.

'Yes, sir. I transferred down about eighteen months ago.'

'Aye. Well.' The superintendent paused for a moment, then seemed to remember why they were all here. He turned to the uniform sergeant who had been eyeing McLean suspiciously throughout the conversation. 'See if you can't find us a couple more of these romper suits will you, Ben? I think it's time we showed our Edinburgh friends the bodies.'

5

They went into the house first. Whether that was on purpose, McLean wasn't sure. He was grateful nonetheless, as the cold had begun seeping into his bones. Heavy wool might keep the worst of the wind off, but it was useless if you were wearing flimsy leather shoes and had forgotten to bring a hat.

Inside, high-powered floodlights chased away even the most tenacious of shadows. Old wooden panelling lined the walls of the hallway from floor to ceiling, shiny under the harsh glare. In the centre, an ornate chandelier hung from a beautifully moulded ceiling rose. It glittered like a starlet's diamonds.

McLean stood in the doorway, taking in the scene as an army of white-suited forensic experts bustled around collecting evidence. Of what, he wasn't entirely sure; there didn't appear to be any mystery to the incident. On the other hand, Andrew Weatherly had been an important man, and other important men would be watching to see he got the treatment they felt he deserved.

'Can we go in?' He directed his attention to Detective Superintendent Tennant, but was answered by the nearest scene-of-crime officer, only her eyes and a stray tuft of auburn hair visible through her coveralls.

'Stick to the marked walkways. Touch nothing.' Brusque, and to the point.

McLean looked at the floor, a black and white chess-board of tiles scuffed by centuries of passing feet. A narrow path had been marked out with silver duct tape, leading straight towards the dark oak staircase. It was plenty wide enough to walk along without trouble, but he still felt that he might overbalance and tumble into the throng of SOC officers as he went.

Upstairs was a wide, carpeted landing not unlike the one in his own home back in Edinburgh. Doors led off to bedrooms; probably a shared bathroom as well. A couple of low dressers were piled up with the detritus of family life: a stack of clean towels waiting to go into the airing cupboard; some children's books in a haphazard heap; a moth-eaten old teddy bear with one eye missing. There were pictures on the walls between the doors, too – modern portraits of Andrew Weatherly's wife, mostly. She'd been a model, if memory served.

The duct-tape walkway continued, narrower up here, leading to an open door at the end of the landing. McLean sensed DS Ritchie a little too close behind him as he approached the room, almost as if she didn't want to be left behind in the gloom. He stepped further into the room than he would have liked, in order to give her space. Then wished he really hadn't.

It was the master bedroom; that much was obvious. Comfortably large, with two windows looking out over the front drive and the temporary forensic tent. Another pair of doors led off to the rear, probably an en-suite bathroom and dressing room. There was antique furniture, but McLean didn't really take it in. Dominating the wall opposite the door through which he'd stepped, a vast four-poster bed held a single occupant, sitting upright, propped up by pillows once white but now stained dark crimson.

Morag Weatherly had been in bed reading when her husband had shot her; the book was still clasped lightly in her hands, nestling in her lap. He must have used a rifle, because apart from the small hole in her forehead, there was no damage to her features at all. The same could not be said for the back of her skull. By the look of the wall behind her, it had exploded, painting blood and brain matter over the flock wallpaper in a dreadful halo. At least she would have died instantly, although if the expression on her pale face was anything to go by, she'd had enough time to realize what was happening.

'Has the pathologist been?' McLean turned away from the grim sight, certain it would take a lot more than that for it to leave him. DS Ritchie stared past him, her face almost as pale as that of the deceased. She had a hand pressed over her face and he could see her swallowing back the urge to vomit.

'Not here yet. Your chum Cadwallader's on his way up from Edinburgh.' Tennant still stood outside the bedroom, away from the view. McLean couldn't really blame him.

'No one nearer by?'

'Oh, plenty. But they sent you up, and we're not exactly short of detectives, either.'

McLean shook his head, partly at the idiocy of it all, partly in a vain attempt to dislodge the memory of Morag Weatherly's startled face. When he looked up again, Ritchie was still transfixed.

'Why don't you go downstairs and wait for Angus, Sergeant?' He reached out and touched her gently on the shoulder. The contact broke whatever spell had fallen over her with a shudder that ran through her whole body. Her gaze flicked to his face as if she'd just snapped out of a trance.

'Sorry, sir. Don't know what came over me. I'm not normally—'

'There's nothing normal about this. Not remotely.' McLean steered Ritchie out of the room and back on to the landing. 'Go see if you can't find whichever SOC van's got the kettle in it. And warn Angus what to expect when he gets here, eh?'

Tennant said nothing as DS Ritchie picked her way along the narrow duct-tape path, disappearing down the stairs into the glare of the spotlights. He waited until she was out of earshot before letting out a pent-up breath.

'Masterfully done. Been a while since I had to extract a detective from a crime scene like that.'

'Just didn't want her throwing up all over the carpet. You know what forensics are like if you so much as touch anything.'

'Still. I'd have expected better from Ritchie. Heard she was . . . what's the expression?'

'Best left unsaid.' McLean almost looked back into the bedroom, managed to stop himself at the last moment. 'Like I told her, not remotely normal, even for the likes of us. And I've a nasty feeling it's going to get worse.'

'I wish I could say you were wrong, Tony. I really do.' Tennant led the way back along the landing, past the stairs and on towards the other end of the house. The parallel lines of silvery tape stopped at another open door, and once again Tennant held back.

'That bad?' McLean asked. The superintendent merely nodded.

This room was smaller than the master bedroom, but not by much. It had two tall windows that looked out over low outbuildings behind the house, then to trees and the snow-covered hill rising up behind. The walls were decorated with an odd mixture of childish pictures of nursery rhyme favourites and posters of the latest boy-band sensations. Or at least that's who McLean assumed the slightly unwholesome-looking and under-dressed teenagers pouting at him were.

There were two beds, side by side but far enough apart to mark out individual territories. On the right-hand bed, the covers had been turned back, as if one of Weatherly's daughters had climbed out in the night, frightened by a noise, or a bad dream. McLean didn't have to look far to see where she had gone for comfort. She lay alongside her twin sister, their two heads poking out from the top of the duvet, nestled in soft, white, funereal pillows. Their faces were slack, identical. At least their eyes were closed, but their stillness and per-fect, pale skin were far more horrifying even than the violence that had been done to their mother.

'How did they die?' McLean noticed that once more Tennant had stayed outside.

'Won't know until the pathologist's been. Best guess is he smothered them with a pillow. Either that or some kind of poison.'

McLean looked around the room again, and noticed the two bedside tables, each holding an empty glass smeared with the last remains of the bedtime milk they had contained. He picked one up, heard the sharp intake of breath from Tennant at the misdemeanour. Ignored it. Sniffed the glass: it smelled of milk just starting to go sour; a touch of nutmeg maybe. Nothing immediately suspicious there. He put the glass back down again exactly where it had been, and turned slowly on the spot, all the while conscious of the tiny dead bodies lying just to his left.

Judging by the indentation in the empty bed, the girls had gone to sleep separately. Had one really awoken in the night, scared enough to climb in with her sister? Maybe so. Maybe she'd been woken by the shot that had killed her mother. Angus would be able to confirm his suspicions at the autopsy.

He took one last look at the girls. At a glance you really could believe they were just sleeping. But only at a glance. The whole room screamed the wrongness of what had happened here; the whole house did. It was no wonder Ritchie felt the way she had. He felt it too. He'd seen far too many crime scenes, far too many bodies down the years, but there was something uniquely horrific about this crime and the place where it had been committed.

Carefully retracing his footsteps, McLean stepped back out of the girls' bedroom to where Tennant waited.

'I guess we'd better go and see Weatherly then.'

The blast of fresh air as they walked out on to the gravel driveway was almost as cold as the stare McLean had received from the SOC officer when he put an over-booted foot on to the silver duct tape crossing the hallway. It was certainly more welcoming.

DS Ritchie was leaning against the bonnet of one of the SOC Transit vans, cradling a mug in her hands. Steam curled gently from the top.

'There'd better be more where that came from, Sergeant. Otherwise I'm going to have to pull rank on you.'

'It's OK, you can have it, sir. I've had one already.' Ritchie held out the mug. McLean was about to take it when another hand reached past and beat him to it.

'I believe superintendent outranks inspector?' Tennant grinned the grin of a man who has both secured a nice hot mug of tea and escaped a terrifying ordeal. He pointed at the pop-up tent in the middle of the lawn. 'Besides, you're meant to be over there, giving us the benefit of your big-city criminal insight.'

McLean sighed away the retort he wanted to give, trudged across the gravel and on to the snow-covered lawn. A uniform PC stood outside the tent, looking cold and miserable. He said nothing as McLean approached, and neither did he attempt to stop him going inside.

The tent had been erected over a stone statue. Some kind of Eros-with-birdbath design as far as McLean could make out. Two white-suited technicians were fiddling with a set of spotlights, the better to illuminate the deceased, but there was plenty of light filtering through the opaque plastic of the tent to see by.

He remembered the last time he'd met Andrew Weatherly. Some police reception he'd been bullied into attending on Jayne McIntyre's behalf. McLean knew of the man's reputation as a ruthless businessman, and vaguely recalled someone intensely interested and focused on you for all of the five seconds it took to be introduced and for him to judge whether or not you were of any use to him. McLean, of course, had been of no use whatsoever, and so was instantly forgotten. It hadn't bothered him at the time; he'd had run-ins with many powerful men over the years and there were plenty more worthy of contempt than Andrew Weatherly.

At least until today.

The MSP for Fife West had sat himself down in the snow, leaning his back against the statue. Shoved the rifle between his legs, the end of the barrel under his chin, and then pulled the trigger. Like his wife before him, the bullet had done most of its damage on the way out, leaving his face oddly slack but otherwise untouched. McLean walked around the edge of the tent, keeping away from the body until he was right in front of it, hunkering down for a better look. Andrew Weatherly's lips were oddly swollen and blistered, as if he'd burned them on something not long before he died. But what was most shocking was the look of utter, abject terror in his eyes.

6

'Sorry I bugged out back there, sir. Don't know what came over me.'

McLean risked a glance over at DS Ritchie as she sat in the passenger seat. You never got much daylight this far north in the winter, and dusk had brought with it heavy snow. Now they were crawling along the A92 in the general direction of Kirkcaldy, but they could have been closing in on the North Pole for all he could see. At least it was warm in the car, and his feet were slowly coming back to life.

'You find out anything useful from the forensics people?'

Ritchie shook her head. 'You know what they're like. Don't want to commit themselves at the best of times. Most of them thought the whole operation was a waste of time anyway.'

'And you don't think that's useful to know?'

Ritchie didn't comment. 'What about you, sir? Did Angus have anything to say? Don't think I've ever seen him looking so . . . I don't know. Careworn?'

Lights flared red through the swirling mess of snow. McLean hadn't been driving fast, but he felt the car slide a little as he dabbed the brakes. They closed on the ambulance they had been following all the way from the country residence of the late Andrew Weatherly MSP, now taking his mortal remains and those of his wife and two children back to Edinburgh City Mortuary. They really should have been going to Dundee; it was closer and had world-class facilities. But the powers that be wanted everything back in the capital. Where they could keep an eye on it.

'Angus has a thing about children,' he said after too long a silence. Then realized just what he'd said. 'Christ, that makes it sound like I don't. Like we weren't all treading on eggshells back there. It really doesn't help that we're being dragged into another force's patch, either. And don't start on about Police Scotland and one big happy family.'

Ritchie said nothing, which only made McLean feel worse about his outburst. The snow eased off a little, and visibility improved by a couple of yards. Without thinking, he pushed down on the throttle, speeding up until they were right behind the slow-moving ambulance. He was checking his mirror and starting to pull out before he realized what he was doing, eased off and let the gap grow to a sensible distance once more.

'That house.' Ritchie chose to say nothing about the driving. 'There was something very off about it.'

'How so?' McLean asked the question not because he didn't agree with her, so much as it was something he'd noticed himself but not been able to put a finger on. 'I mean, apart from the obvious, of course.'

'Well it's old, for starters, and that always makes a place creepy. The setting's pretty bleak too, stuck up the end of that long drive, away from any prying eyes, under that great big hill. How the hell did anyone know Weatherly had . . .' She stopped before uttering the words, as if by not saying them events might un-happen.

'Neighbouring farmer heard gunshots in the dark. He runs the local shoot, so he knew there shouldn't have been anyone out. Especially not at that time of the night. He called it in, and since Mr Weatherly is . . . was . . . such an important man, a squad car went straight out.' That much McLean had learned from Jack Tennant over a mug of purloined tea. 'I pity the poor bastard constable who found him sprawled out on the lawn like that.'

He shuddered, reached out and cranked the heater up to full. The temperature gauge on the dashboard said minus eight now, and had given up flashing. The cold that filled him was deeper still than that. A different kind of chill.

'So what do we do next?' Ritchie asked. 'I take it this investigation is top priority.'

'Until some sod decides they want it swept under the carpet, yes. We'll need to establish a timeline, Weatherly's movements leading up to . . .' McLean found he couldn't say the words either. 'And we'll have to make a stab at finding out some kind of motive, I guess. I'll get Mac-Bride to look into his business dealings. We'll have to set up interviews with his secretary, agent, anyone else in daily contact, really.'

The rest of the journey back to the city was taken up with similar talk. After a while Ritchie even took out her notebook and began scribbling down actions in it. Almost as if the more distance they put between themselves and the terrible house, the less of a hold it had on them. As he pulled into the car park at the back of the station and finally switched off the engine, McLean couldn't help wondering what that hold had been.

He was surprised and pleased to find Mrs McCutcheon's cat waiting for him when he finally arrived home. It sat in the middle of the large kitchen table, cleaning itself in that meticulous way that cats do. Whether it was really interested in him, or only there for the takeaway curry he'd picked up on the way, he couldn't be sure. There was plenty for the both of them anyway, and at least the cat never tried to drink his beer.

He almost dropped the bag and its precious contents when the doorbell rang, so alien was the sound.

'Mine,' McLean said to the cat as he headed out of the kitchen to see who had decided to pay him a visit. It took an embarrassing length of time to get the door unlocked and draw the bolts before he could open it. At least he managed to find the switch this time, bathing both porch and hall in light and revealing a short figure in a long, dark cloak standing on the threshold.

'Inspector. I hope I'm not intruding.'

McLean dredged the depths of his memory, knowing the face but quite unable to put a name to it. It was a friendly face, female and framed with an unruly tangle of greying black hair. She wore overlarge spectacles that made it quite difficult to see any other features, but he knew the voice, too. Then he saw the white dog collar and black shirt just visible through the folds of the heavy woollen scarf draped around her neck. The last time he'd seen the local minister she had been leading carol singers about her parish, but that was two years ago. Now he thought about it, they'd not been back last year.

'Minister . . . I . . . Do come in.' In the circle of light cast by the open door, he could see great clumps of snow not so much floating as plummeting down outside. The back end of his car was already covered.

'Many thanks.' The minister stepped inside, stamped her feet a couple of times on the mat, but didn't unbutton her cloak. 'It's Mary. Mary Currie. Don't worry. I never expected you to remember.'

Except that as soon as she'd started to say it, he had remembered. 'Sorry. I was getting there, slowly. And it's Tony, by the way. Please, come in. I'm afraid it's not much warmer than outside, but you can come through to the kitchen.'

'Perhaps another time. I can't stay long. On my way to visit old Mr Pemberton at number seven. I saw the light as I was passing the drive end, though. Thought I'd pop in. Been hoping to catch you for quite a while now.'

'You're not going to invite me to Sunday's service, are you? Only I do so hate to disappoint.'

The minister smiled. Her glasses had steamed up and she took them off to clean with a white handkerchief she produced from a pocket. Without them obscuring her features, McLean saw an old face, one that had seen a lot of wear. But a welcoming, friendly face, too.

'I know better than to preach to Esther McLean's grandson. You want to come to church, you're always welcome. You don't . . . well, maybe sometime we can have a cup of tea and talk about your donation to the church roof repair fund.'

It made sense now. He'd seen the photocopied flyer someone had posted through his door, read the story and thought 'why not?' He didn't believe in God, didn't really think about it much. But the church itself was a central part of the local community, a building that had stood for centuries. He'd walked past it often enough in his life, had even been inside a few times back when Kirsty was still alive. So he'd dug out his chequebook and sent them a sum that was probably on the generous side.

'How's it coming along?'

'Thanks to you, and old Mr Pemberton, we've made our target. The roofers will be in just as soon as the weather breaks. So really, thank you, Tony. And I mean it when I say you're always welcome. You don't have to pray.' The minister smiled again, and obscured her face by putting her glasses back on. Then she seemed to notice that she was standing in the midst of the post, scattered around the mat where it had been shoved through the letterbox. With a nimbleness that belied the age written in her face, she crouched down and gathered it all together.

'There you go.' She handed the bundle over. 'I'll leave you be now. Goodnight, Tony. And bless you.'

McLean watched her stride through the snow, a latter-day Queen Wenceslas on her way back down the drive to her engagement with lucky old Mr Pemberton. She didn't look back, and had long since disappeared into the darkness when he realized he was letting cold and snow in. Shaking his head, he closed, bolted and locked the door again, flicked off the light and headed back to the kitchen's warm, curry-filled embrace.

'I said that was mine.'

McLean glared at the cat, sniffing around the plastic carrier bag he'd dumped on the counter. It looked at him with an expression that plainly said it disagreed. He dropped the pile of post on the table and went to fetch himself a beer from the fridge. There was one left, which meant that a shopping trip was due in the near future. The thought of it filled him with a greater dread even than the prospect of investigating Andrew Weatherly's violent end.

Drink poured, he turned his attention to the letters. They were, as expected, mostly circulars, junk and catalogues addressed to his grandmother. There were a couple of letters from his solicitor concerning the flat in Newington which he would have to pay a bit more attention to when his mind was less distracted, some bank statements, and other stuff that could be loosely categorized as paperwork. As if he didn't get enough of that at work. Nothing of any great importance.

He transferred most of the rice and curry to a plate, spooning a healthy portion into the cat's bowl to ensure at least a few minutes' peace while he ate. The catalogues addressed to his grandmother were mostly plastic-wrapped and about as interesting as a talk on slugs. One was perhaps slightly better produced though: square-bound thicker card for the cover, and a glossy photograph of a middle-aged woman wearing outdoor clothes that were almost sensible. More for lack of anything better to do than any actual interest, he pulled the catalogue towards him and began leafing through the pages, spooning mouthfuls of Rogan Josh into his mouth as he went.

He nearly choked on a chunk of beef when he saw the postcard.

It must have slipped in between the pages as the postman was tipping the whole delivery through the door. The only reason he didn't immediately think it just part of the catalogue package was that it was so cheap, so obviously a holiday postcard, that he picked it up and turned it over. Saw his address, the tight-packed writing not immediately easy to read, the tiny little scrawled signature down in the bottom corner where the limited space for words had finally run out. A loopy 'E' followed by 'XXX'. Just the sight of those letters sent a shiver down his spine.

A movement to one side was the cat leaping up on to the table. It paid no heed to the remains of his curry, paced deliberately up to the card and rubbed its face against it, as if it were a person's hand. Absentmindedly, McLean reached out and began scratching the cat behind its ears and soon the kitchen was filled with a contented purring. He squinted at the tiny, terrible handwriting and slowly pieced together what Emma had written.

Followed trail across France. We're making good progress but it's early days. Mostly keeping spirits up, but there are days the burden is heavy. Lots of v. helpful people – pls say thanks to Rose for the contacts when U see him next. Thought you might like to know this is where DA first found the book. He's at peace now. No idea how long this will take. Will keep in touch. E XXX

McLean flipped over the card again, saw a series of badly taken photographs of a ruined monastery somewhere in the Pyrenees. That was something he didn't really want to have to think about right now. Bad enough that Emma had left on her mad, strange quest. For a while, a short while, the house hadn't been cold and empty. She'd been there, damaged but cheerful. And Jenny Nairn, too. There'd been food in the fridge and beer in the cellar. Happy days indeed.

He slumped back in the kitchen chair, let the postcard fall to the table. Mrs McCutcheon's cat started to bat it with a paw, as if it might somehow come to life and play. Soon enough it'd knock it to the floor and then lose interest. A glance up at the clock on the wall showed it was late. He could go to bed; it would certainly be more comfortable than the chair. But bed was upstairs in the cold, silent house. At least here he had some company.

The card was just about to tip over the edge when he caught it up, earning an old-fashioned look from the cat. McLean scanned the words again, picturing Emma as he'd last seen her. He'd offered to go with her. No, he'd pleaded with her to let him come. But she'd been adamant that this was a task she needed to do alone. He couldn't even quite understand why she needed to do it at all, or indeed what exactly it was she was doing, but the path she'd set out on was the only thing bringing her back to some semblance of sanity; of the old, bubbly and irrepressible Emma he'd fallen for. He'd let her go, reluctantly, in the hope that she'd get it out of her system, travel Europe on her own for a while. Maybe even further afield. But that was the key point; she was doing it alone.

So who were the 'we' she kept referring to in the postcard?

The answer was staring him in the face. Those few times in their all-too-short relationship Emma had left him a note, she'd always signed it Em. It had been another woman, a long time ago, who'd signed with the first letter of her name. Not an E at all, but a K.

7

'You know if you go digging too deep you're going to find something nasty.'

Grumpy Bob stood at the top end of the incident room, cradling a large mug with a Bugatti logo on it. The smell wafting from the surface of the coffee suggested it hadn't been filled anywhere in the station. McLean knew better than to ask where the sergeant had got it from.

'I rather get the impression that's expected of me.' He watched as DS Ritchie handed out assignments to the gaggle of constables drafted in to the investigation. It made a change to have a lot of manpower to play with, but he wasn't stupid enough to think it could last. He wondered how long it would be before he was called up in front of Duguid to account for his progress, or lack of it. But of course it was the superintendent who had assigned him the case, and precisely so that he would dig deeper than necessary. That would be an interesting conundrum for him.

'Politics is a right bugger.' Grumpy Bob put his finger on the key fact.

'Aye, and office politics is even worse. Still. I'll do what I always do and sod the consequences.'

Whatever Grumpy Bob's response to that was going to be, it was cut short by the arrival of a breathless DC

MacBride. He had a tablet computer of some description clutched in one hand; God alone knew where he'd got it from.

'You look like you've run all the way from Fife, laddie.' Grumpy Bob grinned, then took a sip of his coffee, long and slow in deliberate contrast.

'Just got this in from the Weatherly house, sir. I think you should see it.'

McLean looked at the tablet, puzzled as to how it had made its way down to Edinburgh, and why it wasn't in a clear plastic evidence bag. MacBride paused a moment before realizing what the problem was.

'Oh, sorry sir. Not this. It's a video file you need to watch. Seems Mr Weatherly had a CCTV system in his house for security.'

A large plasma screen had been set up in one of the smaller incident rooms. McLean gathered the detective sergeants assigned to the case together and took them through. Better if they all saw the video at once, though he had a sinking feeling he was going to have to watch it many times over anyway.

The image was blurry, blown up to fill the large screen. It showed the view from four different cameras: one facing the front door from the far side of the hall by the staircase; one showing the living room; one taking in the landing; and a fourth showing the girls' bedroom. As they appeared on the plasma screen, they were paused.

'There's other cameras, apparently.' MacBride tapped and swiped at the screen of his tablet computer. 'They all feed into a hard drive in the basement. Mr Weatherly was very security conscious.'

'What time is this?' McLean peered at the large screen, looking for some kind of clock. It must have been evening, as he could see the two girls in their individual beds asleep, ghostly in infra-red light. MacBride tapped his tablet again, and a timestamp appeared – 11:08PM.

'This is the day before yesterday,' MacBride said. 'You know. When . . .' He tapped the tablet again and the numbers started to climb.

Weatherly appeared at the front door about fifteen seconds in. The cameras were fixed, so all they saw was him walking across the hall, dropping something that was probably car keys into a bowl on a low sideboard just before he moved out of shot.

He reappeared a few minutes later carrying two glasses of milk. He looked straight at the camera as he began to climb the stairs, his face blank and unreadable. Moments later he appeared on another camera, on the landing, then went into the girls' room. The camera went through a rapid white cycle as it adjusted from infra-red to normal recording automatically. Weatherly had turned on the lights, waking his daughters in the process. One of them sat up, stretched and rubbed at her eyes. The other huddled under her duvet as if cold. He must have spoken to them for a while, then he put the glasses of milk down on their bedside tables, and sat on the edge of the yawning daughter's bed.

McLean found himself willing the girl not to pick up the glass, not to drink. But this was all in the past now. These things had already happened. And sure enough the girls took their milk. Weatherly waited until they had both finished, then tucked them in before walking back out of the room. Just before he switched off the lights, he stared up at the camera, his face impossible to read.

There must have been a blind spot in the landing camera, as the next time he appeared it was at the bottom of the stairs, crossing the hall. He disappeared from shot for a good five minutes, but they all watched the empty screen. No one asked MacBride to hit the fast-forward button.

Weatherly finally reappeared, this time carrying his gun. There was no hesitation in his movements as he walked upstairs, leaned the gun against the wall outside the girls' bedroom and went in. This time they didn't respond. They hadn't moved at all since the image had switched from normal to infra-red view with the switching off of the lights. He didn't turn them back on.

Someone watching let out a low, quiet moan as Weatherly picked up a cushion from a chair at the end of one bed and used it to smother his first daughter. He held it over her face for a very long time before taking it away. His other daughter lay on her back, one arm on top of the covers. When he placed the cushion over her face, the hand flapped weakly; a final, useless, desperate struggle. She didn't take long to die, but to the assembled detectives watching the video, it felt like a lifetime.

And then Weatherly stood up. He placed the cushion back on the chair, pulled back the covers from one bed to reveal the still, prone form. Then he picked up the other child, cradling her against his chest as if he were protecting her, even though her head lolled against his shoulder like a drunken man. Or a dead child.

He laid her out alongside her sister and then pulled the covers back up, so that only their heads poked out from the top. For a couple of moments he just stood, staring at them, shoulders hunched. Then he turned and walked out of the room without a backward glance.

The rifle was still waiting on the landing. He took it up, working the bolt as he walked towards the master bedroom. Killing his wife took seconds, mercifully off-camera. Then he was walking back towards the stairs. Once more he looked up at the camera as he approached it; no surprise that he knew exactly where they all were.

The final camera showed the back of his head as he stepped off the bottom of the stairs, strode quickly across the hall and out into the night. He left the front door open, like a man who's just popped out to fetch something in from the car.

'There's nothing after that until the uniforms arrive about half an hour later.' MacBride tapped the screen of his tablet and the big screen froze. McLean was going to have to ask him how he did that.

Nobody said anything for a while. They all just stared at the screen, frozen in time, the two dead girls lying side by side in the bottom right-hand corner. McLean risked a glance across at DS Ritchie. She was pale, her eyes wide. She'd seen Morag Weatherly's dead body, but not the girls. If the expression on her face now was anything to go by, that was probably no bad thing.

*

McLean watched the sergeants leave the room, not chatting among themselves but reflecting quietly on the horrible thing they had all just seen.

'Keep that video secure, will you, Constable? I don't want it leaking out to the press or finding its way mysteriously on to the internet.'

McLean ignored MacBride's look of hurt at the accusation. The video would have to be shown to the rest of the investigating team eventually, but for now he wanted it kept to as few people as possible. Things had a nasty habit of turning up where they shouldn't be, and at the worst possible time. The last thing he needed was the press running horror stories about the two girls before the investigation was over. Just as well there'd been no camera in the master bedroom. Unless there had been . . .

'Was this all the footage? Or were there more cameras?'

'Not sure, sir. This is all I've been sent so far, but given the set-up, I'd be surprised if there weren't more. There's bound to be external cameras as well.' MacBride swiped his screen, bringing up a notepad app and tapping at a virtual keyboard. 'I'll get on to the forensic team and find out.'

'Thanks. I'll be heading out to the house again later today anyway. Need to get a better look at the place now they've moved the bodies.'

'You not going to the PM on the body we found in the glen?'

It took a while for McLean's brain to catch up with the words. 'That's today?'

'Scheduled for half two this afternoon. I sent you an email.'

'Christ, just what I need. Weatherly and his family are scheduled for this morning. And after that video footage . . .' McLean weighed up his options. A drive out to Fife and an afternoon spent wandering around that creepy old house, being scowled at by the forensics team who would really only just be getting started. Or he could stand in the cold mortuary examination theatre and watch a dead man being cut up, his innermost secrets revealed. It wasn't much of a choice, really, but neither was it too hard to make.

'Get in touch with the forensics team about those cameras, OK? I want all the tapes here, secure by the end of the day. We can review what's on them later. I just don't want them falling into the wrong hands.'

He'd still have to go to Fife eventually. Maybe tomorrow, maybe the next day. But given the choice, the city mortuary was a far friendlier place to be.

8

'Subject is male, Caucasian, sixty-one years of age. In general good health, really. Maybe carrying a little more around the middle than he should, but nothing life-threatening.'

McLean watched as the city pathologist Angus Cadwallader carried out his examination of Andrew Weatherly. He'd already performed autopsies on Morag Weatherly and the two girls, and that had been harrowing enough for a little flippancy to be understandable.

'Body shows no signs of obvious interference.' Cadwallader worked his way up the torso in a meticulous, thorough manner. 'Nothing particularly untoward. No signs of drug use or recent injections. Ah, he has a tattoo.'

'He does?' McLean perked up at the news, having let his mind wander. There was still the investigation into the tattooed man to organize. Yet another post-mortem to attend, later in the day. As if he hadn't seen enough dead bodies to last a lifetime and more.

'Nothing exciting.' Cadwallader beckoned McLean over, rolling the dead body slightly to expose the point where thigh turned to buttock. Left-hand side. Weatherly's tattoo looked old and faded. The black ink deep under his skin showed a simple Celtic curl, slightly distorted by age. Probably something he'd done in his youth and regretted ever since, but not enough to go through the painful process of removal.

'Pattern mean anything to you?' McLean asked.

'Ah, Tony. That's your department, if I'm not wrong.' Cadwallader bent over, peering more closely at the design for a moment. 'But no. It doesn't. Looks to have been done by a professional though.'

Having moved in to see the tattoo, McLean found himself uncomfortably close as Cadwallader continued his external examination. Soon the scalpels and saws would come out, and then he'd make some excuse to leave. He probably didn't even need to be here at all; Dr Peachey was acting as witness to the examination, and he could have sent Ritchie, or even MacBride if he was feeling cruel. The report would say Weatherly shot himself, death due to having his brains forcibly blown from the back of his skull and painted over a stone statue in his garden.

'Ah now, this is interesting.'

Cadwallader had moved to Weatherly's head now, or as much of it as was left. The face was slack, barely recognizable as the man on all the news bulletins. Someone had closed his eyes, which was a relief. Cadwallader had picked up a magnifying glass from the tray of torture instruments beside the examination table, and was peering at Weatherly's lips.

'Interesting how?'

'His lips are badly burnt. There's blistering on upper and lower. Recent injury, but ante-mortem.'

'Gun barrel?'

'Well, that's what I thought at first. Wouldn't have

thought it'd get that hot, though. And then there's this.' Cadwallader pointed to the small, black hole below Weatherly's chin. 'He pushed the gun up under there. Didn't shove it in his mouth.'

'Maybe he tried that first, after he'd shot his wife. It hurt him so he took it out again.'

Cadwallader frowned as he mulled over the scenario. 'Possible, I suppose. That would explain why the burns have formed blisters. Oh well. One for the report, I guess.'

The pathologist went back to his examination, tutting and muttering at the mess to the back of the head. When he reached for the scalpel, McLean took a step back.

'Somewhere else you need to be, Tony?' Cadwallader gave him a friendly smile.

'Pretty much anywhere, really. But specifically, a waste of time with everyone's favourite trick cyclist and then half an hour of physio for my leg. Got to come back here again later anyway. For the tattooed man. You'll let me know if you find anything unusual?'

'Don't I always?' The pathologist waved his scalpel in the air above Weatherly's chest, searching for the best place to start his incision. McLean took the hint and fled.

'Come in, Tony. How's the leg?'

Lunchtime and another pointless session with Professor Matt Hilton. McLean tried not to limp as he crossed the spacious room, though in truth his leg was stiffer than he liked to admit.

'Sore. Almost as if it was broken in two places and hasn't fully healed yet. Can we get on with this?'

Hilton had been given his own office along with the fat retainer fee he was paid to assist with profiling criminals and counselling officers traumatized in the line of duty. It was considerably bigger than the shoebox McLean had at the back of the station, and had a nice view from the large window, too. For once, as he settled himself into a firm but comfortable armchair and eased his leg straight, McLean found himself grateful rather than jealous.

'You make it sound like you find these sessions a chore.' Hilton settled himself down behind his desk, leaned back in his own chair.

'That's because they are a chore. I've two new investigations starting up, and I'd much rather be overseeing them than sitting here talking about my feelings.'

'Two?' Hilton raised a surprised eyebrow, leaned forward and scribbled something on a pad lying open on the desk.

'Yes, two. So can we wrap this up?' McLean refused to rise to the bait.

'You know I'm cleared to discuss ongoing cases, Tony. You've not been back at work long since the ... incident.'

'You mean since you lot all think I tried to hang myself?'

Hilton pinched the bridge of his nose and stared out the window. He'd had his ponytail cut off, trying out a DCI Brooks-style shaven head to disguise the receding hairline and encroaching grey. It didn't really work; he looked more like a eunuch than anything else, and an old eunuch at that.

'You still cling to your denial? You know we can't begin to progress until you accept what you did.'

'I am aware of the Four Stages theory, Hilton. I even happen to think it's quite useful. We have a bit of a problem with the denial stage, though. If you won't accept my version of events, if you insist on believing the rumours spread by people who weren't even there, then I can never progress, can I? Unless I lie, of course.'

'Which would be counter-productive, in the end.'

'Exactly so.'

Hilton paused a while before speaking again. It gave McLean a chance to flex his leg. It really was quite sore today. Must be a change in the weather coming.

'You've had a troubled past, Tony. First your parents dying when you were very young. Your fiancée—'

'Look, rehashing the past really doesn't help, you know. You're talking about things that happened years ago. What's the point of picking at the scars?'

'Scabs. You pick at scabs.'

'Yes, and scabs heal in time. If you let them. Old wounds become scars. Since you're so keen on your metaphors, the mark is there but we're able to function well enough. What you're doing isn't a finger rubbing at an itch until it starts bleeding again. You're taking a scalpel and cutting deep to see what's in there. It's not helpful.'

McLean realized he had tensed up as he spoke, and forced himself to relax back into the armchair. He knew all too well what was coming next, but at least if it ticked another of the boxes on Hilton's list then the session could be brought to a close and he could get on with some proper work.

'Anger is good, Tony.' Yes. Right again.

'Is it? I've always found it gets in the way of thinking. Makes you do stupid things.'

'Like trying to hang yourself?'

'I'd say trying to hang yourself was a pretty stupid thing to do, yes.'

'And yet—'

'Gods, it's like listening to a broken record. How many times do I have to tell you, Hilton?'

Hilton gave the smallest of shrugs. 'OK. We'll leave that for now. So these two new cases.' He emphasized the number. 'Anything special?'

'We found a body in the River North Esk in Roslin Glen last week. Still no ID, unless something's come up while I've been stuck in here with you.'

'I see you're eager to get your teeth stuck into that one. That's good, Tony, but don't think throwing yourself into solving cases is the solution to your problems. That didn't work out so well before.'

'The other case, since you're so obviously desperate to know, is Andrew Weatherly and his family. You've seen the news, I'm sure.'

For once, Hilton said nothing. It was almost amusing to see the thoughts flitting across his face, the questions stumbling into each other in their rush to his mouth. McLean waited until he thought the psychiatrist was going to speak, then pushed himself up out of his chair. A shock of pain lanced through his leg, and he covered up the grimace by shaking out the sleeves of his jacket.

'That must be very ... difficult.' Hilton made no attempt to stop McLean as he headed for the door.

'Very. So if you don't mind, I think I'll get back to it.'

'Yes. Yes. Of course. We'll reschedule for tomorrow. Same time.' The psychiatrist stared at him, the thought processes writ large across his face. He'd never make a good criminal: too easy to read. 'You know you can always come to me for help, Tony. Any time. Any thing.'

Humour him, why not? After all, Hilton's signature on a sheet of paper in Duguid's office was the only reason he was back on active cases anyway. McLean nodded his head in understanding. 'I'll bear that in mind.'

Time was he'd hated the Western General Hospital. It was where his grandmother had spent the last eighteen months of her life, slowly shrivelling away like a balloon left over after the party's finished and everyone's gone home. He'd visited every day, then once or twice a week, guilty when he forgot, guilty when he came and only spent a few minutes staring at her. Then she had died and he'd hoped to put the place behind him. But Emma had kept him coming back in the dark days when she'd been unconscious. And then he'd been here himself.

As a patient he'd been dreadful, he knew. The nurses were nice to him, of course. Some thought he'd been close to the edge, and maybe he had been. Their sympathy wasn't really what he'd needed, though. Others just did their job, cheerful around him or simply there, and that had been better. But he'd longed to get out of the place, had discharged himself far earlier than the doctors wanted, earlier even than was wise.

That much he realized now, with the ache in his leg a constant companion. And that was why he'd come to look upon his visits to the hospital with eager anticipation. If nothing else, this was where the really good painkillers came from.

'You've been doing the exercises I set you.' The physiotherapist looked McLean in the eye as she spoke, voicing the words as a statement, not a question.

'When I can.' Well, it wasn't exactly a lie. He had the badly photocopied sheet pinned to the fridge door with a magnet, and sometimes he did some of the stretches while he was waiting for the Aga to reheat his takeaway.

'I can only help you so much, Inspector. The rest you have to do for yourself.' As if to emphasize her point, the physiotherapist manipulated his leg, bending it so that a sharp twist of pain shot through his hip. It was short-lived though, blessed relief coming as she lowered his leg back down on to the bed.

She was called Esmerelda, some cruel trick on the part of her parents. She couldn't have been more than twenty, but she seemed to know her stuff. McLean had started his physiotherapy with a burly man called Steve, but Steve had gone off to work with the Scottish rugby team, leaving him to the tender ministrations of Esmerelda. At first he'd thought she might have been a bit less brutal, but their first session together had put the lie to that one.

'You can put your trousers back on now. We're done. For today.'

'I don't suppose you know what the problem is?'

Esmerelda gave him a look far older than her years. 'Which one? You had a double fracture in your right femur. That's a difficult bone to heal properly at the best of times, but you insisted on going back to work before you were ready. You won't rest it properly, you sit poorly and you don't do the exercises I gave you. If you were twenty and fit, you might just get away with it. You're not twenty, though. And you're not fit.'

McLean felt like Constable MacBride, a deep red blush heating his cheeks, the tops of his ears burning. It was a long time since he'd had a good telling off like that, and the fact that the person telling him off was half his age didn't detract one bit from the fact that she was absolutely right.

'I'll try harder,' he muttered, aware of just how much he sounded like himself as a boy in that horrible English boarding school. Terrified of Matron and her withering stare. At least Esmerelda didn't look like a harridan.

'You do that, Inspector. I look forward to seeing evidence of it next week.'

9

The walk down to the city mortuary was cold, a bitter wind blowing in from the Firth of Forth. McLean tried to stretch his leg as he walked, stung by the physiotherapist's words about his fitness. He couldn't argue with her about his age. Overhead, the clouds had that purple tinge to them that promised more snow. At least it was still daylight, though that wouldn't last long.

Angus had already started on the body, ably assisted by the long-suffering Dr Sharp. Sitting at the back of the examination theatre, Dr Peachey looked bored, most likely because his presence was a legal requirement as witness to the proceedings. McLean thought he'd slipped into the observation area without being seen, but Cadwallader was never easy to fool.

'Nice of you to join us, Tony,' he said without taking his eyes off the cadaver. 'I was beginning to wonder where you'd got to.'

'I was told half past.' McLean looked at his watch, saw that it was a quarter to. 'Sorry. It's been a busy day.'

'No gently easing back into the flow after your enforced leave, I take it.' Cadwallader pulled something dark and slippery out through the large incision in the dead man's chest. Plopped it down on the stainless steel tray that Dr Sharp was already holding out for him. They were a well-rehearsed team.

'What, you don't think Weatherly's an easy case?'

Cadwallader stopped, his hand poised over the body ready to delve in again, and turned to face McLean.

'I would've thought they'd want it all squared away neat and tidy.' Cadwallader shook his head, turned back to the task in hand. 'That's not really your style.'

'Yes, well whoever "they" are, they've pissed off Duguid somewhere along the line. I could've told them that wasn't a good idea. Now he's decided I'm a spanner and he's going to throw me into the works.'

Cadwallader straightened up, handing yet another organ to his assistant. 'You know, that's so cynical it's almost brilliant.'

'You don't have to deal with the consequences though, Angus. I'm the one who's going to get all the shit when it doesn't go to their script. I've already had Jo Dalgliesh bending my ear. Christ alone knows what's going to turn up next.'

'Yes. The term "poisoned chalice" springs to mind.'

McLean saw the CCTV video spool through his mind's eye. The twin girls drinking the milk given them by their father. A shiver ran through him at the thought.

'What about our mysterious tattooed man? Didn't just accidentally fall in and drown?'

'After taking all his clothes off first? If only it were that simple.' Cadwallader stood away from the body, swept his arms wide to take in its full length. 'This, I'm afraid, quite literally has suspicious death written all over it.'

'Literally?'

'Sometimes I wonder how you ever made it to sergeant, let alone detective inspector.' Cadwallader waved his hand at the body, blackened by the intricate web of designs covering every inch of skin.

'The tattoos?'

'Yes, Tony. The tattoos. Unusual enough that someone would go to such lengths. I've read a few stories of full body tattooing, but it's very rare.'

'So this was an unusual person. Should make identification a lot easier.'

'Oh I very much doubt that. Quite the opposite.'

'How so? Surely—'

'These tattoos are all fresh. Some of them are barely healed. I doubt a single one's more than a month old.'

'We're going to need a room. Somewhere not too far from the Weatherly case.'

Back at the station and McLean was feeling the effects of his walk to the mortuary. His thigh ached deep in the bone. He wanted to lie down somewhere comfortable until the painkillers kicked in, but he'd stupidly left them at home. The thought of running two murder investigations side by side was bad enough; it would be unbearable if he had to spend half his time walking up and down stairs between different incident rooms.

'Room five's free I think, sir. It's not very big, but it's just across the corridor.' DC MacBride had a thick wedge of brown manila folders under one arm, his tablet computer clasped firmly in the opposite hand. Not letting such a prize out of his grasp was probably the only way of ensuring it didn't disappear. McLean wondered if he took it home and slept with it.

'Set it up please, Constable.' He leaned back in his

chair, stretching his legs out under his desk in the hope that it might ease off some of the pain. 'I take it we've not had any hits back from Missing Persons about our tattooed man.'

MacBride shook his head. 'Nothing yet. Fingerprints turned up a blank. Still waiting on a DNA profile so we can run that.'

'Angus'll have that by the end of the day, hopefully. You'll need to do the Mis Per all over again, though.' McLean explained about the tattoos being fresh.

'The whole body? In a month?' MacBride's normally pink face went very pale.

'I don't suppose Penicuik turned up anything useful?'

'Said they walked the banks for a mile upstream and down. Nothing obvious, but then the weather's hardly helping. Everything's covered in fresh snow out there.'

McLean tried to remember the area from when he'd mountain biked out that way in his misspent youth. There were a couple of disused railway lines that had been turned into bridleways, if he recalled correctly. Lots of old ruined buildings, and a tunnel.

'You got a map of the river?'

MacBride looked flustered for a moment, then juggled his tablet computer and the folders until he could access the touch screen. 'I can call up Google Maps, sir. There's satellite imagery, too.'

McLean shook his head. 'No. I'm old-fashioned. Give me paper and lines any day. Get something sorted for the incident room. I'll be up as soon as I've managed to find some bodies to fill it with.'

*

Several hours later, with another bruising encounter with Duguid under his belt, McLean entered incident room five, hoping for some peace and quiet. The whiteboard on one wall held a few questions, a photograph of the tattooed man's dead face and a hastily scribbled list of detectives' names – those few who would still work with him and the unlucky ones who'd not managed to find a better excuse in time. It was a very short list; he'd have to draft in some uniforms to help out.

At first he thought the room was empty, but a quiet muttering from behind a stack of folders piled up on a desk at the far end turned out to be DC MacBride.

'Problem?' McLean peered over the folders. MacBride was fiddling with the cables at the back of an elderly computer.

'Oh, sir. Sorry. I didn't see you come in.'

'Too busy fighting technology. Did someone pinch your tablet?'

A second's worry flitted across MacBride's face. He spun around, taking a length of cable with him that probably shouldn't have gone. McLean saw the tablet lying on the desk behind him at the same time as the constable, who grabbed it like a jealous lover.

'Don't even joke about it, sir. You've no idea how many people have tried to nick it. You'd think policemen would be less . . . I don't know . . .'

'Thieving?' McLean offered.

'Yes,' MacBride agreed. 'I've never known so many light fingers as there are in this place. Can't put something down for five minutes.'

'Shouldn't IT be doing that?' McLean pointed at the

61

cable still in the constable's hands. There wasn't a lot of space for anything in the room, but somehow he had managed to get four desks and four computers wedged into one corner.

'Depends on whether you want it done today or next month. Figured it'd be quicker if I did it myself. Just as soon as I can get everything hooked up to the network we can start sorting out those actions.' He nodded at the whiteboard. It wasn't much, but those questions would only multiply.

'You reckon you'll be done by shift end?'

'Should be.' MacBride looked at his watch, then back at McLean. 'No overtime on this one, I take it.'

'Not yet. No. If we're lucky we might get some more help, though.'

MacBride said nothing, but his raised eyebrow showed he was developing the necessary levels of cynicism to survive as a detective. McLean looked back at the whiteboard, reading off the actions quickly. There was one thing missing.

'Penicuik walked the river edge, didn't they?' He searched around for a marker pen before writing 'point of entry?' on the board.

'Mile each way, at least that's what they said.' MacBride flicked a wall switch and the computers clunked into life. 'I was going to get you that map. Sorry, sir, slipped my mind.'

'Don't worry. I've got some old Landrangers at home. I'll dig them out. You'll want to wear something warm tomorrow though.'

'I will?'

'Yup. Good boots, too. You and me are going for a walk along the riverbank.'

10

Cold grey light filtered through the bare tree limbs, reflecting off the thin powdering of snow on the black earth and picking out fringes of frost around the piles of dead leaves. The wind had died down, or turned to a sufficiently different direction to be less noticeable deep in the glen. McLean stamped his feet against the chill, feeling the unfamiliar weight of his walking boots. They were new, like the ski gloves he had bought the evening before. The hat was one of his grandfather's, though, an old tweed deerstalker his grandmother had found in a cupboard somewhere and presented to him when he first made detective. The Meerschaum pipe to go with it had long since disappeared.

'What exactly are we looking for, sir?'

DC MacBride appeared to have kitted himself out from the stores back at the station. His yellow fluorescent jacket was hardly subtle, and it had been built for a constable twice his size. He had what looked like a balaclava nicked from the Armed Response Unit rolled up into a makeshift woolly hat. It was undoubtedly cosy, but nothing could stop the end of his nose from turning red.

'I'm hoping we'll know it when we see it.' McLean slapped his hands together as he turned on the spot, surveying the scene around him. Many years ago, back in his student days, he had bicycled out this way from time to time. The old railway followed the line of the river for a bit, dropping eventually into Penicuik, but first he wanted to walk the other bank.

'This was all munitions factories, back in the war.' He swept an arm over the expanse of car park, empty save for the ticking hulk of his car. His breath misted in the frigid morning air, hanging like the ghost of an idea. MacBride said nothing, perhaps unwilling to open his mouth and thus lose valuable heat.

'They made gunpowder here in the eighteen hundreds. Built the material stores into the cliffside to contain any accidental explosions.' McLean led the way as they crossed a modern bridge over the North Esk. The water was deep and fast moving. Enough to wash a body down to the rocks further along? Looking downstream it was impossible to get to the banks on both sides without cutting a path through the thick undergrowth and weed saplings. A water team with dinghies would get a better view; there was certainly no way Penicuik's uniforms could have done anything more than a very cursory inspection. If they'd done even that much. A single snowflake tumbled lazily down to the rushing black water, no doubt soon to be followed by very many more. McLean found it hard to blame them for taking the lazy option.

At a sharp bend in the road, two heavy stone gate-posts formed an entrance into what a sign proudly declared to be Roslin Glen Country Park. That was new to him; it had never had a name before. The old dirt track had been replaced with a wheelchair-friendly path as well, but the scenery was otherwise much as he remembered. They walked upstream, but even though the trees were leafless it was all but impossible to see the river. This wasn't somewhere you might stumble in by accident.

Further up, and the track ended by a series of ruined buildings. The stump of an old chimney stood to one side, the narrow shape of a wheelhouse nearby evidence of an earlier form of power. The river here was choked by a weir, diverting water to the wheel that was no longer there. McLean clumped down to the water's edge.

'If he'd fallen in further upstream this would have stopped him.' He turned to where MacBride was standing up the slope. 'I'd forgotten this was here. Could've saved us all a bit of time, really.'

'You think Penicuik might've mentioned it.'

'Yes, well.' McLean looked across the river to the trees on the other side. The bank rose steeply, a hundred feet or more, a narrow gully formed by a smaller stream almost directly opposite. Sheltered from the worst of the wind, the ancient oaks and beeches had grown tall and thin. Here and there the earth had given way under their weight, toppling them down to the water. The undergrowth grew thick in the gaps, brambles and gorse fighting for the light. A little further downstream the slope became a cliff of dark yellow sandstone, rhododendrons billowing over the top like spume, cascading down the cracks in the rock.

'His neck was broken, which would suggest a fall.'

'You think he fell down there?' MacBride had followed McLean's gaze across to the cliff, and now the constable shuddered somewhere in the depths of his overlarge jacket.

'Micro-lacerations to the front of the body. Like he'd pushed his way through a gorse bush.'

'With no clothes on? Jesus. What would make someone do that?'

'Being in fear of your life, perhaps?' McLean tapped MacBride on the shoulder, pointed back in the direction they had come. 'Let's go.'

'Where're we going?'

He pointed to the cliff top. 'Up there. Only I don't fancy trying to climb it from this side.'

It took a lot longer to walk than McLean had anticipated. Strange how memory changed a place over time, shortening distances and tidying up reality. Perhaps it would have been easier driving rather than struggling up the narrow lane to Roslin Castle station and then down on to the old railway line. The snow was coming in heavier flurries as they walked along the footpath that was the only good thing to come from Dr Beeching's axe. There were dozens of abandoned railway lines around here, mostly old freight routes for the mines and factories, taking coal and goods to the port at Leith. This one was mostly sunk into a cutting, making it almost impossible to gauge where they were in relation to the ruined gunpowder factory on the other side of the river. The undergrowth to either side was thick, covered with snow and mostly so full of thorns it would have been impossible to get through no matter how terrified or desperate you were, but there were some stands of broom that might give way to someone determined enough.

'When did this snow start to settle?' McLean pushed

at a likely spot and was rewarded with a heavy dump of cold powder in the gap between his coat and glove. Flapping his hand to get rid of it only forced more snow up his sleeve.

'Friday, I think. It's not been properly cold enough to hang around until this week.'

'And best estimate is our man went into the river on Saturday.' McLean pushed deeper into the undergrowth. Somewhere down below, he could hear the water cascading over the weir. They had to be fairly close to the spot he'd seen from the other bank.

'I think that was pretty much blizzard all day. I was processing actions on the Danby case for DI Spence for the whole afternoon and I don't think it let up.'

McLean brushed more snow from the top of the broom, then pushed the branches aside, placing a boot carefully where he thought he'd be able to get a good footing. The edge was nearby somewhere and he really didn't fancy taking a tumble over that cliff.

'So what we're looking at is a naked man, covered from head to toe in fresh tattoos, running through a blizzard and so terrified of whatever's chasing him that he doesn't notice, well, anything.'

'And you think he went over the cliff—'

With hindsight, he should have noticed that the broom's thin, whippy fronds had given way to the bulbous leaves of the rhododendron bushes. Maybe he had, but it just hadn't clicked in his head as to what that actually meant. All McLean knew was that one moment he was standing on firm ground, and the next the bushes had leapt up to consume him. He flailed about, grabbing at the branches with gloves slick with snow. Their padding had been great for keeping out the cold, but now they made it almost impossible to get a decent grip. He twisted around, feeling nothing under his feet now, certain that he'd just stepped into air and a one-hundred-and-fifty-foot drop. He was just beginning to curse himself for such gross stupidity when something clamped hard around one wrist and he jarred to a stop.

'Jesus, fuck!'

McLean whipped his free hand round, used his teeth to pull the glove off. It fell away from him in a lazy arc, bouncing off thin branches before disappearing into the grey. The cold was instant, but at least now he could reach for something a bit more substantial. He looked back, seeing what it was that had saved his life. A gloved hand clamped around his wrist and the pale, worried face of DC MacBride peered through the snow-covered foliage.

'Can't hold on much longer, sir. Can you reach that branch?'

McLean saw what MacBride was nodding at, hooked his free arm around the thick stem and took some of the weight. His feet still hung over nothing, and he suppressed the urge to look down. Concentrated on getting back up the ways.

'Just to your left. There's a rock jutting out. Should be able to get a foot on it.'

McLean inched his left foot over, feeling the boot connect with something solid. He slowly transferred his weight on to it, conscious that the rock might give at any moment. Christ, but he could be stupid sometimes.

'That's it. A little more.'

He felt his back press against the clifftop, brought his right foot over to join the left one. The scramble from there back over the edge, up a short steep slope and then down to the safety of the footpath was inelegant, but McLean really didn't care. It wasn't until he'd collapsed on to his backside on the snowy ground that he realized he was breathing hard, his heart racing. Stupid, stupid, stupid.

'Please don't do that again, sir.' MacBride rested his hands on his knees. He too was panting like a man who's just run a marathon with a fridge tied to his back. His face was white, only the tip of his nose still red from the cold.

McLean looked past him, seeing the railway line curve gently in either direction. True, there was a bank to climb before you got to the bushes, but it was worn away here, not as steep as elsewhere along the route. And that apex in the bend of the line obviously kissed the clifftop. There should have been a fence, or at the very least a sign giving warning.

He pushed himself to his feet, wobbly, dusting the snow and dirt from his coat. One hand was still gloved, but the other was bare. He held it up to his face and watched it shake for a moment.

'I think I know where our man went over.'

The trip back to the station had been conducted in total silence. McLean had never been more grateful to the inventor of the heated car seat as the adrenalin from his near-death experience wore off, leaving him with an unenviable set of aches and pains, not the least of which was the bone-deep throbbing in his hip where it had been broken months earlier. He had visions of being torn off a strip by Esmerelda the physiotherapist at his next session, but frankly he was too happy just being alive to care all that much.

The tinny beep of his smartphone had brought the euphoria to a swift end. Great that you could programme the thing to make different noises for different appointments; he didn't even have to take it out of his pocket to know what it meant. And so here he was, having sent MacBride off to warm himself up with a coffee and a muffin, settling into the chair in Matt Hilton's office for yet another counselling waste of time.

'Are you feeling OK, Tony? You look a bit pale.' Hilton leaned back in his own chair, a look of almost genuine concern plastered across his chubby face.

'Very nearly died this morning. It shakes you up a little.'

'Again?' Hilton raised an eyebrow. 'I hope you're not going to make a habit of it.'

'It was an accident. Stupid mistake. Luckily DC Mac-Bride was to hand and has quick reflexes. I'm fine.'

Hilton paused a moment before answering. 'No. I don't think you are.'

It wasn't a question, so McLean didn't answer. The chair was just the right angle for relieving the strain on his hip; he could quite happily sit there and say nothing for an hour or so. If it weren't for the bruise starting to make itself heard above the other aches and pains in his back . . .

'Tell me what happened. From the beginning.' Hilton took a sip of coffee. His mug looked exactly like one of those large styrofoam cups you get at the expensive coffee chains, but it was made from china. Made in China too, probably. A gimmicky gift for a shallow man.

'Must I?' McLean knew the answer before he'd even posed the question. He tried not to make his sigh too theatrical, probably failed, then told Hilton all about the visit to Roslin Glen, the walk along the riverbank, finding the weir and the cliff. The psychiatrist listened, as he had no doubt been trained to do, nodding his head from time to time and maintaining a disconcerting amount of eye contact. Going over the details helped turn the disquiet at his close shave into anger at his own idiocy, but McLean also found himself thinking about his reasons for going out there in the first place. It would have made far more sense to organize a boat team to scour the river bank for any clues, something he was going to have to do anyway. Yet more expensive man-hours to keep Duguid happy.

'You have a self-destructive streak, you know that, Tony?'

'It was an accident. Could've happened to anyone. I've already phoned the council about getting a fence put up.' Well, he'd asked MacBride to call them, but that was the best way to guarantee it would be done.

'Oh, I'm sure it was an accident. Throwing yourself off a cliff isn't your style.'

'That's right. You think I'm more of the hanging myself type.'

Hilton stifled a smile. 'Actually I've been coming around to your version of events on that one. I'm beginning to think you maybe did fall off that chair accidentally and never meant to hang yourself at all. What you've just told me about the cliff actually helps.' Hilton shrugged. 'Well, in a way.'

'Does that mean we can stop having these bloody meetings? Only I've plenty better things to do with my time.'

'Yes. Like taking Detective Constable MacBride into a dangerous situation without thinking through the consequences. Like going off to visit a crime scene on your own, without back-up, without even telling anyone where you're going. Like . . .' Hilton leaned forward, flipped open a thick folder and began leafing through sheets of paper. 'Like oh-so-many examples dotted through your career as a plain clothes detective.' He gave up, flipped the folder closed again and slumped back into his chair.

'Your point being?'

'Accidents happen around you, Tony. Sometimes they happen to you, but just as often, more often even, they happen to other people.'

'Are you suggesting I'm dangerous? That I shouldn't be allowed out? Maybe shouldn't be a policeman at all?'

'That's not for me to say.'

'You sure about that? I thought that was exactly for you to say. If I'm fit to be a policeman or not.'

Hilton pressed his fingers together into a pyramid, jammed it up under his chin. Started to speak, then realized it wasn't easy with a bunch of fingers shoved in his face.

'Look. I get it,' McLean said. 'I'm not the most brilliant at sticking to procedure all the time. But you know what? Sometimes procedure is more of a hindrance than a help. Sometimes you have to cut corners to get the job done. Sometimes—'

'How are you getting on with the Andrew Weatherly case?'

The change of subject was so unexpected it left McLean momentarily dumbstruck.

'It's . . . It's early days.'

'And is it as horrible as I've heard?'

'That depends entirely on what you've heard.' McLean studied Hilton's face, imagined him asking around the station, digging here and there, trying to wheedle his way into another high-profile investigation. No doubt he saw a book in it, or at the very least a lecture tour.

'Fair enough. I can understand you not wanting to talk about it.' Hilton paused a moment, as if trying to decide whether or not to ask the question he so desperately wanted to ask. 'I can help, you know.'

'Me? Or Weatherly? Only I think he's past helping now. His wife and kids, too.' McLean pushed himself up out of his chair, successfully anticipating the twinge of pain in his hip early enough to stop the grimace from showing. He leaned forward, both hands on the edge of

Hilton's desk as much for support as intimidation. Hilton leaned back reflexively.

'I've been coming to you for months now. Months of wasted afternoons when I could be doing my job. And why? You said it yourself, you believe me when I say I didn't try to kill myself. So I'm accident-prone. Show me a detective in this station who hasn't had the occasional mishap. It's a dangerous profession. How many of them are you seeing on a weekly basis?'

'That's hardly the point—'

'None. Just me. And you've not been doing much profiling of late either. So here's my thoughts on the matter. You've been stringing this out, keeping me going so you can have your nice office and a fat retainer out of our budget.'

'I . . . How dare you suggest—?'

'I don't like you, Hilton. Never have. Don't rate you much as a profiler or a counsellor either, for that matter. I'm only here because I was ordered to be, but like you say, I'm not one for following procedure so I won't be coming back.' McLean turned slowly, all too aware of how falling to the ground screaming in agony might ruin his little speech. It wasn't far to the door, but it seemed to take for ever to reach it. When he looked back, Hilton was still staring from his chair, mouth slightly open in astonishment. It was worth the trouble he knew he was going to get, just to see that face.

She's not done a lot of this sort of thing; interviewing the friends and business associates. There's something very unsettling about this case, too. It's not as unusual as she wishes it was, for a man to kill his family and then himself, but she's never had to deal with it before. And those children . . . She rubs at her eyes to try to dispel the image, never far from her mind. The boss thinks she didn't see. He was too wrapped up in it himself, and how could she blame him? But she saw them, lying side by side like she used to with her own sister back when they were small.

'It's really a terrible business. And such a shock.'

The woman is immaculately dressed, her face almost too perfect to be real. And there's something about her eyes that puts Ritchie on edge. But she's polite, trying to be helpful and friendly.

'You and Mr Weatherly were business associates, I understand.'

'Oh, that and more. Andrew was my friend for many years. I introduced him to his wife, you know.'

'Were you aware of any unusual pressure Mr Weatherly might have been under? He was a very busy man.'

'Oh yes. Constantly busy. But Andrew loved that. I'd be more concerned for his mental state if he weren't running around like a mad thing. Being cooped up for a few months would probably drive him potty.'

They're sitting at an elegant table in a reception room decorated by someone with both taste and an unlimited budget. The chairs are not arranged opposite one another; the woman sits at ninety degrees to her, and perhaps a little closer than Ritchie is comfortable with. As she talks, her hands paint invisible pictures in the air.

'So there was nothing in the business that might have driven him to . . .'

'To kill those poor little girls, Morag, and then himself?' The woman lays one hand lightly on Ritchie's thigh. It seems at once overly familiar and surprisingly reassuring. 'I cannot begin to fathom what would drive a man to do such a thing. Any man. Least of all one I knew well.' She pauses. 'Or at least I thought I knew well.'

A gentle tap at the door, a click as the handle drops and then a secretary pushes in bearing a tray. The aroma of freshly brewed coffee fills the room.

'Ah. Thank you, Sandy.' The woman watches as the secretary puts the tray down on the table, pushes the plunger into the brewing coffee, pours, and offers milk, sugar, biscuits. And all the while her hand is still on Ritchie's thigh. Not caressing or intimate, just anchoring her to the seat. Making sure she doesn't escape.

It's a long time since she's been so unsure of herself. Not since school, really. Not since her sister died. But she's unsettled by this woman, her directness and her power. Ritchie picks up her cup and takes a sip, feels the warm liquid slide down her throat. She needs to get the interview back on track; there are more people on her list still to speak to, a portrait of a family in turmoil to be teased from the memories of others. She meets the woman's gaze, and the question forming on her lips dies.

'That's quite enough about Andrew, don't you think?' the woman says. 'Tell me about yourself, dear. Tell me about your boss.'

12

Moving helped to ease the pain in his hip. It also stopped him from wasting too much energy on being angry with Hilton. Stopped him from getting angry with himself, too. McLean's feet carried him back towards his office, but being alone with a stack of overtime sheets wasn't likely to improve his mood any. He took a left and limped up the stairs towards the Weatherly incident room.

Half the station had been drafted in on the enquiry – at least that's what the press had been told. Truth was there wasn't much to do until the forensic team were finished with the house, and even then it was as obvious as the nose on the end of his face that Weatherly had gone mad, suffocated his daughters, shot his wife and then turned the gun on himself. All they were trying to do was find a reason, and it didn't take a genius to know there wouldn't be one. Not something you could tell people that would let them sleep easier in their beds, anyway.

Standing in the doorway of the incident room, he saw a half-dozen uniforms and support staff manning the phones and tapping instructions into their computers. No detectives around, but then he didn't really expect there to be. It was a PR exercise, nothing more. He turned his back on the inactivity and crossed the corridor.

There were no senior detectives in the incident room

for the tattooed man either, but newly plain-clothes Detective Constable Sandy Gregg greeted him with a cheery smile.

'You just missed Stu . . . DC MacBride, sir. He popped down to the canteen to get some coffee.'

'Busy, is it?' Unlike the room across the corridor, this investigation warranted only one phone line. Gregg was probably regretting having volunteered to man it. She liked to talk and no one was calling.

'It's early days. We've only had the photo out a wee while. I expect someone'll call in soon.'

McLean looked up at the whiteboard. The picture pinned to the top left corner still showed the man as they had found him, face black with swirls and patterns.

'Did we get anywhere with a mock-up photo? One without the tattoos?'

Gregg looked at him blankly, but the answer came from the other side of the room.

'Still waiting for the artist, sir.' DC MacBride pushed into the room with two steaming mugs. A brown paper bag under one arm most likely held muffins at this time of the day.

'Let me know as soon as we get it, OK? I want it put round all the hospitals, shelters, other forces. Someone must've seen him before this was done to him.' McLean peered closely at the photograph on the whiteboard, trying hard not to imagine how much it must have hurt the man. Without thinking, his left hand went up to his right shoulder, rubbed at the patch he'd hardly thought about in over a decade. Kirsty had spent years trying to persuade him to get it done, but it was Phil who'd found the right way of making the dare seem reasonable. It was only a small design, abstract, black, much like those covering the victim's entire body. Even so, he could remember the buzzing of the needle, the pain as the ink was etched deep into his skin, and the long days of burning as it healed.

'You all right there, sir?'

'What? Oh.' McLean turned quickly, winced as a jolt of pain ran up his leg and into his spine. Somehow Mac-Bride had crossed the room without him noticing, and was now standing by his side. The coffee smelled good.

'Reckon we'll find out who he was?'

'Oh, I think so. Have we got the rest of the pathology photos? All the tattoos?'

MacBride frowned. 'I think so. Can get them if not. Why?'

'Get them together quick as you like, Constable. I feel the need to go and see an old friend.'

It wasn't the dingy little backstreet tattoo parlour where McLean had succumbed to the needle all those years ago, egged on by his best friend and buoyed up by perhaps rather more Dutch courage than was advisable. That place had gone bust over a decade past, the building it had occupied long since demolished and replaced with tiny modern apartments for the city's new toiling classes.

Bo's Inks had been around much longer, and would no doubt survive whatever cold winds of fortune came its way. McLean had first come across the place as a beat constable, learning the streets at the side of old Sergeant

Guthrie McManus. Bo and Guthrie had been in the Merchant Navy together, or so he was told. The tattoo parlour was a regular stopping point for a cup of tea and a blether. And if Bo happened to pass on any useful information about who was trying to fence what, then it was just two old chums shooting the breeze, wasn't it?

Bo was long dead, but his son Eddie had taken over and was, by all accounts, a far better inker. He had an artistic flair that his father had lacked, and he'd spent several years in the US, studying how they did things there. Eddie wasn't perhaps as good a source of information as his father, but McLean still popped in occasionally. It was a select crowd that frequented the place, and every so often a case would take him into their midst.

'Tony McLean, as I live and breathe.' Eddie was sitting on a stool at the back of an empty shop when McLean pushed open the door. DC MacBride stood behind him, perhaps a little too close. McLean couldn't imagine the constable having had a lot of experience of such places.

'Looking busy, Eddie.' He crossed the small room, holding out a hand to be shook. Eddie wore a sleeveless vest; you couldn't really call it a wife-beater when he had no wife. It was a garment obviously chosen to show off the intricate swirl of colours and patterns covering both arms and Eddie's neck; all the work of Eddie's partner, George.

'You know how it is, Inspector. Most of my clients come round after dark.' Eddie nodded towards DC MacBride, still standing in the doorway. 'Who's the kid?'

'Detective Constable MacBride, this is Eddie.'

'Pleased. Come on in. And don't worry. We don't ink folk who don't want to be done.'

MacBride closed the door and stepped into the shop. He looked around a bit, taking in the pictures on the walls showing some of the more notable designs done down the years. Then, much to McLean's surprise, he put down his tablet computer, unbuttoned the cuff and rolled up his left sleeve. The pale Scottish skin of his forearm was marked with an intricate swirl of lines that McLean took an embarrassing length of time to identify as a dragon. More Welsh than Chinese, but striking nonetheless.

'Nice,' Eddie said, peering at the tattoo over half-moon spectacles. 'Who did that for you? No, don't tell me. Jake Selden, over in Wardie. Am I right?'

'That's him. Had it about a year now.'

'Well, if you ever want another, Jake's a good man, but you'd do well to come and see me or George. Special rates for our friends in the polis.'

'Thanks. I might do that.' MacBride took his time rolling his sleeve back down and fastening his cuff, all the while trying not to stare too hard at the patterns covering Eddie's arms.

'So, what can I do for you? I'm guessing you're not here just to show us your tatts.'

'Not exactly. Not ours, at least.' McLean noticed Mac-Bride's eyebrow shoot up at that. 'It was tattoos I was hoping you'd be able to help us with, though.'

'Let me guess. Dead body you're hoping to identify.'

'Something like that.' McLean nodded at MacBride. 'Constable.'

MacBride picked up his tablet and tapped at the screen, bringing up the first of a large folder of photos. He turned the device around and handed it to Eddie, who peered at the first image for a while before taking off his half-moon glasses and putting on a different set.

'Jesus.' He swiped a finger on the screen, flicking to the next picture. Then again, and again. Occasionally pinched and zoomed to get a better look at something. McLean was happy to let him take his time. Finally he put the tablet down, took his glasses off and rubbed his eyes.

'Poor bugger.'

'You recognize the work at all?' McLean asked.

'No. Sorry. Christ, it's hard enough to make anything out there's so much going on. And they're all fresh. Well, most of them.'

'Most of them?'

'Aye, there's a few places in there you could see some old designs. He had some inks before this was done to him. Just not many.'

'Can you show me?' McLean picked up the tablet, ready to hand it over.

'On there? Aye. But it'd be easier if I could see the body.'

'The body. You sure about that?'

'I've seen dead folk before, Inspector. Not like that, I'll give you that much.' Eddie gestured at the tablet and its collection of unsettling photographs.

'Well, if you're sure, then I'll have a word with the pathologist, get something set up as soon as possible. Thank you. That's really very helpful.'

Eddie smiled a broad, mischievous grin, and directed a wink at DC MacBride to include him in the conspiracy. 'No worries. I know where to send the bill. And maybe you'll let me sort out that mess on your shoulder like it should've been done in the first place.'

'Didn't know you had a tattoo, Constable.'

Heading back across town, and the traffic was snarled up by the road works in the West End. The little glowing orange light in the instrument cluster told McLean that he was running low on petrol, again. Damned thing seemed to drink its own weight in the stuff every week.

'Not the sort of thing that comes up in conversation often, sir.' MacBride sat upright in the passenger seat, as if slouching were somehow morally reprehensible. His unease at being in the Inspector's Car was palpable, but then he was always like that around senior officers. It was a sharp contrast to DS Ritchie, who rarely seemed ill at ease with anyone.

'Well, I'm glad it did today. Eddie took a shine to you. I'm guessing that's why he's being so helpful.'

'I'll get that all sorted as soon as we're back at the station, sir. Do you want to be there when Mr . . . Eddie comes to see the body?'

'I'll probably have to be. You know what Angus is like when it comes to letting the general public near his bodies.'

MacBride said nothing to that, just peered at his tablet computer, then out the windscreen as the traffic finally started moving. McLean knew the constable wanted to ask something, but didn't know how, or whether he should. He was fairly sure he knew what it was, too.

'What Mr . . . Eddie was saying back there. About your shoulder, sir.'

Right again. 'Yes, Constable, I have a tattoo on my right shoulder. It's very small, impossible to tell what it's meant to be, and I was quite drunk when I got it.'

'No tattoo artist worth his salt would ever ink a drunk subject. You can't even walk in off the street these days. Have to have a consultation, time to change your mind. It's—'

'I know. I know. Let's just say this was done when things were different. And count my blessings I didn't end up with some horrible disease from the backstreet parlour my so-called best friend dragged me along to. Watch your best friend, Stuart. He's the one who'll get you into the deepest shit. And you'll probably forgive him afterwards, once the hangover's gone.'

'So Mr—'

'His surname's Cobbold, but everyone calls him Eddie.'

'Oh. Right. So Eddie. Back there.'

'Yes, I was stupid enough to show him my tattoo. Back when I was a DC, as it happens. He took the piss out of me for months because of it, and when he got bored with that, he started trying to persuade me to let him change it so that it looked better.'

'Why don't you? Let him, I mean. He's good.'

'George is even better. You don't think Eddie did his own arms, do you?' McLean slowed, flashed at an oncoming car, then turned swiftly across its path and into the station car park. The V6 engine growled and the front tyres gave an unnecessary chirp as he spun the wheels a little rushing the manoeuvre. MacBride clutched at the dashboard in alarm, relaxing only once McLean had parked.

'I saw the dragon on your forearm, Constable. It's very good. I can appreciate body art when I see it, but you know, I tried it for myself, didn't really have the best experience, don't really feel the urge to have it all done again. I could get this one removed.' He tapped at his shoulder. 'But it's a reminder as much as anything else. Not to do anything quite so stupid ever again.'

McLean popped open the door and climbed up out of the low seat, feeling the twinge in his hip a moment before the pain. He paused for a moment, resting his arms on the car roof until the throbbing subsided. On the other side, MacBride had already closed his door. He looked like he wanted to say something again, but still couldn't decide whether he should or not.

'I didn't mean to offend you, Stuart. I'm not against tattoos, just against them on me.'

MacBride looked startled for a moment. 'It's not that, sir. It's just, well. I'd not really thought about it for a while, but it was Alison persuaded me to get this. She'd have laughed like a drain if she'd known you had one too.' He tapped at his forearm with the edge of the tablet computer, turned, then walked off to the station. McLean stayed where he was. He didn't think he could move even if he wanted to. The pain in his leg had eased, but the constable's words had sparked off a nasty train of thoughts.

Alison. Alison Kydd. Seconded from uniform to CID and giddy at the excitement of it all. She'd been hit by a van that had been meant for him. She'd pushed him aside, saved his life, at the cost of her own. What had Hilton said? *Accidents happen around you, Tony. Sometimes they happen to you, but just as often, more often even, they happen to other people.*

Damn the man. He hated having to admit he might be right.

13

Grey slush covered the pavement, thrown up from the road by passing traffic. It made walking difficult, but McLean found moving less painful than standing still; a lot less painful than sitting down. The rhythm of his feet helped him to think, and it was always good to get out of the station for a while, even just to clear his head. He'd walked down to the mortuary, hoping to speak to Angus about the tattoo artist coming to see the dead body, a task that could just as easily have been done by phone. Of course, the pathologist hadn't been there, but he didn't mind. It was the walking that mattered, and the thinking.

He noticed the smell first, the aroma of cigarette smoke. It wasn't as if he'd studied the different brands and could identify them like some posh tobacco sommelier. There was just something about this particular smoke, this particular place, that made it instantly obvious who was hurrying up behind him. He didn't even look around as the figure fell into step alongside him.

'Inspector McLean. You're a hard man to track down.'

Jo Dalgliesh wore the same long leather coat that she'd been wearing the last time he'd had the misfortune to meet her. And the time before that, and the time before. It was her uniform, McLean supposed. Either that or her actual skin. That would make sense; she was part lizard, after all. She was a head shorter than him, and wizened like a prune. Her short-cropped spiky hair was perhaps greyer than he remembered, but otherwise she looked just the same.

'Ms Dalgliesh. What a surprise.' He didn't stop walking, would probably have sped up to make life difficult for her, but the twinge in his leg slowed him down. Damn, he'd only just been to the physiotherapist. The next session couldn't come soon enough.

'Call me Jo, please. Even old Duguid does, you know. And he's a lot more stuck up than you.'

'What you and the superintendent get up to is no business of mine.'

Dalgliesh wrinkled her nose, as if she'd just trodden in something unpleasant. 'You don't always have to be such a sourpuss, McLean. We in the fourth estate can be a lot of help to you.'

'Yes, you can. But it usually comes at a high price. I'm rather keen on keeping my soul, thank you.'

'You're looking into old Andy Weatherly and his family, I hear.'

'Goodbye, Ms Dalgliesh.' McLean quickened his pace, then almost immediately had to slow down again as a jolt of pain ran through his thigh.

'That leg still giving you gyp, I see.' The reporter had no trouble keeping up with him. Damn her.

'It's healing.'

'Nasty business, I hear. Up in that attic of yours, with the rope and all. Where'd you get that by the way?'

McLean stopped so suddenly, Dalgliesh was a couple of paces on before she realized.

'What are you talking about?' he asked.

'The rope? In the attic? Where you almost accidentally hanged yourself? Way I heard it, anyway. What were you doing up there?'

'Would it make any difference if I said it was none of your business?' McLean studied Dalgliesh's face for any sign that she was playing games with him. Or at least not the usual hack reporter games she always played. It was difficult to tell; her poker face was well developed.

'Pish and nonsense. Policeman injured in the line of duty. I'm all over that. Course, I could've written something about pressure of work and how a lot of detectives turn self-destructive. But Tony McLean try to kill himself? Nah.' Dalgliesh grinned at him like a shark in a pool full of tuna. It didn't take a genius to work out where she was going.

'What do you want, Ms Dalgliesh?' McLean made no effort to hide the sigh in his question.

'I want to know what's the score with Weatherly. You are investigating, I take it?'

'Detective Superintendent Jack Tennant is SIO on that one, but yes, I'm involved.'

'Why? It's Fife's case, surely.'

'You know there's no Fife Constabulary any more, right? Same as we're not Lothian and Borders?'

'Aye, it's all Greater Strathclyde. I ken that.'

'Weatherly was an MSP. He had a house in the city, and his business is based here. A lot of the enquiries are going to be here, so it makes sense for us to be involved.'

Dalgliesh appeared to consider this for a moment. 'Aye, true enough. But why you? Why no' someone a bit more senior?'

'Thanks for the glowing vote of confidence.'

'Don't get your panties up yer crack, Inspector. You know what I mean. If it's important enough for Fife to put a super on it, why not Dagwood himself at this end?'

McLean only partly stifled the laugh that bubbled up out of his chest. He'd reached the station, where she couldn't easily follow beyond the reception area.

'I'd have thought that'd be obvious to someone like you, Dalgliesh. Think about it, aye?'

'You can't chuck me out of here, laddie. I fought in the war, don't you know.'

McLean had been walking across the reception area, headed for the back door and the station car park. It was late, and he'd quite frankly had enough for one day. Somewhere in his near future he saw a takeaway and some beer. Later there might even be whisky if the painkillers didn't wipe him out completely. But something about the voice stopped him in his tracks.

'They took 'im, they did. I'm telling youse and youse're not listening. The dark angels. They took 'im.'

He couldn't resist it. McLean stopped to see what was going on. The front desk was a magnet for crazies at the best of times, and when the weather turned really cold they'd come in off the street hoping for a nice warm cell for the night. Usually a bit of half-hearted violence was enough to get them what they wanted, but every so often someone played the madness card.

'OK then, sir. From the top.' McLean heard the

long-suffering sigh in the duty sergeant's voice. 'Can I have your name, please?'

'I fought in the war, you know.'

'Yes, sir. You already said. Which war was that, exactly?'

'Bosnia. Iraq. Afghanistan. Fought in 'em all, I did. Served my country I did. Billbo did an' all. And they took him. The dark angels.'

McLean heard the telltale click as Sergeant Dundas put down his pencil on the Formica counter. That was his cue to leave, before he was asked to help out. Turning too quickly sent a spasm of pain up his leg, momentarily stopping him in his tracks. By the time he'd recovered, it was too late.

'Oh, Inspector, sir. Didn't know you were still in.'

McLean turned back more slowly, saw the happy smile on Pete Dundas's face. It was a perfect counterpoint to his own grimace.

'Pete.'

'Don't suppose you could spare a moment? Only this gentleman out here says he's lost his friend.'

'I was just on my way home, actually.'

'It'll only take a minute. Put his mind at ease, aye?'

McLean pinched the bridge of his nose, closed his eyes and let a long, slow breath out through his nostrils. The pizza with his name on it was receding rapidly; at this rate he might as well just skip straight to the whisky and painkillers.

'OK, Pete. But you owe me.'

14

His name was Gordy, and he'd fought in the war. That much McLean managed to ascertain fairly early on in the conversation. What surprised him most about the man was his age; probably about the same as McLean himself. Was that really old enough to have served in so many campaigns? Bosnia, Iraq twice, Afghanistan? It was depressing to realize that yes, it was. So much for the war to end all wars. And the one after that.

It was just as depressing to realize that a man who had served his country for his entire adult life was now living rough on Edinburgh's winter streets. Depressing, but also not altogether surprising. The dropout rate for ex-military was surprisingly high. When you've lived for so long in the discipline and structure of the army, it can be hard to adjust to having to do things for yourself. Throw in the horrific experiences of four different war zones and what was really surprising was that more of them weren't nuts.

'Tell me about this friend of yours.' McLean peered down at the notes he'd been taking. 'Billbo. With two ells?'

'That's 'im. Me an' Billbo go back a ways, you know. We were in the desert with the 'mericans. Saw a thing or two, I can tell you.'

'Did he have another name? Apart from Billbo?'

Gordy scratched at a chin that hadn't seen a razor for a week or so. 'Must've done once, I suppose. Can't say as I remember it, mind.'

'And you say he was taken.'

'By the dark angels. That's right.'

'When did this happen? Last night?'

'Last night. Last night.' Gordy's face took on a slack expression as he spoke, the effort of trying to string some coherent thoughts together requiring all his mental capacity. 'Not last night. So difficult to remember. We were in Afghanistan. I remember that. Helmand. They blew up Bodie and Jugs. Billbo caught some shrapnel in the face, but he was OK.'

OK. Time to change tack. 'You were in the army, Gordy. That right? You and Billbo served together. What was his serial number, his rank?'

'4061470. Sergeant.' Gordy snapped the words out without thinking.

'And yours?'

'4061470. Sergeant.'

McLean sighed. It was never that easy. He looked up at the high window in the interview room. This was the nice room, where they took people who were helping the police with their enquiries. Not like the windowless cells downstairs, with the tables bolted to the floor and institutional beige walls. Outside, the last vestiges of daylight had long disappeared, only the orange undersides of the clouds visible. It wasn't snowing any more, but it was going to be brutally cold out.

'You got somewhere to kip for the night, Gordy?'

The ex-soldier had been studying his hands, as if they

93

were something he'd never really noticed before. Now he looked up, straight at McLean. His eyes were hooded, his greying hair straggly and unkempt. He wore several layers of clothes, all well past their best, but he didn't smell bad. Well, not as bad as some.

'Can look after meself.'

'I'm sure you can. But there's no harm in taking help when it's offered. There's a place down on the Cowgate. Shelter, a bed, food. You don't have to fill in any forms, don't have to stay if you don't want to. I can give you a lift down there if you want.'

Gordy's stare intensified. 'Why'd you do a thing like that, eh?'

'It's cold out. Probably going to snow later. I don't think the streets are such a nice place to be, this time of year.'

'I like the cold. The streets. Long as there's buildings and cars, I know I'm not back there.'

'I can't begin to imagine what that must have been like. Don't really want to, if I'm being honest.'

'Billbo saved my life out there, you know.' The ex-soldier leaned forward and rested his arms on the table. The crazed man from reception was gone, at least for now. In his place was someone who might almost pass for normal, given a shave and a set of clean clothes. But there was something in his eyes; a haunted, far-off look that McLean had seen too many times before. Gordy, whatever his real name was, walked a very fine line between reality and a world of demons, tumbling off it every so often and always the wrong way. He'd been on that side when he'd arrived here, but just for the moment he was skirting back into the edges of normality.

'On patrol. Me, Billbo, Bodie and Jugs. Four-man team, night ops. Stupid thing was, we were on our way back to base. Mission accomplished. Back the way we'd come, so maybe we weren't paying enough attention. Don't know how he knew what was coming. Maybe he didn't, maybe it was just luck. First thing I knew, Billbo'd shoved me hard in the side, knocked me off the path. I was angry with him for all of a second, then it went off.'

Another shudder, followed by a long pause. McLean let the man take his time, all thoughts of pizza and beer forgotten.

'Don't think there's any easy way to describe what it's like. I was covered in blood, bits of brain. Christ only knows what. Thought I was hit, but it was mostly Jugs, I guess. Maybe Bodie. There wasn't much of 'em left but gristle. And the noise. Jesus. Couldn't hear a thing for it. Just Billbo's silent screaming, pulling me up, moving me on. He'd blood pouring from his face then. Looked like something out of a horror movie. Whole fucking place was a horror movie.'

Gordy had been studying his hands again as he spoke. Now he looked up at McLean, his eyes glistening with tears.

'He saved my life then, and he saved it again this time. They weren't after him. The dark angels. They'd come for me. But he was there. He fought them off, just like he did back in the war. Only they had lightning, didn't they. Took him down from behind like cowards. Dragged him off into the night. I ain't seen him since.'

McLean waited for the ex-soldier to say more, but he seemed to have run out of steam. It was an odd story, a sad indictment of the way the country treated its damaged minds, but nothing he'd not heard before. True, the exact form of Gordy's madness was unique, but the fact of it was all too common.

'I'll do my best to find your friend, Gordy, but it would really help me if I had a bit more information about him. You call him Billbo, with two ells. He must have had another name, surely?' McLean started to scribble the nickname down again, stopped when he'd written 'Bill'. 'Was it William? William something?'

Gordy blinked, some ghost of a memory flitting across a haunted brain. Then his eyes glazed over, the old madness coming back in a flood.

'They took him, they did. The dark angels. They took my friend.'

McLean felt he really should have been doing something more for the man, but short of having him arrested and locked up for the night, he couldn't think of anything more constructive. Gordy followed him out through the station to the car park at the back without a word beyond the occasional low mutter of 'I fought in the war, don't you know' to any passing constable.

He looked scared by the massed ranks of squad cars and riot vans, as if they were sleeping monsters that might at any moment awake and devour him. When McLean plipped the key for his own car, the bleep and flashing made him jump visibly. It took a long time, standing in a freezing wind, to persuade the ex-soldier to get in.

The journey down to the shelter was mercifully short. While Gordy didn't smell like someone who had been sleeping rough and getting most of his food from a wheelie bin round the back of Tesco, he wasn't exactly fresh. Fortunately he found the window button and wound it down almost as soon as McLean had started the engine. And leather seats could always be cleaned.

McLean had two reasons for bringing the ex-soldier to the shelter. For one thing, he couldn't just turn the man back out into the night; not with the temperature dropping well below freezing and a forecast of blizzard conditions by the morning. He was also intrigued by Gordy's story. True, the man was a walking advertisement for Care in the Community, but something had happened to him, and recently. And it had been traumatic enough to make him come to the police. He wasn't one of the regulars, either. The duty sergeant would have recognized him if he had been. Chances were that someone in the shelter would recognize him, though. And there was a chance they might know who this Billbo was, too.

The welcoming aroma of hot soup spilled out through the door as McLean led Gordy into the shelter. It must have been piped there from the serving tables, as it was soon overwhelmed by the less pleasant smell of long-unwashed bodies and poor dental hygiene. McLean could sense the ex-soldier tensing beside him as the noise washed over them both, and it occurred to him that bringing a man used to the open air into a room that was a claustrophobe's nightmare might not have been such a good idea.

'We'll get you something to eat, yes? Then maybe see if you can get a bed for the night.'

Gordy followed reluctantly as McLean led him to the serving tables. Hunger overcame fear when he was handed a bowl filled with steaming chunky broth and a thick hunk of brown bread. The serving lady was about to dole some out for McLean too, but he waved her down.

'Jeannie Robertson in?'

The question earned him a raised eyebrow, so he quickly took out his warrant card, showing it as surreptitiously as he could manage. Most of the clients of this particular establishment were less than comfortable in the presence of the police, and on a night like this one he really didn't want to be responsible for them deciding outside was safer.

'I'll just fetch her.' The serving lady shooed a hand at the warrant card in the hope that it would disappear, then hurried off into the kitchen. When McLean turned to see where Gordy had gone, he found the ex-soldier sitting at a table nearby, eating like a man who'd not seen a square meal in a decade.

'Tony McLean. How nice to see you. What brings you here?'

McLean noticed that Jeannie Robertson hadn't called him Inspector, as she did whenever they met at the hospital. As a nurse, she'd tended to his grandmother for eighteen months, but it wasn't until recently that he'd found out she volunteered in the soup kitchens as well. Her generosity made him feel slightly inadequate.

'Just dropping round a new customer.' He pointed to

where Gordy was wiping the inside of his bowl with his bread. 'You know him?'

A frown furrowed the nurse's brow. 'You know what this lot are like. I can't go telling tales to just anyone.'

McLean shrugged. 'Not sure there's really anything I can do anyway. Just Gordy there came into the station earlier ranting about dark angels and how they'd taken his friend. Poor bugger's not had much luck in life.'

'And you thought you'd do him a good turn?' Jeannie's eyebrows rose in mock surprise. Then she shook her head. 'Sadly I can't help anyway. He's new to me. Mind you, this weather's brought a lot of folk in I've not seen before. I don't doubt you lot'll be finding a few dead ones out there soon enough.'

McLean grimaced at the thought, even though every winter brought its share of them. 'I don't suppose you've heard of a man called Billbo? Two ells?'

Again the nurse shook her head. 'Doesn't ring any bells, I'm afraid. I can ask, but this lot can get very defensive if you start prying.'

McLean gave her a weary smile. 'Well, it was worth a try. And at least someone's had a hot meal. Any chance of finding him a bed for the night?'

'We never turn anyone away, Tony. If he wants to stay, we'll give him a mattress and a blanket.'

'OK. Thanks. I'll leave him to your tender care then.'

McLean took one last look at the ex-soldier, hunched over his empty bowl as he pulled apart the last few pieces of bread, shoved them into his mouth. Gordy's eyes darted from side to side, showing his wariness of the other people milling about. He needed medical care;

professional help to get him over the trauma that had destroyed his sanity. And all society could give him was a bowl of soup, some stale bread, a mattress on the floor of an old basement in the dark recesses of the city. Out of sight, out of mind.

15

McLean wasn't sure quite what he'd been expecting, but Jennifer Denton wasn't it. She was small, for one thing. Not so much short as tiny, as if she were actually a little bit further away than you thought. Her manner was distant, too. Not quite rude, but she didn't try to hide the fact that she would rather be somewhere else, and quite frankly found the whole interview process tiresome.

She had arrived on the dot of eight, immaculately turned out. McLean had visions of her poor hairdresser having to schedule an early appointment 'just for Mam'selle'. It was certainly a lot more effort than most of his interviewees went to. When he'd shown her to the interview room she had sniffed the air with a disapproving nose. He had taken some small satisfaction from the knowledge that the last occupant of the chair he offered her had been a mad ex-soldier who'd been sleeping rough.

'You've worked for Mr Weatherly quite a while now, Miss Denton,' he said after the formalities had been dispensed with.

'Twenty years. I started off in his campaign office. Just a summer job to get some experience. When he won the election, Andrew asked me to stay on.'

'What do you . . . What did you do for him?'

'I explained all this to your sergeant. What was her name? Ritchie?'

McLean picked up the top sheet from a pile of papers lying in front of him and made a pretence of reading it. 'I've seen DS Ritchie's interview transcripts. You've been very helpful. All of Weatherly Asset Management have. But there are a few things we need to clear up. It says here you were Mr Weatherly's PA. So what, exactly, did that entail?'

'Everything, Inspector.' Said without a hint of a smile, maybe an edge of weary exasperation. 'Andrew was brilliant, but like most brilliant men he was completely incapable of organizing his life. My job was to make sure he knew where he was meant to be, what he was supposed to be doing, who he was supposed to be meeting.'

'Sounds like you were very busy.'

'I was . . . I am efficient. Busy is a sign of incipient disorganization.' Miss Denton shifted ever so slightly in her seat. 'Show me a busy man and I'll show you someone just barely able to cope.'

Sitting beside him, Grumpy Bob stifled a chuckle, turning it into an unconvincing cough. McLean ignored him as best he could.

'Was Weatherly busy?' he asked.

'Oh, dreadfully. Always rushing around, never taking the time to do things properly.' This time Miss Denton gave him a knowing smile as she answered, as if she were sharing a great secret. It was gone in an instant, replaced with her normal, businesslike facade as she began reciting what was obviously a well-rehearsed list. 'He was on several committees at Holyrood, as you know. The Police Liaison Committee was one. And he ran his business, of course. Two charities he was chairman of the board for, a half-dozen others he was involved with one way or another. He had quite a busy schedule of after-dinner speaking, as well. I've been working through his diary to let everyone know.'

'I suspect most of them have already heard the news.' Grumpy Bob picked up his mug of tea, took a drink. McLean was grateful for the interruption; it was hard to get a word in edgeways when Miss Denton started.

'Did Mr Weatherly have any worries? Anything out of the ordinary, that is?'

'Andrew?' Miss Denton almost laughed. 'Andrew didn't have a care in the world, Inspector. Worries were for people like me, who had to pick up the pieces.'

'So you didn't see anything different in him these last few weeks, months?'

'No. Nothing at all. I was actually meant to meet him that evening. Went round to his flat, but he wasn't in.'

'You have a key?'

'Yes. I expect you'll be wanting to search the place.'

'In due course. Does anyone else have access?'

'The cleaner has a key. And Morag.' Miss Denton frowned slightly, as if the thought of Mrs Weatherly gave her pause. She shook her head. 'No, I don't think anyone else.'

McLean wrote 'cleaner' down in his notebook. When he looked up again, Miss Denton had pulled out a slim smartphone and was tapping at the screen.

'Her name's Muriel. Muriel Jenks. I can give you her number. She won't have been round, if that's bothering you. Only works Tuesdays and Thursdays, and I dare say she'll have heard the news too.'

McLean added the information to his notes. 'Who would you say were Mr Weatherly's enemies, Miss Denton?'

'Oh. Sharp change of subject there, Inspector. Hoping to catch me off-guard, were you?' Miss Denton paused, as if expecting an answer. She didn't wait long to decide one wasn't forthcoming. 'If you mean who might have wanted Andrew dead, well people always say such things, but they rarely mean it, in my experience. And besides, I thought he killed himself.'

'So we believe, though it's still to be confirmed. Mr Weatherly was a high-profile individual, though, so we have to be thorough. No stone unturned.'

'Fair enough. Of course Andrew had enemies. He was a politician, and one with views a lot of people think extreme. He wasn't a fan of independence, for one thing. Not shy of saying so, I think you'll agree.'

McLean looked at his notes. He'd written a half-dozen questions earlier, but they seemed meaningless now. This whole interview was little more than a box-ticking exercise, really.

'Perhaps you could tell me a little about Mr Weatherly's business? He was a financial analyst and fund manager, I understand.'

'A bit like saying the Pope was a Catholic, but broadly speaking, yes.'

'I imagine he dealt with a lot of money.' This from Grumpy Bob, leaning back in his chair as if he hadn't a care in the world.

'I doubt you could begin to imagine the amount of

money he dealt with, Sergeant. At the last audit Weatherly Asset Management was responsible for well over three billion pounds of investments.'

Grumpy Bob let out a whistle. 'That lot going south might put a bit of pressure on the boss man.'

Miss Denton looked at him with an expression mothers reserve for children who have just done something really stupid, but made no comment.

'Sergeant Laird has a point, Miss Denton. Were you aware of any problems in the business? Any deals not working out?'

'It would certainly go some way towards explaining why Andrew did what he did.' Miss Denton paused, as if considering the possibility. McLean was fairly sure it was all just for show. 'But no. There's nothing horrible lurking in the accounts. Business was slow after the crash in oh-eight, but if anything it's been booming recently.'

'So what about his personal life? Was everything OK between Mr Weatherly and his wife?'

'How would I be expected to know something like that?' For the first time since the interview started, Miss Denton looked uncomfortable. A chink in the armour at last, and a very revealing one at that.

'You worked closely with Mr Weatherly for twenty years. You must have known the family, how they got on together.'

'I was Andrew's PA. I wasn't Morag's shopping assistant, or nanny to the girls. If there were problems at home, Andrew never mentioned them.'

Not even when you were lying in his arms? McLean

bit back the question. It was obvious now that he saw it, but the fact that Miss Denton had been Andrew Weatherly's mistress as well as his PA was really not important. Whether Mrs Weatherly had known or not was equally irrelevant. Digging up the man's history, his failings as well as his undoubted success, none of it was going to bring those two girls back to life.

'Well, you've been very helpful, Miss Denton. I can't begin to imagine what this must be like for you. Losing someone you've worked with for so long, a friend even. Having us poking around in his affairs can't be helping.'

There it was, the slightest flinch at the word 'affair'. As if screwing your secretary on the side was all that much of a sin in these modern times. Hell, it was almost a cliché.

'You have your job, Inspector.' Miss Denton gave him the slightest of nods. 'And I have mine, so if you've no more questions.'

'Detective Sergeant Laird will see that you're taken wherever you need to go.' McLean stood, extending a hand to be shaken. He waited until Miss Denton had taken it before adding, 'And if I might trouble you for those keys?'

She paused a moment before asking, 'Do you not need some kind of warrant?'

'Technically, I suppose so. But who would it be served against? If you'd like to be present when we search the place, that can be arranged. But I'd rather do it sooner than later.'

Miss Denton stared at him with that impassive face, and McLean couldn't help but admire her composure.

Maybe she would go home and collapse in tears, or maybe she was simply the type who had no time for such emotional frippery. Did she have some inkling as to why Weatherly had committed such terrible acts? He didn't think so. That didn't mean he wasn't going to do some digging into her own background. Or at least get DC MacBride to do it for him.

'You're right.' Miss Denton opened her handbag and pulled out a bunch of keys, expertly separating two from the bunch before handing them over. 'The alarm keypad is immediately behind the front door as you open it. Code's Andrew's birthday. All eight digits. Please try not to wreck the place.'

16

Andrew Weatherly's city accommodation was not quite the house its Georgian builder had originally intended, but it was more than big enough for a family of four. McLean parked across the road, studying the other cars nearby for signs of the press, but for once they seemed uninterested. Maybe the lone uniform constable stationed at the front door was enough to put them off.

'You got that number?' he asked. Sitting beside him, DS Ritchie took a moment to answer, her mind somewhere else entirely.

'What? Oh. Yes. Sorry, sir. Wrote it down in my notebook.' She sounded bunged up, as if she were coming down with a cold. The constant sniffing suggested it might be a bad one.

'Right then. Let's go and see how the other half lives.'

The constable on watch duty looked half frozen to death. He had his hands shoved deep under his armpits, searching for any warmth that might be lurking up there. McLean was about to make a comment to Ritchie about not remembering to bring gloves, then realized he was hardly dressed for the weather either. At least he had a nice warm car to go back to.

'They relieving you any time soon, Constable?' McLean showed his warrant card, although by the way the PC had reacted on seeing the two of them approach, it wasn't really necessary.

'Shift change at noon, sir. Can't come soon enough. Freezing my nuts off here.'

'Well, you can come inside for a bit. Warm yourself up.' McLean pulled out the keys he'd been given by Jennifer Denton. The deadlock was well oiled, and he was about to push the flat key into the Yale lock when he paused. DS Ritchie was staring off down the street, her back turned to him.

'That number, Sergeant? Only I don't much fancy the alarm going off and letting every journalist in the vicinity know we're here.'

'Oh. Sorry.' Ritchie scrabbled around in her jacket pocket, fumbling the notebook and dropping it to the ground. She and the PC both bent down at the same time to pick it up, with an inevitable collision of heads.

'Honestly. It's like dealing with children.' McLean waited for them to untangle themselves and for Ritchie to find the right page.

'Twenty-two. Oh-seven. One. Nine. Five. Three.'

'You sure?'

'Yup. Checked it on Wikipedia this morning.'

Brilliant. The modern detective. McLean tried not to grimace as he turned back to the door just a little too quickly for his hip. Like the deadlock, the Yale was well oiled. The door hinges too. He pushed it open and stepped inside.

The first thing he noticed was the smell, but he was too busy searching behind the door for the alarm panel to really take it in. He'd been expecting a beeping as it counted down, too, but there was no sound. The panel was a modern device, touch screen showing numbers and a status readout. It took a moment to realize that the alarm hadn't been set after all.

'Come on in.' He opened the door wide for Ritchie and the constable, and finally realized what it was that he was smelling. Old matches struck on sandpaper; hard-boiled picnic eggs, their yolks turning green around the edges; the tang of mustard seeds freshly crushed. The spare room when Grumpy Bob had crashed in it after a night on the beer and curry.

'Ew. Someone forget to empty the bins? It's fair min-gin' in here.' Ritchie wrinkled her nose, the freckles across her cheeks dancing with the movement. Her eyes were red-rimmed and sore now he looked at her prop-erly, and her lips seemed swollen. McLean sniffed the air again, but the smell had almost gone, as if the ghost of Auld Reekie had been trapped in the house and opening the door had let it out.

'You sure about that, Sergeant?'

'I . . .' Ritchie sniffed again. 'No. It's gone. Strange.'

'You smell anything, Constable?'

'No, sir. Well. Not unusual. Some floor polish?'

'Maybe just stale air. Opening the door let it out.' McLean pulled a pair of latex gloves out of his pocket and snapped them on, watched as Ritchie did the same. The constable took up station by the door, apparently unwilling to venture further inside. It was fair enough; the hall was dark, lit only by the pale sun filtering in from the fanlight and down from the stairwell. Shadows hid every corner and painted strange shapes with the antique furniture. It reminded McLean all too much of the house in Fife.

'Let's start at the top and work our way down.' He set off across the hall towards the stairs, stopped when he reached the first step and realized he was alone. Ritchie hadn't moved from the threshold, and as he turned to look, her head was limned with a halo of misty light, her hands paused in the act of stretching one glove around her wrist. 'Come on, Sergeant. We haven't got all day.'

Ritchie started at the noise, as if she'd been sleeping, and snapped the latex. She scuttled across the hall and joined him as he began to climb.

'Are you all right?' McLean asked. 'Only you've been kind of switched-off all day.'

'Sorry, sir. Won't happen again.' Ritchie smoothed the gloves over her fingers. 'What're we looking for?'

'Anything and everything. I don't really know. Let's concentrate on the rooms Weatherly would have most likely used. Bedroom, bathroom, study. That sort of thing.'

The top of the stairs opened out on to a landing lit from overhead by a large glass skylight, oval and spattered with bird droppings. The doors revealed tidy, anonymous guest rooms, the beds made up but the cupboards largely empty. Down a short corridor to the back of the house, a room that had to have been for the girls sat directly opposite a large family bathroom. At the end, the master bedroom opened up with views on to the private gardens behind the terrace. It held a large bed, walk-in cupboards, a low dressing table, a couple of chairs. Nothing you wouldn't expect to find. The bed looked like it had been made by someone in a hurry, a man on his own and not expecting company perhaps. And yet there was something about the place that had McLean's inner alarm bells ringing. A bit like the transient odour at the front door, there was a wrongness he couldn't quite put his finger on.

'Someone's been through here.'

McLean looked over to where Ritchie was standing. She had opened the top drawer of an old mahogany chest of drawers and was rifling through Weatherly's socks.

'What?'

'Someone's been through here. Carefully, and methodically. Searching for something, but not in a hurry like some petty thief.'

'How can you tell?' McLean crossed the room, looked down on a collection of Marks & Spencer's finest Cotton Rich socks remarkably similar to the ones he had back home.

'I'm going out on a limb here, sir, but I'd hazard a guess Weatherly didn't do his own laundry.'

'He had a cleaner. Probably did that for him when she was here. Or his wife, maybe.'

Ritchie shuddered, no doubt recalling the image of Morag Weatherly in her bed. 'Still. When you've done a load of washing, paired up your socks as carefully as this.' She picked out a perfectly folded bundle. 'You put them away neatly. Not all higgledy-piggledy.'

'They look pretty neat to me.' McLean peered at the ranks of socks, nestling cheek by jowl like so many woolly beasts in a hosiery nest. His own socks tended towards the higgled, if not the piggled. But then he didn't have anyone to do his laundry for him.

'Neat, but moved.' Ritchie picked out some more socks, then placed them back in a row. Once she had done that for one half of the drawer, McLean could see what she was on about.

'Anything else been moved?' He went across to the walk-in cupboard, pulled open the door. Andrew Weatherly had owned a great many suits, it would seem. And shoes.

'Here.' Ritchie leaned in past him and he caught the tiniest whiff of her perfume. 'These are all pushed up to one end, as if someone's gone through the pockets one by one.'

'Or Weatherly was just trying to get to the one at the end.'

'It's possible.' Ritchie crouched down and began pulling out shoes from their custom-made cubbyholes. She ran a gloved finger over polished black leather, scoring a line in a thin layer of dust on one. 'You think he suddenly decided to wear a pair of shoes he'd not tried on in a while, too?'

McLean stepped back out of the cupboard and let Ritchie past. He cast an eye over the rest of the room, but without knowing how it had been before, he couldn't really see whether anything had been touched. Should he be getting a fingerprint team in? He really didn't know. No way of knowing if anything had been taken, anyway. 'Let's have a look in some of the other rooms, aye?'

There was nothing obviously amiss in the guest bedrooms, but then the drawers and wardrobes were mostly empty. The girls' room was small, and packed with boxes of toys. Difficult to tell if they'd been messed around with, although the sheets on one of the beds were untucked in one corner. Hardly damning evidence, though.

Back downstairs, the constable had not moved from his spot by the front door. McLean nodded at him before heading through into what turned out to be a large dining room. For a fleeting instant he thought he caught that unpleasant smell again. Perhaps the drains had backed up somewhere nearby. Again, it was gone almost as soon as he noticed it.

The room looked out on to the street, the windows slightly higher than pavement level so that pedestrians couldn't gaze in on the important people inside. The curtains were drawn, but like most of the house it felt strangely dark and oppressive. Nothing in here looked out of place, except for a heavy silver photograph frame, lying askew on the sideboard near the door. McLean picked it up, almost dropping it when he saw the picture of two girls. It was an artfully posed shot, no doubt the work of a skilled photographer, but all he could see were dead eyes staring at him in accusation.

Putting the frame back down on the sideboard, he noticed that its surface was dimpled on one side, as if it had once been soft and someone had gripped it too hard. Or the silver had begun to melt like chocolate in a child's hand. Part of the design? Again, he couldn't tell. It felt wrong, though.

'In here, sir. Think you should see this.'

McLean turned at Ritchie's voice. She had gone through a door at the far end of the room, which on closer inspection led to Weatherly's office. Ritchie was sitting at the surprisingly modern desk, her fingers hovering lightly over the keyboard of a slimline desktop computer. One of those fancy things which were all screen and no obvious electronics.

'What've you got?' He picked his way carefully around the desk until he could see the screen. It was dark, just a small cursor blinking on and off in the bottom left-hand corner.

'It's what I've not got that's interesting.' Ritchie tapped at some keys. Nothing happened.

'Password?'

'It's not that. There's no boot-up sequence, no operating system. Nothing.'

'You tried switching it off then on again?' That got him an old-fashioned look.

'It was on when I found it, sir. Not sure switching it off would be a good idea.'

'You think it's been tampered with?'

'I know it's been tampered with. Look.' Ritchie pointed at the edge of the screen, where a handful of sockets had been artfully designed into the casing. Most were empty, but one held what looked like a cheap USB stick. 'I don't think they meant to leave that behind. If I'm not mistaken it's a wiper. Cleans out the hard drive and fills it up with noughts and ones. There's this, too.' She pushed herself up out of the chair and walked over to a pair of filing cabinets standing beside the wall. Pulled open a drawer.

'First off, they weren't locked. Lots of empty folders. They've taken the little name tags as well.'

McLean turned slowly on his heels, taking in the whole room. How long had it been since the call had first come in about Weatherly's death? He should have guessed, really. The man was important, sat on select committees, dealt with state secrets.

'Bloody Cloak and Dagger Squad have been here already, haven't they?'

Ritchie bobbed her head just once. 'Looks like it, aye.'

17

It was dark when McLean finally let himself in through the back door, but then it had been dark since about four o'clock, many hours before he'd finished writing up his visit to Weatherly's New Town house and adding it to the growing report. No one could accuse them of not being thorough; just a shame they had found out precisely bugger all. But then, he suspected that had always been the intention.

Flicking on the kitchen lights, he was surprised not to find Mrs McCutcheon's cat waiting for him. He knew it slept by the Aga most of the day, but as soon as it heard his car on the gravel outside, it would wake up, leap on to the table and start to clean its arse with its tongue. He had no idea why it would want to greet him every evening this way, but then cats were supposed to be a mystery.

And now it was nowhere to be seen.

He dumped the takeaway pizza box on the table, alongside the pile of folders he'd brought home with him. At least he'd have a bit of peace while he was eating. Maybe if he went and lit the fire in the library now it would be warm enough in an hour or so to sit and read there, too. But first the ritual of picking up the post.

Only when he got to the front door, there was nothing on the mat. He switched the outside light on, opened the door and checked there. Peered through the letterbox, and even under the old wooden chest that was full of mismatched wellington boots and worn-out coats. Nothing. Well, it was always possible there'd been no post. No junk mail catalogues, no offers for credit cards, no charities tugging at his heartstrings with pictures of starving children or abused animals. Possible, but very unlikely. Unless the postmen were on strike.

It was only as he was walking back across the hall to the kitchen that he noticed the light under the library door. It wasn't an electric light, more the flickering orange glow of a fire. A chill blossomed in his stomach that was nothing to do with the snow lying on the ground outside, and everything to do with memories of smoke and heat and a man screaming as the flames melted his skin. He'd had far too much experience of fires recently. But how the hell could anything in there be burning?

He approached the door carefully and quietly, listening out for the telltale sound of flames crackling with glee as they devoured his grandmother's irreplaceable collection of antique books. There was none, and when he placed the back of his hand on the oak panelling of the door, it was as cold as the rest of the room. He twisted the handle quietly, feeling for the point when the latch released, then gently eased the door open as silently as its old hinges would allow. Poked his head around the doorjamb.

'Ah. Inspector. You're home at last. They told me you worked ridiculous hours, but I didn't believe them. More fool me, eh?'

It took a while for McLean's eyes to adjust to the low

light, even longer for him to understand the scene laid out before him. The fire was lit, coals burning merrily and filling the room with a welcome heat. Mrs McCutcheon's cat lay on the tatty old sheepskin rug in front of the hearth, its tail twitching every so often as it dreamed of the death of mice. On the occasional table beside his favourite high-backed leather armchair, one of his bottles of Scottish Malt Whisky Society single-cask malts stood alongside a half-empty glass and a small jug of water. And in the armchair itself sat a man.

He was a stranger, of that much McLean was sure. And yet at the same time he was almost certain he knew who the man was.

'You found the coal. And the whisky, I see.' He stepped fully into the room, closed the door behind him and flicked the switch that would bring the wall lights on. It was low light, but enough compared to the near-darkness of before that the man flinched and squinted his eyes.

'The coal was easy. The whisky less so.' The man took a small sip, tilting the glass to a newly glowing bulb. 'I can see why you keep it hidden, though. Damned good stuff.'

'MI6? MI5? Or is this some new division of Special Branch I've never heard of?' McLean went to the bookcase that hid the drinks cabinet, opened it up and helped himself to a clean glass. The man in the armchair watched him as he poured himself a drink, added a little water, held it up to his nose and let the aroma settle his nerves. Fright had long since turned to anger, but neither would help him here.

'It's not important, really. Should be enough to know we're on the same side.'

McLean let out an unconvincing bark of a laugh. 'You break into my house, steal my whisky and then try to tell me we're on the same side?'

'I don't think you'll find any evidence of breaking in, Inspector.' The man raised his glass in salute. 'But you've got me on the whisky. Anyway. What else was I supposed to do for the past two hours? I thought you were never coming home.'

'You could have phoned. You could have come to the station and spoken to me there. I assume this is about Weatherly?'

'Ah, the incisive mind of the detective. Yes. This is about Weatherly.'

'You lot already went over his flat, wiped his computer. Is that just standard operating procedure, or did he actually have something to hide?'

'Let's just say a bit of both, shall we? Leave it at that.'

'You can say what you like, really. The investigation's done. Case is good as closed. Weatherly killed his family, then topped himself. The whys are for the press to speculate about. We're no longer interested.'

'Oh, but I rather think you are.' The man took another drink, deeper this time, letting out a little gasp of satisfaction as the strong whisky burned its way down his throat. 'I don't believe for a minute that the great Detective Inspector Anthony McLean doesn't want to know why a man like Weatherly would do such terrible things.'

'What I want isn't all that important, really. I want you out of my house, but I don't expect to get that until you've told me whatever it was you couldn't say through official channels.'

'Touché, Inspector.' The man levered himself out of the chair, drained the last of the whisky and placed the glass carefully on a coaster on the table. He was nondescript, the perfect physical shape for his line of work. Average height, average build, no obviously striking features. His clothes were comfortable but tidy: slightly baggy trousers, checked shirt and tie under a V-neck pullover, tweed jacket just a little bit too well tailored for a teacher. He might have been about the same age as McLean, but then again he might have been anything from late twenties to mid-fifties. He was bland, no better way of putting it.

'I came to tell you not to stop looking into Weatherly's case.'

McLean took a moment to process the information. 'Not to stop. You mean to keep going?'

'Precisely. That keen intellect again.' The man smiled like a parent congratulating a child on its first successful solo potty flight.

'I can't once they close the case.'

'Oh, they will. And soon. But when's that ever stopped you before?' The man looked genuinely surprised.

'That's a low blow for someone who wants me to do them a favour.'

'It's true, though. You have something of a reputation.'

'Oh, for fuck's sake.' McLean slammed his glass down on the mantelpiece, startling Mrs McCutcheon's cat awake. 'Go on. Get out before I throw you out.'

'I'm serious, Inspector. You have to keep digging on this one.' The man from the secret service started walking towards the door.

'Dig what? There's nothing to dig. Man goes mad, kills his family, then shoots himself. End of. Now out.'

'You don't really believe that any more than I do.' The man opened the door wide. As if on cue, lights from a car swept across the window looking out from the hallway on to the drive. 'I'll see myself out.'

McLean said nothing, watched the man walk across the hallway with parade square precision. He didn't turn, just stepped through into the porch. A moment later the front door clunked shut, and a moment after that the car crunched away into the night. Only then did Mrs McCutcheon's cat stand up, stretch and yawn, revealing a face filled with far too many teeth. It wove its way between McLean's legs, tail twitching a need to be stroked.

'Turncoat,' he said, stepping over it on his way to the table beside the armchair. He'd run out of latex gloves, but there was a clear evidence bag in one of his jacket pockets. He carefully collected up the empty whisky glass in the bag, sealing it tight for later analysis. Have to beg a favour off someone in SEB. Process it with a burglary investigation. Chances were the prints wouldn't turn up anything, but he was pissed off enough with the lot of them that he didn't much care.

It was as he was picking up the whisky bottle to put it back in the cupboard that McLean noticed the small pile of letters on the table. None appeared to have been opened, but knowing the people he was dealing with, they probably had special laser pens that could read a letter without opening the envelope. It wouldn't have done them much good; these were all flyers and bills.

Except one. On the bottom of the pile, a plain brown A4 envelope had no stamp, no address written on it. Flipping it over, he could see it hadn't been sealed either. Inside was a set of photographs. The first one had him slumping down into his seat, the second and he was reaching for his whisky glass. By the time he'd reached the last one, he knew he couldn't leave the Weatherly case alone.

18

'You wanted to see me, sir.'

McLean stood at the open doorway to Duguid's office. He'd barely arrived at the station that morning when a nervous young uniform constable had scurried up and issued the summons. Given what he and Ritchie had found the day before, and his visit from Special Branch, he had more than a suspicion of what the detective superintendent was going to say.

Duguid scowled; more or less his permanent expression these days. His desk was strewn with papers, a pile of reports stacked precariously at one end. On the floor beside it were more, and a few boxes from the archives. The overall effect was to make him look almost like a detective.

'Come in. Close the door.' Barked orders, sergeant-major style. At least that much hadn't changed. McLean did as he was told, advancing on the desk as if there might be a machine gun nest hiding in among the heaps of folders.

'The Weatherly case. Where are we with it?'

The 'we' didn't go unnoticed, but McLean let it slide. Something was bothering Duguid; best not to poke him until it was obvious exactly what that was.

'We've interviewed all his close friends, business associates, the usual suspects. Forensics are still processing the scene, but there's no doubt he killed his two girls, shot his wife and then turned the gun on himself.' McLean paused, and considered the photographs he'd been given and what he was going to do about them. 'Nothing obvious to explain why he did it. His business is in good shape, politics was working for him. He pretty much had it all to live for, really.'

'So you've got fuck all.'

'A thorough fuck all, sir'

'Don't take the piss, McLean. That's my job.'

'I can keep digging, if that's what you want.'

Duguid's scowl deepened. His anger was obvious, but it wasn't directed at McLean, which was confusing.

'What I want seems to be irrelevant these days. Your report needs to be in by the end of the week. Wrap it up and stick a bow on it for the Fiscal.'

McLean stood silent for a long while as the words trickled through. Not what he'd been hoping to hear at all, and yet exactly what his strange nocturnal visitor had said would happen. If anything, that was worse than having to stop; knowing that the decision had been made some time earlier and he was just a tiny pawn in some greater game.

'You want me to close down the investigation?' he asked eventually.

'What? Did someone just take away your power of reason? Yes, McLean, I want you to close down the investigation.' Duguid rubbed at his eyes with the tips of his fingers, pressing them hard as if he were trying to remove an unwanted image from his brain. 'There's nothing to be gained from digging any further. We can't arrest a dead man, and we're not going to bring those girls back.'

'What about the press?'

'What about them? Soon as the PF OKs it, you can schedule a conference and tell them what you know. Leave it to them to figure out what tipped Weatherly over the edge. That's what they deal in, after all. Supposition, half-truths, outright lies.'

McLean paused for a moment, wondering what was the best thing to do. Given a few days he could get to the bottom of the photographs, slot them neatly into the investigation. But he wasn't being given a few days. That was the whole point. He pulled the envelope full of photographs out of his jacket pocket, unfolded it and threw it down on Duguid's desk.

'Had an interesting visit at home last night. Some spook from Special Branch. Told me the case would be shut down and gave me those.'

Duguid's eyes narrowed as he stared at McLean, no doubt trying to work out whether this was a sick joke or something. 'What is it?'

'Have a look. It's distasteful, but I doubt it'll scar you for life.'

The detective superintendent slowly reached for the envelope, flipped up the flap and peered inside. Then with a sigh he pulled out the photographs. They were creased down the middle where McLean had folded the whole thing over to fit in his pocket. Duguid took a moment flattening them out before really looking at them.

'What the fuck?' He looked up at McLean, anger burning in his eyes. 'Where'd you get these? Who is this?'

'That first photograph is Weatherly with his two children. The woman's not his wife, though, it's his PA. Jennifer Denton.'

'And these?' Duguid shuffled rapidly through the remaining photographs. Images that were most certainly not safe for work. Unless you worked in Vice.

'They come from Weatherly's homes,' McLean said. 'The – ahem – athletic ones with Miss Denton are in his New Town place, the rest are the house in Fife.'

Duguid flicked back and forth through the photographs a couple of times more, then shuffled them all together and slid them into the envelope. Pushed it back across the desk towards McLean.

'Thought you said there was nothing obvious to explain why he did it. Seems pretty fucking obvious to me. Weatherly knew this sordid little secret of his was coming out and couldn't face the thought of losing it all. I'd say look for whoever was trying to blackmail him, but I don't suppose it'll do any good.'

'That was my immediate thought too, sir. And if I was looking, the first person in my sights would be the PA, Jennifer Denton.'

'I sense a but coming.' Duguid slumped back in his chair to a creaking of leather and springs.

'Well, it's obvious. Anyone who's read anything about Weatherly would know he's not the sort of man to give in to blackmail. Not for something like this.' McLean picked up the envelope, folded it over and shoved it back in his inside pocket.

'You're an expert on that then, are you?' Duguid didn't even try to hide the sneer in his voice. 'Knew him well?'

'I met him a couple of times, but no, I didn't know him well. I think you're missing the point though, sir. There's blackmail in these photographs, sure, but it's Weatherly doing the blackmailing, not the other way around.'

'Fuck me, you make things complicated, McLean. What are you going on about?'

'Weatherly was influential. Lots of friends in high places. Lots of influence. I'm guessing this is just one way he went about making sure he got what he wanted.'

'What? Getting caught on camera shagging his secretary?'

'No. Though shagging his secretary when he knew it was being filmed suggests someone who didn't much care if it got out. And that's the point, sir. He knew he was being filmed. You can't look at that last photograph and not see it. He's staring right at the bloody camera. He believes he's invincible, totally in control. If you want to know why he killed himself, then we need to find out what shook that belief. Trust me. It wasn't these photographs.'

'It's all academic, anyway. Like I said before, the investigation has run its course. We can't spend taxpayers' money on some wild goose chase. From what I've read, Andrew Weatherly was a world-class shit. He's taken up enough of our time.'

McLean let his shoulders slump. No point pushing it any further, really. Duguid had been leaned on by someone much higher up the food chain.

'Those two girls deserved more. Their mother too.'

Duguid stared at him with piggy little eyes, red-rimmed

and tired. 'I couldn't agree more. But what we deserve and what we get are rarely the same thing.'

McLean nodded, not sure whether he could say anything more. He turned away, headed for the door. He was about to close it behind him when Duguid spoke again.

'Leave it open, will you.' McLean looked back at the superintendent as he slid the wedge in with his foot. Duguid was scowling again, but there was something different about it this time.

'I know what you're like, McLean. You won't leave this alone. Just don't take any other detectives down with you, aye?'

You probably wouldn't have called it a hive of activity, but the Weatherly incident room was certainly active when McLean walked in half an hour later. Duguid's parting words still rang in his ears, underlining the horrible conviction that he had been used, was still being used. He should have realized that the case was a poisoned chalice the moment he saw it. Actually, he seemed to recall saying as much to DS Ritchie on their way out to Fife. And yet he'd taken it on anyway. Sheer bloody-mindedness. He knew it would be his eventual downfall.

'You got a minute, sir?' Somehow Sandy Gregg had managed to creep up on him unawares.

'I've got all the time in the world, Constable. But if it's anything to do with this case you might want to leave it until I've spoken to everyone. Gather them all up, can you? We'll have a briefing in a couple of minutes.'

McLean watched her scuttle off, determined to shine in her new task. It was nice to see such enthusiasm, even if he couldn't ever remember having been that keen himself. She'd make a half-decent detective, too. Just needed to develop a slightly thicker skin and a protective armour of cynicism.

He walked to the end of the room where the largest whiteboard occupied one half of the wall, a map of the city taking up the other half. Hunkering down brought flashes of pain from his hip, but he was fairly sure one of the physiotherapist's exercises involved squatting, so it was probably good pain. At least that was the lie he told himself. He traced a finger south, up Liberton Brae and on to Burdiehouse. Further down, beyond the bypass, Loanhead was growing ever larger, swallowing up Bilston and threatening to devour Roslin as well. To the east, Bonnyrigg and Rosewell lay on the other side of the glen, linked by the disused railway track. The area was dotted with ancient monuments, mine workings, remains of Midlothian's industrial past. There was history, bloody and violent, written on that map, but nowhere did it suggest a reason for the terrible fate of the tattooed man.

'Ready when you are, sir.'

He stood, wincing as he turned to face the assembled officers. For all that it had been a high-profile investigation, there weren't a lot of them any more. No doubt some had slunk off to other duties, sensing the change in the political wind. Others had probably been nicked by his more senior colleagues to work on their own cases. That seemed to be the way things operated around here. Which just left him with the enthusiastic and the too-dumb-to-know-better. Much like himself, at least on one count.

'OK, everyone. Listen up. I've some good news and some bad news.'

After the briefing, he watched them set about the task of wrapping up the investigation, his little army of uniforms, plain clothes and admin staff. Every so often someone would come up and ask him something, and after a while it occurred to him that this was really sergeant work. He had far more important things to be doing, or at least things that needed to be done that others would consider more important.

Scanning the room, he could see no one above the rank of constable. DS Carter had been part of the team to start with, but his disappearance was hardly surprising. No doubt off brown-nosing with DCI Brooks and DI Spence. Sooner or later Carter was going to get himself promoted to detective inspector. McLean could hardly wait to see the slow-motion train crash that would be, except that he'd be the one left to pick up the pieces.

Grumpy Bob wasn't about, but then that was hardly surprising. The DS had a backlog of unsolved burglary cases that had been dumped on him, and hadn't really been part of the Weatherly investigation from the off. DC MacBride was at the far end of the room, doing something with one of the admin staff's computers, but one detective was notable by her absence.

'Anyone seen DS Ritchie?' McLean pitched his question to the crowd, realizing as he did so that he'd not seen her since they'd been over Weatherly's flat the day before.

'Sorry, sir. Should have said. She phoned in sick this morning.'

'Ritchie? Sick?' Wonders never ceased. She seemed all right the night before, if a little distracted. A bit sniffly, perhaps. It must have been something serious to keep her from work, though.

'That's what I heard, sir.' DC Gregg took the opportunity of the question to stop whatever it was she'd been doing. 'We really closing this down, sir? Now?'

'There's not all that much to close down, is there? Forensics and CCTV say Weatherly did it. The gun was legally owned. There's nothing to suggest he was forced. Those are the facts we present to the Procurator Fiscal. Up to her what she wants done with it after that. Nothing would be my guess.'

'But don't you want to know why he did it?'

For a brief, irrational moment, McLean wondered whether Duguid had put her up to it. That was his way, after all. Getting others to do his dirty work, using people's weaknesses against them. Working away in the shadows to keep his team at each other's throats. All the best techniques of man management. Then he realized who he was talking to. This was DC Gregg. Inquisitive, talkative, gossipy Sandy Gregg who, one day, might make a decent detective, if she learned to talk less and listen more. Her question had been entirely innocent, stemming solely from her own horrified fascination. It was just his growing paranoia that was the problem.

'You know, I used to think I did. Now I'm really not so sure.'

19

The tattooed man incident room was quiet; no one in that early in the morning. Not as if there'd been a great sense of urgency about the case to start with, but with the Weatherly investigation across the corridor killed by edict from on high, there was even less enthusiasm in CID than normal. It didn't help that they weren't even called CID any more. Not really sure what they were one day from the next.

McLean scanned the whiteboard and the scant information on it. There were more questions than answers, perhaps unsurprisingly. They still didn't even have an ID for the man, even if the tattoos meant they were inching ever closer. He needed to get MacBride or Ritchie on to chasing up those DNA results; sort out getting Eddie Cobbold down to the mortuary, if Angus could be persuaded. Then there was the small matter of finishing up the Weatherly report and prepping for what would undoubtedly be a fun press conference.

He was mid-yawn when the door opened, revealing the crumpled form of Detective Sergeant Laird. You could put Grumpy Bob in a perfectly pressed suit first thing in the morning and he'd still look like he'd slept in it by coffee time. Chances were he had.

'You look as tired as I feel, sir. Thought that would

have been a load off your mind.' Grumpy Bob nodded his head in the direction of the main incident room.

'If only it were that easy, Bob. Sure, we've got enough to satisfy the PF, but I don't think the press'll be that happy.' McLean leaned against the nearest desk, taking the weight off his aching hip. 'Damn, this is why Dagwood gave me the case in the first place. He knew it wouldn't be long before someone shut it down. Didn't want to be the one standing up in front of the cameras, telling the world how little we care.'

Grumpy Bob let out a sound that might have been a harrumph. 'You give him credit for more than he's due.'

'Not this time. He warned me at the start. No. There's something more going on here.' McLean unfolded the slim brown envelope he'd already shown to Duguid, handed it over. Grumpy Bob took it, pulled out the sheaf of photographs and shuffled through them. His eyebrows shot up at the first, then tightened into a frown and finally a scowl as he reached the last.

'Do I want to know where you got those?' He handed the envelope with its disturbing contents back.

'Special Branch, at a guess. Or whatever it's calling itself these days.' McLean told Grumpy Bob all about his visit, and about the clues at Weatherly's flat that DS Ritchie had uncovered. 'It's all bloody politics, and you know how much I like that.'

'I'd back right off if it was me. Photos or no photos. Sounds like you've two factions gearing up for a fight up in the high corridors. You don't want to be stuck in the middle of that.'

'Well, it's not as if I haven't got anything else to do.'

McLean stepped closer to the whiteboard, eyes skimming over the words in the hope that some answer might present itself. He still had the photographs in their envelope, noticed he was tapping them against his thigh. Willed himself to stop.

'Talking of Ritchie, you any idea if she's coming in today?'

Grumpy Bob shook his head. 'Haven't heard. Not like her to call in sick.'

'She's been out of sorts all week. Ever since we went to see Weatherly's house in Fife.' McLean shuddered as the image of the two dead girls lying side by side in their bed swam up into his mind. He couldn't stop himself from opening up the envelope and pulling out the first photograph, staring at the image of Andrew Weatherly walking in the park with young Joanna and Margaret. They were all holding hands, swinging off his arm, but the woman holding on at the other side, completing the family picture, wasn't Morag Weatherly. Jennifer Denton looked every inch the mother of the children, not the stern PA they had interviewed just the previous day.

'Don't, Tony.' Grumpy Bob laid a hand on McLean's shoulder. 'You're only doing what they want you to. Let it go. Concentrate on this.' He pointed at the whiteboard.

'You're right, Bob. As ever.' McLean shoved the photograph away. So Weatherly's relationship with his PA was more personal than assistant. It hardly made any difference to the outcome of the case. Just made it all the sadder, and perhaps went some way towards explaining her attitude to their investigation. Of course, there were the other photographs and the story they told. Secrets he'd been given that would surely also be finding their way into less sympathetic hands. How long before the gutter press got hold of them? And what would it mean for him when they did?

'Christ, what a mess.' McLean picked up the marker pen, underlined 'tattoos' and put a question mark beside it. 'See if you can find MacBride can you, Bob? I need to get this Weatherly report out of the way. Then we're going to have a little trip to the mortuary.'

'Well, that's not something you see every day.'

Eddie Cobbold rocked back on his heels, recoiling from the sight in front of him. The city mortuary, late morning. McLean had arrived a few minutes before DC MacBride and the tattoo artist, hoping to have a moment alone with Cadwallader. The pathologist could be prickly when it came to letting civilians anywhere near his bodies. Unfortunately Angus was nowhere to be found, so Tracy had kitted them out with overalls and shown them into the examination theatre. The body had been waiting, covered up with a white sheet. Tracy had so far only revealed the man's head.

'It gets worse, I can assure you.' McLean recognized the voice without turning. Angus Cadwallader crossed the room from the far entrance with long strides, arriving at the opposite side of the examination table, where his assistant was already standing. It felt stupidly like some kind of Wild West stand-off, the medics facing the detectives over the dead body.

'Morning, Angus.' McLean decided to go for the

direct approach. 'This is Eddie Cobbold. Eddie, Angus Cadwallader.'

'Yes, yes. Pleased to meet you and all that. Now can we get on with this? Only I've a stack of examinations to do and this fellow's bed blocking.'

'I thought it best if we didn't start without you.' McLean saw the glint in his old friend's eye and realized that the irascibility was just for show. He too wanted to know the secrets of the tattooed man.

'Well, I'm here now, so shall we start?' Cadwallader nodded to Dr Sharp beside him. 'Tracy.'

She pulled back the white sheet with a practised ease, folding it neatly as she went, revealing the dead man in all his glory. McLean had seen him as he was pulled from the water, and again when the initial post-mortem had begun. He'd seen the photographs as well, but still the sight of the man, up close and personal, was a shock.

'Whoa!' Eddie let out the word with a long whistle, ran a hand through his close-cropped hair in surprise.

'It's quite something, isn't it?' Cadwallader leaned over the body, picked up an arm, turning it to expose the palm of the hand, covered like the rest of the body in swirls and spots of black ink. 'I'm told that's a particularly sensitive spot.'

'It is. Horribly painful.' Eddie peered at the hand. 'Can I touch?'

'You've got gloves on?' Cadwallader asked. Eddie held up his hands to show that he did.

'Be my guest. I'm keen to hear what you think.'

McLean took a couple of steps back as the pathologist

and the tattoo artist huddled over the dead man. Mac-Bride, he noticed, hadn't come anywhere near.

'You rather be outside, Constable?'

'I'd rather be anywhere, frankly, sir.'

'Sensible chap. Why don't you head back to the station? I can take it from here.'

MacBride didn't even protest, just nodded a pathetically grateful 'thanks' and fled. By the time McLean turned his attention back to the examination table, Eddie and Angus were side by side, the tattoo artist manipulating the dead man's leg as he pointed out things of interest.

'See here, the scabs are well formed and even, so that's probably been done a couple weeks back. This swirl here, connects in there, that's newer.'

'Any idea what any of it means?' McLean asked.

'Means?' Eddie looked up at him. 'Haven't a clue. I can tell you what's old and what's new. What it means is for the nutters to decide.'

McLean looked at the painted flesh. He could hardly make anything of it at all. 'When you say old, how old do you mean? Days, months?'

'Oh no. Years. There's a couple of places. Here, look.' Eddie moved up the body to the man's right shoulder, twisted the dead skin around and pointed at a spot not a million miles from the location of McLean's own misguided tattoo. 'This is pretty much the first place most people get done. Our man here's no different. There's markings here underneath the new work, and it's fitted in around it, too. Have you got a magnifying glass or something, Doctor?'

'Angus, please.' Cadwallader took the glass from the tray presented to him by Tracy and handed it over. 'Can you show me?'

The two of them bent to the task, and McLean took a step back again. From what he could hear of the conversation, they were arguing over exactly what form the original tattoo took. It was cross-shaped, but there were wavy lines to either side of it as well. Unless they were something different.

'A dagger maybe,' Eddie said after a while.

'Yes. A dagger. And these look like wings?'

McLean pulled out his phone, checked to see if he'd got a decent signal. There was Wi-Fi in the building, but he didn't have the password. The browser worked slowly as it processed first the search results for the query, then downloaded the photograph he was looking for. Eddie and Angus were still arguing over what was old and what was new by the time he'd found it.

'Is it anything like that?' He held up the phone for them both to see. Cadwallader peered over the rim of his spectacles, squinting, as if that would make the image clearer. McLean stepped closer, handed him the phone. Eddie looked in over his shoulder, then back at the dead man.

'Yup. That's it.' He too squinted at the tiny image on the touch screen before reading out the words. '"Who Dares Wins." That's the SAS, isn't it?'

McLean nodded, took his phone back. 'Have a look on his other shoulder, maybe a forearm.' He tapped the screen again, waiting while the next image came up. 'See if you can't find one of those as well. Wings from the

Parachute Regiment. There's more Paras in the SAS than any other regiment. If you can find that, I'm guessing our man here was a soldier once, rather than a numpty with a military fetish. And if that's the case, we should be getting a hit on the DNA database soon.'

20

He wanted to get straight back to the tattooed man incident room, and make a start on collating information about ex-military Missing Persons. McLean had a couple of contacts he could phone to make more discreet enquiries too; if the man really was ex-SAS then that could narrow the field right down. He wanted to do all of these things, but he had to finish the report on the Weatherly investigation first or face the wrath of Dagwood.

DC MacBride had made a good job of pulling everything together. There were transcripts of all the interviews, a detailed forensic report, the pathologist's findings. Normally he would have expected a sergeant to write up the bulk of the report for him, but DS Ritchie was still off sick. No point dragging in Grumpy Bob; even less giving it to DS Carter, only to have to do it all over again. So it was down to him.

It was nice to have a simple task for a change. The facts of the crime weren't complicated, for all that they were terrible and tragic. It was only the reason behind them that was a mystery. McLean picked up the slim brown envelope given to him by the man from Special Branch. A possible answer to that mystery lay inside, but only a partial one. And he wasn't so naive that he couldn't see the hook and line attached to this particularly juicy worm. They wanted him to look into this, wanted the apple cart upset. He just couldn't quite work out why.

McLean turned his attention back to the report, staring at the cursor flicking on and off on his screen. The brown envelope was still there, the photographs still inside. Some things you just couldn't resist.

He pulled them out, turned the first face down and concentrated on the second. It showed Weatherly and Jennifer Denton, in flagrante delicto as the more prudish papers might have put it. The third and fourth photographs were similar, presumably taken at the same time, and established the fact that Andrew Weatherly was peculiar in his sexual peccadilloes, while Jennifer Denton was extremely accommodating. For all that it was sordid, and he felt rather tawdry being a voyeur at the party, the phrase 'consenting adults' was never far from his mind as he studied the images. Of course, Morag Weatherly had most likely not consented, but adultery was a crime for the priests to deal with, not him.

He concentrated on the background in each of the images: the bed, the windows, the position of the camera. This was not something Weatherly had done for himself; that much was obvious. It looked like the whole event had taken place in his bedroom in the New Town terrace house, but McLean would have to go back and check to be sure.

Then he turned to the next set of pictures.

He'd recognized where these had been taken from as soon as he'd seen them. Stills from the CCTV cameras in the house in Fife, they were of sufficient quality to see what was going on. McLean hoped that the girls had been away, perhaps staying in Edinburgh with their mother, while their father indulged in what could only be described as an orgy. The date stamp in the bottom corner of each photograph put the event back in July, and some of the young women participating looked hardly old enough to be legal, but that wasn't what had struck him most about the photographs. The first thing he noticed was that these were stills from a video. That meant that somewhere out there someone had the full tapes. There were at least half a dozen middle-aged men involved in the antics, possibly more, although he didn't really want to study the pictures too closely to find out. The images were grainy, chosen for angles that made it impossible to see faces, or deliberately obscured. Who had they been, these men, and what were they being asked for to make these pictures disappear?

It was the last photo that puzzled him most, though. The man had stamina, that much McLean could say for Andrew Weatherly. The other thing he could say, which hadn't been evident from the security tape that they had found, was that he had at least one hidden video camera in his bedroom. If there was video of this swinger's party back in July, then there might equally be footage of the night he had walked into the room and shot his wife in the head.

McLean turned the last photograph face down on to the pile, picked the whole lot up and shuffled them back into their envelope. He pulled open one of the drawers of his desk and shoved the whole lot in there, closing it with a grunt of effort, then locking it.

The report was still on his computer screen, the

cursor still blinking. He stared at the meaningless words, trying to concentrate on the facts. Describe what they'd found. Make no suppositions. Hand it all over to the Procurator Fiscal and move on.

Who was he kidding? He unlocked the drawer, pulled out the envelope, hit 'Save' on the document he'd been working on and headed out of the room.

'I thought the investigation was closed now. Isn't that what the Chief Constable said?'

Interview room one, the nice one with an actual window and a radiator that was working. Jennifer Denton sat upright like an A-grade student from finishing school. Today she was wearing dark clothes, widow's weeds. She looked very pale, but McLean could see that was as much to do with foundation as the stress she was under. Nobody's skin was that flawless and white naturally.

'We're just crossing the last few Ts and dotting the Is, Miss Denton. The Procurator Fiscal needs a report, even if it's not going to be taken any further than that.'

The slump in Miss Denton's shoulders was minuscule, but McLean noticed it nonetheless. It confirmed his suspicions.

'So what do you need to know, Inspector?' The tired ghost of a smile flickered across her lips and crinkled the edges of her eyes. She was older than she looked, all made up.

'You were having an affair with Andrew Weatherly.'

'I—'

'Please. Don't insult either of our intelligences by denying it.' McLean cut off the protest written on Miss

Denton's face. 'The fact of it isn't all that important. You're not under any suspicion, Miss Denton, but you were very close to Mr Weatherly. Closer even than his wife, I suspect.'

'Ha. Morag and Andrew were never close. Not for the last ten years, at least. I don't think there was any love in their marriage before that, even.'

The sudden bitterness in Miss Denton's words came as a surprise, as if this were something that had been festering within her for years.

'What makes you say that?' McLean asked.

'Supermodel, the papers called her, but she was more of a gold digger. Hardly did any modelling, then stopped altogether as soon as she was married. Drew was happy enough with that, she was his trophy wife. If it wasn't for the girls, well, I'd have believed it if you'd told me they'd never even had sex.'

'You think Weatherly found out his daughters weren't actually his?' Grumpy Bob asked the question, but it had crossed McLean's mind, too.

'What?' Miss Denton looked momentarily puzzled. 'No. I mean, of course they were his. I didn't mean . . .'

'It might be a motive, I guess.' McLean spoke to the room. 'Weatherly finds out that his wife cheated on him and the result was the two girls he's doted on their whole lives. That would make him angry, maybe enough to kill them all. Then when he realizes what he's done—'

'That's ridiculous. Drew would never have done a thing like that.'

'Are you sure of that, Miss Denton? Can you really know a person that well?'

'Drew wasn't impulsive, Inspector. He didn't get angry. Not like that. And besides, he loved his daughters.'

McLean recalled the first of the photographs he'd been given. A happy family, the father and mother walking with their daughters swinging on their arms. Only it wasn't their mother they were laughing and playing with.

'It's no matter. We're not here to speculate about why it happened,' he said.

'Then why are we here, Inspector?' Miss Denton fixed him with a stare that was more her old self. 'More to the point, why am I here?'

'I need to know Mr Weatherly's movements on the day . . . well, you know. You've already given us his official schedule, but I think there's more you've not told us. Were you planning on joining him later that evening? He was alone in his city house, after all.'

Miss Denton let her gaze drop to her lap. McLean could see the hair where it thinned on the top of her head, the grey strands more noticeable at this angle. They probably had a note of Miss Denton's age somewhere in the files, but he couldn't remember it. The more he studied her, though, the more he saw of the effort she put in to looking young. Was she frightened that Weatherly would trade her in for a new model? Given the photographs he'd seen, McLean thought that unlikely. The politician obviously had access to as much young flesh as he wanted, and was happy to share it with his influential friends.

'Yes, Inspector.' Miss Denton fixed him with a steady stare, daring him to judge her. 'I would go around most evenings Drew was on his own in town.'

'You have your own key, we know that already. So you went round, what time?'

'Ten. No, it must have been nearer half past.'

'That late?'

'I have a life, friends outside of work and ... you know.' Miss Denton's glare intensified.

'Sorry. I didn't mean to imply. Anyway. Half ten. And Weatherly wasn't there, I take it.'

'No. The house was empty. Car was gone from its usual spot out front, too. Stupid idiot had even forgotten to set the alarm, but that's not as unusual as you might think.'

'Absent-minded, was he, Mr Weatherly?' Grumpy Bob shuffled in his seat, grimacing slightly as something caught in his trousers.

'Drew tends to get preoccupied. When something gets lodged in that brain of his, he forgets everything else.' Miss Denton looked at her hands again. 'Forgot, I should say.'

'Would he not have phoned you? Texted, maybe? Just to save you the trip over, if nothing else.'

'Heavens, no. It wouldn't have occurred to him. And besides, my flat's not far. Five minutes' walk.'

'Did he have any other meetings planned that evening?' McLean asked. The question seemed to confuse Miss Denton, as if she couldn't imagine a world where she didn't know everything her boss was supposed to be doing. At least two weeks before he did.

'No, Inspector. He didn't. He had some reports to go over, which is another reason why I wasn't going to go round until later, when he'd finished.'

McLean paused, considered the envelope and its contents lying unopened on the table between them. Was there any point in confronting her with the photographs? She'd already admitted to having an affair with her boss, and any investigation coming from them would be a matter for Jo Dexter in Vice. Not his responsibility, and if he was being honest not somewhere he much wanted to go.

'In which case, I've no further questions.' He stood, holding out his hand to shake. Miss Denton didn't seem to notice for a moment, then struggled to her feet.

'Thank you for coming in.' He felt her small hand in his, warm and slightly damp with sweat. It wasn't overly hot in the interview room, but it could have been the dark, heavy clothing she was wearing. 'Detective Sergeant Laird will find someone to take you home.'

He stood and watched as she gathered herself together, slung her small handbag over her arm and walked towards the door that Grumpy Bob was preparing to open. Only as she was about to leave did he speak again.

'I'm sorry for your loss, truly. And I'm sorry I had to bring it up.'

Miss Denton nodded her understanding.

'I'm afraid the next few days and weeks are going to be hard,' McLean continued. 'It's not taken me long to find out about you and Weatherly. It won't take the press long either. And not just about that.'

He watched her face as he spoke the words, seeing not shock but a tired resignation pass over her. She nodded once more, then turned and left.

21

'Did we ever establish a timeline for Weatherly leaving the city?'

DC MacBride looked up from his desk at McLean's words, confusion plastered across his face.

'Weatherly? I thought that was all done with, sir.'

'Just finishing off the report for the Fiscal. I wondered if we'd put his plates in the PNCR. It'd be useful to know what time he left his city house.'

'I can check.' MacBride pulled over his laptop and started hacking away at the keys. For a moment McLean wondered whether someone had stolen the constable's prized tablet computer, but then he saw it poking out from under a pile of reports. No way MacBride was going to let that out of his sight.

'Here we go, sir. Sandy Gregg ran it. The car was clocked crossing the bridge at a quarter past nine.'

'So assuming he didn't stop off anywhere en route, he'd have left his place about nine, a bit before.'

'I'd guess, aye. Takes what, an hour, hour and a quarter to the house in Fife?'

'Not in that blizzard. It'd be more like two.'

'So that's him arriving any time between half ten and eleven, say.'

McLean scratched at his chin, finding a spot that had missed the razor that morning somehow. 'That fits with the CCTV in the house. The cameras had him coming in the front door just after eleven, didn't they?'

MacBride tapped a few more keys. 'Eleven oh eight, sir.'

McLean looked at his watch, then across at the window. Driving in that morning had been cold and clear, the sky the palest of blues. No more snow for a few days, just freezing cold and ice on the roads. Sometimes he understood why so many detective chief inspectors drove Range Rovers.

'Any word from DS Ritchie?'

'Not today, sir. Word is she's got some nasty flu bug. Doesn't want to be the one who brings it in to work.'

'Very gallant, I'm sure. You fancy a trip to Fife, then?'

'Fife?' A worried frown spread across MacBride's face, as if the Kingdom held special terror for him.

'I need to have one last look at Weatherly's house before it's closed down. Forensics are just finishing off and packing up.' He knew, because he'd phoned them earlier.

'You couldn't maybe take San . . . er, DC Gregg, sir?' The hope in MacBride's puppy-dog eyes as he asked the question was too much to deny.

'Busy, Constable?'

'Very, sir. I've got half a dozen reports needing to be collated by the end of the day. And I'm waiting on the DNA results from our tattooed man so I can run them against the military database. There's a Missing Persons list as long as your arm that I need to go through as well.'

'OK. OK. I'll take Gregg instead.' McLean waved for

the constable to stay where he was. There was no point wasting a day of his time if he was being that productive. It was a shame that he was being taken such advantage of, though. Something McLean would have to look into. There were plenty of other detective constables and a not a few detective sergeants who probably should be doing some of that work. 'The sooner Ritchie gets back the better, though. If I have to spend two hours listening to another story about Constable Gregg's feet, I'll be blaming you.'

The roads were quiet as he sped north from the city, over the bridge and into Fife. McLean's car had a stereo, although it was perhaps more complicated than he would have liked. The salesman had shown him where he could plug in his MP3 player, and apparently the same system that gave him hands-free calling on his phone could also stream music into it. That would have required him to first put some music on his phone, then to work out how the damned thing was meant to play, so he sat in silence, enjoying the gentle burbling of the engine and the roar of tyres on tarmac.

It hadn't been a difficult decision to go alone. Finding DC Gregg would probably have wasted another half an hour, and there would have been no opportunity for thought during the journey. There wasn't really any need to take another officer with him. There wasn't really any need to make the journey at all, for that matter. The case was closed, the report sitting on his desk all ready to be handed in. Just another quick coat of whitewash and it would be done.

So why was he driving north into this rural winter landscape? Why was he going back to the house that had so traumatized DS Ritchie she'd not really been back at work since? Why was he sticking his nose in even when he knew that was precisely what he'd been told not to do, and precisely what people expected him to do anyway? He didn't know, and that more than anything was why he was going.

The motorway had been fine, but as the A roads turned to B, then to unclassified, so the efficiency of Fife Council's fleet of snowploughs diminished. The Alfa might have been comfortable, but it was a heavy old thing, with wide front tyres and more power than traction. Several times McLean felt it sliding out of control, just getting it back before an expensive encounter with one of the rough stone walls that took the place of verges in these parts. Progress slowed to a crawl as he reached the end of the driveway up to the house, the route only passable at all because the SOC vans had worn deep ruts in the drifts.

It had been overcast and grey the day he and Ritchie had visited, but even with a weak sun in a pale blue sky overhead, the house still looked cold and forbidding. Three vans and a couple of squad cars were clustered around the stone steps leading up to the front door. McLean half parked, half slid his car into a space obviously vacated by something a bit larger. He hoped he'd be able to get back out again.

Inside, the chaos of deconstruction was evident all around. Battered aluminium equipment cases were piled by the door, ready to be loaded. A bored-looking uniform constable wandered up as McLean stepped over the threshold, then recognized him from the previous visit.

'Morning, sir. Didn't know you were coming. The Detective Superintendent's in the kitchen out back, if you want him.'

That came as a surprise. McLean hadn't been expecting Jack Tennant to be anywhere other than his nice warm office in Glenrothes. He went through to the kitchen anyway, and found a small group sitting around the table, drinking tea and enjoying the warmth coming from the Aga. Tennant sat at the head and looked up as McLean entered.

'Tony! What brings you back here?'

In the boot of his car, slid into a case folder for the investigation, the photographs he'd been given by the man from Special Branch were the real reason. He wasn't sure why, but McLean didn't want to share them with anyone. He even regretted having shown them to Grumpy Bob.

'I just wanted to have a last look around. Try to exorcize some of the ghosts, you know how it is.'

Tennant put his mug down on the table. The old oak surface was marred by dozens of mug-sized rings. He'd not spent long in here the last time, but McLean couldn't help thinking the table top had been cleaner then. So much for forensic conditions. Or had they done this room first so they could use it to relax in? It wasn't as if Weatherly or his wife were going to complain.

'Knock yourself out.' Tennant pushed his chair noisily

out from the table and got to his feet. 'We're all done here anyway. You've got about half an hour before the vans are all loaded and we lock up.'

'That's plenty more than I need. I'll try not to get in anyone's way.'

McLean backed out of the kitchen, noticing the doorway down to the basement as he did. The stairs opened out on to a surprisingly large space directly under the entrance hall, with several smaller storerooms leading off it. One of these had obviously housed the server where the CCTV camera footage had been stored. There were racks and wires, even a couple of large flat screen monitors, but all the actual computers had gone. He didn't know whether it was worth asking if Fife had them or they'd been spirited away by some shadowy government department. McLean fiddled with his phone until he found the camera function and took a few photographs of the racks anyway. Maybe DC MacBride would be able to look at them and magically tell him how many camera feeds there had been.

Back in the hall, most of the equipment boxes had been moved. McLean went from room to room, barely looking at anything. He wanted to go back to his car and get the photographs, but he'd noticed that one of the uniform constables was following him, discreetly, wherever he went. No doubt Tennant wanted to know what he was up to, and word of his visit would almost certainly get back to Duguid. Hopefully the detective superintendent would stop it from going any higher than that.

McLean went through to the back of the house again, noticing the door that opened on to the small courtyard and outbuildings beyond. Beside it, an open door revealed a downstairs toilet. He went in, shutting the door behind him and making a show of rattling the bolt closed so the constable would be in no doubt as to what he was doing in there. It was a small room, but it had a decent-sized window. After a moment's study, he worked out it had just the one lock, a simple slider that held the two halves of the sash together. So much for all the state-of-the-art camera technology in the place. McLean unlocked the window, flushed the toilet and washed his hands. When he came out of the room Tennant was just walking out of the kitchen.

'You done here, then?' the detective superintendent asked.

'Pretty much. A bit of a waste of time, but you know how it is.'

'I for one can't get out of here soon enough.' Tennant slapped McLean on the shoulder. 'But I know what you mean, Tony. Can't get rid of that niggling feeling you've missed something, eh?'

'Aye.'

They all walked out together. Tennant produced a heavy key of the sort favoured by Victorian jail-keepers and locked the front door. 'That's us. Over to the lawyers now.' He tramped down the steps and climbed into the passenger seat of one of the squad cars.

'I think I'll go for a bit of a walk before heading back to the city,' McLean said, as the constable who'd been following him around the house opened the door on the driver's side. 'Give my legs a bit of a stretch.'

Tennant gave him a look that was half-knowing,

half-surprised. He tapped the heavy iron key against his thigh for a moment, then slipped it into his jacket pocket.

'Good idea. There's a great view from the top up there.' He pointed in the direction of the hill at the back of the house. 'Just don't take too long. The nights drop quickly at this time of year.'

22

The trees at the back of the house were Scots pine, ancient and twisted and gnarly. Granny trees, he remembered them being called in his childhood. He'd never really understood why, except that they were old. The snow had settled in deep piles around the trunks, thinning where a path ran through towards the big hill beyond. It was smooth, though; no footprints to suggest anyone had been this way recently. McLean eyed the summit. From here it looked deceptively close, but who knew how many dips and foothills there were before he got to the top? A last look behind him to make sure no one at the house was following, and he set off into the wood.

The silence was almost total, just the squeaky crunch of his feet in the snow. He'd worn warm clothing, and as he climbed over a stile and stepped from the trees on to open ground, he could feel himself sweating already. There was no wind at all, and the sky was clear, a weak sun low in the southern sky making the white blanket gleam almost too bright. He squinted against it and waded on through the snow, following what looked like it might possibly be a path.

In the end it took almost an hour, but the view from the top of the hill was worth it. To the north, darkening with the dying day, the Tay Estuary opened up towards

Dundee. Ribbons of light marked the A90 as it ran west towards Perth. Further west still, the snow-covered Grampian Mountains reared up like broken teeth, their topmost tips pink and orange as they caught the setting sun. South, McLean could see the Pentland Hills and Edinburgh itself, Salisbury Crags and the Castle Hill both obvious in the clear, crisp air despite being the best part of fifty miles away.

The climb had invigorated him, fresh air driving out the fug of the city. He'd hoped to have time to think about the case as he walked, but found that his mind had been delightfully blank. It was almost as if the further he went from Weatherly's house, the weaker its hold on him became. Not completely broken, though. He knew he'd have to go back. Knew he'd have to uncover its secrets.

A glance at his watch told him it was time to get moving; the light would be almost gone by the time he reached his car, even if going downhill was always quicker. He retraced his steps, noticing how the sparkling light on the snow softened as the sun dipped below the horizon. Head down and mind a million miles away, it wasn't until he reached the final field before dropping once more into the trees that he realized he wasn't alone.

It started with a snort. A sort of cross between a sniff and a deep, rumbling belch. McLean stopped in his tracks, looked to the side and there, staring at him with a belligerent, quizzical expression, was the biggest bull he had ever seen, with thick horns jutting from its head and pointing forward at him. He couldn't begin to imagine how he'd missed it before, nor how it had managed to creep up on him so silently. A rustling in the bushes, and it was joined by another, this one with more slender horns curved upwards and out. It lowered its head as if ready to charge, sniffed the snow. He glanced sideways, trying to gauge the distance to the fence and the trees without actually taking his eyes off the beasts. Now that he was paying attention, he could see that the snow had been kicked around by what must have been a massive herd of them.

For a moment he didn't know what to do. This wasn't something he'd been trained to deal with, wasn't something he'd ever experienced. They were Highland cows, that much he could tell, but he wasn't sure he'd ever been close to one before, if you didn't count a slab of steak on a plate.

Another rustling in the gorse bush, lower down this time, and a calf poked its head around its mother's side. Without the horns and a quarter the size of the bull, it looked harmless and curious. And very, very furry. Like an animated teddy bear. It was difficult to be scared of something so comical.

Moving as slowly as he could, so as not to provoke them, McLean shuffled sideways in the direction of the woods. The cattle followed him, the bull moving with a ponderous gait as its bulk swung from side to side. More appeared from behind the gorse bushes, no doubt eager to see what new thing was happening. If he didn't speed up he'd be surrounded.

The whole herd was following him by the time he reached the stile and climbed over into the woods. He was fairly certain by then that they meant him no harm, but given the size of them and their sharp, pointy horns, he was glad to be out of the field anyway. As he picked his way through the darkening trees, he realized that he was breathing heavily, his heart pumping away as if he been sprinting. Stupid, really. It was just a herd of cows. Or a fold. Wasn't that what they called it if it was Highlands? He'd read that somewhere. Perhaps he'd ask DC MacBride if he remembered.

Darkness had almost completely fallen by the time he returned to his car. Everyone else had gone, leaving just the dead façade of stone and ivy. The windows were lifeless eyes like those of the two little girls huddled together in the one bed. Like those of Morag Weatherly, startled by her husband's final, fatal act.

McLean shook his head to dispel the image. It was just an empty house. Nothing dangerous in it now. Nothing to scare a grown man. He opened up the car, fetched out the envelope with its incriminating photographs, dug a torch from one of the cubbyholes in the boot. Would the moon be out later? He couldn't remember seeing it recently, but then it wasn't something you often noticed in the city.

Slamming the car boot shut, he set off around the back and made for the window he hoped was still unlocked. If not, his trip up the hill and adventure with the cows would have all been for naught.

He needn't have worried about the window. Finding it in the dark wasn't as easy as he'd hoped, but when he pushed at the glass, the sash slid upwards silently, well balanced by its counterweights. Clambering inside took a matter of moments. McLean paused before opening the door on to the back hallway, wondering whether there was some kind of alarm. But he'd seen the mess of the security system in the basement, and Tennant hadn't set anything when they'd left earlier.

Knowing the house was empty didn't make it any less oppressive. There was a feel to the place that the darkness only made worse. The rational part of him knew that it was just superstition, but he also knew people had died here, recently and violently. You'd have to be made of stone not to get just a little scared.

He managed to avoid most of the shin-high obstacles between the downstairs toilet and the stairs. A little evening light filtered in through the large window halfway up, an unexpected but not unwelcome sliver of moon rising over the trees. McLean's eyes had more or less accustomed themselves to the gloom by the time he reached the door to the girls' bedroom. He paused a moment, then went inside.

It was too dark to see anything much, so he finally relented and switched on the torch. Deep shadows sprung out of the general darkness, moving and twisting as he played the light this way and that. The bodies were gone, of course, and the beds had been stripped. Standard procedure for forensics, but it was doubtful they'd be processed now. Most likely someone would accidentally destroy them. That wasn't what he was here for, though.

Popping the torch into his mouth to free both hands, he slid the photographs out of their envelope, shuffling through them until he found the one he was looking for.

Several naked bodies had been caught in all their puffy, unflattering glory, engaged in an athletic collection of sexual acts over the two beds and the floorspace between. The shot was from above, and McLean swept the torch beam up, seeing the chunky security camera in the corner over the door. He stood underneath it, held the photograph up, tried to see the angle but it wouldn't fit. The picture he was looking at had clearly been taken from a different place. He moved over to the foot of the bed, played the beam over the far wall to see if there were any marks from a different camera having been removed. Had he been looking in daylight, he might have missed it, but the torchlight reflected off the tiny lens, buried into the ornate cornicing.

A heavy wooden trunk guarded the end of one of the girls' beds. He pulled it over to the wall, placed a child's chair on top of it and climbed carefully up, all too aware of how he'd broken his leg just a few months earlier. Thinking of it brought a familiar ache that had been missing on his climb to the top of the hill. Perhaps that was all that he needed, a bit of regular walking. Not the mindless stretches and exercises the physiotherapist had given him.

Up close and with the bright torchlight to show up the imperfections, McLean could see where the camera had been inserted into the cornice. A casual glance would easily miss it though, along with the two others he spotted. He stepped carefully down to the floor, put the chair back where it had sat by a desk that would never be used again, dragged the chest over to the foot of the bed. One last sweep of the room with the torch brought only a deep sense of melancholy. Nothing he found in here could hope to change what had happened.

With the photographs to guide him, McLean was able to find twenty more hidden cameras around the upper floor of the house. Some were in the cornicing, others in light fittings, one pushed into an ornate carved scroll on the frame of a large oil painting. In the master bedroom, the wall was still stained with the blood and brains of Morag Weatherly. He tried not to picture her as he compared the scene with the photograph of Weatherly and three very young women sprawled across that same bed.

It took a while to find the back staircase leading up to the attic; Weatherly's house was of an age to have supported quite a staff of servants, but it was also one whose original owners hadn't liked the idea of them being obvious. He eventually located the door hidden in the wooden panelling at the far end of the corridor back past the girls' bedroom. It opened on to a narrow passageway with tiny rooms to either side, pressed into storage use. Steps went both up and down, the latter no doubt leading to the scullery or the boot room. Upstairs opened out on to another narrow corridor with tiny servants' rooms leading off it. Most had clearly not been used in ages, not even as a secret world for the girls to play in. One room had been pressed into a very different service, though.

It had a single window, looking out over the courtyard to the woods and the cows beyond, but that was largely obscured by a bank of monitors, all dead. Racks alongside each wall had obviously held surveillance equipment, hard drive recorders, Christ only knew what. Or maybe Special Branch knew what. Someone had been in and hastily removed everything, just like the equipment down in the basement. But why the two different sets? It was obvious, really. One for the security system; one to keep a discreet eye on the antics of more special guests. It didn't take a genius to realize that the parties must have been fairly regular occurrences, but then he'd assumed that when he'd first seen the photographs.

McLean left the room as he found it. Out in the corridor, the moon was shining through high skylights now, giving more than enough light for him to navigate a safe path back down the stairs. He carried on past the first floor, finding himself in a small pantry just off the kitchen. Back out through the window in the downstairs toilet, and he crunched around the house in snow crusting in the freezing air. Overhead the moon had risen above the summit of the hill, less than half-full, but shedding more than enough light to give the night a magical feel. He took one last look at the house, satisfied that he'd seen as much as he'd ever need to. Far more than he'd ever wanted.

It wasn't until he pulled on to the motorway, almost an hour after leaving the house, that McLean realized how tense he had been. Once more it seemed that distance lessened the effect of the place, as if it exerted some terrible gravity. He'd driven in silence for a while, checking his mirror for signs that he was being followed, even though he wasn't sure who might be doing such a thing. He wouldn't have put it past Jack Tennant to have left a patrol car at the end of the drive with instructions to let him know when the nosy Edinburgh copper left, but McLean had seen nothing obvious. With the roads still covered in snow, there wasn't much traffic about either, which meant detecting a tail should have been easy.

With a clear road ahead, he finally switched on the radio, hoping for some soothing music. He got the news.

'. . . *funeral tomorrow of Andrew Weatherly, his wife Morag and two daughters Joanna and Margaret. Police have concluded their investigation into the tragedy and a report is being prepared for the Procurator Fiscal . . .*'

McLean found the button that changed the station, tuning in to some soft rock so bland it was almost offensive. It was still better than being reminded of where he'd just been. Let alone the work that still needed to be done. And the funeral, of course. He hated the things, but he'd have to go. He wondered if anyone else from work would be there, or any of the blurred faces from the photographs in the boot of his car.

Home was a welcome sight, and Mrs McCutcheon's cat greeting him at the back door even more so. It weaved in and out of his legs as he pushed through to the kitchen, then he saw why it wasn't sitting on the table washing itself as it normally did when he arrived. Propped up against the sugar bowl so he couldn't possibly miss it was another plain brown envelope.

'Oh bloody hell.' He snatched it up, inelegantly ripped the top open and pulled out more photographs. Just what he wanted to deal with. There was a hard case, too, containing a DVD. Just a cheap recordable of the sort you got in boxes of a hundred, all stacked up on a central spindle; it had nothing written on it at all apart from the manufacturer's name.

The top photograph was notable only in as much as he recognized the face of the sweating gentleman in sexual congress with another sweating gentleman. Beyond that, McLean couldn't be bothered looking. He slid the lot into the envelope and put it back where he'd found it.

'Don't know if you lot are watching or listening, but you can fuck right off. I'm not doing your dirty work for you.'

There was no answer, of course, and he doubted whoever it was behind the photographs had bothered to bug his house. They were just going to drip-feed his curiosity and see where it got them. Perhaps he could arrange for the envelope to fall into the hands of the press. But then Jo Dalgliesh would have a field day with it, and probably drag the police into the mess as well. Best to just leave well alone, add the photos to the pile and hope that whoever was sending them got the message.

The hallway was cold and dark as McLean walked over to the front door to fetch the mail. It reminded him too much of Weatherly's house; smaller, but the layout was similar, the dark panelling and chequerboard floor tiles just the same. But then so were countless other houses in the city and all across the country. Scottish architecture could be less than adventurous at times. He shook off the feeling as he bent to pick up the small pile of letters. Flyers, junk mail, catalogues for old ladies' clothing, and a cheap-looking postcard from somewhere in Eastern

Europe. Too many consonants in the word to easily pro-
nounce it.

He flipped the card over, recognized the spidery
scrawl, but couldn't read it in the near-darkness. Back in
the kitchen he put the kettle on, and dumped the bulk of
the post in the recycling bin before reading what Emma
had to say.

*Another one gone. We're making progress but it's hard. So much
has changed since they were here. Heading to Poland in a week or
so, but need to sort out a few things first. Give Mrs M's cat a
scratch from me. Love E XXX*

That was it. He turned over the card in the vain hope
there'd be more on the other side, but it was just a cheap
photograph of a castle, the sky impossibly blue behind
its high towers. Snow capped the mountains on which it
was built, but in the foreground the picture was of
flowers in bloom, a woman in some bizarre dress. He
held it up to his nose, sniffing for any lingering smell of
Emma, but all he got was damp cardboard and the porch
floor.

He stood up as the kettle clattered to the boil, crossed
the kitchen to the cork noteboard by the dresser and
pinned the card alongside the previous one. Perhaps he
should get a map of Europe, plot Emma's progress by
her correspondence. Pins and red cotton thread. But no,
he had enough of that at work. If he was going to waste
his time on anything, it would be puzzling out why he
was being pushed into investigating Weatherly's sordid
past when it was obvious no good would come of it.

Mrs McCutcheon's cat had taken up its habitual spot on the table, sitting beside the sugar bowl and the propped-up envelope of incriminating photographs. He reached over and gave it a scratch behind the ears, and for once it didn't try to claw the veins out of his wrist.

'That's from Emma,' he said, which earned him a purr loud enough to vibrate the spoon in the sugar bowl. McLean smiled, glad of the company, and set about making himself a mug of tea.

23

'Still suffering with the leg, I see.'

Early morning after a fitful night's sleep, visited by nightmares of dead children trying desperately to wake their mother. McLean had hoped for a quiet couple of hours getting to grips with the tattooed man investigation, but his smartphone had chimed the appointment, same as it ever did. He had toyed with the idea of just not turning up. After the last session, he was fairly sure Hilton would let it slide. But annoying though the man was, he did occasionally have insights into the human mind, and there was something McLean wanted to ask him.

'It's healing. Doesn't seem to like the cold weather so much.'

Hilton nodded. 'Wasn't sure I was going to see you today.'

'Wasn't sure I was going to come.'

'So what changed your mind?'

McLean shrugged. 'Nothing better to do, I guess.'

Hilton slumped back in his chair and ran a hand across his stubbly head. 'They closed the Weatherly case down on you.'

McLean managed not to smile as Hilton picked up the thread he wanted followed. 'It'd run its course. We know he did it, where, how, when. Nothing else to do, really.'

Hilton raised an eyebrow. 'You left out why.'

'That's your department, doc. Not mine. What makes a man drug his children and then smother them in their beds? Why would he take a rifle and shoot his wife in the head? And what possesses someone to stick a gun under their chin and pull the trigger?' McLean dangled the details of the case in front of Hilton like bait. He knew the psychiatrist had wanted to be involved from the start. Judging by his expression, he'd not managed to get anything from his usual sources so far.

'He shot himself, you say. With the same rifle he used to shoot his wife?'

'Not long afterwards, if the evidence is to be trusted.'

'And the children. Drugged first? That's . . . interesting.' Hilton picked up a pen, began writing on the notepad that was arranged squarely along the centre line of his immaculately tidy desk. 'And he killed them before his wife?'

'It's not important, though, is it? I mean, he killed them all anyway.'

'Oh, but it's vitally important, Tony. The order is everything. The method.' Hilton scribbled some more, his excitement evident in every movement. McLean was jealous of his enthusiasm, fuelled purely by curiosity and not yet tainted by the politics of the whole thing.

'So what do you think makes a man do something like this, then?' He tried to make the question as casual as possible. It wasn't necessary. Hilton was beyond noticing such subtleties.

'Ah, the eternal question. Despair, of course. But it's more than that. It's a special kind of megalomania.

Almost childish, really. If I can't have it, then no one can.' Hilton made little bunny ear quotation marks with his fingers as he spoke.

'But he had it. He had everything, as far as I can tell. Glamorous wife, successful career, beautiful children. He was even popular, for a politician at least.' McLean counted out the points one by one, putting extra emphasis on the last.

'Then I would suggest that someone threatened to take it all away from him. Blackmail, perhaps. I can't imagine someone like Weatherly wouldn't have had one or two skeletons in his closet. If there was something that could ruin him, something that might even have put him in jail perhaps, then he might well have destroyed it all rather than face the consequences.' Hilton finished writing, put the pen carefully down and leaned back in his chair. 'It's an extreme psychopathy, but all successful men are psychopaths to a greater or lesser extent.'

McLean said nothing, letting Hilton believe he was thinking about what he'd said. It wasn't anything he hadn't already considered, and from a position of having a lot more facts to hand. There was no doubt that someone could have blackmailed Weatherly if they had wanted to, except that from what he knew of the man, Weatherly would more likely have gone public and relished the fight than give in. Even in the face of the photographs, the sex parties.

No, he wasn't at all convinced by Hilton's explanation . . . which was a shame, as it meant he'd have to keep looking.

*

Funerals had never been his thing. He understood the need to remember the dead, comfort the bereaved, but the whole ceremony left McLean cold. He wasn't sure either how Andrew Weatherly could be given a Christian burial, given that the man had taken his own life. Surely he should have been discarded at a crossroads on unconsecrated ground, not afforded the closest thing to a state funeral you could get without actually inviting the Queen.

Perhaps it was the modern way, forgiveness. Or maybe it was the old way back in fashion after two thousand years. Whatever the reason, the church was full, voices raised for the hymns, heads bowed for the prayers. McLean stood in a small side-chapel off the main nave, grateful that all the pews had been taken by the time he had arrived. It gave him the opportunity to scan the congregation for familiar faces.

Jennifer Denton was there, of course. She'd organized the whole thing with the efficiency that must have made her such a good personal assistant. Weatherly had no immediate family beyond that which he had so cruelly dispatched, but from the look of it a few hopeful distant cousins had shown up, no doubt with an eye to any inheritance. Morag McIntosh, as she had been before her marriage, had a sister who could have been her identical twin were she not twice her size. There were a lot of bankers and financiers in the middle rows; he could tell them by the way they kept looking at their watches, glancing from side to side, anxious for this to be over so they could get back to the office and the next deal. McLean wondered why they'd bothered coming at all.

And there were politicians. Lots of them. All accompanied by the many hangers-on, special advisers and whatever else was needed to grease the cogs of state. The only police presence, apart from himself and DC MacBride, were the security teams needed to make sure nothing untoward happened to the great and the good as they celebrated the life of a man who had murdered three people, two of them children. No sign of Detective Superintendent Tennant from Fife, or anyone from the Police Liaison Committee that Weatherly had chaired. Some people obviously had a sense of self-preservation.

McLean found it easy to tune out the service, barely listened to the eulogies and didn't even bother to mime along to the hymns. Religion had never been his thing, and that wasn't why he was here anyway. Towards the end he moved quietly to a position by the door where he could get a better view of the people as they left behind the coffins; two big, two small, carried out to the churchyard and the Weatherly family crypt.

The press were waiting outside like flies attracted by the smell of a well-rotting carcass. Television reporters stood in a line down the pavement across the road, each doing their piece to camera just out of shot of the next. Closer in, the local paparazzi were shouting names and flashing away like it was some celebrity gala or film premiere. So much for respecting the dead. McLean spotted Jo Dalgliesh, leather overcoat tied tight, notebook at the ready as she tried to pump an opposition spokesman for a juicy quote. Her face was alight with the thrill of the chase. Better the politician on the receiving end of that than him.

It was as the assembled great and good were chatting

around the gates, waiting for chauffeur-driven cars to arrive and take them to the wake, that McLean saw the woman. He couldn't have said what caught his attention; just something about her stance, perhaps. She was about twenty yards away, whispering something into the ear of a junior minister, one black gloved hand on the bemused man's shoulder. The junior minister laughed, a braying like a kicked mule that McLean could hear quite clearly despite the hubbub of conversations all around. The woman patted his shoulder once more, then turned away, her eyes scanning over the crowd, looking for someone. They found him and locked on. She frowned, trying to place him, then nodded once and turned away. McLean shook his own head, unsure exactly what had just happened.

'We done here, sir?' DC MacBride's innocent question broke through the chill fog clinging to him. McLean looked around at the departing people. Not many left, just a few still chatting with the priest, who looked like he wanted to get away too.

'Reckon so. You fancy going to the wake?'

MacBride's expression was enough of answer. McLean fished his car keys out of his pocket. Tossed them at the startled constable. 'OK then, you drive. You can drop me off at the hotel on your way back to the station. There's bugger all parking round there anyway.'

MacBride was a nervous driver, constantly fidgeting with the gearstick, the indicator stalk, the steering wheel. He'd spent a fussy age adjusting the seat before they'd set off, but even so he leaned forward, his back not actually touching the leather. McLean knew that the constable had attended an advanced driving course, so it must have been the fact that he was driving the boss's car.

'You heard anything from Ritchie today?' he asked, as they inched forward in heavy traffic.

'What? Oh, no sir. Nothing.'

'Any idea what's up with her? Don't think I've ever seen her sick before.'

'There's a nasty flu bug been doing the rounds. Could be that.'

'I guess.' McLean stared at the grey sky just barely visible between the tops of the high tenements and the edge of the windscreen. It was certainly that time of year when people succumbed. Something to do with the long nights and short, grey days battering the immune system into submission. On the other hand, Ritchie was from Aberdeen; she should have been able to cope with a little snow. 'Hope she's better soon. It's a pain trying to get anything done without her.'

MacBride didn't say 'tell me about it', but McLean could see the words forming in a little bubble above the constable's head. Given that he was probably picking up most of the slack it seemed fair enough.

'We heard anything back from the military about our tattooed man?'

MacBride relaxed a little, back on familiar territory. 'Not yet, sir. It was on my list of things to chase up. Hoping to get the DNA database match done too. Would've been done already but there was some mix-up at the lab. Had to get a fresh sample done.'

'What sort of mix-up? It's not like Angus to get his samples muddled.'

'Way I heard it, couldn't have been Dr Cadwallader.' MacBride sped up to make use of a gap that had appeared in the traffic, then let out a little 'eep' of surprise as the car accelerated a lot faster than he was expecting, the steering wheel twitching in his hands.

'Gently does it, Constable. She's got a bit more grunt than grip, especially on these roads.' McLean grinned once he realized the situation was under control.

'Sorry, sir. Just not used to it.' They were approaching the hotel where Weatherly's wake was being held, and the traffic snarled even worse as dozens of chauffeurs vied with each other to get their cargo as close to the front entrance as possible.

'Pull over, I'll walk from here. Probably be safer that way. See you back at the station in an hour or so.'

MacBride did as he was told, even managing to stop the car just past a large bank of slushy snow. McLean climbed out into fresh, cold air, was about to close the door when something occurred to him.

'You said it couldn't have been Angus's fault, the mix-up. How so?'

'He only deals with dead people, sir. The first sample they tested had the DNA of a goat.'

24

Considerably more people had come to drink Andrew Weatherly's wine than had shown up to pay their last respects at the church. That was the way of these things, McLean supposed. It wasn't as if the man was going to complain. The wake had something of the air of a wedding party, only with more sombre clothes. There wasn't any dancing, either.

'Inspector. How good of you to come.' Jennifer Denton looked tired, but she'd still made the effort to appear smart. People weren't queueing up to offer her their condolences, he noticed. Too busy networking or looking for the next scoop.

'I wasn't sure whether I should. Normally we come along to see who turns up, if there's an investigation ongoing. But, well, it's all officially done and dusted now.'

'And yet here you are.' Miss Denton grabbed a couple of wine glasses from a passing waiter, handed one over and took a sizeable gulp of the other. 'To be honest, I'm rather glad.'

'Are you coping all right?' McLean tried not to make it obvious that he wasn't going to drink his wine.

'Keeping busy's the best thing. I don't like to have to stop and think.'

'You'll have to eventually. I mean, once this is all done, the will sorted . . .'

'That'll give me a year or five then.' Miss Denton took another swig and a single drop of red escaped, landing on her white blouse like a blood splatter.

'That long?' Having not long tidied away the last few pieces of his own inheritance following the death of his grandmother almost eighteen months earlier, McLean was well aware that the wheels of the legal profession ground slow and fine. Still, five years sounded like something of an exaggeration.

'If I'm lucky. Could be ten.' Miss Denton pointed over to the far side of the room, where a cluster of unhappy-looking people were studiously not talking to each other. They looked quite out of place among the politicians and businessmen. 'The jackals are circling. Drew's will's being read out later on, and they're none of them going to be very happy about it.'

'You know what's in it?'

'Of course. I'm one of the executors.'

'And a beneficiary?' The question slipped out before McLean could stop himself. The detective in him taking over. 'Sorry. None of my business.'

'Not supposed to say anything until it's been read.' Miss Denton tapped the side of her nose with a finger. The nail was painted a deep glossy red, but the end of it was cracked and ridged. 'But don't worry. It'll be made public tomorrow. Drew was very old-fashioned that way.'

McLean said nothing, wasn't really sure what he could say. Andrew Weatherly's will was of interest, of course. He'd been a very rich man, so what became of his wealth mattered. Except that the reasons it mattered to McLean were of no importance any more. He wasn't looking for a suspect, so there was no need to seek a motive.

'So why did you come here then, Inspector?' Miss Denton put her empty glass down on a passing tray, swapping it for a full one with a surprising dexterity.

'I rather suspect he's come here looking for me.'

The words cut through him like a stiletto to the soul. The voice was deep, almost husky, and yet unmistakably female. McLean turned to see who had spoken, but he already knew. Close up the woman was striking, that was the best he could manage. She wasn't beautiful in the classic sense of the word; no supermodel like Morag Weatherly had been. But there was something about her that he could imagine men killing each other over. He'd noticed her hair from afar, straight and black like Elizabeth Taylor's wig in *Cleopatra*, only without the gold braids. It framed a face of purest, flawless white skin, high cheekbones and eyes that hinted at a Middle Eastern background. He would have said she was in her early thirties, but something about the way she held herself suggested a much greater age kept at bay by far more effective means than Jennifer Denton's hair dye and foundation. She wore black, unchanged from the funeral. Only her blouse was red, darkest claret as if she had spilled a whole bottle on it compared with Miss Denton's single drop. Her blouse matched her cherry-dark lips, which McLean found he'd been staring at for far too long without realizing. He looked away in embarrassment.

'Jennifer, are you going to introduce us?' The woman spoke softly, but still her voice sounded like it could flay the skin off a man. A sandstorm in the desert.

179

'Mrs Saifre. I'm sorry. This is Detective Inspector McLean.' Miss Denton sounded afraid. She looked afraid, paling visibly under Mrs Saifre's stare and shrinking away from the woman.

'Ah yes. Of course you are. I've heard so much about you.' Mrs Saifre held out a hand and for a moment, McLean wasn't sure what he should do with it. That voice filled his head, chasing away all ability to think straight. Possibly just a little too slow to be polite, he pulled himself together, took the hand in his own and shook it gently. The tiniest flicker of disappointment played around those deep black eyes, and then she smiled, squeezing his hand with a grip that crackled the bones in his knuckles.

'You knew Mr Weatherly?' McLean asked.

'Knew him? I practically made him. Isn't that so, Jennifer?' Mrs Saifre finally let go of McLean's hand. He let it drop to his side, trying to hide it as he flexed his fingers, checking for any broken bones.

'Mrs Saifre was one of Drew's first investors. She's a major stockholder in Weatherly Asset Management.' Miss Denton spoke the words grudgingly, as if she were willing it not to be so.

'Mr Weatherly's death must have come as a shock then, Mrs Saifre,' McLean said. 'The nature of it as much as anything.'

'A shock.' Mrs Saifre rolled the word around her mouth, as if it had a flavour she'd never tasted before. 'Yes. It was. Andrew always struck me as the level-headed type. Not one for rash gestures. Oh, he could take risks, but they were always calculated in his favour. Or my favour, of course.'

'I must go and speak to the First Minister before he leaves.' Jennifer Denton knocked back the last of her second glass of wine. 'Thank you for coming, Inspector.'

'Yes, run along, Jennifer. There's a good girl.' Mrs Saifre dismissed the PA with a casual wave of the hand. It reminded McLean of an old friend of his grandmother's who had dismissed him in similar fashion once he'd been presented to her on one of her infrequent visits. The condescension had hurt him even as a ten-year-old, and yet Miss Denton merely nodded, her eyes flicking to his with a look of horror in them before she turned and fled.

'Such a mousy little thing, don't you think?' The way Mrs Saifre spoke the words, it was all but impossible to disagree. 'Quite what Andrew saw in her, I've no idea.'

'You knew him well?'

'I knew him a long time, if that's the same thing. My late husband left me a great deal of money. Andrew was well placed to turn it into even more. We worked together.'

'And what about play? Did you know Mr Weatherly socially?'

'Ah me, am I being interrogated?' Mrs Saifre let out a tiny laugh like the distant cawing of crows. 'And here I was thinking the investigation was all over.'

'I'm sorry. Force of habit. And you're right, the case is closed. I can't stop myself from wondering why a man with so much to live for would suddenly flip like that, though. I guess I'm just trying to flesh out his character, find out what made him tick.'

Mrs Saifre opened up a black patent leather bag slung over one elbow, and pulled out a business card. That was when McLean realized that she'd taken off her gloves. She handed the card over. 'Here. I'm going to be away on business until the end of next week, but call me after that. You can buy me lunch and I'll tell you all I know about Andrew Weatherly. Investigation or no.' She held out her hand again, and when McLean shook it this time, she merely pinched his fingers lightly, her touch playful now as she dismissed him with much greater panache than she had used on Miss Denton.

'There was just one thing, Mrs Saifre, if you don't mind?' There was that flicker of irritation across the eyes again. McLean hurried to ask the question while his nerve held. There was something about this woman that made him want to recoil. 'My people interviewed every-one involved with Mr Weatherly's businesses, but I don't recall your name coming up.'

Mrs Saifre laughed again, and far away something died. She nodded at the card, still clasped between his fingers. 'I spoke to Detective Sergeant Ritchie. Nice girl. Ask her about me.' And then she turned and left. McLean watched her progress through the crowd, which seemed to part before her. Finally he looked down at the card. Her married name was Saifre, but she'd told him already her husband was dead. Now it seemed she had reverted to her maiden name, and that was what was written on the card in blood-red ink. Jane Louise Dee and a mobile phone number. Nothing else at all.

25

The massed ranks of the press were never a welcome sight. If you wanted their help, with finding a missing person or identifying someone from a CCTV image perhaps, you'd get a small turnout. Unless it was a slow news day or a star reporter had done something stupid and was on punishment duty. If there was no story, then they were nowhere to be seen, and that was how McLean liked them best. This, however, was the other thing.

They'd had to move the press conference down to HQ, with its bigger conference rooms. Any hope that the change of venue might mean some input from top brass was forlorn, though. Looking around the room, Detective Superintendent Jack Tennant was the most senior officer present, and lowly Detective Inspector McLean was next in line.

'Ladies and gentlemen. Thank you all for coming.' Sergeant Dan Hwei, the Press Liaison Officer, kicked things off with the usual instructions about not interrupting, waiting until your name was called before asking questions, where the fire doors were and what to do in an emergency. McLean knew all this was important, but it was also a waste of time. He could almost guarantee he'd be interrupted before five minutes were up, and if there were a fire then it would turn into a bloodbath. These were reporters, after all.

'As you know, we released the bodies of Andrew Weatherly, his wife Morag and two daughters Joanna and Margaret a couple of days ago. They were buried yesterday. I think one or two of you might have been there.' McLean scanned the front few rows of the audience, spotting most of the usual suspects.

'The sharper of you here will realize what that means. Our investigation into the deaths at Mr Weatherly's house in Fife has been concluded and a report has been sent to the Procurator Fiscal.'

'Inspector, can you confirm that Weatherly shot his wife and daughters?'

Not even five minutes. Barely one. McLean sighed, rubbed at his eyes. 'If you'd give me a chance to finish, Mr Truman, I will let you know the results of the post-mortem examination of all four bodies. There were traces of a barbiturate sedative in the girls' blood, but they died from suffocation. It's our belief that Mr Weatherly spiked their evening milk, then when they were too sleepy to resist put a pillow over each of their faces.'

'Was it true they were found together in the same bed?'

McLean didn't recognize the voice, and no one had put their hand up. Almost certainly a tabloid, though.

'How they were found is irrelevant.' Jack Tennant interrupted, his irritation at the question obvious. 'They were only eleven years old, for Christ's sake. Have a bit of respect for the dead.' He slumped back in his seat, looking almost as tired as McLean felt and just as pissed off.

'Thank you, sir.' McLean spoke close to the microphone, his voice echoing about the conference room.

'And in answer to the original question, I will add that I'm not in the habit of describing the crime scene as we found it unless that is pertinent to our enquiries. I've seen some of the more lurid speculation and I'll say this much for you lot, you don't lack imagination.'

There were a couple of muttered comments at the back, but no more interruptions, so McLean continued with his prepared script. 'Morag Weatherly died from a single gunshot wound to the head. Forensic analysis confirms that the bullet was a .243-calibre from a stalking rifle belonging to Mr Weatherly. He had a licence for it, along with a number of shotguns and a .22-calibre rifle for shooting vermin. All these other weapons were found locked up in a gun cabinet on the premises. The keys were in Mr Weatherly's pocket.

'Andrew Weatherly himself died from a single gunshot wound to the head, we assume fired from the same weapon as that used to kill his wife, although the bullet was not recovered from the scene. The evidence as presented in my report suggests that Mr Weatherly smothered his children, shot his wife and then turned the gun on himself. There is no evidence of any outside party being involved.'

'Inspector, can you give us any indication as to why Mr Weatherly would do such a thing?'

McLean looked to the back of the hall, where the question had come from. One of the less sensationalist Scottish papers, if he remembered rightly.

'Mr Weatherly's business was in rude health, and his political career seemed set for better things than being a useful member of the opposition. We've spoken to his friends and associates and there was no indication of pressure being put on him.' McLean swallowed, trying not to think about the photographs and the obvious conclusion the press would draw if they saw them. When they saw them. 'It's one thing to take your own life. Quite another to take your loved ones with you. I can say that Mr Weatherly was a deeply disturbed man, but I cannot, I will not, speculate as to why he did what he did. That's your job.'

That brought a low chuckle from the throng, which was helpful. Always better to keep the press in a good humour.

'Do you think he was being blackmailed?'

'If he was, then he left nothing behind to show that was the case. Of course, he might just have been tired of being hounded by the press.'

That got him another low round of chuckles, but McLean was wary enough not to relax just because things seemed to be going well. That was when the shit usually hit the fan, after all.

'Inspector, were you aware of the rumours regarding Mr Weatherly's sex life?'

Ah yes. That question. And it had to come from the scruffy, leather-coated form of Jo Dalgliesh, of course. Who else would Special Branch leak their tawdry information to? Unless, of course, she was just fishing.

'Which particular rumours would those be, Ms Dalgliesh? Mr Weatherly was a politician, after all.'

Another ripple of laughter ran around the room, louder this time. Dalgliesh scowled in irritation, and McLean realized he'd pay for that jibe later.

'The sex parties, Inspector. The swinging lifestyle. In all your investigations, did it never occur to you to work up a history on the man?'

'I see what you're getting at, Ms Dalgliesh, but as the inspector has already said, our investigations have revealed no evidence of an attempt to blackmail Mr Weatherly. Whatever he may or may not have done in the past, the fact remains that his was the only criminal act here.' Judging by the way he came to McLean's defence, DS Tennant had locked horns with Jo Dalgliesh before.

'Were someone trying to blackmail Mr Weatherly, that would, of course, be a crime. And if you had any evidence to suggest such a thing, I am sure you would bring it to our attention so we could investigate and if necessary prosecute. The fact remains, however, that Mr Weatherly, for reasons unknown, took it upon himself to murder his family and kill himself.' McLean focused all his attention on Jo Dalgliesh, looking for any hint that she knew something she wasn't saying. 'That was the scope of this investigation, and that's our conclusion. Should any fresh evidence come to light, we will, of course, consider it and reopen the case if necessary.'

'Well, I've had worse days.' Jack Tennant leaned back in his chair, hands cupped behind his head for support. 'Can't rightly remember when, but I must have had, sometime.'

'Life must be very quiet indeed in Fife if you thought that was bad.' McLean gathered his papers together, slipping them into a slim brown folder that was probably intended only for a particular kind of archive filing and not as a general carry-all. Somewhere in the building lurked DC MacBride, perhaps the only policeman within five miles who would either know or care.

'Fife has its problems, Tony. But you're right, it's pretty easy really. Can't remember the last time we had a murder wasn't a domestic gone too far. It's mostly speeding tickets and dope these days. A little casual violence at the weekends.'

'Sounds idyllic. Where do I apply for a transfer?'

Tennant laughed, dropping his seat forward and bringing a hand round to his mouth as it turned into a cough from deep in his lungs. It took far too long for him to recover.

'You'd go stir crazy in a week. And besides, what would you do without Jo Dalgliesh to get under your skin? She really doesn't like you, that woman.'

'The feeling's entirely mutual.' McLean stood up, ready to leave. A few journalists were still milling around, talking to camera or manically tapping reports into notebook computers. The last thing he wanted was for someone to approach him for an impromptu interview.

'Rushing back to the front?' Tennant thumped his chest a couple of times, coughed, swallowed and grimaced.

'You OK, Jack? That's a nasty cough.'

'Winters don't get any easier when you're my age, Tony. And this one's been bad.'

'Let me treat you to a mug of Edinburgh's finest tea before you head north, then.'

'You're too kind, but I've tried that pish you call tea

here before. Think I'll wait till I'm home and have something a little stronger.'

Tennant pushed himself up out of his chair with perhaps rather more effort than it should have taken. McLean thought back to the last time he'd seen the detective superintendent, at Weatherly's house just a few days earlier. Had he been so unwell then? He couldn't remember. Maybe it was the same lurgy that had laid Ritchie low. If so, he hoped he was immune. The last thing he needed was a hacking cough and pounding headache to go with his permanently aching hip.

'Well, I need to get back to my own station anyway. There's a stack of paperwork the exact size and shape of my office needs dealing with, and we've got a heavily tattooed corpse we're still trying to identify. No rest for the wicked, eh?'

Tennant gave him a weak smile before picking up his own papers and shuffling them together. Unlike McLean, the detective superintendent was organized enough to have a briefcase to hide them in.

'That question, at the press conference. The Dalgliesh woman,' he said, speaking into the open case rather than face McLean. 'You know the case is closed now, right?'

'Of course. I handed the report over to the PF myself.'

'Only I couldn't help noticing you left the possibility of reopening it . . . well, open.'

'If some new evidence came to light, we'd have to really. Or at least open a new one if it turned out someone had been blackmailing Weatherly.'

Tennant closed his briefcase, clicked the locks shut

and finally turned to face him. 'Yes, of course. If someone brought that to our attention. But we're not going looking for it, are we?'

McLean studied the detective superintendent's face. He'd thought of Jack Tennant as a friend. Someone he could turn to in a crisis, rely on for an honest opinion. But here he was toeing the party line like a good boy. Well, he was due to retire soon. Maybe he just didn't want to rock the boat.

'Not any more. No.'

'So that little trip out to the house the other day. That was just you getting it out of your system?'

'Pretty much.' McLean thought about the photographs locked in the top drawer of his desk, the second set and the DVD still at home in his grandmother's old safe. Someone wanted him to keep looking, someone else wanted him to stop. Stuck in the middle was never a nice place to be. Whatever he did he was going to piss someone off. And get him the blame.

'Good.' Tennant reached up and patted McLean on the shoulder with a hand that looked older than it should have, the skin thinner, bones and tendons showing through. 'I knew you'd see sense, Tony.'

26

He'd switched his mobile phone to silent before the press conference, which was why McLean wasted half an hour wandering around HQ looking for DC Mac-Bride so that he could get a lift back to the station. It wasn't until he'd been to the IT department and been told the constable had gone already that he remembered, and checked the screen to find both a text and a voice-mail message saying he'd had to leave early. Cursing his forgetfulness, McLean set about finding a patrol car headed towards the city centre that he could bully into giving him a ride.

It was always a risk, hitching a lift that way. You never knew if an emergency call was going to come in mid-journey. A considerate driver would at least pull over and let you out, but McLean also had happy memories of attending incidents the other side of town from where he'd wanted to be.

This one at least dropped him in the New Town before heading off up Queen Street with the full Blues and Twos going, its destination the site of a collision between a tourist bus and one of the new trams, which had ground all city centre traffic to a standstill.

McLean shoved his hands into his pockets, hunched his shoulders against the cold and started walking. It wasn't long before he realized he wasn't heading in the right direction. Quite without realizing it, his footsteps had taken him on a slight detour, ending up in the street where Andrew Weatherly's terrace house sat empty, awaiting its fate.

There wasn't really any reason to go and look, other than that he was there. He did anyway, jogging across the road just ahead of a black taxi, his steaming breath hanging behind him in the frigid air.

The house was unchanged from the last time he'd been there, apart from the lack of a uniform constable standing at the top of the steps that led up to the front door. The windows reflected the harsh white brightness of the afternoon sky, and from pavement level you couldn't see inside anyway. If memory served, the backs of all these terraces looked on to a large, private, communal garden that you couldn't easily access, and anyway he hadn't come here to go inside. Wasn't really sure why he'd come, except that the patrol car had dropped him off nearby.

'Thought the Weatherly case was closed. Got your man bang to rights.'

As puns went it was weak, and brought back the uncomfortable image of Andrew Weatherly's dead body, propped up against the statue in the middle of his lawn, the back of his head painted all over the stone.

'Are you following me, Dalgliesh?' McLean replayed the last few moments in his mind, realizing that the black taxi he'd crossed the road in front of had pulled in to the kerb a bit further on.

'That depends on whether you're going the same way as me.' The journalist fished a packet of cigarettes out of her coat as she sauntered up, tapped one out and shoved it in her mouth. Then went from pocket to pocket until she found her lighter. She nodded at the steps and the front door as she lit up. 'You going in?'

'Haven't got the key.'

'What you doing here, then?'

McLean thought about his conversation with Jack Tennant after the press conference. 'Just laying some ghosts to rest.'

'What if they don't want to be?'

'Not my problem. Unless you've got some more evidence you want to bring to my attention?'

Dalgliesh laughed, a crackly cackling sound like a child's nightmare of a witch. 'I've got nothing, and that's God's honest truth. I'll tell you this much for free, though. This isn't finished. Not by a long chalk.'

'That your fine-tuned journalist's instincts twitching, is it?'

'Fine-tuned bollocks. This whole thing stinks. There's no way Weatherly was as pure as driven snow.' Dalgliesh kicked at the grey, salty slush the council hadn't bothered sweeping from the pavement. 'And shutting down the investigation when it was hardly started? Give me a break. Youse lot are covering up something.'

'Come on, Dalgliesh. You just want there to be a conspiracy so you can get your story. We closed the investigation because we were done with it. The evidence was all there. It's not as if someone else shot Morag and suffocated the girls. There wasn't anyone forcing Weatherly to do what he did.'

'You sure of that?' Dalgliesh took another drag on her

cigarette, tilted her head back and let the smoke billow out into the air. McLean watched it climb, noticing the pair of CCTV cameras on a nearby lamp post. One faced away from them, the other seemed angled deliberately to take in Weatherly's front door. Well, he was an important man. Maybe it had been set up that way on purpose.

'Look. We interviewed everyone he worked with, both in business and politics. No one noticed him being under any pressure. There's only so much time we can spare, even for someone like Weatherly with his influential friends. Hell, if we threw all the resources of Police Scotland at it, you'd be writing pieces about dead junkies in Leith not getting a tenth of the attention.'

'It's still a stitch-up, and you know it. Otherwise you wouldn't be here.' Dalgliesh nodded at the building again.

McLean considered explaining exactly how he'd come to be there, then realized it would just be a waste of breath. 'Was there anything in particular you wanted?'

'From you? Not really, no. I was just having a look at the place for background, soaking up a bit of the ambience. I'll be doing a piece on Weatherly for the weekend supplements. Helps to be able to picture the place when you're writing, you know. Really didn't expect to see you here.'

'Well, I'll leave you to your work, then.' McLean shoved his hands in his pockets and started to walk away.

'Why'd they give it to you?' Dalgliesh's question stopped him in his tracks.

'What?'

'Why'd they put you in charge? Man like Weatherly,

you'd think an assistant chief constable would be SIO. I didn't see anyone more senior than you at the funeral. You've headed up all the press conferences.'

'Detective Superintendent Tennant was SIO.'

'Aye, in Fife. And he never made it to the funeral either.'

'It's not in the job spec, you know. "Must attend the funeral of all murder victims." '

'Aye, I ken that. But you do anyway.'

'If we think there's something to be gained from it. If we're interested in seeing who turns up.'

'So why'd you go then? If everything was all fine and tickety-boo?' Dalgliesh accompanied the odd phrase with a wiggly-finger motion that scattered ash from her dying cigarette on to the pavement.

'Professional curiosity?'

'Aye, I heard that about you. Never did know when to let something lie.'

'There a point to all this? Only I need to get back to the station. Just because we're done with Weatherly doesn't mean there's nothing else to worry about.'

Dalgliesh shrugged. 'Just thinking out loud really. No offence, but you're hardly the obvious choice for the job. And Jack Tennant's no' exactly any better. A washed-out super from Fife Constabulary just a few months off retirement? That's hardly putting your best man on the case.' Dalgliesh took a last long drag on her cigarette, holding on to the smoke like a jealous lover before finally, reluctantly, letting it go into the cold air.

'No one up high wanted to touch this 'cause it's got shit all over it. You mark my words, Inspector. They're setting you up for a fall.'

27

Darkness was falling over the city by the time McLean made it back to the station. He'd considered getting a taxi from George Street, then remembered the reason his ride in the patrol car had been cut short and decided walking was better. Judging by the noise of angry horns and the long lines of unmoving cars and buses, he'd made the right decision.

It gave him time to think, too. For all that she was an annoying wee shite, Jo Dalgliesh was a shrewd reporter with lots of good contacts and a knack for putting all the pieces together, however far apart and apparently unrelated they might be. It didn't help that he was all too aware of the political machinations surrounding and directing the Weatherly case, either. He knew damned well that Duguid would have convinced his superiors that he was expendable and so should be put in charge of the case; there to take the fall when necessary. Fife had been fortunate enough to have a more senior officer who was about to leave anyway. That seemed a shitty way to treat a detective of Jack Tennant's long service and good reputation.

And, of course, there was the double bluff that Duguid was playing. It was almost enough to make McLean stick to the rules like a militant shop foreman, but he had to admit, however grudgingly, that the detective superintendent had got the measure of him. There was no way he could leave the case alone until he knew that no stone had been left unturned. As much as anything else, he needed to know everything he could possibly find out in order to protect himself when it all went tits up. Dislike Jo Dalgliesh as much as he did, he still had to agree with her on that point. This wasn't finished yet, and when it did end it wasn't going to be pretty.

He had intended to head straight to his office, use the rest of the day to wade through the never-ending stream of paperwork that flowed through that tiny little room. Then McLean remembered DC MacBride's cryptic text and decided that finding out what the constable had been up to would be infinitely more fun. He pushed his way through the doors to the main first floor corridor, squeezed past the pile of archive files being moved out of the Weatherly incident room to make way for whatever investigation needed it most, and slipped into the much smaller room dedicated to the investigation into the as-yet nameless tattooed man.

MacBride was nowhere to be seen, but another figure sat at his desk.

'Detective Sergeant Ritchie. What a pleasant surprise.'

DS Ritchie looked up from the report she had been reading, and for a moment McLean thought he'd got the wrong person. Her eyes were dark circles, puffy and sore. Her short red hair hung around her face like wet rags. Her skin was pale, just the golden spots of her freckled cheeks to give any colour. She'd only been off a few days, and yet she looked like she'd lost half her body weight.

'Afternoon, sir. Thought you were over at HQ.' Ritchie struggled to her feet.

'Sit down, sit down.' McLean flapped his hands like an old hen, and Ritchie slumped back into her seat with an audible sigh. 'I was going to ask how you were, but you look—'

'Like shit?' Ritchie's smile was something of the sergeant he knew, but it was tired.

'I wasn't going to say it myself, but since you mention it. Yes. You sure you're OK to come back to work? What the hell happened, anyway?'

Ritchie scrubbed at her face with both hands, digging the heels into her eyes and rubbing hard for a moment. It didn't improve how she looked much. 'I've no idea, sir. Must've picked up some lurgy at Weatherly's house. One of the Fife constables came down with a bad flu bug the day after, I'm told. I didn't start feeling sick until the next day myself. We were interviewing friends and business colleagues.'

'That's right. You interviewed Mrs Saifre.'

Ritchie raised a quizzical eyebrow.

'I met her at the wake, yesterday. She said you'd spoken to her.'

'Aye, well. She was the last. Strange woman.' Ritchie frowned, as if she'd been going to say something but had forgotten what it was as soon as she tried to speak. Then she shook her head, let whatever it was go. 'To be honest I was feeling OK by the end of it all. A bit run-down maybe, but you know how it is when you've spent the whole day asking people the same questions over and over.'

McLean did, all too well.

'Next morning I could barely move. Never had a bug hit me like that before. Felt like someone had shrunk my brain and it was rattling around inside my head. I tried to hit it with flu drugs, but I couldn't keep anything down more than a minute. You really don't want to know any more details, trust me on that.'

'I'll take your word for it. It's good to have you back. Even if, you know, you look like you really ought to be still in bed.'

Ritchie stiffened slightly at the suggestion, the tiniest hint of colour deepening her freckles.

'I can manage, sir. Honest. Just don't ask me to go running after any criminals for a day or two.' She lifted the report from her desk, then let it fall back again. 'Paperwork's good.'

'Well, if you get really bored I'm sure I can find you plenty. You seen MacBride about recently?'

'He was here, oh, maybe a half-hour ago.' Ritchie checked her watch. 'Might've gone down to the canteen for a cup of tea. Grumpy Bob was muttering about it being four o'clock somewhere.'

'Actually, tea sounds like a great idea. You want one?'

Ritchie picked up a bottle of spring water from her desk and held it to her forehead. Drips of condensation on the outside glistened in the overhead lights. They matched the sheen on her forehead. 'Having a bit of a hard time keeping tea down at the moment, sir. Water's fine, though. Hurts less on the way back up.'

McLean was going to suggest that maybe she'd be doing them all a favour if she just went home. The last thing he needed was the rest of his team coming down with something so debilitating, let alone getting it himself. But then he'd been at the house in Fife with Ritchie, and he'd shared his car with her all the way there and back. If anyone was going to get what she had then it was him. Before he could say anything, and risk seriously putting his foot in it, the door to the incident room swung open to reveal the twin figures of DC MacBride and Grumpy Bob, each clasping a mug of tea in one hand and a biscuit in the other. The only way you could tell they weren't twins, apart from the obvious age difference, was that while MacBride had a case file slipped under his arm, Grumpy Bob's reading of choice appeared to be the *Edinburgh Herald*.

'Ah, you're back, sir. Sorry I had to leave you at HQ like that.'

McLean eyed MacBride's steaming mug of tea, wondering whether his seniority would allow him to commandeer it, and maybe the biscuit as well, and send the constable back for more. Then he realized that was exactly the sort of thing Duguid would do.

'No matter. I assume it was something important.'

MacBride looked a little sheepish, something he was quite good at. He went swiftly over to the desk Ritchie was occupying, put down his tea, then balanced his biscuit precariously on the edge of the mug before pulling the folder out from under his arm. Grumpy Bob, McLean noticed, was completely unapologetic about his own mug, taking a noisy slurp before chomping on his biscuit.

'I had an email in from the DNA database people.'

MacBride unlocked a drawer in the desk, opened it and pulled out his tablet computer. A couple of swipes on the screen. 'I needed to check with them directly before I spoke to you about it.'

'Why's that?'

'Well, there weren't any matches, sir. Not on the civilian database, certainly.'

'You ran it past the military, though?'

'Yes, and that's where it gets interesting.' MacBride swiped a couple more times, then turned the tablet so McLean could see. He peered at the screen but it was mostly numbers arranged in boxes, along with some tiny text he really couldn't read without giving himself a migraine.

'In words a normal person can understand?'

MacBride's expression was that of a disappointed parent, which was strange given his age. 'DNA matching's not an exact science, sir. It's like fingerprint matching in many respects, only a lot more complicated.'

'I don't need a lecture, Constable, just an answer. Have we got a match or not?'

'Possibly. Only it's unlikely.'

McLean held his breath and counted to ten. MacBride opened his mouth to speak, but Grumpy Bob beat him to the punchline.

'There's a partial match, aye. Above-average probability that it's the same person.'

'So what's the problem? You've got a name, I take it? Request his personnel file, get his address, track him down.'

'There's just the wee inconvenient fact that the person

in question died in Afghanistan four years ago.' Grumpy Bob took another slurp of his tea, shoving the last of his biscuit in after it.

McLean paused for a moment to let that sink in. 'What was his name?'

MacBride swiped at his screen again. 'Lance Corporal William Beaumont, sir. He was in the Royal Highland Fusiliers, apparently. Local boy. The info we got says he trod on an IED during a patrol. Wasn't much of him left to bring home.'

Afghanistan. IED. The words triggered a partial memory, but McLean couldn't immediately put his finger on it.

'The Fusiliers? So he'd have been stationed at Glencorse.' McLean checked his watch, then the window. It was fully dark out now, but the army never really slept. 'Who fancies a trip over to the barracks, then?'

28

Glencorse Barracks, home to the Royal Highland Fusiliers, was sandwiched between Beeslack and Milton Bridge, to the north of Penicuik. Heading south past the bypass, McLean realized that it was just across the river and a little upstream of the spot where their mysterious tattooed man had gone over the cliff. If he'd gone over the cliff. He'd asked for a boat team to search the banks for any clues, but given the weather conditions it was unlikely they'd even been out yet, let alone found anything.

Despite her obvious weariness, DS Ritchie had volunteered to accompany him. It might just have been a ruse to get herself out of the station and sit in a nice warm car for a while. She didn't say much at the start of the journey, and by the time they'd joined the slow snarl-up of commuter traffic on Liberton Brae, she'd fallen asleep. He was happy to let her; should probably have sent her home and forced Grumpy Bob to come with him. He certainly wasn't going to wake her just to make her take down a note about the barracks and its proximity to the river. He could remember that much, surely.

It took far longer to get there than he'd anticipated, and McLean worried that the administrative offices would be closed. They had to wait at security, had their warrant cards taken away for cross-checking and then waited some more for an escort to be found. Then they were led across a vast parade ground, through a maze of passageways and buildings it would be impossible to find their way back from, and eventually into the presence of an elderly gentleman in uniform, sitting behind an old desk in a room straight from the 1950s.

'Anthony McLean. What a pleasant surprise.' The officer stood, walked around the desk and proffered a hand to shake. McLean took it, trying not to look too puzzled. 'Er. Have we met, sir?'

'Of course, you'll have forgotten. Must be, what, twenty years? More, probably. Gilbert Bottomley. Used to live just up the road from your grandmother's place. We played bridge every Tuesday. It was terribly sad when, well, you know.'

McLean was still none the wiser, although he vaguely remembered a group of odd people who would come around and drink too much gin with his gran once a week or so. He'd have been at university by then, living in his own place in Newington. But he wasn't going to pass up the possibility of help.

'She had a good innings, er . . . Major?'

'Ah, you do remember. Splendid. Only it's Lieutenant Colonel now, but please, call me Gilbert. And who is your lovely young assistant?'

Even though she was standing slightly behind him, McLean could feel the tension rise in DS Ritchie. It was heartening to see that she still had that spark, but the last thing he needed right now was a snarky comment.

'Detective Sergeant Ritchie is a valuable member of my team, um, Gilbert.'

'Delighted, I'm sure.' The lieutenant colonel didn't

offer a hand to be shaken this time, increasing Ritchie's hostility by an order of magnitude. Completely oblivious to any offence he might be causing, Bottomley returned to his side of the desk and dropped back down into his chair. 'Now, what can I do for you? I assume this isn't a social visit. Though I'm sure I could rustle up a fourth if you fancied a rubber. You play bridge?'

McLean struggled to keep up with the flow. 'Sorry? Oh. No. Don't really have the time, sadly.'

'Damned shame.'

'Yes. Well. I was looking for some information about one of your soldiers. Ex-soldiers, I should say. Lance Corporal William Beaumont?'

'Beaumont. Beaumont. Rings a bell.' The lieutenant colonel pulled a keyboard towards him, and tapped away at it with two fingers for a moment while peering at a large flat screen quite out of place among the rest of the decor. 'Ah. Here we go. Yes. Lance Corporal William Beaumont. Hmm.'

McLean stood patiently while the lieutenant colonel stared at the screen, occasionally clicking the mouse to scroll down. Every so often he'd let out a little grunt of surprise, or a tut at something that didn't fit in with his narrow world-view. Eventually he slumped back into his chair.

'Why was it you were interested in him?'

'His name came up in a DNA search on an unidentified body we fished out of the river just downstream of here a week or so ago.' McLean had a file with him, and a few photographs, but he didn't want to bring it out unless he had to.

'Well, it's not him. At least not according to this.' The lieutenant colonel leaned forward again, tapped a couple more keys. 'No, according to this—'

'He died in Afghanistan. IED. Yes, I know.'

'Well why'd you come here then?'

'I was hoping I might have been able to speak to someone who served with him. Was also wondering if you had any regimental photographs, that sort of thing.'

'What, like this?' Bottomley swivelled the computer screen around so that McLean could see what was there. It was the front end of some kind of military database, the top left-hand corner of the screen taken up with a mug shot of Lance Corporal William Beaumont. The face looking out at him didn't have tattoos blackening its cheeks and forehead, but it was quite unmistakably the man they'd fished out of the North Esk. Unless he had an identical twin.

'Does he have a brother?' McLean asked.

'No. Nothing under next of kin, anyway. But this.' The lieutenant colonel poked at the screen with a finger. 'This is all wrong. Somebody's been messing with the records.'

'How so?'

'Well, we didn't lose that many men out in Helmand as it was, thank God. But I wrote to the families of all those we did. And this young fellow was not one of them.'

'At ease, Sergeant.'

Fifteen minutes of following Lieutenant Colonel Gilbert Bottomley on a circuitous route around the barracks and McLean was completely lost. Behind him, following on like an elderly but loyal spaniel, DS Ritchie was obviously suffering from the unexpected exercise. The lieutenant colonel had made a couple of phone calls as soon as he'd uncovered the database error, and then in that infuriating way of men used to being obeyed without question, had simply said 'follow me' and marched out of his office. They'd arrived, finally, in what must have been unmarried NCO quarters. It reminded McLean of university halls of residence, only much nicer and without the distant but unshakeable aroma of stale vomit and spilled beer. Bottomley had located a door, rapped hard on it and waited only a couple of seconds before it was opened. The soldier inside had obviously known his commander was coming, and snapped to attention beside an immaculately made bed. Even when he stepped back at ease, he looked tense, but then McLean knew constables who acted the same whenever anyone more senior than a sergeant was in the room.

'Sergeant Grant, this is Detective Inspector McLean and Detective Sergeant Ritchie. They're looking into a suspicious death. Chap found in the river about a week ago. Think he might be connected to the regiment.'

Sergeant Grant said nothing more than a noncommittal 'Sir'.

'You were on the last tour in Helmand, weren't you?'

'Sir.' The sergeant nodded this time, risking a sideways glance at McLean. Somewhere behind him, in the darkness of the corridor, Ritchie was making an odd noise.

'The inspector has a few questions about one of your comrades, William Beaumont. You remember him?'

'Bill? Aye, sir. I remember him. But a ways back.

Before Afghanistan. He wasn't with the regiment when we did our tour out there.'

'What do you mean, not with . . . Oh.' Bottomley did what could only be described as a double-take. 'Oh. I see.'

'Is there a problem?' McLean asked. Something in the sergeant's words had sparked a memory that he couldn't quite get up to a full flame.

'Yes. Well, sort of.' Bottomley looked like a man wrestling with his conscience for a moment.

'He was SAS, wasn't he,' McLean said as DS Ritchie stepped into the light, dabbing at the corner of her mouth with a handkerchief. 'That's what happens. Someone goes off on special duties. You can't say where they've gone, what they're doing. Technically the regiment doesn't even exist. Only, our body's got an SAS tattoo on it, and one for the Royal Highland Fusiliers. I know it's circumstantial. Any idiot can get "Who Dares Wins" and "Nemo Me Impune Lacessit" tattooed on their arms, but I'm right, aren't I?'

'I couldn't say, sir.' Sergeant Grant's eyes darted from McLean to Ritchie to the lieutenant colonel, around his room and then back again, as if a woman in the unmarried men's quarters was something he couldn't quite compute.

'Dammit, yes. He was Air Squad,' Bottomley said. 'Not many of our lot get picked. It's usually the Paras. I thought Beaumont was back by the time we deployed to Helmand.'

'No, sir. He was out there, but with Special Forces. You'd probably have seen him in camp, though. Billbo was always stopping by, stealing our brew.'

'What did you call him?' The spark suddenly flared in McLean's mind. A name he remembered. A frightened homeless man telling tales about his missing friend, seeking shelter from the cold and the snow.

'Billbo. That's what the lads called him. Two ells, though, so nobody thought he was a hobbit.'

'You don't remember a man called Gordy, do you? Would have been friends with Beaumont.'

'Gordy? Aye, that'd be Gordon Johnson. He was Billbo's NCO.' Sergeant Grant shook his head. 'Not heard of either of them for, what, must be three, four years now. Wonder what happened to them.'

'Nothing good, Sergeant. But thank you. You've cleared something up for us.' McLean turned to the lieutenant colonel. 'I wonder if I could beg a copy of that photograph you have on file for Beaumont, sir. No rush, an email copy tomorrow will do.'

'I'd have thought so. I'll have a word with some people. See if we can't come up with a bit more than that for you.'

'Thanks.' McLean looked out the door to the corridor where Ritchie had retreated back into the shadows. 'And if someone could show us the way to the car park?'

Traffic was lighter heading back into town, but heavy flakes of snow had begun swirling out of the sky, making fast progress inadvisable. After her forced march across the barracks, McLean had expected DS Ritchie to be wiped out, but she seemed if anything slightly perkier than when they had arrived.

'You think this William Beaumont is our tattooed man then, sir?'

'I'm almost certain he is.'

'How so? You've come across a Billbo with two ells before, I take it.'

'Exactly that.' McLean told her about the night he'd interviewed Gordy and taken him down to the shelter. 'We'll have to see if we can find him again. Maybe get a bit more out of him. He might be mad, but I think he really did see someone take his friend off the street. If that's the case, then why, and who? And what the hell were they doing covering him in tattoos like that?'

'It's getting weird again, isn't it, sir?'

'Weird?'

'You know. Like all that stuff with Needy and his book.'

McLean didn't answer, concentrated on the road ahead. It wasn't something he really wanted to consider. Ritchie must have got the message, as she said nothing until they were past Bilston and coming up to IKEA.

'I hope they're not too upset with me.'

'What? Who?'

'The army.' Ritchie nodded her head back in the direction of Penicuik, or at least a rough approximation.

'Why would they be upset? Women are allowed in the men's quarters. It's the twenty-first century, you know. And besides, you were accompanied by the barracks commander.'

'It's not that, sir.'

'No? Well what, then?'

'I may have been a little sick in one of their pot plants. Out in the corridor.'

29

McLean dropped Ritchie off at her flat. Not all that far from Weatherly's rather more opulent town house, it was somewhere in among the impossibly high-rise tenements that clustered at the eastern fringes of the New Town. He'd not been in it since she'd moved, wasn't surprised not to be invited this time. Ritchie looked done in. Still fighting whatever lurgy had laid her low.

'We'll have a catch-up and briefing at nine tomorrow. Get yourself a decent night's kip, aye? Look as if you need it.'

Ritchie smiled, giving a little nod by way of thanks for the advice. 'I can look after myself, you know.'

'Sure you can. Night, Sergeant.'

She slammed the car door shut and he pulled away from the kerb. There wasn't much of a view out of the back of the Alfa, but he saw her standing there, outside her front door, staring back at him as he drove away. She was still there, unmoving, as he turned the corner.

Reaching Lothian Road, McLean could have headed home. There was a good Chinese takeaway in Morningside that was only a little bit out of the way and it was late enough that going back to the station was fairly pointless. Instead, he indicated left, swung around into the Old Town, through the Grassmarket and eventually into the Cowgate. The doors to the homeless shelter were closed against the cold, but a welcoming light glowed above it. He parked on a double yellow, only reckoning on being a minute or two.

Inside, the warmth was like being bathed in a light mist of beef soup and unwashed armpits. It wasn't as busy as the night he'd brought Gordy down from the station, but there were still plenty of people who needed all the help they could get.

McLean looked around the open-plan room, scanning the tables for signs of the ex-soldier. A couple of people stared at him, their unfriendly eyes clearly recognizing him for what he was. He ducked away, heading for the serving table and the kitchen. Might as well make this as quick as possible.

'Tony. Didn't think we'd be seeing you again so soon.' Jeannie Robertson stood behind the table, splatters on her apron that made her look like she'd been hacking at someone with a carving knife. She held up a bowl and ladle. 'Soup?'

McLean peered at the lumpy mess in the large metal tureen in front of him. It smelled fine, and the steam gently easing off the surface suggested it would be warming on such a cold night, but the odd lumps floating around in the oil-slicked surface didn't inspire him with confidence. 'No. You're all right.'

Jeannie's face dropped fractionally, her disappointment suggesting that she might well have been the cook that evening. If her apron was anything to go by, whatever had gone into the soup had not done so willingly.

'Slow night tonight,' McLean added, after what was an awkward pause.

'Oh, it's early yet. Wait till about ten, then they'll come trooping in. Mark my words.'

McLean consulted his watch. Half-eight already. Where had the day gone? 'Not sure I can wait that long. I don't suppose you've seen Gordy in here recently? You know, the man I brought in the last time?'

Jeannie frowned in concentration. 'Don't think so, now you mention it. He wasn't a regular. Hang on a minute, I'll ask in the kitchen.'

She dumped the ladle into the soup, causing something suspicious to break the surface, then slowly sink back down again. McLean watched as she walked off to the kitchen, then turned around to look at the room again. A few eyes were on him, but most of this early crowd were busy keeping themselves to themselves. They sat in corners with books, stared at a quietly flickering TV in one corner or just gazed at the floor, their hands, the wall. There wasn't much in the way of interaction, just a general feeling of mistrust and unease.

'You looking for that Gordy fellow, then?'

McLean turned a little too quickly, felt a lance of pain in his hip that hadn't been there for a while. A young man stood where Jeannie Robertson had been, dressed not dissimilarly from the homeless. Baggy hoodie over faded jeans, scarf wrapped around his neck. He was unshaven, but that might have had as much to do with fashion as lack of facilities.

'I was. Have you seen him, Mr . . . ?'

'Ben.' The young man shrugged his hands out of the pockets of his hoodie, held one out across the table to be shaken. 'Ben Chilvers. I run this place.'

McLean shook the hand, recognizing the face now he had a name to go with it. 'Tony McLean. Knew you paid the bills. I didn't realize you slopped out as well.'

Chilvers laughed. 'Does me good to remember. Time was I was on the streets, too.'

'I've read about it. It's still good work you do. Not everyone would.'

'Not everyone would bring a homeless man down here in a snowstorm either, Inspector. Yes, Jeannie told me about that. I was working in the kitchen when you brought him in.'

'You saw him? Gordy?'

'Aye. Spoke to him a while. I try to speak to everyone new. See if there's something I can do to help them more permanently.'

'I take it Gordy wasn't keen.'

'Some people don't like to ask for help, and some get anxious when it's offered. I know. I was that person.' Chilvers had absent-mindedly picked up the ladle and was stirring it around the soup tureen, bringing up chunks of unidentified food like bodies disturbed. 'He stayed the night, but he was gone before dawn. Haven't seen him since.'

Mrs McCutcheon's cat looked up from the old rug in front of the Aga when McLean flicked on the kitchen light an hour later. It had a guilty expression on its face, but then it always did, bobbing its head up and down slightly as if trying to scent his mood. Either that or it wanted some of his aromatic crispy duck and prawn crackers. He'd spent an interesting half-hour chatting with Ben Chilvers down at the shelter before remembering he'd parked on a double yellow line outside. Either the gods were on his side or the traffic patrol cars knew his registration number, as by the time he returned to his Alfa it was covered in an inch of snow, but had no parking ticket.

The snow had continued to fall all the way home, and the further from the city centre he drove, the more it settled on the pavements, the big brown council wheelie bins, the parked cars lining the streets. The hill up to his road had been slippery, making the fat tyres spin a couple of times before he reached his driveway. It was cold outside, but at least the snow had taken the bitter edge off the wind. Still not a night to be huddling in a shop door for shelter.

The cat leapt up on to the table as McLean put the bag with his takeaway in it on the scrubbed wooden surface. It rubbed its nose against his hand, and in that instant of contact he knew someone else had been in the house. He couldn't have said how he knew, just that he did.

His gran had never been much of a baker, but there was a stout wooden rolling pin in one of the kitchen drawers. McLean knew better than to take a knife to confront a burglar; chances were you'd end up getting stuck with it yourself. If whoever had been through the kitchen was still in the house, though, he didn't want to face them completely unarmed.

The hall was silent and dark, just the faintest light from outside filtering in through the windows each side of the front door. He trod silently across to the porch, trying to remember how everything had been when he'd left that morning. A pile of mail lay on the mat, so at least he'd not had another visit from his Special Branch friend.

Unless, of course, he'd not come in that way this time.

Turning back to the hall, McLean scanned the dark shapes of the doors leading off to the various rooms he never used. His grandfather's study, the dining room, the drawing room where his grandmother had played bridge with Major Gilbert Bottomley and others. This house really was too big for just the one person. Judging by the faint play of light below the library door, there was more than one person in it right now.

He'd not lit the fire this time, probably because McLean hadn't brought any more coal in. He had helped himself to some of the whisky, though, and taken one of the old leather books down from the shelves. Not, McLean was pleased to see, the first-edition *Gray's Anatomy* that had caused him so much grief recently.

'Ah, the prodigal son returns.' The man from Special Branch looked up from the book, snapping it closed as he did so. 'Has anyone ever explained to you the concept of the Working Time Directive?'

'Sorry I couldn't be home earlier for you. If you'd let me know you were coming, I'd have cooked something.' McLean walked across to the drinks cabinet, placing the rolling pin carefully down on the table beside the chair as he did. 'Besides, I bet you're putting this down on your timesheet.'

'On the contrary, Inspector. I'm not actually here.'

'Not drinking my whisky, either.' McLean poured himself a rather stiffer one than he perhaps intended. 'What is it that you want? Got some more dirty pictures to share?'

'No.' A flicker of some emotion creased the man's face. Worry, maybe. Or perhaps regret. 'No, I came to tell you that those pictures you have are likely to find their way into the hands of the press soon. Not my idea, but . . .' He spread out his hands in a 'what can you do?' gesture.

McLean took a sip of his whisky, let the Islay peat burn on the tip of his tongue. Then he took another, deeper, drink and felt the liquid as it scratched its way down his throat and into his stomach. It didn't take a genius to understand the ramifications of the press finding evidence of Weatherly's preferred method of relaxation. Shit and fans sprang to mind.

'Why did you give them to me in the first place? Why not just mail the lot anonymously to Jo Dalgliesh and be done with it?'

'It's . . . complicated.'

'Not for me it isn't. Not for Jack Tennant. Soon as this is out in public, they'll be baying for our blood. Did we know? Why didn't we say? And if we didn't know, why didn't we carry out the investigation properly?' McLean threw back another good measure of even better whisky. 'Christ, it's just as well I never wanted a promotion.'

'For what it's worth, I'm sorry. This wasn't—'

'Your idea. I know. You said already. Look, who are you?' McLean studied the man's face, trying to find any feature that would make it easy to describe him to someone else. There was nothing. He was bland, almost as if whatever secret department he actually worked for had managed to clone an average person.

'It's best you don't know.'

'Really? Best for who? For me? For you? For Joanna, Margaret and Morag fucking Weatherly?'

The man squirmed uncomfortably in his chair. 'Look, I'm really not supposed to—'

'I don't give a shit what you're supposed to do and say. You come into my house, meddle with my investigation, fuck me around. The least I deserve is an explanation of some sorts. If only so I can look my team in the eye and apologize to them when their careers are flushed down the toilet because of your stupid fucking politics.' McLean threw back the rest of his whisky, managed to get most of it in his mouth. The effort of hiding the choking fit that it caused brought tears to his eyes.

'We watch men like Weatherly. Powerful men. We . . . protect them.'

McLean's choking reflex vanished with surprise. 'You what?'

'Weatherly is . . . was . . . important. He wasn't a nice man. He had some shocking vices, as you know. But he had power and influence. And he controlled a very large amount of money. Our . . . my job was to keep an eye on him, stop things from becoming public. Or if they had to, then manage the process to minimize the damage.'

'You dropped the ball on that one a bit.'

'Tell me about it.' The man rubbed at his face with tired fingers. 'It's not an exact science, but we profile these people.'

'People? You mean there are more like him out there?'

'Don't look so surprised, Inspector. The world's full

of perverts and sociopaths. It's a sad truth but it's the nasty people who get things done.'

McLean poured himself another large whisky, added a bit of water to it this time. 'So you profile them. Why?'

'In order to anticipate what they're going to do next. It works, most of the time. But Weatherly went off-radar when he . . .' The man seemed unable to finish the sentence. McLean considered filling in the details, then decided the irony would be wasted.

'So why involve me? Why give me those photographs?'

'Because other people wanted the investigation shut down quickly. We were concerned that if you did as you were told, then you'd never find out about this.'

'I wish I never had.'

'Do you? Do you really?' The man picked up his own glass, still with a good inch of liquid in the bottom, and twirled it around, savouring the play of light through the whisky before taking a sip. 'Would you have been happy finding it all out from Ms Dalgliesh and her like?'

McLean had to admit that the man had a point, at least to himself. He wasn't going to say it out loud.

'We needed time to get things in place. Needed you to know . . . what you know. The next few days, possibly a fortnight, are going to be . . . uncomfortable for you, Inspector.' The man knocked back the whisky, put the glass down and pushed himself up out of the chair. 'I really am sorry about that, and I'll do all I can to limit the fallout. It'll all blow over in time, and we'll avoid the financial damage that could have been done had this happened differently. And before you start muttering about the money, you should realize we're talking fall-of-nations, going-to-war amounts, not just a couple of upstart billionaires playing who can piss highest up the wall. Weatherly needed careful managing when he was alive; he needs even more careful managing now he's dead.'

McLean watched the man walk slowly across the room towards the door. As he opened it, and was about to step out into the hall, McLean asked: 'You spin the same rubbish to Duguid?'

The man stopped, turned to face him, a puzzled look on his face. 'Duguid?'

'He was the one first told me to keep digging, even after the case was officially closed. I assume you put him up to it.'

'Oh no. Charles Duguid would be useless for our needs. We've had nothing to do with him.' The man paused, as if considering something. 'And yet he wanted you to keep on investigating. Interesting. We may have underestimated him.' He smiled at some secret and very personal joke. 'Goodbye, Inspector. You won't be seeing me again.'

30

'You've been a naughty boy, Inspector. Keeping things from me like that.'

Early morning, and the city was blanketed in snow. McLean had just popped out for some decent coffee and a bacon butty for his breakfast. He'd momentarily forgotten the warning from his nocturnal visitor, and now cursed himself for not being content with the substandard fare the station canteen was producing these days.

'I have nothing to say, Ms Dalgliesh.'

She must have been waiting for him, slouched in a pub doorway, unlit cigarette dangling from her mouth. She sparked up as he walked past, falling into line alongside him like they were old chums.

'You sure about that? I mean, you must have known, right? What he was up to?'

He stopped so suddenly that Dalgliesh had taken another step and was halfway into the next before she realized.

'Just what exactly are you trying to say, Ms Dalgliesh? Only, I'm a busy man. Can't stand and chat all day.'

Dalgliesh gave him a look that suggested disbelief. Given that he was walking back to work with a cup of coffee and a greasy brown paper bag clutched in his hands, he could see her point.

'Seems Andrew Weatherly liked to play away from home. Or should I say he liked to play at home when the wife and kids were away?'

'We've concluded our investigation into Mr Weatherly's death, and his family. My report is with the Procurator Fiscal as we speak.'

'Aye, I know. I was at the press conference. But does your report mention the fact Weatherly held regular orgies at his house in Fife? Does it mention he had sex with women a third his age in the bed where he shot his wife?'

McLean tried to hide the surprise at that little detail Dalgliesh had let slip. Judging by the look of triumph on her face, he hadn't quite succeeded.

'We haven't released details of where Mrs Weatherly was when her husband shot her. You're just guessing and trying to get me to give up something lurid you can print in your bloody paper.'

Dalgliesh pulled her large shoulder bag around so she could unzip it. She fought with the contents for a couple of minutes, until they reluctantly released a slim brown envelope. This one was A5 size, the photographs she pulled from it smaller than the copies he had. But there were more of them. Stills from the orgy, he'd seen before, but the pictures of Morag Weatherly being shot were new to him. Three stills, and more detail than any horror movie could possibly hope to give.

'Where'd you get these?'

'Come on. You don't expect me to tell you that.'

'Let me guess, they just appeared in your inbox this morning.'

The look of hurt on Dalgliesh's face was so obviously manufactured McLean knew he was right.

'It doesn't change anything, really,' he said.

'Are you mad? This changes everything.' Dalgliesh flapped the photographs against her hand, then began flicking through them as she spoke. 'This is why he did it. Someone got hold of this, threatened to go public with it. Don't know what they wanted from Weatherly, but he couldn't take the pressure. The thought of losing it all was too much for him, so he killed his family then shot himself.' She ended up with the picture of Weatherly's corpse leaning back against the stone statue in the snow, his rifle gripped between his knees.

'Can I have a look at that?' McLean reached out and took it before Dalgliesh could stop him. There was something about the photograph that set his internal alarm bells ringing. It was different from most of the others, for a start. Not taken from a CCTV image, it was sharper. He could see the flakes of snow in what remained of Weatherly's hair, on his cheeks and nose. When he'd seen the body himself, it had been clear of snow, covered over by the Scene Examination Branch plastic tent. This picture had been taken before that had been put up. But by whom? A forensic photographer? Or had the man from Special Branch got there first? He'd have to go through the crime scene photos and check for anything similar. It wouldn't be the first time something like that had leaked.

'I'd be very careful what you do with those, Ms Dalgliesh.' McLean handed back the photograph. 'I don't think it's quite the scoop you think it is.'

'You think you can cover your arse that easily, Inspector?' Dalgliesh finished her cigarette, dropped it to the pavement and ground it out with her heel as she fumbled the photographs back into her bag. 'This is dynamite. This is what caused this whole tragedy, and who knows what else? And you didn't even mention the possibility of it existing at the press briefing. That either means you didn't know about it, which doesn't say much for your skills as a detective. Or you did know about it, and kept it secret. Either way it doesn't look too clever from where I'm standing.'

McLean resisted the urge to arrest her for littering. It would have been easy enough; they were only a few hundred yards from the station. And if her photographs went missing whilst she was being processed, well, these things happened, sadly. But he had enough experience to know that arresting journalists, however much they deserved it, rarely worked. And no doubt copies of the pictures would appear in someone else's inbox in short order. No, this was a problem that could only be solved by tackling it head on.

'I'm not prepared to comment on what I did and didn't know about Weatherly. I've made my report and its recommendations, and it's up to the PF to decide where to go next. I'll tell you this for free though, since you're already halfway there. Andrew Weatherly had his whole house rigged up with hidden CCTV cameras. All the bedrooms, the corridors, everything. It was all recorded on to hard drives. We found the control centre in his basement.'

'I know this.' Dalgliesh swung her bag around to indicate the photographs hidden within.

'Well, think about it a bit, then. It was his house, his cameras. He knew he was being filmed. And yet he didn't try to hide anything.' McLean nodded towards the reporter's bag. 'Leastways, not if those are anything to go by.'

Dalgliesh didn't say anything for a while, which McLean took to mean she was thinking.

'So you don't think Weatherly did what he did because he knew these were going to be made public.'

'Nope.'

'Why do you think he did it then?'

'Like I said at the press conference, I don't like to speculate. That's your job.'

'Oh, come on. You must have wondered. Must have asked during your investigation.'

McLean gave her a weary smile. 'Of course I have. But you're asking the wrong question. You shouldn't be asking why Weatherly killed his family. I don't think we'll ever know that. Not really.'

'OK. What should I be asking then?'

'Those photographs. Who sent them to you? Why now? What are they hoping to achieve? That's what you should be asking about. That's your story.'

MacBride was on the phone when McLean finally made it back to the incident room. He had the receiver clamped hard against one ear, his free hand covering the other, as if there were some very loud noise in the room. Looking around, McLean could see no other detectives anywhere, and the silence was almost deafening, so it must have been the other end of the line that was the problem.

The detective constable looked up for a moment, saw McLean and mouthed some words that could have been anything. Then he shouted 'I'm sorry, I can't hear you. Could you repeat that?' into the mouthpiece, so loud McLean winced. You could probably hear it on the fourth floor.

He turned his attention to the whiteboard. They had a photograph of Lance Corporal William 'Billbo' Beaumont without his tattoos now, pinned up alongside the death mask shot. The body they'd found was thinner than he had been in his army days, but then living on the streets would do that to a man. McLean looked at the disparate lines of investigation all centred around the man. True, they had an identity for him now, but that was about it. No timeline, no last movements, no real idea of anything, if he was being honest. He'd been so distracted by the Weatherly case he'd let this one slide, and now the trail was going very cold indeed.

A shouted 'Thank you. Bye.' A click as the receiver was put back down again. McLean turned away from the board, back to where DC MacBride was sitting.

'That was the homeless shelter in Bonnyrigg.'

McLean winced again. 'I'm just here, Constable. No need to shout.'

MacBride reddened about the cheeks. 'Sorry, sir,' he said in a more reasonable voice. 'It was a crap line. I—'

'Never mind. Bonnyrigg homeless shelter. What about it?'

'I put a word out round all the shelters in Midlothian. About the man you were looking for. Gordon Johnson.'

'Gordy? You found him?'

'Think so, sir. There's a bloke answering his description anyway. Probably worth having a look.'

'Bonnyrigg, you say. I wonder . . .' McLean turned back to the whiteboard, scanned the empty wall beside it. He could have sworn there'd been something pinned up earlier. 'You ever get that map, Stuart?'

MacBride's chair legs scraped against the floor as he stood up. It didn't take him long to walk across the room to where McLean was standing.

'I did, sir, pinned it up right there.' Now he looked carefully, McLean could see the holes in the wallpaper.

'Only some bugger's gone and nicked it.'

'The thieving wee . . .' MacBride approached the wall, peered at the obviously empty space. 'I swear, this place. You can't leave anything lying around.'

'Never mind. I've got my own copy at home. You seen Ritchie about?'

A little flicker of worry spread across MacBride's innocent round face. 'She phoned in about nine, sir. Sounded proper poorly. Don't think we'll be seeing her today.'

McLean remembered the night before, dropping Ritchie off at her tenement flat. She'd not been right then.

'I'll give her a call later. Make sure she's all right.'

'Might be better if you texted, sir?' MacBride pulled his own phone out, holding it up as if he thought McLean might never have seen one before. 'You know. If she's asleep or something.'

'Good point, Constable. Thanks.' McLean tried to keep the sarcasm out of his voice. It was a good point, after all. Just annoying having it pointed out to him by someone just out of school. 'And for that you get to come with me.'

'I do?' MacBride fumbled his phone back into his pocket in hurried excitement. 'Where are we going?'

'Bonnyrigg. Where else?'

31

He was old enough to remember when Bonnyrigg, Loanhead, Eskgrove and Polton had all been separate places. As Edinburgh continued its never-ending growth, so the housing estates had burst through the bypass and started to fill in the gaps between the old mining villages, merging everything into one. McLean drove carefully; the roads were still slippery with a mush of salty snow and road grime. His hip ached, too, which suggested there was more foul weather on the way. If the darkness of the early afternoon was anything to go by, it was going to be another fine snowstorm. Just what the city needed.

MacBride gave directions, peering at his tablet computer, which seemed to have satellite navigation as one of its many features.

'Where'd you get that thing?' McLean asked as they edged slowly down the steep hill out of Loanhead, down to where the narrow Polton Bridge crossed over the North Esk.

'One of my pals in IT sorted it. They're running a trial to see if they're any use in the field.' The detective constable tapped at the screen again and through the corner of his eye, McLean saw a frown spread across his face.

'Problem?'

'Well, the map's held on a central server. Makes sense as it's easier to update that way. But as soon as we lose a signal . . .' He twisted the tablet so McLean could see the blank screen. Just a green arrow blinking away in the middle, everything else a grey grid.

'Phone signal's always rubbish down here. Just as well I know where we're going, aye?'

'You do?' MacBride asked. 'Then why did you ask me to give you directions?'

'Because you're a nervous passenger. Gives you something to concentrate on.' McLean indicated, turned left into a small square of houses and shops. Most of the latter were boarded up. One showed signs of having been torched at some point in its recent past. The council hadn't done much to clear the snow here, even less in the side street he turned down next. Eventually McLean stopped the car, pulling as far to the kerb as he dared without getting stuck in the pile of ploughed snow heaped up away from the centre.

'It's just up there.' He pointed through the windscreen to a house that didn't look all that different from the others. 'We'll walk, I think.'

The shelter was busy; a shuffling line of people queueing up in the main room waiting to be given bowls of soup and floury baps. McLean couldn't help noticing that almost all of the clientele were male, though given the many layers of elderly and patched clothing, the woolly hats and gloves, you'd be hard pushed to tell were it not for the beards. He also couldn't help noticing the unfriendly stares directed towards him and DC Mac-Bride as they kicked snow off their shoes in the tiny porch.

'You filth?' one of the nearest men asked as they pushed through to the main hall. He was taller than McLean, and as wide as a door, although that might have been down to the many layers of coats he was wearing.

'If by filth you mean polis, then yes.' McLean pushed past the man, hoping that MacBride would have the sense to keep up. The rest of the group gave grudging way and soon they were at the far side, the door through to the kitchen. He knocked, then opened the door and went in.

Steam filled the air with an aroma of boiled cabbage and onions. It reminded him horribly of his schooldays. An enormously fat man with a bald head, sweat sheening his ruddy pink skin, stood over the cooker, stirring a vat of soup. Further away, a pair of YTS dropouts were chopping vegetables to feed the army outside. McLean shut the door with a heavy clunk, the noise finally reaching the fat man. He turned with surprising grace, putting his ladle down on a plate beside the burner and peering through round wire-rimmed spectacles turned opaque.

'Tony! Tony McLean! Jesus, man. Where've you been? It's been years.' Recognition plastered a smile on the man's face. He wiped his hands on a cloth tucked into a belt big enough to hold up the trousers of three normal men as he advanced across the kitchen. Before he could react, McLean found himself in a bear hug that brought a twinge of pain to his ribs. He'd thought them healed long ago, but perhaps they weren't quite up to that kind of abuse yet.

'Bobby. Good to see you.' McLean extricated himself from the chef's embrace. 'Still running the place, I see.'

'Folk've gotta eat. Not everyone can afford a posh night out.' The chef eyed the nervous DC MacBride, still standing by the door. 'Who's the queenie?'

'Don't be mean, Bobby. This is my colleague Detective Constable MacBride. I think you may have spoken to him on the phone earlier. Or was that Eric?'

'They not feed you at work, MacBride?' Bobby held out a hand to be shaken.

'You're Bobby Innes?' MacBride shook, found his hand immediately engulfed by Bobby's other one.

'Ah. This one's a fan!' Bobby pumped MacBride's arm up and down until the constable shook, then took a step back and looked him up and down, still holding him by the outstretched arm. 'Strange, you don't look like you eat at all.'

'Saw an article about you in the *Scotsman*.' MacBride retrieved his arm. 'You got a Michelin star for your place down in Leith. I'd no idea . . .' He let his words tail off, eyes roaming over the kitchen.

'This is where it all started. Well, not here exactly, but in Bonnyrigg. My dad ran the chippy in the High Street. But you'll know the story. Everyone likes rags to riches, eh?' Bobby turned to the two young lads with the vegetables. 'Keep an eye on that stock, all right? I'm just going to find Eric.'

He led them out of the kitchen, back through the hall of patiently queueing homeless, and into another big room beyond, talking all the while.

'It's been far too long, Tony. Why you never come to the restaurant any more? You find someone else to cook your favourite food now?'

'Kind of lost the habit of eating out after Kirsty died, Bobby.'

'It shows, you know.' Bobby slapped his enormous gut. 'Lucky I eat enough for two, yes?'

The room they had entered was painted in institutional beige, with a big picture window looking out on to a darkening back garden covered in snow, glimpses of the Pentland Hills through the tall cypress trees that delineated the boundary with the neighbouring property. Several tables took up one end of the room, arranged like a restaurant with half a dozen simple chairs around each. At the other end, a welcoming fire crackled in a large open fireplace, sofas and comfortable armchairs circling it like a wagon train. There were very few people in here; most of them queueing up for their soup in the hall outside. One table was occupied though, two people sitting not quite side by side. McLean recognized them both. Eric was Bobby's partner and the brains behind the business. Like Bobby, he was a large man, but most of his bulk was muscle rather than Michelin-starred food. He had a small laptop computer and a mobile phone on the table in front of him, but was talking to the other man, who looked up as they all came into view.

'Inspector.' Gordon Johnson, Gordy as he'd introduced himself before, looked better than the last time McLean had met him, but he still had a haunted look in his eyes. He sat on the edge of his chair, tense, ready to flee at the slightest sign of trouble. No fight left in him, McLean could see that. This man who had served his country in countless battles was broken, utterly.

'How're you doing, Gordy? They feeding you enough

in here?' McLean took one of the remaining seats, pulled it out and settled himself into it. Nodded at the other man sitting at the table. 'Eric.'

'Long time, Tony. You want a minute alone?'

McLean saw Gordy stiffen at the question. 'No. I'm not here to cause any trouble. Just wanted to let Gordy know we'd found his friend, Billbo.'

Gordy's eyes widened, darted from McLean's face to Eric's, then to the point where MacBride was standing a few paces behind, before returning to McLean. 'He's dead, isn't he?'

'Yes. I'm sorry.'

'Told you. It was the dark angels. They took him. They were coming for me, but he stopped them. They took him instead.'

'We're trying to find them, Gordy. The dark angels. We need to know where you were when they came for you and Billbo.'

'Wasn't here.' Gordy looked up at Eric. 'Safe here.'

'Was it in the city? Nearer the centre?' A nod. Which would explain why he'd ended up at McLean's station, rather than rambling on to someone in Loanhead or Dalkeith.

'You reckon you're up to showing us?'

Gordy's eyes widened even more, the fear threatening to tip him back over into full-blown madness. Eric reached out and placed a hand on his arm, gently. The contact seemed to give the ex-soldier strength, at least a little.

'In your shiny car?'

'It's not so shiny, but yes. In my car. If you can show

us where it happened, you won't even have to get out. I'll bring you straight back here, or take you to the barracks if you'd prefer.'

Gordy looked at his hands, clenched into fists on the table top. They were shaking for a while, but he brought them under control before shifting his gaze back up to McLean, his eyes clear with determination.

'Aye, I'll do it. I'll show you where it happened.'

32

'How on earth do you know Bobby Innes, sir?'

It was just as well that DC MacBride wasn't tall. He'd squeezed into the back of the car without complaining, but McLean could see that there wasn't a lot of room. Gordy sat in the passenger seat, stiff and upright, his madness and fear bubbling just below the surface. McLean didn't want to think what was going through his fractured mind.

'He used to share a flat with Kirsty, back when we were both students. We helped him decorate his first restaurant. Christ, I've not thought about that in a while.'

McLean stared through the windscreen, watching the first flurries of snow fall between the street lamps. It shouldn't have been dark for another hour yet, but the sunlight hadn't really managed to penetrate the thick cloud all day and now seemed to have given it up as a bad job. Even so, they'd made reasonably good time back into the city, only to be stuck in the slow crawl of traffic now they were near the centre.

'Never realized he ran a soup kitchen. And out in Bonnyrigg of all places.'

'It's a bit more than a soup kitchen. More of a halfway house. Somewhere people can stop a while if needs be, get themselves back together. I'm guessing that's what you were doing out there, eh Gordy?'

The ex-soldier flinched at his name, eyes going wide as if he'd been sleeping with them open and had been rudely woken. 'Eh? What?'

'You were at the shelter in Bonnyrigg,' McLean said. 'Trying to get yourself sorted out?'

'Trying to get away from the dark angels. City's not safe for the likes of us.' He dropped his head low, craning his neck to look up at the invisible monsters that lurked on the roofs of the tenements. 'Not safe for anyone.'

'Well, we'll make this as quick as possible, OK. You want to tell us where they took Billbo?'

'That way.' Gordy pointed towards the West End and the New Town. 'I'll know it when I see it.'

It took another half-hour just to get to the far end of George Street and down towards Dean Village. With each passing set of traffic lights slowly negotiated, McLean's suspicion deepened that he knew exactly where they were headed. When he took the next turning without any instruction from Gordy, it was confirmed. They drove slowly past Andrew Weatherly's empty terrace house. Its windows were dead eyes staring up at a snow-filled sky.

'Here, on the right.' Gordy's flailing hand almost smacked McLean in the face. He braked a little too hard, felt the car slide on snow-greased cobbles, overshot the narrow alley he wouldn't have been able to get down anyway. For a moment he thought he was going to hit a black Transit van parked half on the pavement, but he missed it by just a few inches.

'Down there?'

'Aye. Down there.' Gordy's voice was cracked, an edge of hysteria breaking through. McLean checked his rear-view mirror, and found it full of detective constable. It wasn't as if you could see much out of the back anyway. There was a space up ahead, though, probably double yellow lines but obscured by the snow. He pulled over and switched the engine off.

'I'm going to have a look, OK? You want to come, or stay here?'

Gordy's answer was to pull the door handle, unclip his seat belt and haul himself out into the street. A blast of cold air filled the car, sending a shiver through McLean's whole body. He got out, tilted his seat forward to let MacBride follow him. By the time they'd sorted themselves out, Gordy was already halfway down the alley.

'They're not here now,' he said as they reached him. McLean didn't need to be told. The alleyway cut between the terraces, giving access to the large private gardens at the back. Ornate wrought-iron gates stopped any riff-raff from getting in, a heavy chain and padlock hanging around the bars. Off to one side, a smaller service gate had a sophisticated entry phone and camera system. Looking up, McLean saw a security camera trained on the main gates too, but he didn't hold out any hopes that there'd be footage available.

'Where exactly were you, Gordy?'

'Over there.' The ex-soldier pointed at a doorway, partly blocked in by large wheelie bins. McLean walked over to the spot, turned around a couple of times, then hunkered down. It was sheltered, well out of the view of the camera, and best of all a ventilation duct blew warm air out into the night. Sure, it smelled bad, and there was a constant noise from the fan, but it was warm and dry. He shuffled into the doorway itself, then looked back towards the gates. You could barely see them, just the tops, and the dark trees beyond, skeletal branches reaching up into the night sky like bony fingers. Fat flakes of snow spiralled out of the black, caught briefly in the light from the street lamp, then disappeared again into shadow.

'How did you find this place?' McLean stood up, walked back out into the cold alleyway. 'It's a bit off the beaten track, isn't it?'

Gordy's eyes glinted in the darkness as he turned his head to face McLean. He'd been staring at the gates as if they opened up on to hell. 'You get to know the city's hiding places if you walk its streets long enough. You should know that, copper. Tramps and polis, we're the ones who know where everything is.'

McLean had to concede that the man had a point. 'Why's no one else using it, then?'

'Marked it, didn't I.' Gordy pointed at the stonework beside the door. Sure enough, now that he'd been shown them, McLean could see the dark charcoal lines scratched on to the building.

'Staked your claim?'

'No. That's a warning. Anyone who knows how to read the signs would keep well away.'

'So what happened here, Gordy? Where did they come from, the dark angels?'

At the words, the ex-soldier stiffened. His hands started to shake and he looked around the alleyway as if only just realizing where he was.

'They came out of the walls. They were everywhere. Their eyes glowed red like fire and they had tails that sparked and crackled and stung. I was stuck there, couldn't move. It was just like the war. Thought I was back there. And then Billbo comes in roaring like a . . . like a . . .' Gordy trailed off, his words having exhausted him. His shoulders slumped and McLean thought he was going to drop to his knees, but he just stood there, swaying slightly as fat lazy snowflakes spiralled down all around him, slumped like a puppet thrown over the back of a chair, waiting for its master to come back and take up the strings once more. When he approached, McLean could see tears running down his cheeks.

'Come on,' he said. 'We've seen enough. Let's get you away from here, aye?'

Gordy turned his head slowly, sniffed. 'They'd come for me. It was my turn. But Billbo went instead. Why'd he do that?'

33

McLean watched the squad car drive out of the station car park, turn right and head south towards the bypass and Bonnyrigg beyond. He'd have taken the ex-soldier himself, but the drive there and back would have eaten up yet more of the day, even if he could get in and out of the place without being accosted by Bobby or Eric. They'd always been Kirsty's friends more than his, and he'd shunned her friends more even than his own when she had died. When he'd realized where Gordy was hiding out, he'd thought it would be awkward seeing them again, that it would bring the pain and the despair back. Instead he'd found himself wondering why he'd never made the effort to catch up with them before.

'McLean. My office. Now.' Detective Superintendent Duguid might simply have been passing by as he stepped through the back door, or more likely he'd been lying in wait for just this moment. Either way, his flat, unemotional tone brooked no argument. A raging, unreasonable Dagwood he could deal with; the cold, calm manner McLean found more difficult to manage.

'If this is about Detective Sergeant Ritchie—'

'Not here. My office.' Duguid cut McLean off midsentence, turned away and headed up the back stairs at a speed surprising for one of his advancing years. McLean followed, the ever-present dull ache in his hip turning into a series of sharp stabbing pains with each further step. He was soon several paces behind his boss, the irony of the role reversal not lost on him at all. When was his next physiotherapist session? Not soon enough.

'You just can't do it, can you, McLean?' Duguid slumped into the seat behind his overlarge desk when they finally reached his office. McLean stood, not that there was much option.

'Sir?'

'Subtlety. It's not your style.'

'I'm sorry, sir, but I really don't know what you're talking about.'

'Dammit, man. This.' Duguid picked up the newspaper that had been lying at one corner of the desk, folded up. He flicked it open and dropped it down in front of McLean with a smooth action. The headline was answer enough. 'Family Slaughter MSP in Sex Romp Scandal!' It looked like the senior editor at the *Evening News* was on holiday again.

'This case was meant to be closed. Tidied away under the rug with Minimal Fuss. Does this look like Minimal Fuss to you, eh? What the fuck did you think you were doing handing those photos to the press?'

'What? You think I—?'

'You spent an hour this morning with Jo Dalgliesh. This evening she hits us with this.' Duguid picked up the paper, then threw it down on his desk again. 'Where else did she get her information from?'

'Oh dear God.' McLean pinched the bridge of his nose, closed his eyes, hoped that when he opened them again, he'd be back at home and all this just a bad dream. It didn't work, of course. Never did.

'I spoke to Dalgliesh this morning, yes. I'll admit it. But it was five minutes, maybe ten max. Bloody woman jumped me in the street as I was coming back here. Hit me with all this stuff about Weatherly. Thought if I told her to try to find out who was feeding her the pictures it might keep her off our backs for a while. Looks like she went for the easier option of giving us a good kicking.'

Duguid's eyes narrowed, his face darkening as the hamster strained to squeeze out a thought. 'If you didn't give them to her, where did she get them from then?'

Good Christ, they put this man in charge. McLean rocked on his heels, trying to puzzle out what was at the root of Duguid's current angry bluster.

'Probably the same place I did, sir. Plain brown envelope delivered anonymously. No context, no accompanying notes. Just carefully selected images to push an agenda.'

'But . . . If they'd already handed them to us . . . Why would they do that? What's to be gained—?'

'Other than fucking me and my team over? Making life bloody awkward for you? Uncomfortable for the Chief Constable? I'd have thought it would be obvious.'

Duguid's scowl was a small reward. Not enough to make up for the bollocking, though. 'Enlighten me,' the detective superintendent said.

'The man who gave me those photographs told me to keep digging even when the case was closed. He was Weatherly's handler. Part of a team who managed his excesses. They tolerated what he did as long as he was useful. Tried to make sure he didn't get too far out of line.'

'Well, they fucked that one up pretty spectacularly, I'd say.'

'So it would seem. There's more to it than that, though. Someone searched Weatherly's town house before we got there. They stripped all the hard drives out of his security systems except the ones they wanted us to see. They drip-fed us information, manipulated the investigation.' McLean remembered his conversation after the last press conference. 'I even think they've got Jack Tennant working for them, and that's not something I ever thought I'd see.'

'But that doesn't make sense. Why give you this stuff if they want the case to go away? For fuck's sake, why give it to the press?'

'It's all about the timing, I think. Something like this was bound to come out sooner or later. They just needed the process managed. Delayed until they were ready to deal with it. Weatherly's not the only one in those photos. There's bound to be others who need to be protected. Or dumped.' Another possibility occurred to him as he spoke, and McLean felt that familiar cold churning in the pit of his stomach as the ramifications began to form behind it. 'Either that or we've got two sides fighting a war, using us as proxies.'

'Fucking politics.' Duguid picked up the paper again, flicking it open so hard the front page tore. 'Christ, but I hate being played like this.'

From anyone else, McLean would have been surprised, might even have protested that he shouldn't dish it out if he couldn't take it. But this was Dagwood, and the point would be completely lost on the man. Instead he just tried to let it all wash over him, suppressing his reaction until all that escaped was a quiet sigh. The torn page slid slowly to the floor, turning over a couple of times before coming to a rest at his feet. Upside down, the smug face of Andrew Weatherly looked up at him, a playful smile on his lips as if he were enjoying the trouble his actions had caused.

'Me too, sir. Me too.'

'Good Christ, what are you doing here, Sergeant? I thought you were meant to be on sick leave.'

McLean had popped into the CID room on his way from Duguid's office in the hope of finding Grumpy Bob. Instead the pale, sniffing form of DS Ritchie looked up at him from her desk, eyes sunken, face thinner than could possibly be healthy. She gave him a weary smile.

'Sorry, sir. Thought this was more important.' She nodded at her laptop, then winced.

'And people say I'm a lost cause . . .' McLean walked over to the desk and peered at the screen. At first he thought it was a criminal record profile page, but the mug shot in the top right-hand corner didn't look right. Then he saw the Wikipedia logo, and the title of the entry. Jane Louise Dee.

'Mrs Saifre?' He recalled the woman he'd met at Weatherly's wake.

'That's what she calls herself these days, but this is

who everyone remembers.' Ritchie tapped the screen with the flat of her fingernail.

'They do?'

'Honestly. I thought you had a well-rounded education, sir. Jane Louise Dee. The Scottish Bill Gates. Invented half of the stuff that makes all our computer networks run properly?'

'That's her?' McLean shook his head, feeling a slight rush of embarrassment as his mind went back to their conversation. He had heard of her, now that Ritchie mentioned it. Surprised how the name hadn't meant anything to him when she'd handed him her card. His hand went up to the breast pocket on his jacket, the same one he'd been wearing that day. Sure enough, the card was still there. Just the name and that mobile phone number. Nothing else.

'I interviewed her a while back. About Weatherly. At least I think I did.' Ritchie pulled open her desk drawer and took out a large plastic pot of painkillers, shook it to see if there was anything left inside. It relinquished a pair of reluctant pills, washed down with a swig from a two-litre plastic water bottle. McLean noticed three more pill pots in the drawer before Ritchie closed it again.

'You think you did? Aren't you sure?'

'Well, that's the odd thing. Can't find my notes anywhere. There's nothing in the folder, nothing in my notebook. But this . . .' Ritchie picked up a sheet of paper, bearing the logo of Weatherly Asset Management and a list of names, all scored out, with little annotations in Ritchie's spidery handwriting. 'This tells me I did. And I sort of remember it.'

'Sort of?' McLean asked.

'It's stupid. My head's so thick most of the time. I'm sure I interviewed her. Just ... Well ... Can't seem to remember any of the details other than coffee and biscuits.'

McLean could only sympathize. 'I've had days like that.' He took the sheet of paper from Ritchie's damp grasp, peered at the names. 'Gone through lists like this. After a while, asking the same questions, getting the same answers, it gets difficult to remember who said what to whom. Add in some Fife lurgy and it's a miracle you even remembered her name.' He dropped the sheet back on the top of an open investigation folder.

'Still bugging me, sir. I should've had all this stuff finished ages ago. I mean, I know they closed down the case, but what with all the stuff in the press, and—'

'Go home, Kirsty.' McLean reached past the detective sergeant and gently eased down the lid of her laptop. The face of Jane Louise Dee stared at him as he did so, almost begging him not to be so cruel.

'But my report—'

'Can wait. You're right. The Fiscal's going to want another report now. We'll have to reopen the investigation even though it won't do us any good. But you're no good to anyone here. You need rest. This'll still be here for you when you get back.'

Ritchie looked up at him and sniffed. 'Will it?' she said. 'That's a shame. I was rather hoping it might all just go away.'

34

The thought of locking himself in his office and hiding behind the ever-growing stacks of paperwork there had rather lost its appeal after his conversation with Ritchie. McLean knew he had a brief respite before the powers that be read the *Evening News* and the shit hit the fan. If he was lucky, he might keep his job, but it was going to be an uncomfortable time. That was what his nocturnal visitor had said. Well, McLean wouldn't starve if they kicked him out of the force, but his team deserved better. Maybe they could deal with the inevitable criticism by solving a completely unrelated case.

He headed for the small incident room they were using for the tattooed man investigation. It was just across the corridor from the larger room, where the Weatherly case had run its very short distance. Perhaps it would be reopened, perhaps not. But for now it was empty. Why he decided to go in, McLean couldn't really be sure. There was no one else in there, which might have been a good reason if it weren't for the fact that the other room would likely be empty as well.

At first, he didn't even turn the lights on, just relied on the scant orange illumination coming in through the window wall from the street lamps beyond. The snow that had been just the occasional flurry all day was settling into something altogether heavier now that the light had gone, the temperature dropped. At least there wasn't the strong wind to throw it all about this time.

A large conference table took up most of the centre of the room, desks pushed back to the walls. McLean ran a finger over the wooden surfaces as he walked slowly around the room. It was quiet in here, peaceful. He couldn't remember a time recently when he'd been able to just sit and think. Or stand and think, for that matter. When he'd climbed to the top of the hill behind Weatherly's house in Fife, perhaps? Despite being chased by a fold of Highland cattle.

He smiled to himself at the memory. They hadn't really been chasing him, just curious as to what he was doing in their midst. If he'd not been in a hurry to get back, he'd probably have stood his ground, waited until they got used to him.

Still standing in semi-darkness, McLean finally realized what it was that he'd been staring at all this time, what his subconscious had probably made him come into this room for in the first place. The end wall was split in two, one half whiteboard still scrawled with notes and questions relating to Andrew Weatherly. The other half was corkboard, to which had been pinned a large-scale map of the city and the surrounding area.

Whether it was the map MacBride had pinned up in the room across the corridor, he couldn't be sure. It didn't really matter. It was a map and it was fairly new, so should be reasonably accurate. McLean flicked on the lights then crossed the room and crouched down, peering at the area to the south until he found Roslin and the river. Then he unpinned the map, folded it and carried it over to the big table, where he could see it without having to squat.

The bypass snaked around the city to the south, cutting it off from Loanhead, Bilston, Roslin and further still Penicuik. McLean traced the River North Esk with his finger, upstream from Dalkeith, Polton Mill and into Roslin Glen. Even with the overhead lights he had to peer closely to see the chapel and castle, identify the spot where they'd pulled the body out of the river. It annoyed him that they'd not already done this, and all because someone had nicked the map before they'd had a chance. Some way to run an investigation. No wonder Duguid thought so little of him.

McLean traced his finger further, finding Glencorse Barracks, the remains of the old gunpowder works, the railway cutting, the country park. Somewhere along there, their tattooed man, William Beaumont, had tumbled over the cliff and ended up in the river. At least that was the best guess he had. He'd been covered in scratches from the gorse bushes, so it was likely he'd been running. If someone had simply chucked him over the cliff to get rid of him, he'd not have had so many thorns in his legs and arms. So where had he come from? Couldn't have been far, not in that weather, naked. No matter how terrified you might be, that kind of cold would slow you down soon enough.

Off to the northeast, Rosewell and Bonnyrigg were too far, and McLean doubted the man would have run naked through a populated area without at least someone noticing. It had to be closer in. His finger hovered over the complex of buildings that made up Rossketle

Hospital. It had been a psychiatric hospital, if memory served, but was closed now. Derelict. Probably worth going to have a look around, though. If the snow ever eased off.

McLean folded up the map, shoved it under his arm and left. Stepping into the corridor it felt like his ears had popped. Noise flowed back that he hadn't realized had been missing before, the quiet spell of the empty room broken.

'Stealing again, McLean?'

He turned to see the portly form of Detective Chief Inspector Brooks filling the corridor. Bobbing along behind him, little DI Spence looked like he'd fit right in on *The Muppet Show*.

'Didn't think anyone was using it.' McLean flapped the folded-up map against his thigh. 'And someone lifted it out of my incident room anyway.'

'Ah yes. Your mysterious tattooed man. How's that going?'

'We know who he is now. Know where he was last seen alive and where he died. Just need to fill in the gap between.'

Whatever Brooks had been expecting McLean to say, this obviously wasn't it. He had closed the gap between them now. Sneered as he barged past, forcing McLean into the door to the smaller incident room. 'Better hurry up then. I'd be surprised if you were still here by the end of the week.'

Not for the first time, he wondered why it was he persisted with the job. It wasn't as if he needed the money, after all, and dealing with the likes of Dagwood and Brooks on a daily basis was an unusual kind of masochism. On the other hand, as he pinned the map back on to the wall in the small incident room, smoothing it over and tapping his finger on the tiny knot of buildings at Rosskettle, he couldn't help but feel a little surge of excitement. This was the best part of the job. The hunt for clues, the slow puzzling out of just what had happened. And hopefully, when all was said and done, justice for the victim.

It was only as he stepped back from the board to get a better look at things that he realized he wasn't alone in the room. A soft snore rose up from behind a large flat-screen monitor on a desk at the back of the room, next to the radiator. It gurgled at the end, transforming into a snort as Grumpy Bob awoke from his slumber. McLean glanced at his watch. Almost six already. Where had the day gone?

'Evening, Bob. Making sure that chair doesn't go anywhere, I see.'

Grumpy Bob stretched, yawned and scratched at the grey stubble on his cheek. 'You know what it's like with these internal reports, sir. Just dozed off thinking about the thing, let alone reading it.'

He picked up a sheaf of papers, stood with much creaking of joints and shuffled around the desk so that he could hand them over.

'No thanks. You can keep it. I've no problems getting to sleep.' McLean held up his hands to ward the document off. 'What is it, anyway?'

'Report from the boat team.'

'Boat team?'

'Aye, you know. Roslin Glen. The river.'

'Oh, right. I didn't think they'd get out in this weather.'

'Can't imagine they were all that pleased about it, but they went. Found something, too.' Grumpy Bob handed over the file again, and this time McLean took it. There were some photographs, close-ups that hadn't survived the laser printing process well.

'The executive summary?'

'It's all couched in maybes and probabilities, but it's pretty much where you and the lad thought it happened.'

McLean remembered the cliff, DC MacBride's firm grip the only thing between him and painful death. 'What's the evidence like?'

'Well, there's lots of broken branches. Not conclusive, of course. Could've been made by anything. But they also found scraps of what they think are skin on the rocks at the water's edge. Covered in snow, but then everything was. Samples have gone off to the lab. We should know by the morning if that's what they are. Confirming it's our man will take a little longer, but I can't seen anyone else barking their shins on that side of the river any time recently.'

'The east bank, I take it.'

'That's the chappy.'

McLean went back to the map, found a red marker pen and circled the spot.

'What do you know about Rosskettle Hospital, Bob?'

Grumpy Bob scratched his head through thinning grey hair. 'Rosskettle? Not much. Loony bin, wasn't it?'

'I think the preferred term is psychiatric hospital, Sergeant.'

'Aye, well, it's closed now, in't it. They moved everyone to the new place out at Little France.'

'Find out, can you? Only I think we need to pay it a visit first thing tomorrow.'

Grumpy Bob raised an eyebrow. 'Don't you have to go see your favourite therapist tomorrow morning?'

McLean looked at his watch again, noting the day as well as the time. True enough, he was due his weekly waste of time with Matt Hilton at eight.

'Sod that, Bob. I'll go see if he's in now. You never know, he might be able to shed some light on the hospital. And if not, then I'll just have to tell him to reschedule. I'll pick you up here at eight.'

Hilton was locking the door to his office when McLean turned the corner. He must have caught the movement out of the corner of his eye. He looked up startled, a frightened, guilty expression on his face. McLean had seen that expression so many times before, usually on the faces of the innocent, those witnesses called in to give statements and other helpful citizens not used to being in the company of policemen. Criminals, at least the hardened kind, never worried about the laws they might be unknowingly breaking.

'Tony. Hi. I wasn't expecting to see you till tomorrow.' Hilton covered his unease with a smile that made him look a little deranged. How long had he been working with the police? And yet he still had this slightly uncomfortable manner if you caught him off-guard. Either that or there was a dead body in his office he didn't want anyone to know about.

'Yes, about that. I was wondering if we might be able to reschedule.' McLean watched the smile turn into a frown, cut off Hilton's response before he could give it. 'Also wanted to pick your brains about something. Rosskettle Hospital. You know it?'

Hilton managed to go from frown to hurt in a move that would have done an actor proud. 'Know it? Certainly. I did a lot of my training there. Really sad when they closed it down, but the facilities were getting quite dated. And it's so isolated. That's why they put it there, of course. Back in the mid-nineteenth century, I think. When we used to lock up our problems and forget about them. Attitudes to mental illness have changed a bit since then, thankfully.'

'Any idea what's happened to the site?'

'I'm not sure.' Hilton finished locking his office door, shoved the keys in his pocket and picked up his heavy black briefcase. 'Mind if we walk? Only I've got to get going.'

'Of course.' McLean stood to one side, let the psychiatrist past, then fell into step with him. 'It's still NHS Scotland, then?'

'Actually, now you mention it, I think I did hear something about it being sold. Probably being turned into exclusive apartments or something. You thinking of heading out there, are you? That why you want to reschedule?'

'It's part of the investigation into the tattooed man. We reckon he fell off the cliff into the river not far from the hospital. There's not many other places round there he could have come from. Unless someone drove him out there, of course.'

'Clutching at straws, Inspector? That's hardly like you.'

'I prefer to think of it as being thorough. But I'd like to go at first light, if the snow's cleared. I get the feeling the afternoon's going to be mostly dealing with the press about bloody Andrew Weatherly.'

Hilton smiled at that. 'Yes, I'd heard. Don't really envy you.' He stopped at the top of the stairs that would take him down to the back door and the staff car park. 'Don't worry about tomorrow. That's fine. We'll catch up next week. I'll make some calls, ask about Rosskettle for you, too. Let you know if I find out anything useful.'

'Thanks.' McLean watched as the psychiatrist trotted down the stairs, surprised at him being actually helpful for a change. Perhaps that was all he needed, to be involved in something. A shame he had to be such a tit all the time.

'That you sorted for tomorrow then, sir?' Grumpy Bob joined him at the railing, leaning over and peering down. For a moment McLean thought he was going to hawk and spit.

'Eight sharp. I'll pick you up from here. That you off for the day?'

'Aye. Shift ended over an hour ago and it's not like there's any overtime these days. What about you?'

McLean had intended going back to his office and spending at least a couple of hours ploughing through forms. A couple of hours would inevitably become four, and then he'd finally go home and share his takeaway curry with a disapproving Mrs McCutcheon's cat. That was what he'd intended doing.

'Sod it, Bob. Fancy a pint?'

35

The early morning sun hung low in the southern sky, painting the glittering snow in shades of white and gold as McLean drove out of the city towards Dalkeith. He'd forgotten to put his shades back in the car after the last time he'd needed them, and was forced to squint to see anything ahead. Beside him in the passenger seat, Grumpy Bob had given up and just closed his eyes. Any excuse for forty winks; the man was a living Womble.

Climbing up on to the Midlothian plain, the roads were narrower, less frequently used and bordered on both sides by high banks that trapped the snow into deep drifts. McLean had often wondered why so many DCIs and superintendents drove big four by fours; he'd have given good money to be in one of them right now. As they neared the hospital though, the road became clearer, the snow turned to grey-black slush by heavy traffic. Turning the final corner to the entrance gate, he saw why.

The NHS Scotland sign was still there, proudly proclaiming the existence of Rosskettle Hospital, but alongside it a new sign had gone up. McLean had never heard of Price Developments. Apparently they were turning the site into a science and technology park, with funding from the EU and a dozen other quangos whose logos had probably cost a king's ransom in taxpayers' money to design. A barrier hung across the driveway, and a fluorescent-jacketed security guard approached with a clipboard and a frown as McLean pulled the car to a halt in front of it.

'Private site, sir. No visitors allowed,' he said, as McLean lowered the window.

'I was wondering if I could have a word with the site manager, actually.' McLean held up his warrant card for inspection and the security guard's frown deepened.

'One moment please.' He bustled back to the control booth, a Portakabin with a wide glass front. Inside, McLean could see him pick up a phone. A lengthy conversation ensued, during which time the nice warm air inside the car was replaced with cold, dry air from outside. He was about to raise the window again, reached across to rack up the temperature and point it at his feet, but the guard finished his conversation, pressed a button that raised the barrier and bustled out again.

'Sorry about that, Inspector. If you'd like to follow the drive to the main house, the boss will meet you there. Please don't go wandering off, though. A lot of the buildings are in a dangerous condition. We had one roof fall in just last week. Miracle no one was hurt.'

'Thanks. We'll be careful.' He raised the window and drove into the site. Before he'd gone more than fifty yards he had to pull hard over to the verge to let an enormous truck past the other way. Craning his neck, he could see it was filled with bits of scrap metal, twisted hospital bed frames, iron balustrades and other rubbish. Everything had a value these days; no doubt this lot would be melted down and turned into something useful.

The old buildings at the centre of the complex came into sight, three storeys high and looking every inch the Victorian asylum. They were surrounded by trees, the large old oaks and beeches looming over hundreds of whippy little weed saplings. No groundsmen had worked here for a few years, it appeared. McLean parked in the yard between a rusty Transit minibus and a brand new Range Rover, shiny black with tinted windows. Looking around as he climbed out of the Alfa, he could see that it was very much out of place among the cheap and dirty cars and vans of the work crews. Someone important was visiting the site. It didn't take long to find out who.

'Inspector McLean, we meet again.'

She walked slowly down the stone steps from the front entrance, looking for all the world like a 1940s movie star in her long black coat, lined with sable fur around the collar. The door she had come through was vast, its surround made from enormous blocks of red sandstone, the keystone of the lintel arch an ornately carved coat of arms that looked more suited to some ancestral home than a lunatic asylum. Following behind her, two enormous men in expensively tailored suits and wearing mirror shades were more likely bodyguards than builders.

'Mrs Saifre. You're back from your business trip, then?'

'And you haven't called. I was so looking forward to lunch.' She gave him a Marilyn Monroe pout.

'I'm afraid us lowly detective inspectors don't get much time for lunch.'

'Dinner it is, then. I'll send a car to pick you up at eight.'

McLean studied the woman's face, trying to tell

whether she was joking or not. He had a terrible feeling she was not. Then she broke into a broad smile.

'I'm so sorry. I shouldn't play around. What do they call it? Wasting Police Time? You might lock me up.'

'I take it Price Developments is one of your concerns, Mrs Saifre?' McLean asked, anxious to get the conversation on to more stable ground.

'Please, call me Jane Louise. All my friends do. And yes. Price is one of mine now. We have such plans for this place. So what brings you here? Obviously not me.' She arched a perfectly shaped eyebrow at him.

'Just part of an ongoing investigation into an incident down in the glen.' McLean nodded in what he thought was the right direction, although given the twists and turns in the road here, he might have been indicating Fife. 'I remembered this place from when I was a student. Heard it had closed, and wondered if anyone had been squatting here.'

Mrs Saifre gave a theatrical shiver. 'Don't much fancy it in this weather. Half the windows are gone and there's nothing much to burn in the fireplaces. You're welcome to have a look around if you want. Just be careful, and avoid the outbuildings. They're pulling a lot of it down at the moment.'

'Thanks. I don't think we'll be here long.'

McLean watched as one of the bodyguards pulled open the Range Rover door for Mrs Saifre, then went around to the other side to drive. The second bodyguard climbed in the back and they reversed out of the parking space. The window wound down as they were about to leave.

'Eight o'clock, Inspector. Karl will pick you up.' And before he could say anything in reply, they were gone in a waffle of V8 engine and steaming exhaust.

'Friend of yours?' Grumpy Bob stood beside McLean's car, his elbows resting on the roof, a familiar grin plastered over his old face.

'Hardly. She's . . . was one of Andrew Weatherly's associates. I met her at the funeral. Well, the wake to be precise.'

'And there she is inviting you out to dinner. Seems you have all the luck.'

'That's just some strange kind of joke. At least I hope it's a strange kind of joke. Come on. Let's have a look at this place, since we came all this way.' McLean set off across the parking yard in the direction of the snow-covered fields and the collection of outbuildings beyond.

'Aren't we going inside?' Grumpy Bob asked.

'No. There's nothing in there worth seeing, unless you've a thing for derelict buildings. I'm far more interested in the stuff they didn't want us to look at.'

36

There wasn't much left; that was the first thing McLean noticed. Half a dozen large diggers were busy ripping down buildings, filling up an endless line of trucks with rubble and steel. They had churned up the previous night's snow over a small area, but it was easy to see the scope of the work they had already done. Separate blocks where the smooth surface turned bumpy over some disturbance below must have been four or five outbuildings, probably identical to the one that was coming down now and the three still standing entire.

'Which way's the river from here, Bob?'

'Search me, sir. I'm useless at directions.'

McLean squinted up at the sun. At this time of year it never got very high in the southern sky. Through the skeletal trees to his right he could just make out the Pentland Hills, which meant that the river must be in that direction, too. He walked that way, boots crunching deep into the snow, giving the buildings and the diggers a wide berth. No one shouted at them to keep away or ran over to accost them as they worked a slow, wide arc, ending up at the boundary between the hospital grounds and the surrounding farmland. A thin band of trees opened up on to a flat field, probably ploughed and sown under its blanket of white. Beyond that more woodland marked the edge of the glen itself. The developers had put up a three-metre-high temporary fence to stop anyone wandering on to the site by mistake. If it circled the entire complex it must have cost a fortune.

'How long d'you reckon this has been here?' McLean reached out, grabbed the nearest section of fence and gave it a good shake. No matter how terrified he was, a naked man wouldn't have been able to get over it.

'Hard to say with this snow.' Grumpy Bob walked over to where two sections connected, sturdy poles slotted into a heavy concrete block. He kicked at the slight drift that had built up against it. A bit further along, an old oak tree had fallen down long enough ago to have been partly sawn into logs. Here the snow had been heaped high by the wind, carved into an elegant curve at the top. 'Not long.'

'What I thought. Come on.' McLean trudged back to the nearest undemolished building. It was a single-storey prefab of the kind thrown up in haste just after the Second World War. Never intended to be used for as long as they had been. Thin walls, no doubt featuring asbestos heavily in their make-up, windows up too high to see in from the ground, single glazing, minimal insulation. They were a product of a time when heating oil was cheap and cold air at night was meant to build up your moral fibre. He remembered the miserable school nights he'd spent in similar accommodation, the frozen tooth mug of water on the bedside table every winter morning. The happiest days of his life. Aye, right.

A concrete ramp led up to double doors, but they were locked from the inside, no handles on the out. McLean walked around the building looking for another way in, Grumpy Bob trudging along behind him like a reluctant servant. At the end of the wall they were following they would come into view of the digger operators and other workmen on site, and for some unaccountable reason, McLean didn't want to be seen. At least not yet.

'Give us a leg up, will you, Bob?'

'You're not going in there, are you? They could start smashing it down any minute. And besides, we've not got a warrant.'

'It's just a wee look-see. I wasn't planning on going in.'

Grumpy Bob grumbled a bit about getting his hands cold, but he crouched down anyway. McLean clambered up and reached the windowsill, pulling at the edge of the frame. Something snapped, clattering to the floor inside, and the window swung open.

'Bit higher, eh, Bob.'

'Thought you weren't going in.'

'Didn't think I'd be able to.' McLean hauled himself up and over the sill, then lowered himself carefully down to the floor inside, not trusting it to take his weight. The room he was in took up about a quarter of the building, its ceiling collapsed near the centre. Snow had come in through the hole in the roof and been spread around in the wind, covering everything in a fine white powder. He could still see the chairs and tables, a row of benches along one wall, whiteboards fixed to another. The windows that would have looked out on to the next building had been painted black at some point in the past, which meant that he couldn't be seen by the workmen. It also meant he couldn't see the diggers when they approached. He'd have to rely on the sound coming in through the roof. And Grumpy Bob's nervous grumbling.

Keeping to the edge of the room, McLean walked carefully around to the door opposite where he had climbed in. It opened up on to a dark corridor that smelled of damp and cold. He guddled around in his pocket for the pen torch he always carried, flicked it on and played it up and down the way. At the end facing the main building complex, the corridor widened out into a small reception area, with a desk, shelves and a few uncomfortable-looking armchairs scattered around. The windows here were painted black too, as if whoever had been sent to this building had been terrified of the light. Looking back the other way, the corridor ended with the double doors they'd not been able to open before. On his side of the passage there was one other door; opposite him there were four, evenly spaced.

McLean tried the door on his side first. It opened on to a room similar to the one he'd just left. Some kind of communal area, only this one had a basic open-plan kitchen in it as well. The windows were all blacked out again, and a dark stain on the ceiling tiles suggested it wouldn't be long before the roof collapsed in here too.

Across the hall, three of the rooms were small dormitories, containing four narrow iron-framed beds, one in each corner. The final door opened on to a bathroom. McLean played his torchlight over the heavy-duty shower heads that poked from one wall. The toilet cubicles alongside the showering area had no doors on them;

communal living at its most primitive. But who had lived here, and what had become of them? He had no idea.

Coming back out of the bathroom, McLean heard the sound of diggers ever closer. At the same time he noticed the small metal ring in the floor. It sat in a little recess and had been covered with a thin plastic-backed runner that lay crumpled against the wall nearby. Playing the torch around, he could see the edges of a trapdoor, and there on the wall a catch to hold it open. He pulled on the ring, but the door seemed stuck fast. Nearby the sound of the diggers was even louder, heading straight for this building. He knelt down and studied the trapdoor and ring more carefully, looking for some kind of keyhole but finding none. And then it dawned on him. He twisted the ring through a half turn, then pulled.

The door opened with a terrible crashing noise. For a moment, McLean couldn't work out what was happening, then he realized that the diggers had begun their work on the front wall of the building. Light flooded in through the collapsed door at the other end of the corridor, bringing with it billowing, powdery snow. He hefted the trapdoor up and latched it against the wall, then shone his torch into the darkness beneath. Concrete steps led down to a corridor that followed the line of the one above it, breeze-block walls with modern-looking light fittings bolted to them, a freshly painted door just visible.

Another crash of demolished wall, and this time a chunk of the roof collapsed into the corridor. McLean covered his eyes and mouth as a wave of asbestos dust smothered him. It was time to go. He retreated reluctantly to the double doors at the back of the building as another crash roared in from the room to his right. How many diggers were they using, for Christ's sake?

A kick at the bars, and the doors popped open. Grumpy Bob stood a few yards away, his face a picture of horror, turning to relief as he saw McLean run down the concrete ramp. He had his mobile phone out, hand poised over it to make a call, whether it was for back-up or an ambulance, McLean couldn't be sure, but he waved his hands to stop him as he trotted down the ramp.

'Don't call it in,' he said as he reached the sergeant.

'But they just carried on knocking it down. Stood in front of the digger and that fat bastard just drove on like he hadn't seen me. Had to get out of his way sharpish.'

'Like you said, Bob, I wasn't meant to be in there. We were warned, and we've no warrant.' McLean turned back to watch as three diggers converged on the centre of the building, their buckets making short work of the flimsy walls. The rate they were going it would only take a half hour or so to flatten the place and load it all into the waiting trucks. Carted off to landfill somewhere or crushed into the foundations of the new Forth Road Bridge. Any evidence of wrongdoing long gone.

'Come on. Let's get out of here.'

37

'Ah, Constable, good. You're in. I need you to get on to NHS Scotland, see if someone in their Buildings Department's got plans of Rosskettle Hospital.'

The drive back to the station had been an interesting one. McLean had felt jittery the whole way; partly the adrenalin rush from his near escape, partly the feeling that he was on to something, if he could just work out what. Grumpy Bob, on the other hand, had for once lived up to his name, cradling his phone in his lap and every five minutes or so threatening to call in some uniforms to go and arrest the digger drivers. As soon as they arrived, McLean sent him off to the canteen for coffee and bacon rolls, but mostly to get the detective sergeant out of his hair.

'Rosskettle? That not the psychiatric hospital?' DC MacBride had been working at his tablet computer, but he put it to one side and picked up his phone.

'Was. It's closed now. Being redeveloped by an outfit called Price Developments. See what you can dig up on them too, will you?'

'On it, sir. Oh, there was a call came in for you about an hour ago. I tried to put it through to your mobile, but it was just going to voicemail. Took a message instead.'

McLean could only wonder at the technological know-how involved in such a thing. 'Who was it?'

'Your friend Mr Cobbold. The tattoo guy.'

'Eddie? What did he want?'

'To talk to you, sir. He wouldn't tell me what it was about. I took down his number, though.' McLean expected MacBride to fetch a Post-it note out from among the papers arranged neatly around his desk, but instead the detective constable took up his tablet, swiped the screen and tapped a couple of times. 'Here you go.'

'Thanks.' McLean took the tablet from MacBride's slightly reluctant grip, peered at the note on the screen, then wrote it down on a Post-it and handed the tablet back. 'I'll give him a call. Hopefully he's got something useful for us and doesn't just want to persuade me to go under the needle again.'

'Booked in for a session myself, sir. Got a killer design in mind, and Mr Cobbold said he'd do me a special rate.'

'I don't need to know any more, Constable. Thank you. Just get me that information. Soon as possible, aye?'

McLean left MacBride doing the thing he did best, ferreting out secrets from the electronic world. He set off for his office, dialling the number on the Post-it note as he went. It rang twice before being answered.

'Bo's Inks.' Not Eddie, unless he'd had a sex change.

'Is Eddie there?'

'Just a minute. Can I ask who's calling?'

'Tell him it's Tony McLean. He called wanting to speak to me earlier.' McLean negotiated the stairwell, pushed through a gaggle of uniforms just off shift, nodded and smiled at a couple of support staff he recognized and made it to his office before the phone was answered a second time.

'Tony. Hi. Thanks for calling back.'

'You called first, Eddie. I take it this is about our tattooed friend?'

'Aye, it was. Been thinking about it since, well, you know . . .'

'And?'

'Well, it's like, there's tatts and there's tatts. Sometimes you can tell who's done the inking just by how it looks. Your wee friend MacBride. I clocked it was Jake Selden down in Wardie'd done him, soon as I saw the design.'

'Thought you said you couldn't tell who'd done the work on our body, though?'

'No, at first. There was just too much to take in, you know?'

McLean could appreciate that. He was depressingly used to seeing dead bodies, but even so, William Beaumont had shocked him more than he would admit.

'I know what you mean.'

'Aye, well. Angus gave me a set of photos and I've had another look. Think I might know who did it. Not sure, but you can maybe go and see him? Bring him in for questioning?'

McLean sensed what Eddie Cobbold was getting at. 'Make him fall up and down the stairs a few times?'

'It's not natural, what was done to that poor bastard. Might be wrong. It might not be him at all, but if it is . . .'

'Just give me a name, Eddie, OK? I'll take it from there.'

Gentrification of the city had happened in chaotic waves over his lifetime. Sometimes it was intentional; the bulldozing of slum tenements to make way for modern apartments and office buildings. More often it was by accident; an area becoming popular with students because it was cheap would be dragged upmarket by them graduating and deciding to stay. There wasn't often any discernible pattern to it. A road might be lined on one side with renovated terrace houses fetching upwards of half a million, and yet still have run-down tenements opposite, populated by the unemployed and the unemployable.

Areas once prosperous could just as quickly fall into disarray. Sometimes all it took was a change of priorities at a set of traffic lights; a once-peaceful street turned into a main road feeding the city with its endless diet of lorries and cars. Those grand houses would soon be split into ever smaller units, let to those who could only dream of being able to afford somewhere quiet.

And some areas simply refused to improve, no matter what. The freshly painted railings would soon be daubed with graffiti, the expensive children's playpark littered with spent needles and used condoms, the bus stops turned into little fiefdoms by the feral youth that presumably lived in the anonymous social housing all around.

It was to one of these areas that the man whom Eddie Cobbold had named had perhaps inevitably sunk. McLean wished he'd been able to secure a pool car as he drove his Alfa along the street looking for Barry Timbrel's address. Half the vehicles parked at the kerbside were on bricks. A couple were burnt out.

'Nice part of town,' Grumpy Bob observed as they pulled into a space littered with broken windscreen glass, glittering in the slushy snow like fake diamonds.

'Let's not linger, then.' McLean climbed out, tasting a sharp tang to the air that had more than a whiff of illegal substances about it. The estate was made up of a dozen or so two-storey housing blocks, four flats in each. They'd probably be a decent size inside, and the uPVC double-glazing would have at least kept out the worst of the noise. There was no snow on any roofs, though, so likely not much in the way of loft insulation. Or heating.

Barry's flat was up a flight of stone steps, open to the elements at the bottom and leading straight to a narrow landing. McLean had been expecting to find a wheel-less bicycle frame chained and padlocked to the railings at the top, but this part of town obviously wasn't that sophisticated. There was nothing except a couple of soggy cardboard boxes that had once contained whole-sale quantities of cigarettes, a smell of stale urine and damp.

'Which door?' Grumpy Bob asked, walking towards the one on the left. Neither had any kind of identifying marker.

'Give it a knock. See if anyone's in.' McLean approached the door on the right to do the same, but as he lifted his hand to the flaking paintwork, he noticed that it was slightly ajar.

'Forget it, Bob. Horrible suspicion this is the one.' He bent down to inspect the lock, saw no sign that it had been forced. Still, he pulled on a pair of latex gloves. If for nothing else then to avoid getting that smell on his hands.

Pushing open the door let an even less pleasant odour

out. It brought with it a half-memory, though McLean couldn't immediately place it. Sulphurous like a recently struck match, only stronger. It went straight to the back of his throat. Straight to the back of Grumpy Bob's too, if the cough behind him was anything to go by.

'How the other half lives.' The open door revealed a narrow hall littered with more cigarette boxes. Empty pizza squares and foil containers for Chinese takeaway or curry poked out of the top of a couple of black bags that had yet to make it down to the big wheelie bins outside. Clothes hung over a long radiator to dry, although even McLean knew it was better to wash them first. Any or all of them could have accounted for the smell, but there was still that nagging feeling he'd come across it recently. Or something very similar.

'Hello? Mr Timbrel? Anyone at home?' He took a tentative step into the flat, listening for any sign of inhabitants. There was no reply, so he picked a path through the detritus to the first door off the hall. It opened on to a bedroom that was messy, but not dirty. The bed hadn't been made in a while by the look of its tangled sheets and blankets. A chest of drawers vomited underwear from an open top drawer, spilling it to the floor. Alongside it, a closet filled with shirts and trousers, most fairly well worn and firmly in the casual jeans and lumberjack mould. Several pairs of heavy boots were strewn about the base, spilling out on to the floor from the space where the door had once been. That was leaning against the wall a few feet away, turned around so that the full-length mirror that had been on the inside now faced the world.

It was the same in the other rooms. Signs of recent habitation, general chaos that you might associate with bachelor living, if you had no self-respect. The only place that broke the rule was the small second bedroom, which confirmed this was indeed the apartment of Barry Timbrel. Either that or there just happened to be two tattoo artists sharing this level of this particular council block. There were neatly stacked shelves, lined with supplies for Barry's shop, design books, spare equipment. The floor was even clear enough to show the faded red carpet.

'Looks like your man's not here.' Grumpy Bob peered in through the open door. 'Left in a hurry, too. If the kitchen's anything to go by.'

'And the front door. You don't leave that unlocked if you've got stuff like this stored here.' McLean wandered back to the kitchen. He'd only given it a brief glance before, but now he looked more closely he could see a pattern to the mess. Barry's last takeaway had been a curry, and he'd at least made the effort to scrape it on to a plate. A can of cheap lager made up the ensemble, all arranged on the small table, in front of the only chair. The curry was half-eaten, and when he picked up the can there was still some beer sloshing around in the base of it. A cigarette had been placed on the edge of an ashtray in the middle of the table and then forgotten, burning a perfect tube of ash before dropping the butt to the Formica tabletop. All the signs of someone who had been disturbed at his meal.

'No sign of a struggle, though,' McLean said, turning slowly on the spot, looking for something that didn't look like it had been dropped in apathy. The place was a mess, true, but it was a cultivated mess. Work had gone into getting it that way, and time.

'No.' Grumpy Bob agreed. 'Reckon he just got up and walked out.'

38

The tinny buzzing of his office phone shook McLean from his reverie. He'd been staring at the wall opposite his desk, trying to untangle all the knotted strands in his head and mostly succeeding in making things worse. They'd put a call out for Barry Timbrel, but chances were he was gone, or had been taken. Nothing he could do about it now, which was almost more frustrating than not knowing who he was in the first place. Whether this new distraction was a good thing or not, he couldn't be sure. At least it was something to focus on.

'McLean,' he said into the receiver, as if whoever was on the front desk didn't know that already.

'Evening, Inspector. There's a bloke here says he's come to pick you up.'

'This another one of your jokes, Reg? Only the last one kind of backfired?'

'No joke, sir. Honest injun. There's a bloke here, must be six foot eight if he's an inch. Built like a brick shit-house too, but one that's been dressed by its mum. Muttered something about dinner? I don't know. Doesn't really seem your type, if I'm being honest. His accent's not the easiest to get either.'

Dinner. McLean looked at his watch. Eight o'clock. He stuck his hand in the breast pocket of his jacket, dug out the card that was still there from Andrew Weatherly's funeral. Jane Louise Dee. Mrs Saifre. He thought she'd been joking that morning when she'd said she'd send someone round to pick him up. But no, that was just what his brain had told him. If he'd thought about it, he'd already known she wasn't a woman to joke about something like that. Nor was she someone who was prepared to take no for an answer. She was used to getting her own way.

Well, two could play that game. There were questions he wanted to put to her, and if he could do that at some nice restaurant over a good meal and a glass or two of wine, then so much the better. He looked at the pile of forms, reports and as yet unidentified folders spilling over one side of his desk. It was smaller than it had been before he'd started, but still bigger than he'd have liked. On the other hand, if he polished off the whole lot, there'd only be the same again waiting for him in the morning.

'Tell him I'll be down in ten minutes.'

Reg was right about Mrs Saifre's bodyguard; his accent was almost completely impenetrable. McLean thought his name was Karl, but that might have been an instruction to get into the waiting car. It wasn't the black Range Rover from earlier. That was presumably kept for trips outwith the city limits. This was a vast whale of a Rolls-Royce, its interior almost as big as the office he'd just vacated.

Karl closed the door as McLean settled himself into a soft, contoured seat. The silence was almost total, broken only by the rustling of his coat against leather. Overhead, tiny little lights had been set into the lining, a constellation of stars that lit the entire cabin without casting shadows. It was an unsettling effect, made worse by the deeply tinted windows that meant it was almost impossible to see out. He only knew they were moving because of the gentle pressure forcing him back into his seat, and the relatively clear view out through the glass that separated him from the driver, and the windscreen beyond.

McLean looked around for something that would allow him to communicate with the front. There was nothing obvious, but when he examined the armrest he found the top of it hinged open to reveal controls for the windows, a phone keypad and many other buttons whose purpose he couldn't immediately divine. There was one button with a loudspeaker icon on it, which he pressed more in hope than expectation.

'Can you tell me where we're going?' he asked. Something must have worked because Karl looked briefly in the mirror, then reached for a button on the dashboard.

'Is not far. Please to have drink.' He pressed another button, and lights came on around a concealed door. McLean found a latch artfully hidden in the polished veneer surface, and opened it to reveal a refrigerated compartment. A pair of champagne flutes nestled in little compartments designed to hold them safe, and alongside them a bottle of champagne. He pulled it out, noticing that it had already been opened. Dom Perignon Vintage 1973. McLean had no idea whether it was a good year or not, but just its age would suggest a value somewhere north of a detective inspector's monthly salary. It seemed a shame to let it go to waste, but he closed the cabinet without helping himself nonetheless.

After a while fiddling with the various buttons in the armrest, McLean finally found the button that switched off the overhead lights. He still couldn't see much out of the side windows, but the view forwards was much clearer. They were moving slowly in traffic heading south and west. Making for a chic brasserie in Morningside, perhaps? But the car continued, picking up speed as the road ahead cleared. As they turned down one street then another, McLean had a sickening feeling he knew exactly where they were going. His suspicions were confirmed when they slowed at a set of heavy wrought-iron gates. Karl hit another button to open them, and then they were crunching up the gravel drive to a house McLean had not thought to see again.

The last time he'd been here, it had belonged to Gavin Spenser, billionaire industrialist and probably the murderer of a young woman in the mid-1940s. McLean had wrestled with Spenser's bodyguard, too late to save the man himself from a fate just as grisly as that he had meted out on his young victim. Of course the house would have been sold. Spenser had died intestate, no family to inherit what was a massive fortune. It seemed somehow inevitable that Mrs Saifre would have ended up buying it.

She met him in the entrance hall, a champagne glass in one hand. She was dressed in her customary crimson blouse, this time over tight black leather trousers and calf-length boots. It was warm in the house, McLean noticed as he took off his coat, handing it to the waiting Karl.

'No champagne?' were Mrs Saifre's first words. She scowled at Karl, who shrank visibly under her gaze and cast a worried glance McLean's way.

'Thank you. It was offered, but I wasn't sure I was in the mood for it,' he said.

'Not in the mood for champagne? My dear Inspector, what have they done to you?' Mrs Saifre advanced on him, kissed the air a few inches away from his cheeks in the French style, then held out her arm for him to take. 'Come. We will find something that you are in the mood for, no?'

McLean found himself led through the house into a large room at the back. A log fire roared in a huge fireplace, but his attention was drawn to the windows and the patio beyond. He'd sat there not so long ago, drinking coffee with a man offering him a job. He'd been tempted then; what was he going to be tempted with this time?

'We have whisky, beer, gin, wine? I could make you a cocktail perhaps. Poor old Mr Saifre. He wasn't good for much, but he taught me how to make the perfect martini.'

'Orange juice?'

Mrs Saifre pouted, but opened up a fridge artfully hidden in the wood panelling that lined most of the room. She pulled out a bottle and poured. 'Sure I can't put some vodka in it?'

'Orange juice is fine.' McLean took the glass, pretended not to notice the way Mrs Saifre's fingers brushed his.

'Come, sit with me by the fire.' She walked towards the flames, hips swaying seductively. Her trousers creaked against the leather cushion as she settled herself down, took another sip of her champagne. McLean hadn't moved, and she frowned at him when she realized. 'Don't be shy, Inspector. I won't bite.'

'What is it you want, Mrs Saifre?'

'Please, call me Jane Louise. May I call you Tony?'

'It's my name.'

'Well, come here, Tony.' She patted the edge of the sofa. 'Tell me about yourself. I've heard so much but people do embellish.'

McLean finally relented, crossed the large room and took the offered seat. There was a low table in front of the sofa, and he placed his glass of orange juice carefully down on a small coaster before speaking again.

'I don't suppose there's any point in my asking who they are,' he said.

Mrs Saifre smiled, the merest edge of white teeth showing between her dark red lips. 'The Chief Constable for one. You've crossed swords with a few notables over the years. I knew Gavin Spenser, too. Not well, mind you. So sad what happened to him. Oh, and Jack Tennant sings your praises.'

McLean had been about to ask Mrs Saifre about her connections with Spenser, but the last name she gave up derailed his train of thought, like a breeze block lobbed off a railway bridge.

'Jack Tennant? How on earth do you know him?'

Mrs Saifre gave a low, throaty chuckle. 'Oh me and Jack go way back. Before I met Mr Saifre even. When I was just plain old Jane Louise Dee. He was a beat constable then, helped me out with a spot of bother. We've been friends ever since. After a fashion.'

McLean looked at Mrs Saifre's face again, her neck, trying to see the signs of ageing that cosmetics and surgery tended not to hide. He'd put her age as much the same as his, maybe a little older. Mid-forties at the oldest. And yet she'd have to have been older than that to have known Jack Tennant at the start of his police career. Unless she was very young at the time. Still just a child.

'I'm older than I look, Tony. But then, aren't we all?'

McLean said nothing. Mrs Saifre took a long drink from her champagne flute, her dark eyes on him all the while. He reached out for his orange juice almost without thinking. Picked up the glass, then put it down again.

'Why did you really ask me here?'

'For dinner, of course. And because you interest me.' Mrs Saifre put her glass down on the carpet. She didn't so much stand up as unfold herself from the sofa in an impossibly lithe movement. McLean had seen cats more clumsy. In two steps she was at the mantelpiece, where a collection of intricate and expensive statuettes had been carefully arranged. She picked up a stone-carved fertility goddess, all rounded buttocks, swelling belly and fat breasts. Caressed it with thin fingers. 'I collect things that interest me.'

'Not sure I like the idea of being collected. That usually means being put on a shelf somewhere and forgotten about.'

'Oh, I don't think you need worry about that.' Mrs Saifre put the carved stone down on the mantelpiece and came back to the sofa, sat herself much closer to McLean this time. There was a heat radiating from her that was nothing to do with the flames roaring in the fireplace. She gave off an aura of desirability almost too perfectly attuned to his senses to be anything but manufactured. Her face, her clothes, her scent, her behaviour. It was all a show, and yet he could so easily have surrendered himself to it.

'We're not so different, you and me.' She put a slim hand on his thigh, leaned her body against his. McLean tried to cover up the flinch. Probably failed. 'We're both outsiders, don't like to play by the silly rules others put in our way, have no ties binding us. We both of us want to see justice done.'

McLean was about to say something, but a vibration in his pocket cut him short. It was followed almost instantly by the trilling electronic ring of his mobile, an uncannily accurate reproduction of the noise the old dial-fronted Bakelite phone in the hall of his gran's house made. He pulled it out, peered at the screen. DS Ritchie calling. Beside him, Mrs Saifre stiffened and frowned.

'Sorry. Work. Policemen are never really off, and that goes double for detective inspectors. I have to take this.' He lifted the phone to his ear. 'Thought you were off sick, Sergeant. What's up?'

'Can't sit around in my flat all day, sir. Going stir crazy.' At the other end of the line, Ritchie sniffed loudly. She sounded blocked up. 'Everyone else is off, anyway, so Reg called me in. They've found a body. Think it might be that tattoo artist you were looking for. Barry Timbrel?'

Beside him, Mrs Saifre stood, walked back to the fireplace and picked up the statuette again. She had a frown on her face as if she knew what was going to happen.

'OK. I'll get there as soon as I can.' McLean hung up, slipped the phone back into his pocket, never more grateful for its interruption, or for someone to have died. Mrs Saifre's gaze locked on to his; not concern on her face, nor annoyance at an evening ruined. More the frustration of a child who can't understand why the world isn't working the way it's supposed to.

'I'm so sorry—'

'But you have to go. I know. It's true what they say, we can't always have the things we want the most.' Mrs Saifre reached for a cord that hung from the ceiling close to the fireplace, tugged it once. 'I'll have Karl take you wherever you need to go.'

'That's very kind. Thank you.' McLean stood up as the bodyguard appeared through a side door. 'Perhaps another time, then.'

Mrs Saifre's eyes reflected the leaping flames as she smiled at him then. Either that or there was fire in her soul. 'Oh, I think so, Tony. You don't get away from me that easily.'

McLean followed Karl out of the room, back across the hall and out to where the Rolls-Royce was waiting. It was only once he had settled back into the soft leather seat that he realized he'd left his glass on the table by the fireplace, the orange juice inside it untouched.

39

It took an hour to get back to the station, pick up his own car and then drive across town to Cramond. All the while, McLean couldn't shake the feeling that he'd just survived a horribly dangerous situation thanks purely to blind luck. There was something not right about Mrs Saifre, and it wasn't just her blatant attempts at seduction. He felt no physical attraction to her. No, that wasn't being honest. The base part of his nature couldn't help but be physically attracted to her; she positively screamed sexuality. But he knew that, understood it, compartmentalised it. He wasn't looking for a relationship anyway, casual or otherwise. But she was fascinating. Dangerously so. And for some reason she was fascinated by him, too.

Ritchie met him in the car park on the edge of Drum Sands, but in the pitch black of a cloudy, moonless night they could have been anywhere. The lights of distant Dalgety Bay and the South Fife coast across the Firth of Forth cast an odd glow, suggesting something sinister lurked in the space between. The darkness and mist in the air made it impossible to tell what, leaving it for the imagination to fill in the void.

'Sorry to spoil your evening, sir. Only I thought—'

'Trust me, Sergeant. You've nothing to apologize for. Saved me from a very tricky situation.' McLean pulled a pair of boots out of the back of the car as he spoke, shucked off his shoes and slid his feet into them. Ritchie was already wrapped up in a huge padded jacket, the hood pulled tight so that he could only see her nose. 'Where's this body then?'

'Out on the sands a ways. We'll have to get a move on, sir. Tide's on the turn.' Ritchie hurried away and McLean followed, on to the causeway that linked the mainland with Cramond Island. It was a fair few years since last he'd been out this way, but he remembered the tall concrete pillars of the breakwater, marching out across the beach. The track alongside them speared arrow-straight into the darkness, not at all inviting.

'Is it far?' McLean asked as he quickly caught up with Ritchie. She was breathing heavily, and stopped for a moment to choke out a long slippery cough. The answer soon appeared ahead of them, a faint light in the murk. Closer in, McLean made out three head torches and a brighter handheld arc light, all pointed at the gap between two of the heavy concrete pillars. Ritchie quickened her pace for the last few tens of yards, and McLean could see why. Thin waves of seawater were lapping over the sand, each one coming closer as the tide rose. Soon it would be over the causeway, and by the time it turned again anything loose would have been swept away, out into the North Sea and gone for ever.

'Who found the body?' he asked as he finally reached the spot. Two familiar figures crouched down beside a crumpled, naked figure. Angus Cadwallader looked up at the question.

'Evening, Tony.' He nodded once, then went back to examining his patient.

'Young couple got stuck out on the island,' Ritchie said. 'Walking their dog. Happens quite a lot, I'm told. They had to wait for the tide to go out before they could get back. Dog found this as they went past.'

McLean leaned over beside the pathologist to get a better view. The body was naked, which made him shiver at the cold. It was obviously a man, scrawny and thin. He had tattoos over his arms, legs, back, one spiralling up his neck and on to his face, but he wasn't completely covered in them like the body in Roslin Glen. He'd been carried by the retreating tide, tumbled over the causeway, but had stuck up against one of the concrete pillars, hugging it as if he'd been alive and clinging on.

'Can we get a look at his face?' he asked of no one in particular.

'Don't think we're going to get anything else here.' Cadwallader leaned forward, took a firm grasp of one of the dead man's arms and eased him away from the pillar, on to his back. The corpse moved with an odd sucking noise where the wet sand had begun to pull him down. McLean took the portable arc light from the uniform constable who had been holding it over the scene, stepped carefully down to where the body lay. His hair was plastered over his face, and Cadwallader smoothed it away with practised fingers.

'Dear God. What's happened to his mouth?'

Cadwallader's assistant Tracy spoke the words, but it could have been any of them. McLean recognized the face of Barry Timbrel, tattoo artist, from the photographs they'd seen at his flat. He'd not been in the water long; the fish hadn't started on him. His eyes were white though, as if he'd been suffering from cataracts for many a year, and the tattoos on his neck were faded and old. In many ways he looked peaceful in death. Except for his lips, which were burnt and blistered, cracked brown teeth showing through ragged gaps in the flesh.

'You seen anything like that before, Angus?' McLean asked. He knew the answer, of course, even if the implications of it left an ice-cold churning in his gut that had nothing to do with the weather.

'Indeed I have, Tony.' Cadwallader levered himself up to a loud popping of knees. 'Indeed I have.'

Blue flashing lights spiralled lazily on the top of the ambulance as a couple of crime scene technicians loaded the body into the back. The crime scene itself was underwater now, time and tide waiting for no man. McLean looked out over the choppy sea to the far side of the Forth and the lights of Dalgety Bay. But for the grace of God, and two unlucky dog walkers, the body of Barry Timbrel would have been out there too, food for the fishes.

'What're the chances? Finding a man like that?'

'Chances? Slim to nil, I'd say. 'Till it happens, of course. Bit like winning the lottery.' DS Ritchie stamped her feet, then started coughing.

'You really shouldn't have come in, you know. There's a reason they call it sick leave.'

'Was in anyway,' Ritchie said, once she'd managed to stop coughing. Her voice sounded hoarse and nasal. 'It was doing my head in being stuck at home. And this is on the way out anyway.' She waved a gloved hand at her face, then started coughing again.

'Doesn't really sound like it, you know. Have you seen a doctor?'

Ritchie finished her coughing fit with a throat-clearing bark, then spat on the ground in a most unladylike fashion. Rubbed at her lips with the back of her glove. 'Gave me antibiotics and said take some rest. They make it sound so easy, but you know as well as I do it's a pain. Seem to recall you clumping around the station on crutches for a month or so, getting up everyone's backs.'

McLean considered the dull ache in his hip, not helped by the cold and salt air. It was the tail end of an enforced period of leave that he'd fought against with every trick he knew. He could hardly blame Ritchie when he'd not exactly been a model patient himself.

'What do you make of this, then?' He shrugged his head back in the direction of the ambulance.

'I read Grumpy Bob's report on Timbrel. All Stuart's stuff about the tattoos, too. Wasn't much else I could do for a while. Definitely your man, but Christ only knows what happened to him to get in that state. Out there.'

'Christ and Angus Cadwallader, hopefully. At least tomorrow morning once he's done the PM.' McLean looked at his watch, noticed that it had stopped being late and was now early. 'This morning, I should say.'

Ritchie started another rumbling cough, and slammed a gloved fist into her chest a couple of times until it went away.

'You drive down here?' McLean asked.

'No, got a lift.' Ritchie turned around just in time to see the ambulance pull away. A quick look around the beachfront showed a distinct lack of squad cars. 'Bugger's gone and sodded off without me, though.'

McLean shoved his hand into his coat pocket, dug out his car keys. 'Come on then. I'll take you home. And I don't want to see you back in until you've shifted that cough.'

40

Thin, watery sunlight struggled to fight its way through the heavy cloud overhead and down into the cavernous depths of the Cowgate. It was early, and McLean hadn't slept well. His dreams had been filled with fire and brimstone although he'd been cold. It had taken a full ten minutes in the shower, the temperature turned up as high as he could bear, just to get the chill out of his bones.

Even though they'd found the body of Barry Timbrel just the night before, Cadwallader had insisted he would carry out the post-mortem first thing. Someone else would have to be shuffled away to make a space in the schedule, but then it wasn't as if they were going to complain.

All the way from the station, McLean kept having to suppress the urge to look around, convinced in some paranoid corner of his mind that he was being watched, followed. Even the cars seemed suspicious, passing him slowly as if to give the drivers a chance to check him out. They were driving that way because of the road conditions, of course. Snow still piled up on the pavements and against any car that had been parked for more than a couple of hours. Gritting lorries and snowploughs had been along this road many times, but so far the weather was winning that particular battle.

Stepping into the city mortuary was a relief both from the cold and from the sense of foreboding. McLean nodded at the security guard as she buzzed him through to the business end. The building was always quiet, but at this time of the morning it was almost entirely silent, just the faint whoosh of air in the ventilation system and the squeak, squeak, squeak of his shoes on the shiny linoleum floor.

Angus Cadwallader had already started, ably assisted by Dr Sharp. Another doctor McLean didn't know was sitting a little way off, witness to the proceedings and quite obviously unhappy about being dragged out of his bed so early in the morning. He was young, rumpled black hair and bristly chin making him look more like a med student than a fully fledged pathologist.

'Ah, Tony. You made it. Good.' Cadwallader barely looked up from his grisly work. McLean stepped forward to get a better look, then wished he hadn't. Barry Timbrel lay on his back, his chest opened up in a neat, bloodless Y cut. Half his organs had already been removed and weighed. Now they sat in little plastic containers to one side, waiting for Tracy Sharp to put them all back again.

'You said eight o'clock start, Angus.' McLean glanced at his watch: ten past.

'Yes, well. Couldn't sleep last night, so I thought I'd come in and get started early. Tom here was kind enough to agree to witness.'

The young doctor stepped down off his stool, held out a hand for McLean to shake. 'Tom MacPhail. You must be Detective Inspector McLean.'

'Thanks for doing this.' McLean nodded at the body on the slab.

'Aye, well, Angus didn't exactly give me much of an option.' MacPhail grinned, then went back to his stool. He looked half-asleep, and McLean wondered where exactly it was that Cadwallader had found him.

'So what's the prognosis then, doc?' It was a half-hearted attempt at a joke McLean realized he'd used far too many times before.

'There's no evidence of foul play. I can tell you that much.'

'None?'

'Externally, he's clean. Well, you'd expect that from being in the water. Reckon he'd been there eight, maybe ten hours tops. He didn't drown, though. There's no water in his lungs.'

'So foul play, then. Someone stripped him and threw him in?'

Cadwallader waved a gore-smeared hand. 'Not necessarily, no. He didn't drown, but he might have jumped.'

'Jumped?'

'You'll have heard the schoolboy saying that if you jump off a high building or something similar you'll be dead before you hit the ground?'

McLean nodded. Best to let Cadwallader go when he had an idea in his brain.

'It's nonsense, of course. Most jumpers die from massive deceleration trauma. Broken bones, smashed skull, the shock of impact. Most, but not all.'

The pathologist turned back to his patient, and plunged his hands into the open chest cavity in a manner

294

that made McLean glad he'd not had time yet for break-fast that morning. A couple of seconds and then Cadwallader pulled them back out again, this time cradling something red and slippery.

'Some. You might say the lucky few, except what's lucky about a man who jumps off a bridge, eh? Some have a heart attack before they reach the ground. Or the water. This is what killed our man here.' He held the shiny mass up to the light. McLean already knew it was a heart; not the first one he'd encountered up closer than he would have liked.

'Heart attack?'

'Myocardial infarction. Coronary. Heart attack. I don't think any of them really do justice to what happened to this poor fellow.' Cadwallader stroked the heart gently with one latex-gloved finger, then handed it over to Tracy to be weighed. 'This man's heart pretty much exploded.'

'Is that natural?'

'It's unusual, Tony, if that's what you mean. It's not the first time I've seen it, though. I can tell you this much. He died in an instant. Probably didn't know what had hit him. If he'd been fully clothed in the water I might have suggested that he'd just been unlucky enough to be walking along the beach when it happened. But he was completely naked, and this really isn't the time of year for skinny dipping.'

'So you reckon he jumped off the bridge.'

'A bridge, certainly. He was found at Cramond, so he might well have jumped into the river rather than the Firth. Been swept down that way.'

'What about the burning to his lips?' McLean recalled

295

the sight from the night before, the light shining on the dead man's face for the first time, the mess of blisters and ripped flesh around his mouth.

'What indeed.' Cadwallader turned to MacPhail. 'What do you make of it, Tom?'

The young pathologist jumped down off his stool and went to inspect the body, bending down close to the head before straightening up again. 'Looks like he's kissed a red-hot poker. The water's washed it pretty clean, but you can see some evidence of charring, and the blisters are consistent with third degree. Must've happened not long before he died. There's no sign of healing.'

'Seen anything like it before?' McLean asked.

'Can't say as I have. Must have hurt like buggery, though.'

'I have, and recently.' Cadwallader went over to the wall screen, then realized his gloved hands were still covered in ichor. 'Tracy, can you bring up the Weatherly photos.'

Dr Sharp sighed, removed her own smattered gloves and set to tapping at the keyboard. In a matter of seconds a larger-than-lifesize photograph of the dead Andrew Weatherly's flaccid face appeared on the screen. A click of the mouse and the image zoomed in on the lips. Another few clicks and a second image appeared alongside it; live feed from the camera mounted over the body. Dr Sharp went back to the table, adjusting the direction and focus until there were two sets of damaged lips side by side. It was hard to imagine that the damage hadn't been caused by the same thing.

'Well, there's something you don't see every day,' Dr MacPhail said. 'I don't suppose we've still got him in here.' He pointed at the first image, Andrew Weatherly.

'No. He was buried a week ago.' McLean felt that all-too-familiar churning in the pit of his stomach as the implications built up in his mind. 'I suppose you're going to want us to dig him up again now.'

41

'Are you out of your fucking mind?'

As responses went, it was fairly predictable. McLean stood on the wrong side of Detective Superintendent Duguid's desk, hands behind his back, trying not to bounce up and down on his feet with impatience. He said nothing, though. Best to make the initial request, then let Dagwood work his way through at his own speed.

'The man's only just been laid to rest and you want to go digging him up?'

Actually, his body was lying in a crypt, so removing it would be easy. He'd already pointed that out though, so probably not a good idea to do it again.

'And this investigation is closed, for fuck's sake. You told me yourself it was done and dusted. No complications. How the hell am I supposed to take this up with the Deputy Chief Constable? What's going to happen when the press get a hold of it?'

Hide from them like you did before, most likely, McLean thought. Leave it to a detective inspector to take all the flak.

'What do you even need to see the body for? Didn't your ghoul of a friend Cadwallader take enough photographs?'

Objections voiced, now Duguid was getting into the detail. McLean considered it safe to answer.

'The injuries to the dead man we pulled out of the Forth yesterday evening are too similar to those we found on Weatherly just to be coincidence, sir. Angus wants to get a sample for tests. He's not even sure what caused the damage in the first place.'

'And you only bother telling me this now.' Duguid ran spidery fingers over his face, pulling down his lower lip as they went past to reveal yellowing teeth with large gaps between them, the legacy of a long and dedicated career as a heavy smoker.

'It was in . . .' McLean began to say, then shut up. No point telling Duguid what he already knew. 'Look, we can probably do the exam in situ. The coffin's in a crypt. We just need a Sheriff Court order. Get the timing right and no one need know we were even there.'

Duguid looked at him like he was an idiot, which McLean reckoned was probably fair that time. 'I should never have given you the bloody Weatherly case in the first place. Spence would've done what he was told and left it at that.'

'I thought you wanted justice for his two girls, sir.'

'Justice? That's a fucking laugh. They're past justice, McLean. Can't you let them rest?' Duguid slumped back in his seat, his initial burst of anger at the request worn out. 'What's this all leading to, anyway? Who is this man you found last night, and what's he got to do with Weatherly?'

'His name's Barry Timbrel, sir. He's the tattoo artist we were looking for about the body we found in Roslin Glen. Only, soon as we start looking for him, he turns up dead, and with injuries very similar to those Weatherly had. Well, apart from the gunshot wound, obviously. There might be nothing to it. Christ, I really hope there's nothing to it. But the last thing we want is someone else turning up dead with blistered lips and everyone screaming at us for not doing our jobs.'

'You're going to keep on at me until I say yes, aren't you, McLean?' Duguid rubbed at his eye with the palm of one hand, leaned forward and grabbed a notepad, scribbled something down. 'OK. I'll back your request. But if the Sheriff Court throws it out, that's it. We're not going to fight it.'

'Thank you, sir.' McLean knew he couldn't ask for more, was surprised he'd got as much. 'I'll keep you in the loop.'

'Please don't. It's bad enough as it is with the DCIs bleating at me every day. But you know that already, or you'd have gone to one of them first.' Duguid gave McLean the briefest of smiles, an expression so alien he thought the detective superintendent might be ill. It didn't last, though.

'Go on. Get out. Some of us have got better things to do than going off on wild goose chases.'

'Got those plans you were looking for, sir.'

McLean stopped on his way past the large incident room, still unoccupied since the Weatherly investigation had been wound up. How long that state of affairs would continue was anyone's guess, although he had a hunch it wouldn't be quite the enquiry it had started out as. Across the corridor, DC MacBride must have seen him through the door to the smaller room set aside for the tattooed man investigation, and bustled out to stop him.

'Plans?' McLean scrambled around in the mess of thoughts and things he was supposed to be remembering until he finally got it. 'Oh yes. Plans. Rosskettle. What've you got then?'

He followed MacBride back into the tiny room. The constable went to his desk, now sporting the largest flat-screen computer monitor McLean had ever seen. He tapped a few keys and clicked the mouse, bringing up a grainy image.

'One of these days you're going to have to tell me how you get all this kit, Constable,' McLean said.

'This old thing?' MacBride tapped the side of the monitor. 'They were going to throw it out. I persuaded Zoe in the IT department to let me have it. The interface is several generations out of date, but then so's half the kit we're running it on. I found something that fitted, and this is easier than trying to blag a projector and screen.'

McLean ignored the technospeak. 'Zoe? Have I met her?'

MacBride's ears reddened at the lobes. 'She's new, sir. Probably not. Bright red hair? About so high?'

McLean shook his head as much to stop himself from laughing as to suggest that he hadn't met the diminutive Zoe yet. He leaned forward to the screen, trying to make sense of the slightly blurred lines and indecipherable text. 'What's all this about, then?'

'Plans of Rosskettle. Scans of the originals. Best

we could do at short notice. They're something like A-nought or bigger. Huge rolled-up things. The NHS Buildings Department keep everything, it seems. Even plans of buildings they've sold.'

'Can we zoom out a bit? Get an idea of what I'm looking at?'

MacBride clicked the mouse a couple more times, coming up with a site plan that only took a couple of minutes of squinting and head twisting until McLean could work out what was what. 'These buildings here.' He pointed at the plans where the modern units he'd seen being demolished were outlined in a neat arc. 'Can we zoom in on them?'

MacBride squinted at the screen, then with a couple of clicks the first image was gone, replaced by a clearer outline showing just the buildings he wanted. 'First picture's just an index. There's individual plans for everything.'

McLean stared at the shapes until he could work out the layout. He identified the room he'd climbed into, the corridor separating it from the dormitory rooms opposite. The buildings were all the same, all self-contained units that were presumably some sort of sheltered housing for patients not yet ready to be trusted to Care in the Community, but neither needing the sort of twenty-four-hour attention they'd get in the larger, main building.

'Have we got any plans of the lower level?'

MacBride frowned. 'Lower level, sir?'

'There was a basement level in at least one of these buildings. I saw it myself.'

MacBride clicked and scrolled, finding a box of text that would have been at the bottom right of the original plan. 'No mention of a lower level here, sir. I've looked through all the files they sent over, and I don't remember seeing anything.' He clicked back to the original image of the building. 'There's no mention of any stairwell or trapdoor on here either.'

'Strange. It was definitely there. Won't be any more, mind you. The whole site will have been razed by now.' Which was, he suspected, the whole point.

'I found out about Price Developments too, sir. Well, as much as I could.'

'Let me guess. They're a new outfit only recently registered.'

'Pretty much. But they're based at the same address as a couple of other developers who've been around a bit. There's an outfit called Saifre Holdings. It's a shell corporation. Fingers in a lot of pies all over the place. Not just Scotland.'

McLean wasn't at all surprised to hear the name. 'What about the other one?'

'That's more interesting, sir. Or maybe not, depending on who you are.' MacBride tried to raise his eyebrows towards the ceiling in a suggestive manner. At least that's what McLean thought he was doing. He might just have had an itchy nose.

'Go on.'

'Well, the site's being developed by Price, which is basically owned by Saifre. But it was originally bought by another company, owned by Weatherly Asset Management.'

42

'Any chance I could have a word, Tony?'

McLean looked up from his desk, confused by the voice. He was used to DC MacBride, DS Ritchie and Grumpy Bob coming to see him in his office. Occasionally a lost PC would find their way there too, and in the good old days Jayne McIntyre had sometimes wandered down for a chat. Everyone else seemed to expect him to go to them, which suited him fine. The sight of Matt Hilton standing uncertainly at the threshold was a new one for him.

'Sure. Come on in.' McLean closed the file he'd been trying to read without much success, leaned back in his seat and tried not to grimace at the stab of pain that shot through his thigh. 'Have a seat if you can find one.'

Hilton took a couple of steps into the space, looked at the chaos within. In theory there was a chair for him to sit in, but it would be a day's archaeological dig to find it. 'I think I'll stand.'

'Fair enough. What can I do for you?'

Hilton didn't immediately respond; he seemed to be worried about something. He stared back down the corridor outside, then firmly closed the door before leaning against it. No chance of being interrupted.

'How've you been getting on lately? I hear your workload's been increased, what with the Weatherly investigation, and now two bodies, is it?'

'The tattooed man, and now the tattoo artist we thought might have done it to him.'

'The tattooed man. That would be the one you thought might have been out at Rosskettle.'

'That's him. William Beaumont. Ex-SAS. He was living on the streets in the city centre when someone took him, but he ended up in the river at Roslin Glen. Somewhere in between he was covered from head to toe in tattoos. Black, strange swirls and patterns. Nothing recognizable. The thing is, whoever did it to him must have worked flat out; he was only missing about three weeks.'

Hilton ran a chubby hand over his shiny bald pate, rubbed a finger under his nose. For a psychiatrist, he wasn't very good at hiding his unease. There was something he wanted to say, but he couldn't quite find the way to say it. McLean would have found it amusing were it not eating into his already precious time.

'Look, I don't—'

'If you've got—'

Both of them spoke at the same time, then fell silent. McLean waited a second before motioning Hilton to continue. The psychiatrist paused briefly, then decided to jump right in.

'I've been getting a few calls recently. From people higher up the food chain. Asking specifically about you and your mental state.'

'And what have you been telling them?'

'You don't want to know who they are?' Hilton wore his incredulity like a fine actor.

'Come on, Hilton. You wouldn't tell me if I asked.'

'No, no. But still . . .'

'Of course I want to know, but there's lots of things I want that I can't have. More pertinently, why are you telling me this?'

'Well.' Hilton pushed himself from the door as if he were going to sit down, then realized there was no seat and slumped against the wall directly opposite McLean's desk instead. 'You'll probably find this hard to believe, but I do have a code of ethics.'

McLean kept silent. He wanted to laugh out loud, but doing so wouldn't really help. Not with Hilton coming over all confessional.

'So when someone tells me to do something that goes against that code. Well, it kind of pisses me off as much as anything else. Abuse of power, and all that.'

'Someone's been leaning on you to get at me?'

'Pretty much. I've had more than one senior officer casting doubt on your fitness for work. It's fairly obvious they want me to back that up.'

'Are you going to?'

Hilton looked hurt by the question. 'Of course not. I wouldn't say you were a poster boy for good mental health in the police service. You have deep-seated problems that you need to address, but in many ways they inform your character and make you the detective you are. There are other officers in this station much less fit for work than you. Besides, I don't like being told what to do.'

'What if they take away your office?' McLean nodded towards the door. 'This gig must be worth a bit to you.'

'Yes and no. It's good money for not too much stress.

At least it was until recently.' Hilton fished around in his inside jacket pocket, pulled out a folded slip of paper. He didn't hand it over. 'I've plenty of work elsewhere to keep the wolf from the door. And there's always the books.'

The books. McLean had almost been warming to the man. At the very least he'd had some sympathy for his current dilemma, having been there all too often himself. But the mention of books brought back all the old rage. He might be older now, but this was still the same Matt Hilton who had made his name and fortune on the back of Donald Anderson and his victims. The same Matt Hilton who had co-authored the book that told the world in gory, intimate detail how Kirsty had died.

On the other hand, he was putting himself on the line. Maybe not exactly risking his career, but certainly making life unnecessarily harder for himself. Not enough for redemption, perhaps, but at least a start.

'Look. I appreciate you telling me this. But what are you really after, Hilton?'

'After?' Hilton tapped the folded paper against his arm. 'I suppose that's a fair enough question. I wouldn't believe me capable of altruism either. Here.' He pushed himself away from the wall, took a step to the desk and handed the paper to McLean. 'This is what I've managed to dig up about Rosskettle. What's been going on there since it was closed down and sold. A bit before then, too. I don't think it's any coincidence that I started getting calls from on high as soon as I started asking questions about that place. There's a name. Don't think you'll be all that surprised it keeps coming up.'

McLean took the paper, but didn't open it up. He held

Hilton's stare, trying to read the chubby face and failing. 'Thanks,' he said finally.

Hilton nodded, turned to leave. As he opened the door, McLean spoke again.

'Look, Hilton. We don't see eye to eye. Don't suppose we ever will. But this?' He held up the paper, even though he didn't know yet what was written on it. 'Well, thanks.'

Hilton smiled, and for an instant he looked less like a bald old fat man and more like a mischievous schoolboy. 'Don't worry about next week's session. Or any after that. I've just sent in your final evaluation report. Far as I'm concerned you're as fit for duty as anyone in this madhouse.'

McLean sat and stared at the door after Hilton had left, unsure whether he was waiting for a crowd of people to burst in and start laughing at some complicated prank or just rendered speechless by the psychiatrist's strange behaviour. It was only after a few minutes had passed, and the echo of the conversation had died away, leaving just the tick, tick, ticking of the wall clock and the distant city roar, that he realized he was still holding the folded sheet of paper.

It was handwritten, notes squeezed on to the page in densely packed but neat script. McLean couldn't remember having seen Hilton's handwriting before, just his bloated ego of a signature on medical notes and in the front of his bloody books. It made sense that someone as self-obsessed and anally retentive would try to cram everything into one side of one page. Or maybe he just wanted something that would be easy to get rid of should the need arise. Whatever it was, it made for difficult read-ing. McLean had to squint, then pull the desk light over. Finally he began to piece it together and his squint turned to a frown.

Rossketle Hospital was closed because it was too far away from centres of population – the same reason why it was built there in the first place. Times change, and with them attitudes to mental illness. I only spent a couple of years there, and I was never a per-manent member of staff, but I ate in the canteen and got to know a lot of the orderlies well. By then they'd pretty much stopped using the sixties prefabs to the west of the main house, although there were one or two elderly patients who were left in the nearest, num-ber six, mostly because they became agitated and difficult to manage every time they were moved.

The other five units were empty, but only number three had a padlock on the front door. Every so often groups of important people would come out to view the hospital. Sometimes one or two, sometimes a dozen at a time. Mostly they'd get a tour of the place and then go back home, but I do remember one time when I was working late seeing that about ten of them had gone into number three. The padlock was open and I could see lights at the back. I didn't think all that much of it, to be honest, but I do remember Andrew Weatherly was one of that particular group. He was one of the most regular visitors during my time there, which made sense as a company he owned was responsible for managing all non-clinical aspects of the site. I didn't leave the hospital until near enough midnight that night, but the cars were still there then. I was at the university the next day, so I don't know when they left. I do know that when I mentioned it to one of the older orderlies, he told me that if I knew what was good for me I'd forget I'd ever seen anything. I got the impression from him that it wasn't that unusual an occurrence.

There were stories among the orderlies of parties during the sixties and seventies, where some of the long-term patients were taken to one of the remote residential units and sexually abused. Individual cases of sexual abuse by hospital staff are, alas, not uncommon. The gossip, however, was of what might loosely be termed 'swinging' parties, attended by some of Edinburgh High Society's more notorious members. There is every possibility that the stories were, in some small part, true.

The hospital was earmarked for closure in the nineties, and patients were moved to other facilities as and when they became available. It finally closed in '02, and was left derelict for a couple of years before being sold to a development company. No development happened, of course. The rumour was that it was another of Andrew Weatherly's companies that had bought the place, and he was simply keeping it as it had been when he was growing up there as a child.

Of the dozen or so psychiatrists I knew from the place who are still alive, most were very reluctant to talk about it at all. One was quite blunt in his refusal. Many told me just to forget about it. I may be a fan of conspiracy theories, but I don't think it too much to assume that something untoward was going on there, had been for quite a long time, and that Andrew Weatherly was involved. It's no coincidence that as soon as I began asking questions, questions began being asked of me. And of you. There is no smoke without fire, as the saying goes.

I would appreciate it if you destroyed this note once you have read it, and tell no one where you discovered the information here.

McLean read the note twice; the second time was easier than the first, though the meaning of the words still largely eluded him. Or he didn't want to accept them, the places they took him to in his mind. One particular statement stood out. Andrew Weatherly keeping the hospital 'as it had been when he was growing up there as a child'. The way Hilton had written it made it seem like common knowledge, but it was the first McLean knew of it. Finally, when he was sure there was nothing more to be gleaned from the page, he folded the sheet carefully and tucked it into his pocket. It'd be time to go home soon enough, and when he got there he'd light a fire with it.

'I'm not even going to bother asking you about your exercises, Inspector. It's obvious you've not been doing them.'

McLean lay on the couch and stared up at the ceiling as Esmerelda the physiotherapist manipulated his leg. She had warm hands and a gentle touch, but there was nothing subtle about the way she lifted, twisted, bent and pulled, all the while studying his face to see his involuntary grimaces of pain. It didn't help either that she was fully clothed, while his trousers were draped across a chair back on the other side of the room. Put him at something of a disadvantage.

'There's never enough time . . .' he began.

'That's what they all say. Then when they're stuck in a wheelchair there's far too much.' Esmerelda gave his leg another tweak. Something clicked, sending a bolt of pain through his hip and up his spine as if he'd been wired to the mains and the switch flipped. It was all McLean could manage not to scream.

'See. Seized up completely.' Esmerelda let the leg down again. 'You can put your trousers back on now.'

McLean sat up slowly, expecting another shock at any moment. His leg hadn't really been giving him all that much gyp for a few days. Except when he sat down at his desk. Or climbed in and out of the car. Or went to bed. He'd not have bothered coming to the session were it not for the fact that they'd obviously given him the wrong painkillers the previous time. These new ones looked just the same as the old, but they didn't work as well, or last as long.

The floor seemed a long way off as he let himself slowly down from the couch. The echo of that last click made him tense, expecting a repeat as his foot touched ground and he stood up as gingerly as a man twice his age venturing out on to slippery ice. The lack of any noticeable pain was almost a disappointment.

'I want to see you again. Same time. Tomorrow.' Esmerelda spoke to the medical file she was annotating rather than to McLean himself. He was too busy testing each step across the room in the quest for his trousers to really take in what she had said. It only registered as he was pulling them on, fastening the button and zip.

'Tomorrow? I can't possibly—'

'Tomorrow, Inspector. Or I make a call to your boss.' This time Esmerelda turned to face him, her eyes locked on his, not a smile to be seen. 'Seriously. You should be completely over these injuries by now. I've never met anyone who treated themselves so badly.'

'I just missed doing the exercises for a couple of days.' McLean looked down at the floor where his shoes lay, a million miles away. Why the hell had he worn lace-ups today? 'It's not like I'm overdoing it or anything.'

'My point exactly. You're not overdoing it. You're not doing it at all.'

'But surely that's a good thing. I mean, rest's what the doctor ordered.'

'Only up to a point. And you're past that now.' Esmerelda consulted her medical file again. 'I'm not going to give you any more pills, and if you've still got any I'd suggest you stop taking them.'

'I . . . What?'

'They're not helping. You need to feel the pain and work through it. That's the only way you're going to get back to normal. Tomorrow we'll go through your exercises together. It'll only take a half-hour. Then we'll do it all again the next day, and the day after that.'

'I can't possibly . . . I mean . . . I've got work—'

'Tomorrow, Inspector. Same time as today.' Esmerelda gave him a cheery smile now. 'See you then.'

43

'I'm not going to tell you where I got this information, but I think you all need to hear it.'

Early morning. Perhaps too early to be comfortable. McLean stood in front of what had been reassembled of the original Weatherly investigation team. He was glad to see that those missing were those he could most easily do without. DS Carter, for instance, and the gaggle of detective constables who followed him around as if he were some seasoned font of detective wisdom rather than a pale and useless streak of lazy piss.

'It concerns Andrew Weatherly. In particular some facts about his childhood and early career that aren't common knowledge. You won't find any of this on Wikipedia.'

At the back of the darkened room, Grumpy Bob gave McLean a slight nod of understanding. The rest of the assembled crew merely looked at him expectantly, like a bunch of first-year students in a particularly engrossing lecture. The effect was enhanced by the video projector with remote control that DC MacBride had rigged up painting a bright image on the whiteboard; only a few half-hearted actions scribbled down to muddy the picture. It showed a picture of the MSP for West Fife, taken from a newspaper article published a few months back.

'Andrew Weatherly was born in Rosskettle Psychiatric

Hospital in 1953. His mother had only recently been admitted herself; records say she was suicidal and hysterical, but the best guess is her family paid to have her locked up when she managed to fall pregnant without bothering to get married first. She was only seventeen at the time, and came from a very important family. I dare say her father thought the scandal of having a mad daughter was less than that of having a bastard in the family.'

'Could they do that? I mean, back in Victorian times maybe, but the fifties?' DC Gregg's face was a picture of outrage as she asked the question.

'They could do it today if they had enough money. Back then it wasn't even owned by the NHS, remember. Weatherly's grandfather was a senior partner in one of the larger city law firms, owned a fair chunk of Midlothian. His family pretty much built the hospital in the first place, so calling in a few favours wouldn't have been hard.'

McLean clicked the remote and the image changed: a blurred photocopy of a birth certificate.

'Weatherly lived with his mother until he was eight. As far we're aware, he was never christened and the Weatherly family disowned him completely. He was even given a different surname. Andrew Theobold.'

'Who was Theobold? His dad?' DC MacBride asked.

'Possibly. His grandfather had influence and money, so it might just have been the first name that came to mind when he was telling the registrar what to write down. It doesn't really matter, except to show the lengths to which the Weatherlys went to stop this child from being associated with them in any way.'

'Seems a bit over the top, really. I mean, what's so bad about having an illegitimate child? My mum and dad never bothered getting married.'

McLean raised an eyebrow in DC Gregg's direction at this piece of family gossip shared. 'Different times, different values. I agree with you, Constable, it's madness, but that's what happened. The family were so shocked, they did everything in their considerable power to make sure Andrew Weatherly went away. Not that it did them much good.'

Another click, another picture. This one a graduation photograph; the faces so indistinct it could have been anyone in them. Only the grainy colours, the clothes and the hairstyles suggested it might have been taken in the decade time would like to forget. The 1970s.

'His mother died when he was eight, after which he was fostered out. We don't really know much about him until he surfaced again fourteen years later, graduating with a first-class degree from Edinburgh University. By this time he was calling himself Andrew Weatherly; changed his name by deed poll when he was sixteen. You might call it a statement of intent.'

'Sounds like a right nutter.' This from Grumpy Bob, who already knew the story.

'You won't find me disagreeing with you there, Bob. Seems Weatherly had something of a grudge against his estranged family. I can't really blame him for that, after what they did to him. Still not sure I'd have been quite so single-minded in my revenge, mind you.'

'Revenge?' MacBride asked.

'Can't really call it anything else. Weatherly was always

good at finance. You don't build a company managing billions without knowing your way around a spreadsheet. He used that skill to systematically bankrupt the Weatherly family and buy up all their assets on the cheap. His grandfather died in a miserable little care home without two coins to rub together. He had a couple of uncles and they fared no better. Everything the Weatherly family owned, the estates in Midlothian, the properties in the city, the house in Fife. He grabbed the lot. There's a rumour he even managed to break up the law firm; it certainly doesn't exist any more.'

MacBride let out a low whistle. 'That's some revenge.'

'It is indeed. And I think it gives you some measure of the man. Which makes the nature of his death all the more difficult to understand. You've all seen the pictures doing the rounds. There's video footage too, though I'd suggest you don't watch it if you don't want to have to go and bleach your mind afterwards. The press are shouting blackmail as a reason for what he did, but Weatherly wasn't the sort of man who ran away from blackmail. And besides, he knew about the pictures, the video footage. He took the bloody things in the first place. That was him blackmailing others. Gaining leverage. Making sure his friends in high places never forgot who put them there. No, this . . .' McLean clicked the button and moved on to the final image. He'd picked it with care, not wanting to offend the sensibilities of the younger officers, even though he knew they would probably be the least shocked. It still showed rather more flesh than was decent. 'This isn't what made Andrew Weatherly take the lives of his wife and children before he shot himself.'

'So what did, then?' DC Gregg asked, her head tilted awkwardly to one side as she tried to make sense of the picture. Fair enough; there were more buttocks in it than you'd expect.

'That, Constable, is what I want you all to find out.'

'Have you got a minute, sir?'

Heading back to his office after the briefing, McLean stopped mid-limp and looked up from his phone. He'd been trying to programme it to remind him of his changed physiotherapist appointment schedule, but was so far having little joy. DC MacBride had a sheaf of papers clutched in one podgy hand, but there was nothing so odd about that. The half-smiling, half-worried expression on his face was unusual, though.

'Anything has to be better than trying to figure out how this damned thing works.' McLean slipped the phone into his pocket. 'What have you got?'

'Been going over the paperwork for the demolition at Rosskettle.' MacBride held up his handful. 'Just got all these copies through from the council planning department.'

McLean raised an eyebrow. 'How on earth did you manage that?'

MacBride's face dropped in disappointment, and he took a deep breath, about to launch into an explanation. McLean stopped him. 'No. How's not important right now. What's the story?'

A slump of relief in the constable's shoulders, then he spoke. 'It might just be a cock-up. We're talking about the council here, after all. But see here?' He held up one sheaf of papers that might or might not have been permission from the council to demolish buildings at the Rosskettle Psychiatric Hospital. Pointed a chubby finger at the date. 'This is after Weatherly . . . Well, after.'

'And? We know the application had been approved before the bulldozers rolled in.'

MacBride shuffled the papers around, finding another letter, another variation on the council logo. 'Yes, I know. But see here. This is the Building Control letter. Sets out what reporting needs to be done during the work, stuff like that.'

McLean took the sheet from the constable and scanned it, seeing only the officialese that these things were written in. A mindlessly self-important language that gave the impression of authority without actually meaning anything. It all seemed above-board, though, nothing suspicious. And then he saw it.

'The date.'

'Exactly, sir.' MacBride beamed like a schoolboy who's got the answer right in front of the whole class. 'It's the same as the planning letter.'

'And that's unusual?'

'I'd say unheard of, sir. Building Control wouldn't have received the application until planning was done. Even if they got it the same day, there's no way they'd have done this so quickly.'

'But it's not impossible.'

A worried frown scuttered across the detective constable's face. 'Not impossible, no. But someone would've had to be leaned on. Or offered a wodge of cash.'

44

The cold, thin light of early morning painted the pale blue sky with streaks of purple and grey. Clear now, but the serious threat of snow later. McLean sat in his car with the engine burbling away to itself, feeding much-needed heat into the cabin as he waited outside the church. Every so often he'd look around, trying to see if there were any reporters on lookout. As yet he'd not spotted any, although that was no real assurance they weren't there. At least the cold would keep the casual passers-by to a minimum.

A battered old Vauxhall Cavalier slowed as it went past him, then pulled into a space a few yards further on. The oily black smoke from its tired diesel engine was still hanging in the air when the driver's door opened and a scruffy young man climbed out. He was dressed in heavy-weight winter walking gear, with a bright red woolly hat pulled down over his ears, so McLean didn't immediately recognize him. When he turned to stare over the grave-yard, then down the street as if waiting for someone, McLean finally clicked. Dr Tom MacPhail wasn't the pathologist he'd been expecting.

'Time to go.' He turned off the engine, and nudged the snoozing Grumpy Bob in the ribs. The detective ser-geant let out a great grunting snore as he woke, rubbed at his nose and then ran his fingers through what was left of his hair.

'Already? I was having a nice wee kip.'

'I had noticed. Come on.' McLean pushed open the door and climbed out into air cold enough to freeze his lungs. Grumpy Bob hauled himself out the other side. The slamming of doors alerted Dr MacPhail to their presence. He spun around, almost losing his footing on the icy road.

'Inspector McLean. Angus sends his apologies. He's had to jet off down to London to fill in as key speaker at some tedious symposium. Seems the man they wanted was so desperate not to go he had a heart attack and died.'

As introductions went, it was a good one, McLean had to admit. 'I'm sure he's loving every minute of it. You know what we're here to do?'

'More or less.' MacPhail pulled open the rear door of his ancient car and hauled out a black bag. Most physicians McLean knew carried them filled with medicines and equipment for saving life. He couldn't help thinking this particular bag wouldn't be much use in an emergency.

'Right then. Sooner we can get this done, the less chance there is some numpty from the press catches us at it.' Grumpy Bob said the words, even though McLean was thinking the same thing. Out of his car he felt much more exposed. There could be long-lens photographers in every tree, ready to spread his picture over the evening news. 'Mad cop in grave-robbing scandal' or maybe 'Dead MSP still not giving up his secrets.'

Looking around the snow-covered scene, he couldn't see anyone. Just the hulk of the church rising up into the greying sky, the graveyard with its headstones poking up like crooked, broken teeth.

'You got the key, Bob?' McLean asked. The detective sergeant nodded, producing a huge iron lump from one pocket.

'Right then. Come on.'

The gates were unlocked, and at least one person had been to the front door of the church since the last snowfall. A narrow strip of footprints marked a passage each way. No one had been into the graveyard with feet bigger than a fox, though; the route to the Weatherly crypt was crisp underfoot. McLean hadn't paid it much attention at the funeral, but it was something of a Gothic monstrosity. Large square slab sides formed a plinth, with a carving on top that would likely have given even quite large children nightmares. Death in all his skeletal, scythe-bearing finery bore down on the prone figure of a buxom woman. The carving was well executed, but the combination of Auld Reekie's soot and the soft white snow made it even more lifelike, as if the whole tableau had been real, petrified by an unfortunate glimpse of the Gorgon.

Snow had piled deep in the hollow where stone steps led down from the path and into the crypt. McLean took the key from Grumpy Bob, then regretted it when his foot, then his lower leg, disappeared. He landed heavily, a twinge of pain shooting through his hip. Only a steadying hand from Dr MacPhail stopped him pitching forward into the heavy iron door.

'Careful there, Inspector. I'm a bit out of practice with living patients.'

Once he'd found the keyhole in the intricate wrought ironwork, McLean was pleasantly surprised to find that the lock was well oiled, as were the hinges on the door that swung open on to more steps and darkness. It made sense, of course. The crypt might only be used occasionally, but the last occasion had only been a couple of weeks ago. No doubt someone had been along to prepare the place for its newest inhabitants, and they'd had the foresight to bring a can of oil.

'You got that light?' McLean had hardly spoken before a powerful torch beam speared into the darkness, chasing the shadows into the corners. There were half a dozen steps, then the crypt widened out into a small room, stone shelves lining all the walls, most filled with ancient coffins.

'This the Weatherly family vault then?' Grumpy Bob asked. 'He bought this too?'

McLean considered the heavy stone carving, the solidity and permanence in death only money could secure. 'Seems that way,' he said.

'Surprised he didn't turf all the old folk out then.' Grumpy Bob raised an eyebrow, nodding towards the interior. It was a good point, given the lengths Weatherly had gone to in destroying the family that had disowned him. But then it had been his grandfather and uncles he'd ruined. Maybe there were limits to his thirst for revenge after all.

McLean stepped down carefully, then pulled the plan out of his pocket. The exhumation order was in there too, just in case anyone queried what they were doing. He'd already spoken to the church authorities, though, assured them that he was going to do very little to disturb those who should have been resting in peace. In many ways it was a lot easier than digging someone up. That almost always upset people.

'Should be the third on the left, one shelf up.' McLean squinted at the coffins as Grumpy Bob's torch played on them. It was easy enough to see who had been put here most recently, but he didn't want to open up Mrs Weatherly by mistake. No chance of doing that with the two girls; their coffins were tellingly small. 'That one, I think.'

There was just enough room between one shelf and the next to open the lid. Dr MacPhail joined him, and together they unscrewed the heavy brass fittings and levered off the dark wooden lid. McLean wasn't sure what to expect. A sudden rush of wind gusting the spider webs perhaps, or a distant scream of terror. The crypt smelled of cold stone and still, stagnant air. He thought perhaps there'd be some odour of corruption, or the formaldehyde stench of the mortuary. Instead there was no drama, no smell at all, nothing.

The coffin was empty.

'What the fuck do you mean, gone?'

There had been no way this was going to be easy. They'd spent another half-hour in the crypt, checking the other coffins even though they had permission only to disturb one. Morag Weatherly and her two daughters were where they should have been, but Andrew Weatherly's last resting place was quite clearly somewhere else.

McLean had sworn Grumpy Bob and the wide-eyed Dr MacPhail to silence on the matter, and gone to tell Duguid. Now he stood on the wrong side of that desk, like he had done so many times before, weathering the storm as best he could.

'I put my career on the line getting you that exhumation order, you know?' Duguid's face was a study in scarlet blotches and terrifying spots of bloodless white. 'How could you fuck up something like this?'

'With respect, sir—'

'Don't you fucking "respect" me, McLean.' Duguid leapt out of his chair, fists pummelling the top of his desk with an effort that should have launched him into the ceiling. 'If you'd left well alone none of this would have happened.'

'None of what, exactly? I didn't spirit Weatherly's body away. Think yourself lucky we've found out so soon it's gone. Lucky it was us found out and not someone else.'

'I . . .' Duguid opened his mouth to speak, then realized he had no answer.

'Exactly.' McLean took the momentary lapse to go on the offensive. 'In case you'd forgotten, I had a good reason to look at Weatherly's body again. I'm just as pissed off as you are that it's disappeared. But it does rather underline the point I was making before. There's more to this whole thing than meets the eye.'

Duguid squeezed at the bridge of his nose with a thumb and forefinger, as if trying to force something out of his brain. 'Jesus wept, McLean. This was supposed to be a simple enquiry. Man goes off the rails, kills his family and himself. End of story. That's the script you were meant to be following.'

'I thought you wanted me to get to the truth, sir. For the girls and their mother, if no one else.'

'The truth?' Duguid slumped back down into his chair, his anger spent. 'How long have you been a detective, McLean?'

'I . . . What?'

'Twelve years is it? Fourteen? And you're still convinced there's something called the truth. Christ, I wish I had your naivety some days.'

'There's a solid line of evidence linking Andrew Weatherly with—'

'Solid my arse. You deal in supposition and conjecture. Ghosts and fairies, for fuck's sake. You see links where there are none. Burnt lips. What does that even mean? I should never have got you that bloody exhumation order in the first place.'

Good God, they put this man in charge of CID. 'Sir, I'm sorry if the disappearance of Andrew Weatherly's body is inconvenient to you, but don't you think it's better we know now rather than later?'

'Better we never knew at all. Better he stayed where he was supposed to be. Best he never fucking well existed in the first place.'

'I'll give you that. Except we'd all look bloody stupid if it turned up somewhere unexpected, wouldn't we?'

Duguid looked up at him with a piggy-eyed, quizzical expression. 'You think you know where it is?'

'Supposition and conjecture, sir. Ghosts and fairies.'

'Don't get fucking clever with me, McLean.'

'OK, how about this then? Andrew Weatherly owned the company that has managed Rosskettle Hospital for NHS Scotland for the past twenty years. He also owned a different company that bought the place when it was no longer needed. Now a third company owned by one of his closest business partners is redeveloping the site.'

'What the fuck's Rosskettle got to do with anything? It's a loony bin, isn't it?'

'It was a mental hospital, yes. It's been closed for about twelve years now. But it's the most likely place our tattooed man came from. William Beaumont. Some of the outbuildings are only a few hundred yards from where he went over the cliff into the glen.'

Now the puzzled face. Well, he'd been expecting that.

'What are you getting at?'

'I'm saying there's a link between Andrew Weatherly and William Beaumont, sir. It means that Weatherly was doing far more than having sex parties at his house in Fife while his wife was away. It means he was into something I don't begin to understand, but which is responsible for the deaths of two people I know of and God alone knows how many more. It's probably what pushed him over the edge to do what he did. The thought that this secret was going to come out. And it means that even as we speak all evidence of it is being bulldozed and carted off to landfill.'

Duguid slumped back in his chair and ran a large, spidery hand over his head, ending up scratching at his neck. McLean said no more, letting the detective superintendent come to his own conclusion and in his own time. He'd laid his cards out on the table. Nothing else he could do now.

'You can't tell anyone about this,' was Duguid's eventual response. 'Make it clear to Grumpy Bob and that pathologist friend of yours. No one can know that Weatherly's body has gone missing. Not now.'

McLean tried to keep an upright posture, but inside he was slumping in disappointment. No, worse than that, frustration. He knew there was pressure from above to cover up all this stuff, but surely Duguid wasn't important enough to be mixed up in it.

'You'll need a warrant to search the hospital. I'll make a couple of calls. Keep it away from the usual channels so it doesn't put up a big red flag.'

'I . . . What?'

'You want to search the hospital, right? Before it's completely obliterated? That's what I'd do.'

It was McLean's turn to do the stupid impression. 'But I thought . . .'

'Me too. I thought they wanted a quick investigation because Weatherly was friends with powerful people. Wasn't happy about it, but I've not got many years left and I really don't want to retire on a constable's pension.' Duguid fished around in his jacket pocket, pulled out a small black notebook and leafed through it, looking for something. Found it, and reached for his phone. 'I'll cover up a lot of shit for a quiet life, but this is going too far.'

45

'You seen Ritchie recently?'

McLean was still reeling from his encounter with Duguid, the second person in as many days to defy his expectations and turn out to be, if grudgingly, helpful. It was almost as if the end times were upon them and people were finally taking sides in some great battle. Only the ones he'd expected to be siding with the enemy turned out to be coming to his aid. He hoped the opposite wasn't going to turn out to be the case with his friends.

'Still off sick, sir.' MacBride had been tapping dolorously at the screen of his tablet computer, his face a picture of despair.

'Still? I thought she was getting better.' How long had it been since he'd seen her last? When he'd dropped her off at her flat after they'd been out at Cramond. It felt like weeks ago. True, she'd looked ill, but not enough to put her out of action this long, surely.

'So did she, sir. Had something of a relapse, apparently. She's got an appointment at the doctor's later on this afternoon. Said she'd try to pop in after. Not sure I particularly want to be here if she does. Not the way she sounded on the phone.'

McLean knew what MacBride meant. It was always the way with some people. Martyrs to their work. They'd drag themselves in with one leg hanging off rather than let down the team, and frankly that was fine. Less helpful was coming in dosed up to the eyeballs with flu remedy, sharing their germs with everyone else so the whole station could go down one by one.

'I'll go and see her later. Meantime you get promoted to acting detective sergeant.'

MacBride's eyes lit up, his slumped back straightened and a grin started to form on his face. 'I do?'

'Only in my head, alas. I need you to organize a search team. Might need the Armed Response Unit on standby just in case it gets lairy.'

MacBride slumped again, but only a little. He had a task, and that was usually enough to keep him happy. 'Where are we going, sir?'

'Rosskettle Hospital. Just as soon as Duguid sorts out my warrant. We'll go in first light tomorrow.'

Some might have said there were more important things to do, but McLean would have been happy to argue the point with them. He'd left MacBride in charge, which meant that the details would be attended to. Grumpy Bob was on containment, making sure that only those officers – particularly senior ranks – who needed to knew what was planned for the morning. That also meant that he'd only be getting in the way if he hung around. There was always paperwork to do, of course, but somehow he knew he wouldn't be able to keep his mind on it with everything building up to the morning raid. And besides, there was more to man management than making sure the overtime sheets were all filed away.

Even though she'd been warned he was coming, it still

took Ritchie a long time to answer when he pushed the buzzer in the doorframe of her basement flat. McLean didn't really know what to expect; she'd sounded tired and hoarse on the phone and she wasn't the type to throw a sickie on a whim. Still he was surprised at the terrible apparition that opened the front door. She looked shrunken, wrapped up in a huge towelling dressing gown, feet enveloped in great big fluffy slippers. She peered up at him with eyes dark and sunken, sniffed, then dissolved into a fit of coughing that would have put a lifelong smoker to shame. It took a long time for her to get her breath back.

'Sir.' She motioned for him to come in.

Now he'd seen her, McLean wasn't quite so sure he wanted to share that same air, but he'd come to see how she was and bring her up to speed on their ongoing cases. It would have been rude to turn tail and flee.

'I was going to ask how you were. Seems a bit stupid now.' He stepped into the hallway, closed the door. Ritchie sniffed again and muttered something that might have been 'this way', then shuffled off towards an open door leading to the back of the building. McLean followed, finding himself in a large living room with a surprisingly high ceiling. The end wall opened out onto a tiny garden surrounded on all sides by more tenements. It was white with deep snow at the moment, but must have been a wonderful place to sit of a summer's evening, cocooned from the bustle and noise of the city.

'Think it's getting better.' Ritchie dropped into a large, soft leather armchair close to a small gas fire that almost looked like it might have been burning real wood. This was obviously her default position, given the barricade of scrumpled-up tissues surrounding her. She pulled another one out of a box on the arm of the chair, honked something wet and slippery into it, then scrunched it up and set it among its friends. 'You want some tea?'

'It's OK. You stay there. I'll get it. Kitchen this way?' McLean hadn't sat down. He went back out into the hallway, noticing the boxes piled around and still not unpacked. How long had Ritchie been in here?

More boxes cluttered up the tiny kitchen, but the kettle was on the counter by the sink, along with mugs and a caddy of teabags. He busied himself with his task, only noticing Ritchie standing at the door as the water began to rumble to the boil.

'Lemsip's good. Cupboard up there,' she said, then started coughing again.

'Sounds like you need something stronger. You seen a doctor?' McLean found the box, tore open a sachet and poured the yellow-green crystals into a mug.

'This morning. Told me to rest. Got a note if you want to see it.'

'Christ, no, that's not why I'm here.' He poured the water, stirred the foul-smelling liquid. Maybe they worked, these cold remedies. Mostly they hid the symptoms so you could go back to work and spread your disease. And then they could sell more cold remedies to all your colleagues. Brilliant, when you thought about it.

'Keeping out of Dagwood's way then?' Ritchie tried a smile, but only half succeeded. McLean handed her the mug of Lemsip which she sniffed, wrinkling her nose. 'Ugh. Disgusting stuff.'

'Just wanted to see how you were, really. Not like you to get sick.'

'Tell me about it. Can't remember ever feeling so fucking useless.'

'Well, I won't say you're not missed.' McLean pulled the bag out of his own mug, found a bulging milk carton in the fridge door, then decided he really liked his tea black, all the while bringing Ritchie up to speed. She slumped against the doorframe as he spoke, the effort of standing leaving her too short of breath to reply for a while.

'I don't get it,' she said finally. 'What's out at the hospital that's so important Dagwood got you a warrant?'

McLean didn't answer straight away. He had a hunch, of course, but he liked to keep those to himself just in case they didn't play out.

'To be honest, I didn't think he'd go for it. He's starting to get pissed off at being told what to do by headquarters, though. This is his little way of rebelling.'

'Drops you in the shit a bit, though, doesn't it?'

'What, you mean when it all goes tits up? When we raid an empty building site and find fuck all?' McLean was pleased to see that for all her weariness and disease, Ritchie's brain still seemed to be working.

'Well, you are kind of being set up for a fall here, aren't you?'

'From the minute I was handed the Weatherly case.'

That brought a raised eyebrow. It didn't stay up long, though. Like everything else that took any kind of effort, even being cynical was beyond her.

'What, you don't think I knew?' McLean cupped his hands around his mug, feeling the warmth of the tea seep through into his bones. For all that she was ill, Ritchie kept her flat surprisingly cold. Just the fire in the living room to cheer things up. 'It's not the first time I've been made the scapegoat. Part of being a DI, of course. I'm not so senior that it would destroy my career, not so junior I can blame someone else. Bear that in mind when it's your turn, aye?'

Ritchie smiled at that, and for a minute McLean could see past the illness to the detective sergeant he was used to having around. Then without warning her eyes disappeared upwards into her head and she collapsed like someone had cut her strings. The full mug of Lemsip fell from fingers suddenly limp, tumbling to the floor in a slow, messy spray of cold remedy. She folded into herself, slumping down against the doorframe just slowly enough for him to be able to catch her before her head could clatter off the floorboards. Instinctively, he felt for a pulse. It was weak and erratic, much worse than he would have expected even from someone with the flu. Her skin was clammy to the touch, almost burning hot. He looked around the hallway, saw the half-open door into what must have been her bedroom. For an instant he considered carrying her there, tucking her up, sitting with her until she woke or maybe phoning someone to come round and help. But it was way past that, whatever illness she had. Time to bring in the big guns.

He pulled out his phone, brought up the number pad on the screen, and dialled for an ambulance.

Much later that night, McLean let himself in through the back door and on into the kitchen. He'd gone with Ritchie to the hospital, sat in an uncomfortable plastic chair in the waiting room while she was seen by the doctors. They were as mystified as him about what was causing her ailments, but agreed to keep her in for observation. It had taken him a long time to realize that there was nothing constructive he could do beyond going home and getting some rest.

Weary, he dumped his briefcase on a chair, the take-away curry on the table. Mrs McCutcheon's cat stared at him from its bed by the Aga, sniffing the air to be sure both that it was the human it deigned to share its house with, and that said human had brought the food. With a baring of the whitest teeth, it yawned, reached out a single paw with claws extended, then unfolded itself from its bed. A long stretch turned into a jump on to the kitchen table, with no discernible manoeuvre in between. It padded across the scrubbed wooden surface towards him, head and tail up in anticipation of some cosseting. McLean leaned forward to scratch it behind the ears. Her, he remembered, not it. Mrs McCutcheon's cat might have an ungainly name, but he knew what sex it was now.

That was when he noticed the envelope.

He probably should have seen it before; it wasn't exactly inconspicuous. Propped up against a dark pottery biscuit barrel he may or may not have left in the middle of the table. Inside there would be more incriminating photographs of Andrew Weatherly, sickening and pointless and heading to a journalist near here soon. He picked it up, slid a finger under the flap and tore it open. He was sick of the bloody politics of it all, the tiresome games. If they had something to say, then why couldn't they just bloody well get on and say it?

Only they weren't photographs of a dead politician having sex with his personal assistant.

It was probably the sky that caught his attention. All the earlier pictures had been from video taken indoors. These were proper photographs, and they showed a scene that took him a while to recognize. Perhaps it was because all the buildings were there, rather than just the couple that were left by the time he'd first visited Ross-kettle. Or maybe it was because they had been taken in summer, with the mature oak trees in full leaf.

Either way, it was clearly a set of pictures of the prefab buildings that Price Developments were busy demolishing. That was if they hadn't finished already.

McLean settled back in his chair and leafed through the collection again, more slowly this time. The pictures had that slightly faded quality about them that suggested they'd been taken a while ago, and they were true photographs rather than digital prints. There were no people visible in any of the pictures, and the more he studied them, the more he realized that they all focused on one building in particular. Some were close-ups of the windows and doors, others wider-angled shots, all with that same building right in the centre. He couldn't have said how he knew, but he was sure it was the building into which he had climbed just a few days earlier. The one that had been bulldozed even while he was still inside. The one with the basement that wasn't on any of the plans.

'Supposed to be a hint, is it?' McLean asked, of no one but the cat. She looked up at him with an expression that suggested she thought him an idiot, then went back to washing herself.

46

Darkness still. Dawn wouldn't be with them for at least an hour. Just the cloudy, moonless sky and the dull orange glow cast from the city to the north. McLean checked his watch for the hundredth time. A quarter past six and they were already late starting.

'Where's that bloody ARU got to?' Grumpy Bob gave voice to the thought occupying McLean's mind. The rest of the team was ready to go; just the armed unit holding everyone up. They probably wouldn't be needed anyway, but in hindsight it had been a mistake to suggest as much at the briefing.

Headlights swept across the parked car, momentarily dazzling McLean. The black Transit van pulled to a halt alongside them, wound down a window.

'Sorry about that, sir. Got a bit lost in the glen.'

McLean bit back the retort he wanted to give. 'Right, let's get this done.'

He nodded to Grumpy Bob, sitting in the passenger seat, and started up his engine as the sergeant relayed the go command on his Airwave set. They'd parked up at the top end of the lane leading to the hospital site, and now McLean led the convoy of Transit vans and squad cars down to the gates. Lights shone from the security guard's hut, and the barrier was down. McLean pulled in at the side of the lane, letting the vans past, then climbed out of his car as a sleepy guard came to see what was going on.

'Private property, mate. You can't go in there.' Blind as well as sleepy.

'Police. I have a warrant to search this site.' McLean held up the sheet of paper, thankful for whatever strings Duguid had pulled to get it. 'You can either lift the barrier now, or we'll drive through it.'

McLean followed the guard as he scurried back to his hut. Grumpy Bob was already there, and pressed the button to raise the barrier as they both entered. The guard went straight for the phone, but McLean held down the receiver with a finger. 'Not until my men have secured the site.'

'But . . . My boss—'

'Will find out about this just as soon as we're happy to let her know.' McLean paused until the guard sat down, then took his hand off the phone again. 'Shouldn't be long.'

The three of them waited in silence. Through the window of the guard hut, McLean could see past the skeletal trees to the shadowy bulk of the main building a hundred yards or so away. After a few minutes, spotlights lit up the stone facade. Not long after, Grumpy Bob's Airwave set buzzed the all-clear.

'OK then. Let's go see what they've found.' McLean let Grumpy Bob lead the way out before speaking to the hapless guard. 'You can phone your boss now.'

'Site's empty, sir. No one here.'

DC MacBride met them at the drive end. He was dressed up in full protective gear, though not armed.

The ARU officers were milling around at the back of their Transit, an air of disappointment boiling off them as they checked their weapons back into storage and shucked off their Kevlar kit. McLean breathed a sigh of relief that they'd not been needed.

'What about the rest of the site?' he asked.

'This is the site, sir. Everything else has been levelled, far as we can tell.'

McLean looked past MacBride to the imposing three-storey bulk of the old hospital. Overhead, the sky was starting to tinge with the coming dawn, the scene slowly revealing itself as the shadows retreated. Where he stood, the ground was tarmac, a large parking area funnelling into the driveway. Narrow lanes curved through the trees to where the other buildings had been, but almost every-thing had gone. A churned mess of snow and mud was evidence of the haste with which the site had been cleared. How long was it since he and Grumpy Bob had been here before? Couldn't have been more than three days. They'd been going at it some to get the site cleared so quickly. Not Edinburgh workmen, for sure.

'The other van arrived yet, Bob?' McLean asked as the detective sergeant ambled up.

'Just on its way from the gatehouse, sir.'

Headlights swept over the trees and on down the lane, then a panel van swung into view, pulling up a distance away from the car park already full of police vehicles. By the time McLean had walked over to it, a young uniform officer had climbed out and opened the back, releasing a pair of very excited spaniels. He stopped a distance away, not because they posed any great threat so much as he

339

didn't really want to get muddy pawprints all over his clean trousers.

'Constable Fraser?'

The officer growled a command and the two dogs instantly sat. Only when she was happy they were behaving did she turn to answer. 'You'll be Detective Inspector McLean, aye?'

'Yes. Thanks for coming at such short notice. I just hope these two are as good as I've heard.'

In the half-light of dawn it was hard to tell if Constable Fraser was scowling at that. She was short, not plump but rather stocky in build, and had a no-nonsense air about her that suggested Young Farmer.

'If there's a dead body then Eilidh and Maisie will find it. You've no worries there, sir.' She looked up at the building, her neck craning as she took in the size of the place. 'I'm no' saying it'll be quick, mind. That's a big wee hoose.'

'Don't think there's much point going through there, to be honest.' McLean pointed off to the side of the building, where the light was starting to reveal something of a battlefield. 'A wee bird tells me what we're looking for's going to be over there.'

The spaniels busied themselves quartering the ground as McLean and Constable Fraser picked a careful route across the building site. It took a while for him to build the picture in his head, digging up the memory of his brief visit just a few days earlier. He had the photographs, of course, but half the trees were missing, as well as all the outbuildings. There was no sign at all of the single-storey blocks that had stood in an arc around the west end of the main house; just a sea of broken earth, ankle-breaking chunks frozen as hard as rocks. In the pale light of dawn, he identified the fallen tree, still half-buried in drifts of snow and close to the metal perimeter fence. Working back from there brought him and the dogs and the constable to a point he was fairly certain marked the entry to the basement he'd not been able to investigate. Maybe within fifty yards either way.

'Somewhere around here.' He pointed at the ground around his feet. Fraser gave another growl of a command, and the two dogs came to attention. Another, and their heads went down, tails up as they set to working. Back and forth with the single-minded intensity of something mostly imbecilic, but very, very good at doing just one thing.

It didn't take long. First one of the dogs stopped, quivered and started barking. Within moments its companion had done the same. They didn't dig, which impressed McLean almost as much as the sniffing. Instead they just sat side by side, looking from their handler to a point on the ground in front of them and back again.

'X marks the spot, Inspector. I'm impressed.'

'You think there's something down there?'

'I'm sure of it. You sometimes get false positives, but these two are my best, and if they agree on something then I'd put money on it being a body.' She took a handful of biscuits out of her pocket and gave the dogs a reward; lots of patting on the head and encouragement, too. McLean hoped they'd earned it.

*

'Jesus, this stuff's like concrete.'

Detective Constable MacBride was wielding a pickaxe with all the skill of a navvy, and two uniform constables were scraping away soil as best they could with shovels, but there was no getting away from the fact that it had been below freezing, even in the middle of the afternoon, for several days now. The earth was as hard as iron, and when it did break, it formed clumps too heavy for one man to lift. They'd been at it for half an hour now, but you'd be hard pressed to tell if you hadn't watched them from the start.

'Can't be too deep. Should get softer as you go down, too.' McLean wasn't sure if this was true, but he felt the need to give encouragement. The day was as light as it was likely to get now, almost half-past seven in the morning and a dull grey cloud blanketed the distant Pentland Hills, freezing fog clinging to the nearby woodland.

'You sure you don't want a go, sir?' MacBride asked, offering up the pickaxe handle.

'Wouldn't want to deny you your workout, Constable.' McLean cradled a mug of coffee in his hands, courtesy of Grumpy Bob. Where DS Laird managed to magic the stuff up from he had no idea; he was just happy to feel the heat of it in his belly. He had been savouring the rich aroma too, but a waft of something much less pleasant reached his nose at the same time as one of the uniform constables let out a yelp.

'Got something here, sir. Oh, sweet hairy—' he stopped mid-sentence, dropping his shovel in his haste to scramble out of the shallow pit. To his credit, he made it at least ten yards from the scene before vomiting.

'I think we've found our missing body, sir.' MacBride handed up his pickaxe again as the second uniform constable clambered out more carefully. McLean took it this time, hauling the detective constable up by the business end. With all three of them out of the way, he could peer down and see what the sniffer dogs had found. It wasn't pleasant.

Encased in mud as if he'd been thrown there while it was liquid, a man's face peered up from the bottom of the hole. His lips were blistered and torn, teeth showing through the ragged, pale pink and burned black flesh. His eyes were gone, black holes filled with mud where once eyeballs had been. You might have thought it would be hard to recognize a person from such a small bit of their face, damaged, bloodless and blind. But there was no mistaking the identity of the man whose body they had uncovered. Andrew Weatherly.

'Looks like you were right, sir.' Grumpy Bob sidled up, looked into the hole. 'You going to tell me how you knew?'

McLean thought about the page of notes Matt Hilton had given him, and how it had crackled and burned in his fireplace. It was cold outside in the fog and the pale dawn light, but that wasn't what sent a shiver right through him.

'To be honest, this wasn't what I thought we'd find, Bob. Not going to complain, mind. Let's get Scene Examination Branch in here, eh?' He cast a glance over to where MacBride and the two uniform constables were huddled together shivering.

'Think they can dig the rest of him out, don't you?'

47

He heard the commotion long before he reached the parking area in front of the main house. McLean didn't need to see the shiny Range Rover with its black-tinted windows or the hulking forms of Karl and the other bodyguard to know who was making it. Part of him was impressed that Mrs Saifre had come to the site herself, and that she had made it there so quickly, but another part of him wondered how it was she hadn't known long beforehand.

'I want to speak to whoever is in charge. This is quite outrageous, young woman.'

Of all the plain clothes officers she could have picked on, Mrs Saifre had chosen DC Gregg, probably thinking that as she was both young and female she would be easy to push around. That, McLean realized as he approached the scene, was her first mistake.

'I'm very sorry ma'am, but I cannot let you go any further. This is a potential crime scene and it's imperative we keep contamination to a minimum. We wouldn't want to have to take your clothes away for forensic examination now, would we?'

'Do you have any idea who I am, young lady? What's your name, your rank? Who do you report to? I will be taking this up with the Chief Constable himself.'

'Mrs Saifre. I must say I didn't expect to see you here.'

McLean half-shouted the words, anxious to defuse the situation even though he was still too far away. Or at least turn it on himself and away from his junior officers. If there was one thing he couldn't abide it was people in authority bullying the underlings. That was his job.

'Detective Inspector McLean. Tony. Surely there has been some mistake here.' Mrs Saifre flashed him a smile that would have weakened the knees of any red-blooded male. Except that McLean could see the artifice in it; could see this woman for the parasite that she was.

'I'm afraid not.' He finally reached the little group of people, noticing that several uniform constables and a couple of the Armed Response Unit sergeants had formed a loose semicircle around DC Gregg. With only Karl and her other bodyguard behind her, Mrs Saifre was quite clearly outnumbered, for all her bluster about connections in high places. McLean took the search warrant from his inside jacket pocket, unfolded it and handed it to her.

'We had reason to believe a man was held against his will and tortured on or near these premises. This gives us permission both to search the entire grounds and to exclude anyone from them while we carry out that search.'

'*Had* reason?' Mrs Saifre picked up on McLean's use of the past tense. 'So you've conducted your search already.'

'Oh, we're not finished yet. No. We've only just begun. Tell me, Mrs Saifre, how involved are you in the day-to-day running of Price Developments?'

A dark scowl creased Mrs Saifre's brow, her eyes flashing with a red flame that must surely have been a reflection of the rising sun. The cold air seemed to chill even further and McLean felt the pain in his hip twinge. Through the corner of his eye, he noticed several of the collected officers take a step back, as if they had been standing too close to a bonfire that had begun to burn more vigorously than expected.

'I am the money, Detective Inspector,' Mrs Saifre said eventually. 'So naturally I take an interest in anything that might affect the bottom line. Technical aspects of the development are left to the engineers and architects.'

'And yet here you are. Where are they?'

'I own this land.' There was something about the verb, the way Mrs Saifre voiced it, that put McLean on edge. It was as if she were saying she owned someone's soul. Where had that thought come from? He felt a growing pressure to back off, to order everyone to pack up and leave. But that was mad; they'd only just got here and a couple of hundred yards away DC MacBride and Grumpy Bob were helping a couple of uniform constables to guard a dead body that was somewhere it really shouldn't have been.

'Then ultimately you are responsible for what we find on it. Is that not so?' McLean held Mrs Saifre's gaze even though it actually hurt to look into those black, bottomless eyes.

'You have no idea what you're messing with here, Detective Inspector McLean.' She looked away, cast her eyes over all the assembled police. 'None of you do. This will go badly for you all.'

'Please don't threaten my officers, Mrs Saifre.' McLean took a step forward. He had been going to take her arm and guide her back to her car, but the way the two body-guards stiffened made him think twice. He looked at Karl, who gave him the most minimal shake of the head. Not so much a discouragement as a warning. McLean turned the touch into an open-handed gesture, pointing with his other hand back towards the Range Rover. 'I'll have to ask you to move off the site until the forensic team have finished their examination. We will, of course, keep you informed as to our progress.'

Mrs Saifre glowered at him and again he felt that pressure building up in his head, his whole body. There was a heat boiling off her that should have melted the icy ground all around them, driven off the freezing fog. But it was a heat only felt inside, a warning of the rage that was yet to come. McLean felt a momentary pity for the two bodyguards, whose journey back to the city was going to be difficult to say the least.

'You haven't heard the last of this.' Mrs Saifre stalked back to the car, climbed in. McLean followed her over.

'I don't doubt it. I'll be wanting to talk to you anyway, so don't go far.'

Karl the bodyguard and chauffeur closed the door, the black tinted windows making it impossible to see Mrs Saifre's angry glare any more. As he turned and opened the driver's door, ready to climb in, McLean caught the expression on his face. A more complete and horrifying terror he had never seen.

'Just exactly what have you been up to, Inspector?'

The physiotherapist's room was warm after a morning spent out in the freezing fog. McLean lay on the padded bench, trying not to wince as Esmerelda manipulated his leg and hip. It hurt far more than he was prepared to admit. Far more than it had even the day before.

'Standing in a cold field watching forensic experts dig up a dead body, if you must know.'

Scene Examination Branch had arrived not long after Mrs Saifre's departure, taking over the site in short order in that efficient manner of theirs. McLean was happy to let them get on with it, and to hand responsibility over to Grumpy Bob. By then the cold had really begun to bother him; far more than he would have expected given the amount of extra clothing he'd been wearing. When his phone had beeped the one-hour reminder of his physio appointment, he'd leapt at the opportunity to leave Rosskettle. Well, maybe not leapt.

'Charming.' Esmerelda forced out the word as she put her weight behind her work. McLean wasn't fighting her, but he could feel his leg stiffening as it bent, as if the joint was no longer the right shape. 'Feels like you've been for a twenty-mile hike in boots that are two sizes too small.'

Something went pop and McLean screamed. It was a small scream, but a scream nonetheless. The pain was excruciating, then as soon as it had arrived it was gone. He reached out and touched his hip, expecting it to be tender. Instead it felt perfectly normal, and for the first time in weeks he realized just how wrong it had been feeling before.

'What was—' Esmerelda began.

'What did you—' McLean's question came at the same time. 'What did you do?' he asked in the eventual silence.

'That really shouldn't have hurt.' The physiotherapist

gave him a look that was part suspicious, part incredulous. As if his sudden burst of agony were somehow a criticism of her ability.

'Believe me, it did. But now . . .' McLean swung his legs off the bench and lowered his feet to the floor. He was tense, expecting at least the old stiffness and pain to settle in as soon as he put weight on his hip. But there was nothing. He took a step, then another. Two more brought him to the door, so he turned and walked a swift circle around the therapy bench. Esmerelda watched him all the while, a puzzled frown on her face.

'That's incredible,' she said at last. 'You're hardly limping at all now. Just muscle compensation on the opposite leg. Please. Up on the bench again.'

McLean did as he was told, letting the physiotherapist take his leg again and manipulate the knee and hip. They moved loosely, freely. No feeling like there was wet sand clogging up the ball joint. No constant dull ache.

'Must've been a trapped nerve.' Esmerelda gave him his leg back. 'That last push probably popped it back out to where it was meant to be. That'd explain the yelp, I guess.' She looked like she was trying to convince herself more than anyone else.

'Yelp?' McLean asked.

'Well it wasn't much of a scream. Not really.'

McLean fetched his trousers off the chair in the corner of the room and pulled them on without first having to sit down. How long had it been since he'd managed that? He couldn't remember.

'You'll still want to take it easy for a few days. Maybe a week. Don't want to undo whatever it was I just did.'

349

'I'll be careful.' McLean sat down to put on his shoes, just to show he understood. 'Does this mean I don't need to come again tomorrow?'

'No. I think we can go back to the old schedule,' she said.

McLean stood up, flexed up and down on his feet in a manner he wouldn't have been able to half an hour earlier. The physiotherapist looked at him slightly askance, as if she couldn't quite believe her own skill. And that was when McLean noticed the chain hanging around her neck. Thin, silver; he thought at first that it was some form of pendant, but the end was actually a simple cross. It must have slipped out when she was working on his leg earlier and now it hung loosely over her top. Her hand went to it almost reflexively, slipping it away with a guilty smile.

'Next week then.' McLean shoved his hands in his pockets to stop them doing anything untoward, gave Esmerelda the slightest of nods, and fled the room.

48

'I must say, it's not often I get them back a second time.'

McLean stood a few paces away from the examination table, watching Angus Cadwallader set to work on the pale, naked form of Andrew Weatherly. The journey from crypt to burial in ice-hardened ground hadn't done the dead MSP any favours. His arms and legs had been broken in several places, and while Dr MacPhail and Tracy had done their best to lay him out in the semblance of a man on his back, there was no denying that several bits were missing. Forensics were even now excavating the site further, and DC MacBride was leading a team of officers trying to track down where the endless truckloads of landfill had gone. Somewhere in his future there was a difficult meeting with Detective Superintendent Duguid scheduled, which was probably why he was hiding down here in the mortuary.

'There enough of him for you to get the sample you needed?'

Cadwallader bent over the cadaver, peering closely at Weatherly's battered face and damaged lips. Dr MacPhail looked on, hands twitching slightly with an eagerness to help. McLean wasn't sure of the protocol here. It wasn't exactly a post-mortem – that had already been done. On the other hand, if they discovered clues from his remains that pointed to whoever had taken Andrew Weatherly from his crypt and buried him in the grounds of Ross-kettle, then the evidence would have to be corroborated. And for that the young pathologist would have to observe but not assist.

'Wheel the other fellow out, will you, Tracy.' Cadwallader straightened up, then set about examining the rest of the body while his assistant went to the cold store. He lifted up arms, inspected the left hand, then the pale, bloodless stump where the right had been removed. Weatherly's right foot was gone, too, along with a wide chunk of his midriff that looked horribly like it had been bitten out by an enormous mouth. Something had unstitched some of Dr Sharp's careful needlework up the chest, too.

'Any idea what's missing from inside him, Angus?' McLean had a horrible feeling he knew the answer already.

'Patience, Tony. I'll get there. First there's the small matter of why we wanted to look at him again in the first place. Ah, here we go.'

Tracy appeared from the far side of the examination theatre, pushing Barry Timbrel on a metal trolley. At least, McLean expected it was Barry Timbrel. Covered in a white sheet it was hard to tell. She lined the trolley up alongside the examination table already occupied by Weatherly, then turned down the sheet to reveal the waxy head of the tattoo artist. Cadwallader picked up a large magnifying glass and peered close to the dead man's lips. Stood up and turned back to Weatherly, giving him the same close attention.

'Fascinating.' He selected a weapon from the stainless

steel collection close by. To McLean it looked like a particularly sharp and sinister needle; the sort of thing you might use if extreme knitting were a sport. Cadwallader used it to pry a little skin from Weatherly's lips and place it on a small sample dish. He did the same with Timbrel, then took both over to the workbench, sliding them under a microscope one after the other. All the while he muttered to himself. McLean had seen him like this before, but only when particularly absorbed by a problem.

'Tom. Have a look at these and tell me what you think,' Cadwallader said eventually. Dr MacPhail repeated the exercise with the two samples, taking less time than his senior, and not making any noise.

'Acid?'

'That's what I thought. But here and here –' Cadwallader pointed with the needle at the dead men's lips. 'There's charring that suggests great heat. I can't imagine anything that would burn with acid and fire at the same time. And while they were still alive, too.'

Something clicked in McLean's brain then. He took a step forward before realizing that a closer look at either body wouldn't answer his question but would probably put him off his tea. 'You say they burned their lips while they were alive?'

'Burned them, or had them burned. It's possible this was done to them by someone, rather than them doing it to themselves.'

'And you think they're both caused by the same thing?'

'Thought Weatherly might have put the barrel in his mouth just as he fired it. Burned himself that way. But the shape of the blistering's all wrong, and now I've looked at it again . . .' Cadwallader pointed at Weatherly's battered and muddy face with his needle. 'If it had been charring – burning with heat – alone, then there'd be a very slim possibility of it being a strange coincidence. But this –' He swept the needle in a wide arc until it pointed at Timbrel, narrowly avoiding taking out Dr MacPhail's eye. 'Acid and heat together? Suggests something unusual, something . . . bespoke.'

'How long have you owned the Rosskettle site, Mrs Saifre?'

The radiator in interview room one had never worked very well, either heating the room to a fair semblance of hell or leaving it cold enough to worry a brass monkey. Today it was the former, the air thick enough to make breathing a struggle. McLean had already taken off his jacket, and sweat stuck his shirt to his back. Beside him, Grumpy Bob was struggling to keep his composure, beads of sweat clearly visible in the thinning mess of hair on his head. Across the table, Mrs Saifre looked like she was somewhere else entirely, not a hair out of place, her face pale. Only the glare in her eyes gave the lie to the air of calmness she was projecting.

'Me?' She raised a single eyebrow. 'Since dear old Andrew's last will and testament was read, I suppose.'

'That was after the funeral, if I recall.' McLean remembered the conversation at the wake. The first time he had met this unusual woman.

'Yes. It was. Andrew left me all of his business assets, of which Rosskettle was just one.'

'You didn't waste any time getting the bulldozers in.'

'Ah. No. That wasn't me.' Mrs Saifre smiled like a piranha, a mouthful of teeth that looked for a moment as if they were filed to points. Just a trick of the light.

'Your company, though.'

'No. That was Andrew. He had such plans for the place. Obsessive about it. Really such a shame what happened.'

McLean rubbed at his forehead, feeling beads of sweat just below his own hairline. Christ but he'd like to have found the person responsible for building maintenance and given him a stiff kicking.

'I'm sure Mrs Weatherly and the two girls feel the same way.' He shook the anger away, not really quite sure where it had come from.

'Oh they do, Detective Inspector. They do.'

Despite the excessive heat, the words sent a shiver of cold down McLean's spine. 'So all the demolition work and site clearing that's gone on since the funeral was work commissioned by Weatherly when he was still alive?'

'Exactly so. Glad I could clear that up.'

'And it didn't occur to you to maybe stop things while all the legal work was carried out?' Grumpy Bob gave a little asthmatic cough at the end of the question, as if it had taken all his breath just to voice those few words.

'My dear Detective Sergeant Laird. You should get that seen to.' Mrs Saifre's head turned so smoothly as she changed the focus of her attention that McLean could have been persuaded she was some kind of machine. Certainly not human, anyway.

'It's still a valid question, Mrs Saifre.'

'You were going to call me Jane Louise, Tony. I had such plans for us.'

McLean felt the return of that gaze and knew what the man who feeds the coals into the steam engine must feel like every time he opens the furnace door. The heat was playing havoc with his mind. He needed to get the interview back on track.

'Much as I'd like to keep this interview informal, Mrs Saifre, this is a very serious matter. A body was found buried on property you own. Property you are currently developing.'

'A body?' Mrs Saifre raised a slim hand to her throat in a gesture of mock horror. 'Whose?'

'That will come out in due course. I can tell you that it was a man's body, not long dead. We found it in the ground where your outbuildings were so recently demolished. Have you any idea how it might have got there?'

'Dear me, no. How horrible. But like I said, the demolition wasn't my doing. Rosskettle was Andrew's project. I've barely had time to visit the place, let alone look over the plans he had for it. Have you spoken to the builders?'

'Were you aware that Andrew Weatherly was born in Rosskettle, Mrs Saifre?' McLean dropped the question hoping to take her by surprise. If he had, she didn't show it.

'Who on earth told you that?' Was that a hint of worry behind the actress smile?

'It's a matter of record.' McLean wasn't going to let on that it had been Matt Hilton who'd put him on the track, DC MacBride who had waded through a mountain of old NHS Scotland files. 'His mother was a residential patient there. Far as I can tell he spent several years in the place before being fostered. I expect for a young lad it would be quite the adventure playground. Of course, no friends his own age.'

'Well, you learn something new every day. It certainly explains why Andrew was so attached to it. I never really understood that.'

McLean doubted that was true. It struck him that there was very little Mrs Saifre didn't know about Andrew Weatherly, including what his dead body was doing out of its crypt.

'How long have you known him? When did you meet?'

Mrs Saifre rolled her eyes, tossed her head back in mock ennui. 'Must we go over all this again? I already told that nice Detective Sergeant Ritchie all about Andrew and me. What was it, weeks ago?'

'Humour me, please.'

'Oh very well. But you still owe me dinner.' Mrs Saifre settled back in her chair, taking her time to speak again. 'I first met Andrew when he was still at university. I'd not long married Mr Saifre, rest his soul. Andrew had ideas but no money; Mr Saifre had money but no ideas. They were ideally matched, really.'

'And you brought the two of them together.'

Mrs Saifre nodded, a glint in her eye that put McLean on edge. 'Yes. Like I told Detective Sergeant Ritchie. I offered to make some introductions for her, too. But she declined. You have your troops well trained, Tony.'

McLean's response was cut short. A single, hard tap, then the door was pushed open. There weren't many people he wouldn't have torn a strip off for interrupting an interview like that, but one look at Detective Superintendent Duguid's face was enough to extinguish any residual anger. His gaze shifted nervously between McLean and Mrs Saifre, as if his eyes couldn't quite believe what was going on.

'I need to see you in my office, McLean. It's urgent.'

Had Duguid barked it as an order, McLean might have made a fuss. As it was, the detective superintendent voiced it more as a reasonable request. Obviously the man was incapable of being polite, but then you couldn't expect miracles. It was remarkable he'd shown as much restraint as this.

'I think we're done here anyway.' He stood up, extending a hand towards Mrs Saifre to suggest she did the same. 'Thank you for coming in and clearing this up.'

Mrs Saifre took the hand as she stood. Her touch was even hotter than the room, like grasping a glowing poker. McLean had to stop himself from dragging his hand back, stifled the cry of shock. Mrs Saifre saw it in his eyes, though. Smiled at her small victory.

'Will I have my building site back soon?' She released his hand, much to McLean's relief.

'That's a matter for the forensics team, and how we get on with questioning the construction crews. I'm sorry, but I can't be any more specific than that at the moment.' McLean's hand still tingled. He wanted to check it, makes sure the skin wasn't peeling and blistered by that touch. Instead he held Mrs Saifre's gaze for just a moment longer. Duguid took the silence as his cue to wade in.

'I'm very sorry for your inconvenience, ma'am. Detective Sergeant Laird will escort you back to the car park. I understand your man is waiting there?'

Mrs Saifre gave Duguid the curtest of nods, then strode out through the open door. Grumpy Bob bustled to keep up. McLean stepped out into a blissfully cool corridor, took in a deep breath of air that a half-hour before he would have said smelled badly of unwashed police officer and boiled cabbage, but now was the sweetest thing he had ever known. He lifted up his hand, inspected it closely. There was no sign of damage, even though it still felt strange.

'Enough dawdling, McLean.' Duguid's voice broke through his stupor. 'My office. Now.'

'What the fuck were you thinking bringing her in here like that?'

Duguid's office looked like a whirlwind had blown through it, or at the very least the Chief Constable. The desk was a mess of folders, strewn about the usually spotless space as if someone had been searching desperately for a single piece of information among the millions of carefully thrown-together words of obfuscation. Box files were piled about the floor, but the detective superintendent paid them no heed as he paced back and forth, toppling and spilling and trampling as he went.

'I mean, couldn't you have interviewed her at home? Couldn't you at least have had a senior officer present? Have you any idea who she is? Who she knows?'

'Mrs Saifre came in of her own volition, sir.'

'What if she goes to the CC with this? What if she

takes it up with complaints? What if . . . what?' Duguid's brain finally stopped for long enough for his ears to get through with their message.

'She came of her own volition, sir. I offered to interview her at her home or office, but she said she was in this area anyway. Don't believe a bit of it, but then I've long since given up trying to work out what her angle is. Or who the hell she is for that matter.'

'You don't know?' Duguid asked, a look of incredulity spread across his florid face.

'Oh, I know who she is. Jane Louise Dee, the Scottish Bill Gates was what they used to call her back in the eighties. Married some Middle East financier who didn't last long. Has been building her business empire ever since. Probably the richest woman in the world.' McLean ticked off the results of his most recent Wikipedia search on his fingers. 'For some reason she seems to have taken an interest in me recently. Flattering, I'm sure, but she's not my type. Like I say, not sure really who she is at all.'

Duguid's mouth had fallen open, which meant he slurred his first few words trying to get control of it again. 'She's what? How do you mean "taken an interest in you"?'

'You've met her, I take it? Before today?'

'Briefly. At official functions. Can't say as we've exchanged more than a couple of words. But . . .' Duguid tailed off as the thinking part of his brain demanded all the processing power available.

'Look, sir. If you think it'll help, I'll go and apologize to her in person, but if we'd found Weatherly's body on anyone else's building site we'd have them down in the cells right now, sweating. OK, so she's powerful, but she's not that powerful. She can't make this go away.'

'You actually believe that, don't you?' Duguid slumped down into his seat, sending another stack of papers cascading to the floor. Someone was going to have a lot of fun sorting out this lot later.

'Look at this place.' He flicked a clumsy hand at a folder on the desk. 'You know why I've had to dig this lot out and go through every single fucking one of them?' Duguid paused, but not long enough for McLean to answer. 'Because the Deputy Chief Constable wants to know details of every single investigation you've been involved in while under my command. That's why.'

McLean said nothing, just swept the room with his eyes. He tried to remember when Duguid would first have been his superior officer. There'd been at least half a dozen different superintendents in charge of CID in the station since he'd first made detective, but Duguid had always been somewhere in the pecking order as well. Even so, looking at the collected folders, it seemed an awful lot of cases for them to have both been involved in. But then again, it had been a long time.

'Why does he want to know that, sir?'

'Why do you fucking well think, McLean?'

Because he's worried. Because he's in someone's pocket and wants to make sure he's got everything covered. Or someone even higher up is leaning on him.

'Exactly.' Duguid took McLean's silence as understanding. 'I've had politicians from every party on the phone.

City councillors, too. Christ, I even had some nob from Holyrood calling. And you know what? They're all fucking scared of that woman. She's got leverage on every single one of them. And you brought her in here for questioning.'

McLean was about to explain once again that he hadn't brought Mrs Saifre in. That she had come of her own volition. He'd been meaning to interview her, yes. But she'd beaten him to it. Then he saw the edge of a smile on Duguid's face, something he couldn't really recall ever having seen before. Not like that.

'I've always said you're trouble. You know that. Christ alone knows this lot needed kicking up a bit.'

'You want me to call her back in?'

'Fuck, no. Leave her alone.' Duguid's smile disappeared, his hands shooting up to his chest as if the very thought of Mrs Saifre in his station was enough to give him a heart attack.

'And Weatherly?' McLean took the unprecedented occurrence of goodwill from Duguid to press home his advantage. Probably a mistake, in hindsight. The detective superintendent's face darkened once more. Normal service resumed.

'He's dead. Worst thing you've got is interfering with a corpse. If you can pin it on anyone. If I thought we could get away with it I'd say stick him back in his crypt and hope no one noticed he was gone.' Duguid shook his head; they both knew that would never work. 'No. You rattled the cage, now you'd be best to leave things alone a while. Don't push your luck.'

49

It was a sad but inevitable part of his job that McLean spent far too much time in hospitals. More often than not, the victims of the crimes he investigated ended up either here or the mortuary. Sometimes both. All too often recently it had been his personal life that had brought him down these familiar corridors. He wasn't entirely sure how DS Ritchie fitted into that. She was a work colleague, but also a friend. And she'd saved his life, which had to count for something.

He found her in a quiet ward at the end of a long corridor lined with an odd mixture of modern art and medical warning posters. She looked like she was asleep, a saline drip the only medical intervention evident. As McLean approached, she stirred, looked up at him with tired eyes. Her expression turned to fluster as recognition dawned.

'Sir. I . . . Sorry—'

'Take it easy, Kirsty. You're not at work here. No need for any of that "sir" nonsense.' McLean found a chair, pulled it across so he could sit beside her on the opposite side of the bed from the drip stand. She looked like shit; there was no other way of putting it. Her face was sunken, dark bags around her eyes. Even the speckled blotches of her freckles had faded away almost to nothing in the greyness of her skin. Her hair hung lank from her head, tightening up into rings where she'd not been looking after it properly. Lying by her sides on top of the covers, her bare arms were thin and weedy.

'Fainted,' she said as he settled into the chair.

'I was there, remember?'

A moment's confusion, then a look of consternation narrowed her eyes. 'It's nothing. I'll be up and about in no time. Just need to shake this bastard flu.'

That sounded like the old Ritchie, but her voice was thin, wavering. Looking closer, McLean could see the damp of sweat on her forehead, feel the heat radiating off her.

'Doctors know what's wrong with you, then?'

A slight shake of the head, followed by a wince as Ritchie discovered that perhaps shaking her head wasn't a good idea. 'They've sent some blood off to the labs. Pumped me full of antivirals. Hope they work it out soon.'

'Me too. And not just because we need you back at work.' McLean saw the ghost of a smile flit across Ritchie's face, but the effort was obviously too hard to maintain for any length of time.

'How's everything going there?' she asked. 'You were getting ready to raid Rosskettle or something?'

McLean settled back in the chair and brought her up to speed on their investigations. About halfway through, she closed her eyes. He stopped talking once he'd noticed, but she just said 'Go on' in a quiet whisper. It reminded him painfully of the long hours he'd spent sitting at his grandmother's hospital bed, talking to her while she lay unresponsive in her coma. On the other hand, it had helped him then, to marshal his thoughts by talking them through without interruption. As he spoke to Ritchie about Billbo Beaumont, Barry Timbrel, Andrew Weatherly and his mysteriously wandering body, Rosskettle Hospital and the hurried demolition of the outbuildings, a picture began to form in his mind as to how, and why, it might all fit together. How it all seemed to hinge around the strange figure of Mrs Saifre. Jane Louise Dee.

'Remember interviewing her. At Weatherly's office.' Ritchie's voice was sleepy, her eyes still closed.

'She said she'd spoken to you. Asked how you were, actually.' Now McLean mentioned it, the concern seemed odd.

'Haven't been right since I left that place.' Ritchie opened her eyes, struggled upright and started coughing. She pulled the clean white sheet to her face as she did so, and when she had finished, McLean saw that it was speckled with red.

'You want me to fetch a nurse?' He leaned over the bed, unsure what to do. Ritchie waved him away.

''M fine. Getting better, honest.' She dropped into her pillows, face waxy, arms flopping back to the blankets, exhausted after the effort of seconds.

'You never were a good liar, Kirsty.'

'Meant what I said, though. I felt a bit rough after we got back from Fife, but the next day I was pretty much OK. Only started to get sick after I'd left the office. After I spoke to that woman. Ask in there. See if anyone else's been off a while. Whatever I picked up there's proper nasty.'

'You know, I—' McLean began, but was cut off by a

365

buzzing from his pocket as his phone rang. He looked around the ward guiltily as he pulled it out. He couldn't swear he'd remembered to turn it off when he came in, despite knowing better. The caller ID told him it was DC MacBride on the other end, and he couldn't see any of the officious 'No Mobile Phones' signs about like there were in the ICU. Ritchie had barely raised her head, but he could see the look in her eyes that suggested she would have rolled them had she the energy.

'It's MacBride,' he told her. Then thumbed the screen and raised the phone to his ear. 'Constable?'

'Ah, sir. Good. Hoping I'd catch you.'

'I'm in the hospital. Can't speak long. Is it urgent?'

'Scene Examination Branch phoned. Seems they've found something at Rosskettle. Need you back on site as soon as possible.'

One thing to be said for the endless snow that was gripping the whole of the country that winter: it meant the traffic was generally light. On the other hand, McLean's new car was hardly designed for cold weather driving. He'd left Ritchie to the tender ministrations of the nurses and hurried south as fast as he dared, but it was still almost dark by the time he turned down the narrow lane to Rosskettle. At least there was a uniformed officer at the entrance where they'd met the security guard when they'd first raided the place, keeping the general public out. He couldn't help noticing the parked cars a short distance away, little clumps of dog-ends on the ground below the windows, long lenses glinting behind windscreens. Someone had tipped off the press and now they were circling like jackals.

A half-dozen Scene Examination Branch vans filled the parking space in front of the main building. They'd even brought their big truck, which didn't normally get wheeled out unless something serious was up. McLean found a space to park close enough that he wouldn't have to walk for miles, but far enough away that no one would reverse into him, then went in search of someone in charge.

He found Jemima Cairns directing a small platoon of SOC officers armed with spades. Her face spread into a wide beam when she saw him, quite out of character for the dour woman he was expecting.

'You got the message, I see.' She dismissed the last of the SOCOs, who all traipsed off in the direction of the area where they'd found Weatherly's body that morning.

'You said you'd found something interesting.' McLean shook the hand that was proffered, half-expecting to be grasped in a bear hug by the short, round woman. She'd helped him in the past, and had a thing about knots, he remembered. But her reputation was not one of great humour and bonhomie.

'Indeed we have. Not often we get something like this to investigate, either. You've made my year, Inspector. Possibly my decade. Grab a bunny suit and follow me.'

Intrigued as much by the casual reference to full protective gear as Miss Cairns's obvious excitement, McLean did as he was told, pulling on the white paper suit and slipping his feet into a pair of spotlessly clean rubber wellies. The two of them walked through snow churned by countless feet to the point where they had dug up Weatherly that morning. A set of arc lights illuminated the ground around a deeper hole. McLean stopped to peer in, but Miss Cairns motioned him on. A second, larger array of lights had been set up to illuminate an area close by the fallen oak tree and the temporary fence. A team was struggling with the largest tent frame he had seen in a while.

'Those cadaver dogs you got in went crazy over here.' Miss Cairns walked with surprising speed over the ice-crusted snow. Looking at her, McLean had thought she'd crack the surface and disappear up to her thighs, but she seemed to have a way of walking that meant she floated over the surface. Not so himself, and he found out soon enough that the SEB-issue rubber boots were not as tall as the snow was deep.

'We did a preliminary dig and came up with some very old bones. Thought it might have been historic. You know there's been a mental hospital on this site for centuries. The dogs wouldn't have smelled them, though. So we kept digging.' They approached the lit area, stepping from late afternoon gloom to a sparkling whiteness that hurt McLean's eyes. In the middle of it all, the snow had been shovelled back, the grass with it, and several feet of rock-hard earth. Now the SOCOs were working with tools you might see on *Time Team*, gently picking at the soil to reveal what looked like a cemetery in a country where coffins hadn't been invented yet.

'What am I looking at?' McLean asked after several minutes of stunned silence.

'So far? Twenty-two bodies. All male, adult. They've been buried carefully, but this isn't a Christian graveyard. They're all facing the wrong way for starters. Some are very old, even I can tell that. Others, less so. That's what got the dogs going.'

McLean let out a long, slow breath, the steam rising in the frigid air to surround him like his own personal cloud. 'Foul play?'

'Your friends from the city mortuary'll have to decide that.' Miss Cairns nodded at a point a few yards in where two figures were kneeling around a set of bones. 'At the very least, we've got an unregistered burial ground that's been used some time in the last ten years. Reckon we've a good fortnight's work here. Maybe even a month's. Congratulations, Inspector. You've hit the jackpot.'

50

'Jesus Christ, this is a mess. Thirty bodies. Thirty fucking bodies! Have you any idea what kind of grief I'm getting?'

The morning after the gruesome discoveries at Ross-kettle Hospital, and McLean wasn't at all surprised to find himself hauled up in front of Duguid. He pulled out his phone, flicked it on and held it up for the detective superintendent to see.

'Not just you, sir. I've had sixteen calls from Jo Dal-gliesh in the past three hours, and she's not even supposed to have this number.'

Duguid rubbed at weary eyes with his prehensile fingers. 'You really do know how to fuck things up, don't you?'

'Why does everyone think this is my fault? Not like I put all those bodies in the ground myself.'

'No, but you had to go and dig them all up, didn't you?'

McLean bit back the retort he wanted to give. No point descending to Duguid's level. 'I can't un-find them, sir. We have to investigate. And there's one small bit of silver lining in all this.'

'There is?' Duguid looked genuinely surprised.

'Aye, there is. The press are so excited by this mass grave they've completely forgotten about Andrew-bloody-Weatherly.'

'How long's that going to last, though?' Duguid muttered to himself, pulled some folders across from the mess all over his desk. 'It's a major incident now. That's official. So you'll be handing over to DCI Brooks. I have oversight of the whole thing for now, but it might go higher yet.' He shook his head as if that might make it all go away. 'What the fuck's actually happening out there?'

'Best guess so far is that there's been an unofficial burial ground there for as long as the hospital. Maybe even before. If they were all ancient, then we'd just get the archaeologists in, but some of these burials are recent. At least in the last ten years or so.'

'So who are they? Dead lunatics?'

Nothing like sympathy for the victims. 'Could be. The older ones almost certainly. We won't know until the pathologists have finished with them.'

'Well, hurry them up, McLean. We need answers fast, or this is going to blow up in our faces.'

'Always thought you were one to watch.'

He should have gone straight to DCI Brooks's office and then organised a major incident room for the investigation. Instead, McLean had taken his opportunity, and dashed out for a decent cup of coffee and something to eat. He should have known better, of course. That was how she'd caught him the last time.

'I've nothing to say to you, Ms Dalgliesh.' McLean ducked into the coffee shop, only to find a queue snaking its way up to the counter. Dalgliesh slipped in behind him. Trapped.

'C'mon. I'll buy youse a coffee if you just give us the heads-up.'

'You don't know already?' Despite himself, McLean couldn't help rising to the bait.

'Oh, aye. Lots of SOC vans and the likes out at the old loony bin. Ten vans heading back to the mortuary. University archaeology team wandering about the place talking about an ancient burial site not mentioned in any of their precious history books. Sounds like a mystery to me.'

Trust the civilians to speak out of turn. Either that or Dalgliesh was making stuff up in the hope he'd fill in the gaps for her. On the other hand, she'd had someone following the vans taking the remains back to the mortuary. Chances were she'd had a few unattributable tip-offs too. Amazing what a little bit of cash could do if you found the right officer to flash it at.

'We're having a press conference this afternoon. Can't you wait until then?'

'And miss my scoop?' Dalgliesh looked genuinely hurt. 'I know you've found bodies. Lots of them. I'm just looking for a few more details. Like how old they are.'

'It's only been a day. Let the pathologists do their job, aye?'

'So they're old then. Twenty years or more?' Now she was fishing.

'This is a major enquiry. I can't say anything until we know what we're dealing with.'

'Major enquiry, eh?' Dalgliesh's eyebrow shot up. 'So you're no' the man in charge.'

'Not even close. I report to DCI Brooks. Duguid's

Gold on this one. At least for now. You never know, it might escalate beyond even his enormous capacity.'

'And the archaeologists?'

'Should learn to keep their mouths shut.' McLean had reached the head of the queue, ordered his coffee, gave his name and added, 'She's paying.' Dalgliesh scowled, but pulled out a crumpled ten pound note from the pocket of her leather coat and handed it over with her own order.

'Look, you've got to give me something.' Dalgliesh leaned against the counter, waiting impatiently for the barista to do her business. 'What were you looking for out there, anyway?'

'That's part of an ongoing investigation, so I really can't discuss it.'

'Oh, come on. You must have had a reason to go poking about down there.' Dalgliesh scratched at her face with a yellow fingernail. 'Your tattooed body wasn't all that far away, was it? Washed down the river. You reckon he was a loony?'

'The hospital's been closed almost twelve years. William Beaumont was living on the streets, but he wasn't ever a patient at Rosskettle.'

'So that was why you were there.' Dalgliesh had a grin on her like the Cheshire Cat's idiot half-cousin. 'And you reckon whoever did for him did for all these others. And them going back hundreds of years.' Maybe not such an idiot.

'Look, Dalgliesh. I can't say much because I don't know much. Not yet, at least. Yes, I can confirm we've found bodies, and some of them have been in the ground a long time. Foul play, or just an unregistered burial ground used by the mental hospital before everything became more regulated? Who knows? I aim to find out, and that would be a lot easier if you held back from publishing your usual lurid speculation. The last thing I need is the conspiracy nutters wandering on to a potential crime scene.'

'Conspiracy nutters. Can I quote you on that?'

McLean grabbed his coffee the moment it arrived, somewhat startling the lady who handed it to him. He felt bad about that until he realized she'd spelt his name 'Maclean', like the toothpaste. Dalgliesh's own drink hadn't been made yet and he leapt at the chance to escape.

'Print what you want. You just make it all up anyway.'

He left the journalist standing at the counter, preparing her response. Hurried out the door before she decided badgering him for more answers was worth more than an abandoned latte. Everything was going to hell anyway, what did it matter if he pissed off the press now?

51

Two days later, and things were going from bad to worse. Scene Examination Branch had so far found the remains of twenty-nine bodies, neatly buried a couple of hundred yards away from the old outbuildings of the hospital. All adult, all male, some were little more than bones, but three were more recent. Dr MacPhail, for all his apparent youth, had spent a couple of years helping to identify bodies from mass graves, and was now overseeing the whole process with a macabre glee that suggested when older he would fit the Angus Cadwallader mould well. The senior pathologist seemed happy to let his underling shine, less happy at the growing number of bodies now filling up his mortuary.

As yet, none of the bodies had been identified, but one thing was obvious enough from what they had found. All of them that still had skin were extensively tattooed; intricate swirls of black ink covering them from head to toe. It wasn't hard to see the picture forming: a regular killing, structured, well organized, sacrificial. What McLean couldn't work out as he sat alone in his office, late into the night, was what the sacrifices were for.

Of course, poor old Billbo Beaumont had escaped. After the tattoos had been done, but before the final act. Not that it had done him much good, alone and terrified, probably half crazy from whatever drugs they'd used to sedate him, the other half crazy already. In the dark and snow, running naked through fences and gorse bushes until his fear took him over the cliff. But how long had this been going on before that happened? Twenty-nine bodies, Billbo number thirty. One a year? Probably one every ten, by the age of some of them. Nearly three centuries' worth.

McLean shuddered as he stared, unseeing, at the report on his screen. The press were having a field day, not helped by the tendency of the archaeological team brought in to help the forensics effort to talk long and loud about their latest theories in the pub every night. He'd spoken to their boss, a wannabe Indiana Jones-type with a stupid hat and an even stupider faith in his own abilities. This hadn't worked, of course, and the lack of support from his superiors had only made things worse.

At least the disappearance and recovery of Weatherly's body seemed to have passed without notice, but that didn't mean the question didn't still need an answer. Who had taken his body to Rossketle? Why had they buried it there in the grounds so close to all those others, just waiting to be found? Almost as if it had been a signpost for them. It was far too big a coincidence, and anyway McLean didn't believe in coincidences.

A knock on the open door startled him out of his thoughts. DC Gregg stood in the doorway, looking somewhat uncertain about whether she could come in or not. Moving to plain clothes seemed to have quietened her down a bit, which had to be a good thing.

'You still here, Constable?' McLean tried a weary smile, got one back in return.

'Don't think anyone's going to be doing much sleeping for a while, sir.'

McLean shook his head gently in reply. 'Anything I can do for you?'

'There's a woman in reception asking to see you. Duty sergeant's tried to put her off, but she's insistent.'

'Does this woman have a name?' McLean glanced from the detective constable to his desk phone, wondering why no one had called up. It wouldn't have surprised him to find out the switchboard was buggered and all his calls were being routed to a cupboard on the fourth floor.

'Said her name was Jenny Denton, sir. Keeps going on about the devil being in the details. Least, I think that's what she's saying. She's not exactly dealing from a full deck, if you get my meaning.'

It was the same interview room where he and Grumpy Bob had interviewed Mrs Saifre, and yet while then it had been stifling hot, now it was as if there were no walls and they were sitting out in the frosty night. McLean had sent DC Gregg off in search of warming tea, and perhaps a few biscuits. Now he sat alone with Jennifer Denton, both of them huddled into their jackets against the cold.

At least Miss Denton was dressed for the part. McLean couldn't remember how long it was since last he'd spoken to her, but the days had not been kind. He remembered a woman in total control, well turned-out and proper. It had surprised him to find out that she was doing anything so tawdry as having an affair with her boss. Now she looked haggard, her hair unwashed, face completely without make-up. She was greyer than he remembered, and she looked as if she were suffering from some terrible wasting disease.

'You have to stop, Inspector.'

McLean shivered, although whether it was at the cold or Miss Denton's voice, he couldn't be sure. She spoke in a hoarse whisper, quite at odds with the confidence bordering on arrogance of before.

'Stop? Stop what?'

'You have to leave it alone. No good will come of it. No good at all.'

McLean tried to catch Miss Denton's eye, but she wouldn't look straight at him. She'd avoided his gaze almost from the moment she'd seen him come into the reception area at the front of the station, staring at the floor or her hands for most of the time.

'Miss Denton. Jennifer. You came here to see me. You obviously wanted to tell me something. Has someone been threatening you?'

At that, she looked up, just briefly. A thin smile ghosted across her lips. 'I'm beyond threats, Inspector. I'm damned whatever I do. I just don't want any more people getting caught up in it.'

'Caught up in what?'

'I've not been home, you know. Not since the funeral, the wake.' Miss Denton studied her hands again, and McLean could see that they were dirty, black marks under the fingernails. 'Not a good time of year to start sleeping on the streets. Safer there, though. Least I thought it was.'

'You've been living rough—'

'Saw in the papers that you'd found the bodies. Buried out at the hospital.' Miss Denton stared at him now, as if it had taken her this long to summon up the courage. 'Always thought Drew was up to no good. That place had an unnatural hold on him.'

'You knew? That he was born there?'

Miss Denton gave the most minimal of nods. 'It wasn't common knowledge, but it wasn't exactly a secret either. I take it you know the story?'

'His mum was locked in there for getting pregnant, disgracing the family name. Yes, I've heard the story.'

'And you know the kind of man it made him into. What he did to them when he found out.'

'Seems he wasn't one to take no for an answer.'

'That's a very kind way of putting it, Inspector.' Miss Denton scratched at her eyelid with a quivering finger. Her whole arm was shaking like she had the DTs. McLean recalled the wake, her swift disposal of two glasses of wine. That single red drop on her pure white blouse. It was very possible she might be a functioning alcoholic who'd not had a drink in days. Perhaps not at her most reliable, then.

'So how did he find out? About his true family, that is?'

'I expect his mother told him, before she went mad. You'd think that would put him off the place, but he always had a thing for that hospital. Spent so much time there.'

'Did you ever go with him?'

Miss Denton's shakes disappeared for a moment, a look of genuine shock on her face. It didn't last long. 'Me? Heavens no. That was Drew's place.'

'But you knew what went on there.'

'I . . .' Miss Denton hesitated, either unable or unwilling to speak.

'We found his body buried in the hospital grounds. Someone took it from the crypt and put it there, close to all those other bodies. Almost as if we were meant to find him, and them.' McLean placed his arms on the table, leaned forward. 'You know who did that, don't you Miss Denton.'

'I . . . I can't . . . To name it is to summon it.'

Miss Denton shook her head violently from side to side, plunging her hands into her lap and hunching over like a small child trying not to be forced into doing something.

'But you know.'

McLean let the words drift into silence, waited until Miss Denton calmed enough to nod. When she looked up again, there were tears in her eyes, tracks clearing the grime off her cheeks.

'I'm going to hell, Inspector. There's nothing I can do about that. You can't save me, but you can save others. Save yourself.'

'Save myself? From what? How?' McLean leaned forward across the table, trying once more to catch Miss Denton's eye. There was something not right about her now, even more so than when she had first come in. She was twitching like a person with advanced Parkinson's disease. What he'd taken to be a shaking of the head to indicate that she couldn't say now looked more like an involuntary muscle spasm.

'You have to leave it alone.' The words were coming in gasps now; Miss Denton was having some kind of seizure. McLean leapt up, took two steps around the table to get to her side. At the same moment, the door opened and DC Gregg appeared in the doorway, three steaming mugs in her hand, packet of biscuits clamped under one arm. Her eyes widened in surprise, the biscuits tumbling to the floor.

'Get help. And call an ambulance.'

Gregg paused only to put the mugs down, slopping hot coffee on the chipped Formica before she turned and fled. McLean felt a hand grab his arm, shaking it hard as the spasms ripped through Jennifer Denton's small frame. She pulled him close, forcing words out through clenched teeth.

'If. You. Keep. Digging. More. Will. Die.'

52

'She's in intensive care, but the doctors aren't very hopeful. Looks like she had a stroke.'

McLean sat at one of the empty desks in the tattooed man incident room, half-listening as DC Gregg brought the rest of the team up to speed. The rest of the team being DC MacBride and Grumpy Bob, as far as he could see. Everyone else was across the hall in the Weatherly room, although now it was re-purposed for the Rosskettle investigation. Everyone except DS Ritchie, of course. She was still off sick, cause unknown. He'd have to find time to pay her a visit.

His own brain felt like it was only half there. Following the ambulance to the hospital and watching helplessly as they tried to do something, anything, to save Jennifer Denton, had taken him to the small hours of the morning. He'd gone home, tried to get some sleep, grateful for once that Mrs McCutcheon's cat had decided he needed company in the night. Even with her reassuring presence he'd not had any rest, and the alarm set for six hadn't helped.

'You got a moment, sir?'

McLean snapped his head up, not realizing until he did so that he'd been half-dozing. Sergeant Dundas stood at the door, a worried expression on his face.

'What is it, Pete?' He struggled to his feet, aware that the impromptu briefing had come to a halt.

The sergeant shifted, cast his eye over the rest of the room, saw Grumpy Bob over by the radiator. 'It's . . . Well, Bob, you might want to hear this too. Don't know if the youngsters need to be bothered.'

'No secrets in here, Pete,' Grumpy Bob said, even though it wasn't strictly true.

'It's Jack. Jack Tennant.'

'What about him?' McLean asked. 'Not like you to be so reticent where there's a nice bit of gossip to pass on.'

Dundas let out a weary sigh. 'He's dead, sir. Last night.'

'You what . . . ?' McLean rocked back on his heels, sending a shock up his spine and into his neck. 'How?'

'Way I heard, it was cancer. Didn't tell anyone he was sick, the daft bastard.'

That much sounded like Jack Tennant, but surely you couldn't go from looking pretty much fine to keeling over in such a short time. McLean thought back to the last time he'd seen the detective superintendent: the press conference when they drew a line under the Weatherly case. Well, the first line anyway. He'd been unwell then, but nothing life-threatening, surely.

Then he remembered Tennant's warning, how keen he had been that the Weatherly case be done and dusted. No chance of it being re-opened in the light of new evidence. And a later memory of him too, referred to as an old friend by someone who'd probably never had any.

'Shit.'

'Couldn't have put it better myself, sir.' Pete Dundas grimaced. 'There'll be a good few of us heading up to the funeral once it's announced.'

McLean didn't have the heart to tell the sergeant that

wasn't what he'd meant. He'd be going too, if nothing else got in the way. Jack Tennant had been his mentor early on in his career. A friend, too, albeit a distant one. But somewhere in the past, the detective superintendent had chosen a side, and McLean couldn't help but think that choice had come back to claim him.

'Do us a favour, will you, Pete?' McLean took a step towards the door as he spoke, forcing the duty sergeant back out into the corridor and away from the earshot of the others. No secrets in there, but out here anything was game.

'Sir?' Dundas asked.

'See if you can get me a copy of the pathologist's report, once it's done, aye?'

'Jack Tennant's report?' Dundas looked puzzled, perhaps understandably. 'What you want that for?'

Good question. McLean couldn't really put the reason into words even for himself. It was just that niggling feeling in the back of his mind that something, or someone, was playing fast and loose with the rules. And it all revolved around Andrew Weatherly. How many were dead, or as good as, because they'd had something to do with the politician? How many more might still die?

'Just do your best, aye?' McLean slapped the duty sergeant on the arm, and left him standing in the corridor as he headed back into the incident room.

McLean felt the blast of warm air from a fan heater on his cold cheeks as he stepped into the little office just off the examination theatre. He'd walked down to the mortuary from the station, taking the time to mull over the news about Jack Tennant. It was difficult to take in the idea that the healthy-looking man he'd last seen a week or so ago could have succumbed to cancer so fast. But of course Tennant hadn't been all that healthy-looking, really. He'd had that nasty cough, for one thing. And he was just obstinate enough to have ignored any medical advice to take it easy. Probably hadn't even been to see a doctor at all.

'Inspector McLean. Good to see you again.' Dr MacPhail appeared from the back of the office, where he'd been hiding behind a large flat-screen computer monitor. He was dressed in heavy green overalls flecked with little bits of something probably best left unidentified. There was a powerful smell of loam about the place, a far cry from its usual mix of antiseptic cleanliness and the whiff of decay.

'Angus told me you brought him the most interesting cases. I can see he wasn't lying. Come.' MacPhail indicated for McLean to follow him and led the way into the depths of the building. They passed along corridors he had never seen before, the impression of being deep underground heightened by the way the modern plastered walls gave way to a white-painted arched brick tunnel. Eventually MacPhail opened a heavy door, revealing a scene from another century.

'We use this place when things get tight in the new block. Your little discovery was too much for the cold store, so we've got them in here for analysis.'

McLean shivered at the cold and the view laid out in front of him. It was an old basement, carved out of the rock beneath the Royal Mile, or perhaps a remnant of one of the many vennels and closes that had been built on top of as the city grew over the years. Heavy stone pillars held up arched ceilings, and arranged around the spaces in between were dozens of examination tables, each with a black plastic body bag lying on top. Towards the centre of the room, a set of LED arc lights had been arranged around one of the tables, a couple of trolleys of tools alongside and a familiar couple hard at work. Perhaps alerted by the noise of their arrival, Angus Cadwallader looked up, grinning like a schoolboy.

'Tony. Thought you might be along soon enough.'

McLean picked a careful trail through the bodies until he reached the impromptu examination centre. He'd been expecting to see a corpse laid out, but when he finally saw what Cadwallader had been working on, it was just a skeleton.

'The fresher ones are in the cool store. We don't want to stink this place out.'

Now that Cadwallader mentioned it, McLean realized that there wasn't the kind of smell here that he would have expected. The temperature was low – both pathologists and their assistant Dr Sharp were wearing gear more appropriate for working outdoors – but it wasn't so cold as to be uncomfortable.

'What was the final count?' He did a slow turn on one heel, trying to count the body bags. Got to twenty before Cadwallader answered.

'They found twenty-nine bodies in all. Three of them still had some flesh on them. The rest have been in the ground at least thirty years.'

'Thirty years?' McLean emphasized the last word,

hoping that perhaps Cadwallader had meant months. Looking at the brown-stained assortment of bones on the table in front of him, he realized it was a forlorn hope.

'Sorry, Tony. It's early days, but my best guess is this one is a hundred years dead. Maybe more. And it's not the oldest by a long shot.'

'So they could just be patients from the mental hospital? People who maybe died without anyone to claim them? Cheaper to lay them out in the grounds than give them a pauper's burial.'

'Well, it's possible. That's your department anyway. I'm just here to try to work out what killed them.' Cadwallader reached out a latex-gloved hand and helped himself to something that looked like a neck vertebra. 'In this case, it's not all that difficult. See?'

He held up the bone, angling it in the light. McLean was no great expert, but his grandmother had been a pathologist, and he'd witnessed too many post-mortems in the line of duty not to recognize the scratches on the surface as knife marks. Even after a century it was fairly obvious that the man whose bones these were had died violently, with a knife to the throat, deep and swift.

'Murder, then.'

'Looks like it. And not just him.' Cadwallader put the bone back in the wrong place, Tracy quickly moving it to where it should be while he swept the room with one arm, indicating the collected bones. 'Every single one of them's exactly the same.'

53

'The Weatherly family owned most of the land around Bonnyrigg and Roslin in the eighteenth and nineteenth centuries. They made their money in the munitions factories, mostly. Some sugar trading, slaves, stuff like that. It was Josiah Weatherly who built Rosskettle Hospital, back in the late 1800s. Well, I say built. He was on the Midlothian and Peebles District Lunacy Board. Pushed for the hospital to be built. Provided the site and a lot of the funds, too. The main building was originally one of the family homes. Been remodelled a bit over the years.'

The small incident room was quiet, just McLean, Grumpy Bob and constables MacBride and Gregg. The core team. He'd called a meeting to bring everyone up to speed with the investigations, but MacBride seemed to be the one with all the facts.

'How is it you know all this, laddie?' Grumpy Bob asked. MacBride simply grinned, the tips of his ears reddening at the praise, then continued reading from his tablet computer.

'There's been a fair number of Weatherlys in the asylum down the years. Josiah's younger brother, Nathan, was the first on record. I suspect that might have had something to do with his enthusiasm for the project in the first place. The last one there was Annie Weatherly, born in 1936. She was committed in late 1952. By then it was part of the South Eastern Hospital Board. NHS Scotland, basically. She died in 1961.'

'Andrew Weatherly's mother?' This from DC Gregg.

'The very same.' McLean took up the story, pieced together from what Matt Hilton and Jennifer Denton had told him. 'They basically locked her away for getting pregnant when she was just sixteen. I know it's a rite of passage in some parts of the city these days, but it was frowned upon back then. Andrew Weatherly was born in Rosskettle. Spent his first eight years living there. Got fostered out when his mother died.'

'You think that's why his body ended up back there?' Grumpy Bob asked. 'That how you persuaded Duguid to get you the warrant?'

McLean paused before answering, trying to get his thoughts about it in order. 'I had a suspicion. There was too much linking him to the site, and I needed to move before the bulldozers erased everything. I never really expected to find him. Thought there'd be something, though.'

'The other bodies?' Grumpy Bob raised a laconic eye-brow. 'That's some leap, sir.'

'Didn't think there'd be so many.' McLean shook his head, leaned back against the desk. 'But I was working on the assumption William Beaumont wasn't the first. You any idea how many people go missing from this city every year?'

'But why?' DC Gregg asked. 'Why the tattoos? Why bury them in the grounds?'

'Why do people do the things they do? Money? Power? Madness? Weatherly grew up in a lunatic asylum, remember. His family has a history of mental illness.'

'It's still a bit of a stretch, isn't it?' Gregg asked. 'I mean, yes, the bodies are there, but you really think Weatherly killed them? I thought some of them went back centuries?'

'Everything's a stretch, Constable. But it makes most sense that Weatherly was behind it all. He controlled that hospital for years, even while it was part of the NHS. Bought it as soon as it was possible. He grew up there, had the run of the place. Who else would know all its secrets?'

'But he was only just sixty.'

'Don't think I don't know that.' McLean rubbed at his forehead, hoping it would ease the headache. It didn't. 'Let's not mess about here, these are sacrificial killings. Someone's been offering up the mad or the homeless for a hundred years and more. The sophistication suggests it was well organized and protected from prying eyes. Weatherly was just the latest to do it, almost certainly with a great deal of help.'

'And he killed his family because he thought his secret was going to come out?' Gregg asked.

'That's the most obvious conclusion, and that's what we'll offer to the press.' McLean pushed himself up from the desk, signalling to the team that their impromptu briefing was over. 'Not much else we can do, really.'

Now all he had to do was break the good news to Duguid.

*

'What the fuck are we looking at here?' Duguid slumped back into his seat like a man defeated by circumstance. It had taken a while for McLean to realize it, but now he looked closely, he could see just how tired the detective superintendent was. How worn down. Even his normal abrasive anger was tempered by a terrible weariness. And it was terrible, something that could break even Duguid's intemperance.

'To be honest, I don't know. And that worries me.'

'Ha. The great Detective Inspector McLean baffled.' Duguid tried to make a joke of it, but it was too much effort. McLean looked around the office, wondering whether he could get away with sitting down. The only chairs other than the one currently occupied were over at the far side of the room, arranged around a small conference table. No informality in here.

'There's a possible link between Andrew Weatherly and William Beaumont, sir.'

'Beaumont?'

'The tattooed man. He was living on the streets. Ex-military. You'd be surprised how many there are. Seems he was dossing down for the night in a prime New Town spot, him and an old service friend of his, Gordy Johnson. The two of them were attacked. Gordy called them "dark angels" and said they shot lightning from their hands, so I'm guessing black clothing, tasers, professional.'

'That's a bit of a leap, isn't it? From the ravings of a madman?'

McLean bit his tongue to stop the obvious retort coming out. Best to humour Duguid when he wasn't being deliberately obstructive. 'I'm just trying to build a scenario here, sir. Next thing we know, Beaumont's naked, covered from head to toe in fresh tattoos and drowned in the North Esk, just downstream from Roslin Chapel.'

'Oh Christ, not the bloody Templar conspiracy. Thought you had more sense, McLean.'

'Funny you should say that, sir. DCI Brooks was telling me much the same thing earlier this morning.' McLean paused for just enough time to let Duguid start speaking again, then interrupted him before he could get the words out. Petty but satisfying. 'I think the proximity to the chapel's coincidence, for what it's worth. The body was washed downstream by the floods, so where we found it's irrelevant, really.'

'It is?'

'Yes, sir. It is. The important thing is the tattoos themselves. From what I can gather, Beaumont had a few tattoos from his service days, but nothing you'd notice unless he took his shirt off. And yet somehow in the space of a couple of weeks he ended up covered in them, quite literally head to toe.'

'Someone else did this to him.' Duguid's weariness sloughed off a little as his brain began to engage.

'Exactly so. And they must have kept him sedated. It's not exactly painless getting a tattoo.'

That got him a raised eyebrow. 'You an expert, are you?'

'Not as much as Detective Constable MacBride, sir. But you're missing the point. It takes years to do a whole body, not weeks. Beaumont would've been in agony if he'd been conscious.'

Duguid said nothing for a while, which might have suggested that he was thinking. McLean knew better than to be too hopeful.

'Where are you going with this, McLean?'

'Well, I think it's fair to say Beaumont didn't volunteer for this. Someone took him off the streets reckoning no one would miss a homeless person. And they covered him in tattoos for a reason, however far-fetched. This was organized and efficient. With Andrew-bloody-Weatherly smack bang in the middle of it.' McLean reluctantly let the loose carriages in his train of thoughts join up, promising to take him to a place he really didn't want to go. 'Only whatever crazed reason, whatever ceremony he was performing, I've a nasty suspicion it went wrong this time.'

'What are you suggesting, then? Beaumont escaped?'

'Exactly that. He was ex-SAS. I don't think they realized what they'd let themselves in for. He woke up, freaked out, ran. Somehow he ended up in the river. The other bodies were all buried in the hospital grounds.'

'So Weatherly knew his little secret was about to come out. Topped his wife and kids, then turned the gun on himself.' Duguid nodded to himself as he spoke, as if this made perfect sense. McLean didn't buy it, though. It just didn't fit the profile of the man.

'But why?' Duguid continued. 'Why did he want to kill this Beaumont fellow in the first place?'

'I never said it made sense, sir. Murder rarely does. I think it's probably something Weatherly got involved in when he was a boy, growing up at Rosskettle. Some sort of cult, secret society or something.'

Duguid stared at him for just a little too long, the expression on his face inscrutable. 'Jayne warned me about you, McLean. Said you were a weirdness magnet. I thought she was making excuses for your poor record, but damn it if she wasn't right.'

McLean said nothing. Not sure there was anything he could say.

'So they took this man, Beaumont. Hauled him off the streets for this fucking ceremony of yours. Covered him in tattoos. I'm guessing he wasn't meant to come out of it alive.'

'Doesn't look that way, no. Not if the other bodies are anything to go by.'

'Christ, yes, the other bodies.' Duguid rubbed at his temples with his fingertips. 'That's a fucking mess right there. What are we supposed to make of them?'

'Tattoos on the bodies that still had skin, not a Christian burial, all of them with deep cuts to the throat?' McLean ran a quick precis of the initial forensic reports he'd read.

'A sacrifice, then.'

'That's a reasonable assumption.'

'Reasonable.' Duguid let out a bark of humourless laughter. 'Nothing about this is in any way reasonable. But here's a question for you. If your tattooed man was a ceremonial sacrifice, then what the fuck was Weatherly hoping to get out of it?' Duguid fixed McLean with a stare that was all the more alarming for the sudden insights that came with it. 'What the fuck was he sacrificing Beaumont to?'

*

Duguid's question preyed on his mind all the way to his tiny office, tucked away at the forgotten back end of the station. It was a good place to sit and think; people rarely visited unless by mistake. Which wasn't to say they didn't occasionally drop by on purpose. Someone must have done on a regular basis to keep adding to the piles of paperwork, unless those really were breeding of their own accord. And someone had put a plain brown envelope in the centre of his desk recently enough for it not to have been buried.

Heart heavy at the thought of yet another load of disturbing photographs, McLean pulled the envelope towards him and pulled out the contents.

Not something from Special Branch or whoever the man in the tweed jacket worked for, but a detailed pathology report for the late Detective Superintendent Jack Tennant. Top marks to Pete Dundas for getting a hold of it so quickly; he owed the duty sergeant a pint or two.

McLean had read enough PM reports in his time to know that they weren't exactly filled with joy. Even so, the list of problems that had finished off his old friend made for grim reading. The lung cancer had been relatively recent, apparently, but was just the last metastasis of something that had started in his bones a long time ago and had even spread to his brain. The pathologist came to the conclusion that, like a lot of men of his age, Jack Tennant had ignored the early signs of his illness, missing the point at which anything could have been done about it. If anything ever could have been done about it. Nevertheless, he was surprised at how far-reaching the cancer was, how many vital organs it had attacked. A sample was being sent to a top research laboratory for genetic analysis, just in case it was something they needed to know about.

He skim-read most of the report, saddened by how unfair life could be sometimes. The Jack Tennant McLean remembered had been full of energy and intelligence, with a deadpan sense of humour that caught everyone out most of the time. He'd been just months off retirement, though whether that was a good thing or bad, McLean couldn't really be sure. Either way, it seemed just bloody unfair that he drop dead now.

A sentence near the end of the report caught his eye. McLean had put his feet up on the desk, the chair tilted as far back as it would go before smacking against the wall. Now he dropped forward with a loud crash. Held the final page up to the light, squinting at the words as if he'd misread them the first time.

Subject's lips were swollen, with signs of recent blistering consistent with the application of excessive heat. It is estimated that this injury was sustained two to four weeks ante-mortem and was beginning to heal.

Four weeks. What had Tennant been doing four weeks ago? Heading up the Fife end of the Weatherly investigation. Interviewing friends and work colleagues of the deceased. Weatherly himself had shown a similar injury, but if it had been Weatherly behind the abduction of William Beaumont, Weatherly who had employed Barry Timbrel to tattoo his entire body, then why had Timbrel been damaged the same way? Unless the burnt lips were the mark of a third party. What was it Duguid had asked? What was William Beaumont being sacrificed to?

What did Weatherly expect to get in return? But what if that was the wrong way to look at it? What if the sacrifice was meant to keep something away?

A shiver ran from his head down into his gut as the implications of the question started to come together. There was someone else who had fallen ill recently, suffering from a mysterious ailment that had the doctors baffled. He gathered up the papers with hands so shaky it was almost impossible to get the report back into its envelope. Folding the whole thing lengthways, he shoved it in the inside pocket of his jacket. Pete Dundas had gone out on a limb getting it in the first place; no point dropping him in the shit by leaving it lying around where any Tom, Dick or detective superintendent might find it. Checking everything else was in order, he headed out the door. DCI Brooks might want him collating the forensic and pathology results coming in from the Rosskettle investigation, but right now there were much more important things to do.

54

She was asleep when he entered the ward, head sunk into the pillows as if the bed were slowly swallowing her. It wasn't official visiting hours, but even so the other patients were all awake. McLean approached quietly once more, taking in the changes that had occurred to DS Ritchie in just a few short weeks of illness. Her skin was dry and cracked, her hair a mess of grease and sweat. Her eyebrows had never really grown back after the fire she'd pulled him out of a year or so back, and now the lines where they had been were white. The nutrient drip on a tall stand beside the bed suggested that she was still having a hard time eating anything, as did the faint dribble of bloody mucus around her mouth. As he leaned in close, he could hear her breathing ragged and forced. A smell rose off her quite unlike the faint perfume he would always associate with her presence. More rotting compost than rose water.

He was staring at her face, trying to see whether there was any swelling or bruising about her lips, when she slowly opened her eyes. A puzzled frown grew across her face, then she started coughing, leaning up out of the pillows and bent almost double with the effort of clearing whatever it was that clogged up her lungs.

'Easy now.' McLean pulled a clean handkerchief from his pocket and handed it to her, knowing full well the stern lecture on hygiene he'd get from the nurses if they caught him. Ritchie took it, shoving it so hard into her mouth he thought for a moment she was going to swallow it. Eventually the spasms subsided and she slumped back into her pillows. Held up the hankie for him to have back, then saw what it looked like and dropped it to the floor.

'How're you feeling?' McLean couldn't stop himself asking the question, even though he knew it was perhaps the most idiotic thing he'd said since he was a teenager.

'Like that hankie.' Ritchie dropped her gaze to the floor, then dragged it back up to his face with considerable effort. 'Was sleeping. Dreaming. Woke up and it looked like you were going to kiss me.'

'Don't flatter yourself, Sergeant.' McLean pulled up a chair, sat himself down beside the bed. 'What were you dreaming about?'

Ritchie stared up at the ceiling. 'Not really sure. I was somewhere hot. Stifling. Couldn't breathe properly, but that's not really surprising.' She coughed again, and McLean could see the effort she put into stopping it turning into another fit. He probably shouldn't have been bothering her, but he had an inkling of an idea what was going on, and before he did anything rash he needed to know he was heading in the right direction. Or losing his mind.

'You said you thought I was going to kiss you. I didn't think I was standing that close.'

'You weren't?' Ritchie's eyes narrowed in concentration, the frown opening cracks in the dry skin on her forehead and cheeks. 'No. You weren't. That was someone else. The dream, maybe? I'm so fucking tired the whole time, it's hard to tell what's real and what's not.'

'What about your interview with Mrs Saifre? You remember that?'

Ritchie's brow furrowed again, the memories obviously hard to sift from the mess going around in her head. McLean hadn't seen any doctors on his way here, just slipping down the corridors unchallenged, using his familiarity with the hospital and its staff to his advantage. He had no idea what was wrong with her, but assumed it couldn't be that contagious otherwise she wouldn't have been on an open ward.

'Funny you should mention her,' Ritchie said eventually. 'Was thinking about that after your last visit.' She coughed again, and struggled to free herself from the sucking embrace of her pillows so that she could give her lungs a good clearing. McLean wanted to help her, but didn't know how. Not like him to be so useless. Maybe it was the delicate hospital gown she was wearing, the thinness of her arms and the curve of her neck. Whatever it was, touching seemed inappropriate, probably also inadvisable. So he sat like a lemon and waited for her to tell him what had happened. She took a long time to get her breath back, and when she did speak her lips were blue with hypoxia.

'Must have blanked it.' Ritchie gasped in a couple of shallow breaths before continuing. 'The interview. Was weird. I asked questions.' More shallow breaths, a pause for a coughing fit. 'She answered a few, but nothing much. Then she started asking about me, about work, you. She was nice. Seemed nice, anyway. Something about her I couldn't . . . She offered me a job. Can't even remember what it was now, but it sounded too good to be true. 'Sides, I'm happy enough with what I've got, really.' Ritchie coughed again, rattling loose something slippery. 'Well, I was.'

'This is going to seem like an odd question, Kirsty.' McLean paused, knowing what he was going to ask was mad. 'But did she kiss you?'

Ritchie's brow furrowed. 'Kiss me?'

'Mrs Saifre. Did she kiss you?'

'She put her hand on my leg. I remember that now.' The furrows on Ritchie's brow grew deeper, the effort of digging up the memories bringing a damp sweat to her forehead. 'Seems bloody weird now, but it felt perfectly natural then. But kiss? I . . . Why would she?'

'I don't know. It's like I've got a box full of pieces to half a dozen different puzzles. No matter how hard I try, I can't get them to fit together.'

Ritchie settled back into her pillows, weariness dragging her eyelids down. McLean sat silent for a while. He could tell himself that he'd come to see her because he was concerned, but the truth was he was looking for answers as much as anything. Or maybe just looking for someone to bounce theories off who wouldn't think him insane.

'I keep coming back to William Beaumont,' he said after a while. Ritchie nodded her head almost imperceptibly to show she was listening, but said nothing in reply.

'We know he was taken off the streets. We know he was prepared for some sick ceremonial sacrifice. We're working on the assumption he escaped before it could happen. Now we've got loads more bodies, going back several centuries, but some in the last two or three decades. Looks like they've all been through the same thing.'

'Cult?' Ritchie's voice was little more than a whisper.

'Cult. Secret society. Could be anything, really. But well organized, influential enough to remain unnoticed, and centred on the old mental hospital. That's shocking enough in itself, but the unanswered question is: what were they trying to achieve? Duguid had it right, damn him. We really need to know why they were doing this. What were these men's sacrifices meant to do?'

Ritchie said nothing, and when McLean looked at her face he couldn't tell whether she was awake or sleeping. Maybe it was easier if she was sleeping.

'You're wondering why I asked if you'd been kissed.' His voice was low now, talking to the semi-darkness of the night-time ward. 'Well, people keep turning up dead with badly damaged lips. I thought Weatherly'd maybe put the hot gun barrel in his mouth, but Barry Timbrel didn't try to shoot himself. And Jack . . .'

'Beaumont's lips weren't damaged.' So Ritchie was awake. And listening.

'He was the sacrifice. He'd have had his throat cut if he hadn't escaped. No, the lips are something else. Something new.' McLean paused again, not so much because he was bringing the strands of thought together as because what they formed was too terrible to contemplate. 'What happens if the sacrifice doesn't go as planned?'

'Whatever they were sacrificing to gets angry? Stops protecting them? Comes after them?'

And there it was; the link he'd been trying so hard not

to see. Three hundred years or more they'd fed this particular beast. Was it any surprise its return was marked by chaos and carnage?

It had been dark when he left the hospital, late enough that it wasn't worth going back to the station. Nothing there but politics and paperwork anyway. So McLean had driven across a snow-frozen city, enjoying the relatively light traffic that made his journey home much quicker than normal. The V6 engine made a fat cat purring noise and the leather seat hugged him like a warm lover as he sat staring at the unlit edifice of his grandmother's house, silhouetted by the orange and purple of the low night-time clouds. It was a good place to sit and think, the car. Enclosed and safe. Just a pity that his thoughts of late were taking him to dangerous places. Uncomfortable places, both physically and mentally.

A trill from his phone broke the moment. He pulled it out and looked at the screen. A text message: *Let's try again, shall we? Dinner at eight. Will send Karl. Jane Louise.* McLean let out a sigh; the woman never gave up. A quick glance at the clock at the top of the screen showed him that Karl would be around in a little over half an hour. There was no point hiding or putting her off, even if he knew he'd get it in the neck from Duguid when he found out. A company now owned by Mrs Saifre was under investigation, after all. He was SIO for the bloody crime scene. He shouldn't be talking to her at all, except at the station, with legal representation and two tapes recording everything.

But there was no way he'd ever get anything to stick to

her. She was too powerful, too well connected. No, she wanted something from him and wouldn't leave him alone until she got it. Well, two could play that game. He thumbed through his address book, wondering at the serendipity that had reunited him with an old acquaintance so soon before he needed a favour. A single call should do it.

55

Karl turned up in the Rolls-Royce twenty-five minutes later. McLean knew it was him, mostly because he wasn't expecting anyone else that evening, but also because Mrs McCutcheon's cat, which had spent the intervening time rubbing her head against his hand and arm, suddenly stiffened. Her fur stood up, not quite on end like she'd been electrocuted, but certainly making her twice her normal size. She looked towards the door through to the main hall, and hissed a couple of seconds before the doorbell rang.

'Don't worry. I have a plan.' McLean patted her on the head, left her on the kitchen table and walked out of the front door into the night.

Karl was standing by the open passenger door. McLean nodded at him before climbing in, surprised to find Mrs Saifre already sitting inside.

'I wasn't sure you'd come.' She patted the seat beside her like a good seductress, and was dressed for the part, too. Her outfit was shimmering gold and black. It covered everything, but clung to her body like it was painted on, accentuating curves and casting shadows of allure. As he settled into the warm, soft leather of the seat, McLean caught a whiff of something expensive and fragrant. It might have been intoxicating, but then so was cyanide gas, so was brimstone. The thought surprised him and the merest hint of a smile must have brushed his lips. Certainly Mrs Saifre mistook it for encouragement, moving closer to him as he sat.

'I probably shouldn't. You are connected with an ongoing investigation, after all.' McLean tried to relax as Karl closed the door, locking him in with the monster.

'Rules are for the little people though, aren't they, Tony?' Mrs Saifre leaned forward, her tight clothing moving like a second skin as she opened up the drinks cabinet. McLean had to admit that she was in every way the most intoxicating woman he had met, and yet at the same time he found it easy to ignore that aspect of her, see it for the plastic that it was.

'Drink?' It was voiced as a question, but at the same time, she handed him a glass filled with champagne. McLean took it, raised it in salute as she did the same with her own, then pretended to take a sip.

'I wanted to make up for . . . well, everything,' he said as Mrs Saifre was still drinking from her own glass. 'So I called in a few favours and got us a table at Chez Innes.'

Mrs Saifre's eyebrow arched at this, though whether with annoyance or incredulity, he couldn't tell. Whatever it was, she accepted it after only a few seconds' thought. Tapped the window and issued a command to Karl to change their destination.

'Thought you couldn't get a table there for love or money. I've offered Bobby the world and it's still a three-month wait.'

'Maybe you've been offering him the wrong thing.' McLean settled back into his seat, cradling his glass to avoid spilling champagne on his suit as they motored back into the city. Round one to him; could he hope to keep it going?

If he'd been hoping to get in unnoticed, he'd not counted on the tenacity of the local paparazzi. Even on a freezing night in early February, they were camped outside the restaurant waiting to see who might turn up. It was a sad indictment of society that pictures of rich people going into and coming out of what was just a glorified chippie with delusions of grandeur were more newsworthy than famine in Africa or climate change-induced natural disasters around the world, but judging by the artillery barrage of flashguns that went off as he led Mrs Saifre through the understated entrance of Chez Innes, that was the case. McLean hoped that they were just snapping everything that moved in the general direction of the restaurant, but he had a horrible feeling they knew exactly who she was, and probably a fair idea who he was too. Gossip would inevitably ensue. Well, it wouldn't be the first time he'd been the brunt of it at work.

'Tony. Finally you grace us with your presence.' Bobby greeted him in the entrance hall, dressed up in his soup-spattered chef's whites. He switched his gaze from McLean to Mrs Saifre, bowing theatrically. 'And now I can see why you have waited so long. Madame de Saifre, welcome to my humble restaurant.'

Eric appeared on the scene before Bobby could make a fool of himself, a half-scowl on his face as he welcomed them both. He led them across the restaurant to a small nook with a couple of comfortable sofas arranged around a log fire. McLean waited until Mrs Saifre's back was momentarily turned before whispering to him.

'You got the message, I take it?'

'Yes. It's all taken care of. I hope you know what you're doing, Tony. She's—'

But whatever she was, he never said. Mrs Saifre had been studying the picture above the fireplace, but turned back to face them. 'Is that really an original Elspeth McKenzie?'

'Madame has a good eye. It is indeed.'

'How on earth did you get it? She never sold anything. I thought she burned most of it before she died.'

'All she still had, but that was a gift.' Eric produced a couple of menus. 'Your table will be ready in a minute. Would you like a cocktail before dining?'

McLean could still feel the sensation against his lips where he'd raised the glass of champagne but not drunk. 'That would be nice, Eric. A martini, perhaps.' He turned to his companion. 'Mrs Sai— . . . Jane?'

'Jane Louise. The Scottish way. No hyphen.' Mrs Saifre frowned for the briefest instant before smiling again. 'Yes, a martini would be lovely.'

Eric retreated, leaving them alone. He was barely out of earshot before she spoke. 'How do you know these people? Have you any idea how long I've been trying to get in here?' For a moment, she reminded McLean of a different person entirely; a young woman excited and impressed, genuinely thrilled at this new adventure and the handsome hero with whom she was embarking upon it. But she wasn't young, for all she looked barely thirty. He knew that. She'd been a postgraduate electronics engineer in the early eighties, so had to be in her fifties now. Or she could be as old as time. That was the whole point.

'Bobby was my fiancée's flatmate, way back. We helped him set up his first place.'

'Fiancée?' Mrs Saifre raised a perfect eyebrow. McLean swallowed. This was always going to be the hard part.

'She died. It was a long time ago.'

'I'm so sorry, Tony. You must have loved her a great deal.'

'I did, yes. Still do, really.'

'Is that why you live all alone in that big old house?' Mrs Saifre took his hand, guided him to the sofa and sat down. He sat beside her, feeling the warmth from the fire, a deeper heat radiating from Mrs Saifre. Before he could say anything in reply, Eric returned with two martinis on a small tray. He set it down on the table in front of them, putting out two coasters and placing the glasses on them. One in front of each of them. Mrs Saifre took hers, lifting it in toast. McLean took his and did likewise.

'To lost love and that still to be found,' Mrs Saifre said, and took a long sip of her drink. 'That's a fine martini.'

McLean sipped at his own drink, tasted only ice-cold water. 'Indeed it is.'

'Your table is ready whenever you are.' Eric gave him a big wink, picked up the tray and sauntered off.

It was a long time since he'd properly eaten out, at a fine restaurant, sitting opposite a beautiful woman who was both witty and intelligent. Not since before Kirsty had died. That was perhaps the only melancholy aspect to the whole evening, if you overlooked who it actually was he was dining with.

For her part, Mrs Saifre was the perfect dinner date. Her conversation was interesting, she flirted with him every so often, smiled a lot. He found it strange that for all her obvious physical perfection, all her advances, he felt no attraction to her whatsoever. Every so often McLean caught a look in her eye that might have been irritation. He took a little satisfaction from that, but was careful not to let down his guard.

The food was everything he had expected and more; there was no doubt that Bobby deserved his Michelin stars. Still, as the evening progressed, McLean found it harder and harder to enjoy. This wasn't pleasure, he realized after a while; it was work. And work for which he wouldn't be paid, nor receive any kind of recognition. More likely he'd be hauled over the coals for it. Mrs Saifre was linked to an ongoing major incident investigation, after all. Such was life.

When it came to the pudding, an elegant concoction of chocolate soufflé and rich dark sauce, McLean realized he'd quite lost his appetite, despite the intoxicating aromas rising from the plate. Mrs Saifre fell upon hers with greedy abandon.

'This. This is why your friend is a genius.' She spooned another mouthful between her lips, tongue flicking at the edges where melted chocolate bubbled and glistened. 'I would pay anything to have him come work for me.'

'You could offer, but I doubt he'd be interested. Bobby's very much his own man.'

Mrs Saifre smiled. 'A bit like you, if what I hear is true.'

'Oh yes?' McLean raised an eyebrow. 'Been digging up the dirt on me, have you?'

'Just a few questions here and there. You know I'm on first-name terms with the Chief Constable.'

'Does he even know who I am?'

Mrs Saifre paused while she finished another mouthful of soufflé, devouring it in a manner that would make any man weak at the knees. 'The great Detective Inspector Anthony McLean. Of course he knows who you are. And he worries about you.'

'Worries about me, or that I'll do something really stupid?' Like taking the boss of a firm under investigation out to dinner, perhaps.

'A bit of both, I'm sure.' She placed her spoon delicately on the side of her empty plate, took up her napkin and dabbed at her lips once more, then dropped it on the table in an untidy heap. Then she slumped back in her chair, arms drooping by her sides in a parody of sexual exhaustion. Her face glowed in the candlelight, her raven-black hair loose now, slightly dishevelled, as if it had grown inches in the time it had taken them to eat dinner. She reminded McLean of nothing so much as a cat that has just had its fill of mouse and now intends sleeping for eighteen hours while digesting it.

'That was delicious. We should do this more often.' Even her voice was languorous.

'It's not often I have the time.' McLean put his own spoon down. He'd done no more than prod his pudding around a bit. 'Work has a habit of interrupting at the most inopportune moments, as you know. Still, you look like you've enjoyed yourself.'

'I always do.' Mrs Saifre pulled herself upright again. 'But perhaps this place has done its job. Time to move on?' She lifted a hand and in an instant Eric was at the table.

'Tell Mr Innes if he ever needs a job I'll pay handsomely.'

'Madame is too kind.'

'Madame hasn't even started being kind yet.' Mrs Saifre sat up straight, going from flirt to businesswoman in an eyeblink. 'I know this was Tony's invitation, but I want you to bring the bill to me. I asked him out, after all.'

Eric looked briefly at McLean, kept his best poker face. 'I would love nothing more than to do as you say, Madame de Saifre, but Tony McLean is an old friend. Bobby wouldn't dream of charging him for a meal. Nor anyone he chooses to dine with.'

The room seemed to cool, just for an instant. Mrs Saifre had gone very still, her face unreadable. Somewhere in the back of his mind, McLean imagined he could hear the wailing of tortured souls. He'd have put it down to the wine, were it not for the fact that Eric had been carefully topping his glass up with coloured water all evening.

'You're too kind, Eric. Bobby too. But I know better than to try to argue. I'll make it up to you some other way.'

Eric half-smiled, his gaze shifting from McLean to Mrs Saifre and back again before he answered.

'I'm sure you will, Tony. I'm sure you will.'

56

Mrs Saifre was perfectly charming from that point onwards, but McLean could see a difference in her, in the way she looked at him. They didn't stay long in the restaurant after that, and when he climbed into the Rolls-Royce beside her, she maintained a few inches of distance between them. As far as he was concerned that was fine. It had been an exhausting act and he looked forward to getting some sleep with only Mrs McCutcheon's cat for company.

They made small talk as the car drove swiftly across town. Out of the corner of his eye, McLean noticed that every light changed to green at their approach, as if some invisible hand were controlling them, speeding their progress. For a moment he thought he was going to be taken back to Mrs Saifre's house, prolonging the awkwardness yet further or perhaps forcing the issue, but Karl slowed as they approached the turn into the quiet street where his grandmother's house stood.

'You can drop me off anywhere here. I wouldn't mind walking a bit. Get a bit of fresh air to counteract that fine wine.'

'It was very good, wasn't it?' Mrs Saifre's voice was warm and sleepy. 'You sure I can't interest you in a nightcap?'

McLean smiled away the suggestion, knowing it wasn't really meant. 'Maybe next time.'

'I'll hold you to that, Tony.' She tapped the glass screen separating them from the driver and the car pulled in to the pavement. Before he could even find the door handle, Karl had stepped out and opened it from the outside. McLean didn't waste any time in exiting, pleased to see that Mrs Saifre didn't climb out after him. She lifted a lazy hand, and he took it in his, raising it as close to his lips as he dared but not actually letting it touch.

'Till next time, then.' He closed the door and waited as the car pulled away, disappeared into the night. Then let out a long, cloudy breath of relief.

He'd walked this street countless times in his life; knew all the buildings, the trees, the positions of the street lamps. He knew the church too, its dark stained stone, squat tower and arched windows. He'd never attended a service in there; his grandmother had been a devout atheist all her life, and something of that had rubbed off on him. True, recent experience had given him cause to re-evaluate some of the sweeping generalizations he'd made growing up, but all the same McLean was confident that the God represented by that building did not exist.

Which wasn't to say that there were not forces beyond his ken, as the poet would have it. Just that kneeling every Sunday in front of a slightly sinister statue of a man being tortured to death didn't strike him as a very constructive way of fighting evil.

Without quite knowing why, he found that he'd

stopped at the entrance to the churchyard and was staring at the dark, forbidding building. There was no obvious sign of work on the roof, he noticed. But then again, there wouldn't be. Not until the weather cleared; that's what the minister had said. One of the gates was ajar, almost as if beckoning him in. Looking up the straight paved path to the church door, he saw a low light in the stained glass windows, too.

The church door was unlocked, but when McLean went in he couldn't see anyone around. It was cold inside, possibly even colder than the snowy night outside. The light he had seen through the windows came from a half-dozen large candles, burning away on the plain stone altar. He walked slowly up to it, conscious of the echo of his footsteps on the flagstones, worn-down dedications to the dead people interred beneath his feet. Bones in the ground.

The interior of the church was not ostentatious, but neither was it as dour and plain as the Presbyterian kirks he'd been in. The Church of Scotland, Episcopalian, call it what you will. The Scottish offshoot of the Church of England was no-nonsense in its approach to devotion. The pews were well carved, but not ornate; a solid quality was their most obvious feature. The altar itself was a simple stone affair, decorated with nothing more than a damask cloth. There was a large cross, McLean noted, but no tortured Jesus weeping blood from his wounds.

He'd never really known what to do in churches. Some people, Kirsty among them, had always bowed a head, knelt, mouthed some silent prayer to the grey-haired old man in the clouds. He just stared for a while, then as his eyes adjusted to the gloom, he turned slowly and drank in the atmosphere of the place. It was peaceful, he had to admit that much, and after the evening he had just had, he needed some peace.

When he saw the font, at the opposite end of the nave to the altar, he finally realized what it was that had brought him in here. It was much older than the church; he seemed to remember someone telling him that once. Legend had it that Saint Columba himself had carved it, that it had been saved from the devastation when Vikings raided the monastery on Iona, brought here to the capital and finally to this unassuming church in what was then a wealthy estate, not even part of the city. McLean didn't know if that was true or not, but it was certainly older than the building surrounding it. The stone was different, and carved with intricate Celtic symbols.

The wooden lid that covered the font was old too, a simple construction of narrow planks, dotted with woodworm holes and chewed at the edges as if this were the home of some large Labrador rather than a church. Two heavy iron rings set into the top made it easy to lift off, and there within it was the Holy Water, still as a prayer, reflecting the dim lights behind him.

'It doesn't work if you steal it.'

McLean turned too suddenly at the voice, almost dropped the lid to the floor. The minister stood about ten feet away from him, a gentle, knowing smile on her face.

'Umm. I . . . That is . . .' He really couldn't think of anything to say. 'Sorry.'

'It's all right. Inspector. I know you're not going to

416

steal anything.' She came a little closer and he saw that she was dressed in her priestly robes, white dog collar over black shirt. Had there been an evening service or something?

'I saw the lights. Not really sure why I came in at all.'

'And yet here you are, peering into the font as if the answer to all your troubles lies within.' She stepped up to the edge of the stone urn, producing a small bottle from her cassock as she did so. She dipped it into the water, bubbles gurgling out with an eerie, echoing sound as it filled. Stoppered and wiped dry on her sleeve, she handed it to him.

'A gift. May it help you in your endeavours.'

McLean took the bottle almost reluctantly. Now he thought about it, he felt rather silly. 'It's not for me,' he said.

'I know it's not.' The minister smiled. 'And that is why it will work.'

The hospital never entirely stopped, but this late at night it was quiet, especially on the wards, where all but the most unlucky of patients were sleeping. McLean took the back route, hoping to avoid as many nurses as possible, but he still had to get past the ward sister before he could reach his destination.

'She's sleeping, Inspector. You can't disturb her.'

'Would you like me to go back and get a warrant? Come in here with a half-dozen uniforms and wake everyone?'

It wasn't Jeannie Robertson working the night shift. That would have been too easy, McLean supposed.

'This is impossible. I'll be having words with your superior officer, you know. Sergeant Ritchie is very sick. Critically sick. She needs her rest.'

'Believe me, I know just how ill she is. I'm trying to help her. And I'll keep it short, OK?'

The nurse glowered at him, but relented. He slipped as quietly as possible into the ward and across to Ritchie's bed. He needn't have worried about making a noise, though. She was bent double, hacking up her lungs and wide awake. She must have seen his shoes approaching, looked up as he neared her bed.

'Seeing me at my best, sir.' A tired smile and then she was coughing again. No attempt to hide the blood that was coming up with each hack now.

McLean saw the glass, half-filled with water on the bedside table, a jug nearby. While Ritchie was otherwise occupied, he tipped the contents of the bottle the vicar had given him into the glass. It was only a few drops, really. By the time he was done, Ritchie was too.

'Here. Drink this.' He crouched down beside her bed, held the glass up to her blood- and spittle-flecked lips. 'It'll help.'

'Who're you, my mother?' Ritchie glared at him, but took the glass anyway, sipped and swallowed gingerly.

If he'd been expecting miracles, then McLean was disappointed. The water soothed Ritchie's throat for a few seconds at most before she started coughing again. He took the glass from her before she spilled any, waited patiently for her to finish before handing it back again.

'You need to drink all of it.'

'Yes, Mum.' Ritchie grimaced, but did as she was told.

This time the coughing was less, and she lay back in the pillows drowsily.

'It's not looking good, sir.' She wiped at her mouth with the back of her hand, smearing her face.

'How no? You'll be fine.'

'You can see it in their faces. The doctors and nurses. Christ knows, I've seen enough of these places to get that.'

'You're imagining things, Kirsty. It's just the flu messing with your head. Rest up. Get well. I'll come visit in the morning.'

Ritchie frowned at his words, her eyes sliding from his face to take in the rest of the ward, only just realizing that it was night, not visiting hours at all.

'What—?' she began to ask, but he put a hand on her shoulder, pressed her down into the pillows.

'Relax. Sleep. Rest,' he said. 'It'll all be fine tomorrow.'

She didn't struggle against the weariness that closed her eyes and settled her breathing. McLean stayed where he was for a few minutes more, watching her relax into a deep sleep. He'd just given a very sick woman a drink of water of questionable purity. Who knew how many babies had pissed in it? Christ, he hoped he knew what he was doing.

Outside in the corridor, McLean nodded his thanks to the ward sister, feeling that conversation would be unwise. He'd remembered to turn his phone off – that would have been one sin too many. As he reached the reception area, he pulled it out of his pocket and turned it back on again. Almost immediately it started buzzing messages at him, most from DC MacBride. He looked at his watch, wondering what the detective constable was doing up at an hour so late it was early.

He was fairly sure it had been overcast, with the threat of yet more snow, but when McLean stepped out of the hospital, heading in the direction of the car park, the sky was clear. A thin crescent moon hung over a landscape of white, tiny pinprick stars fighting to be seen past the city lights. MacBride answered his phone almost before it had rung.

'Sorry to wake you, sir. Thought it was important, though.' In the background, McLean could hear shouting, machinery, the busy noise more associated with daytime.

'You didn't.' He was about to say that he'd been in the hospital, then realized that would only worry MacBride unduly. He'd done all he could for Ritchie; her fate was in the hands of others now. No point fretting over what he couldn't control. 'What's happening that's got you up at this hour, Constable? Sounds like a bomb went off.'

'You're not far wrong, sir. It's Rosskettle. Someone's set fire to it, and it's—' But what it was, McLean never learned. Something exploded at the other end of the line, and then the call went dead.

57

He could see the flames from Bonnyrigg, a mile and a half away from the mental hospital. McLean had already pulled over to let almost every fire engine in the region past him, full flashing blue lights and sirens on the go. There were squad cars too, even though at this hour they weren't really needed to clear the road ahead. The ambulances were more of a worry. The hospital was empty; there should have been no need for them.

Closer in and an explosion rocked the car, a huge rolling ball of flame and black smoke boiling up into the air above the bare trees. They stood stark against a backdrop of hell, flames tearing through the buildings as if they were made of paper and card, not sandstone and mortar. There was no one at the guard house as McLean drove past. Everyone was at the main building.

He parked a good distance away, at a spot on the drive where he wasn't blocking anything, and well beyond the scorching heat of the fire. Even so, it was uncomfortable; brought back memories of another fire not so far from here in which he had almost died.

All the snow had melted for a hundred yards and more from the building, the ground softening and steam rising from the dead grass in devilish wisps. At least a dozen fire engines had piled into the area immediately in front of the building. They were pouring water on to the flames with no obvious sign that it was having any effect. Quite the opposite, in fact. The closer he came, the fiercer the fire seemed to rage. Firemen ran about in well-choreographed chaos. There were paramedics and a few uniform officers standing about, but no sign of DC MacBride.

McLean spotted a familiar figure, standing head and shoulders above the crowd. Big Andy Houseman had been based in his own station until recently, and now worked out of Gilmerton. If even he was here, then the blaze must be serious.

'You seen MacBride?' McLean asked once he'd pushed his way through the crowd. He had to shout over the roaring of the flames, shielding his face from the heat.

'Over there, sir.' Houseman pointed to an ambulance a few yards back. 'He was a bit closer in when the first explosion happened.'

'First? What the fuck's going on in there?'

'Christ only knows.' Big Andy shook his head. 'Don't think they've got a hope of putting it out, either. Lucky it was empty, really.'

Before McLean could say anything, another explosion shook the ground around them. Flames burst from the burning windows, sending showers of glass out across the cars and fire engines parked closer to the building.

'Pull everyone back, Andy. At least to the treeline. Let the firemen do their stuff, but I don't want anyone getting hurt.'

'It's a crime scene, sir. Shouldn't we be—'

'It's my crime scene. I'm SIO. And I say safety first. Pull them back, and let the senior fire officer know too.

If all they can do is contain it, I'm not going to ask for more.'

'Aye, sir.' Big Andy gave a curt nod and then started shouting orders. McLean headed over to the ambulance, noticing as he got closer that its windscreen, facing the blaze, was cracked where something had hit it at speed.

DC MacBride was lying on a stretcher in the back, a bandage wrapped around his head with a dark red blotch in the middle of it. He tried to sit up when he saw McLean, but sank back down with a groan when he realized just how painful that was.

'Take it easy, Stuart.' McLean climbed into the ambulance as the paramedic who had been tending MacBride turned to face him.

'We're pulling everyone further back,' he said. 'Judging by your windscreen it's not exactly safe here.'

'Soon as we get this lad sorted, I'm out of here.' The paramedic went back to tending to MacBride.

'He's going to be OK?'

''M fine, sir.' MacBride's voice was woozy and faltering.

'You're not fine. You're lucky to be alive,' the paramedic said. 'That glass hit you an inch to the left . . .'

McLean watched the ambulance as it pulled away, taking MacBride to the hospital. Bad enough to have one of his team down and fighting for her life; the last thing he needed was for him to lose two. For a moment paranoia got the better of him. What if someone was picking off his team one by one? He'd taken out his phone, begun scrolling through the contacts list for Grumpy Bob and

Sandy Gregg before he realized that madness lay there. Worse madness than he'd already embraced that night. And even if it were true, Grumpy Bob could look after himself. DC Gregg wasn't to be trifled with either.

The fire hadn't abated at all in the few minutes he'd spent in the ambulance. If anything it was just getting started, raging as if a hole had appeared beneath the hospital leading straight into another hellish dimension. The stone walls still held, but the roof was gone and the windows looked like the eyes of the damned. The air was getting hard to breathe, unsatisfying. It seared his lungs, making him cough and wheeze.

The chief fire officer was a short man, but he made up in volume and presence what he lacked in stature. The other firemen paid attention when he shouted at them, and he didn't look like the sort who was prone to panic. McLean had met him before at fires much closer to population centres than this, which made his obvious distress even more remarkable.

'What the fuck's in that building?' were his first words on seeing the detective inspector approach.

'It should've been empty. Just a few old bits of furniture.'

'Could've fooled me.' The fireman winced as another explosion crumpled in the night air. 'It's like bloody Greek fire. The more water we pour in, the hotter it gets. I've seen munitions dumps burn more peacefully.'

'We're going to have to let it burn,' McLean said. 'It can't go any further. Just fields out there.'

'SIO's not going to be happy we let his crime scene burn.'

'I'm SIO. And believe me, nothing I might find in there's worth risking a life for.'

'That's all I needed to hear.' The fire officer turned away. Bellowed an order and his men started to pull back from the flames. McLean scanned the area, using his hands as best he could to shield his face and eyes from the scorching heat. Most of the police cars had gone now, and all the ambulances. Only fire engines ringed the remains of the hospital. Fire engines and one other car.

It was parked right up close to the steps leading to the front door. He'd not noticed it before, but he recognized it as soon as he saw it. A black Range Rover with tinted windows. How it hadn't melted, or exploded, in the heat, he had no idea.

'That car.' McLean grabbed the chief fire officer by the arm, hauled him round and pointed. 'Anyone check it out?'

'Empty. Locked. We broke a window just to be sure.'

'What about the driver?'

'If he's in there,' the chief fire officer pointed at the blaze, 'he's dead. I'm not risking my men to go fetch a corpse.'

'Not going to ask you to. Any chance we can get a line on the car and drag it away, though?'

The chief fire officer gave him a world-weary look. 'See what I can do. Wait here.'

He hurried off, called over a couple of firemen. A brief conversation, during which faces turned towards him with glowering expressions made even worse by the hellish firelight. Another loud explosion rocked the night, and McLean was about to shout out to them not to bother, but then a heavily suited fireman appeared with a loop of rope over his shoulder. In moments he had run to the Range Rover, uncoiling the rope as he went. He looped it around the towhook on the back of the vehicle and then scurried back to the relative safety of a nearby fire engine. Moments later, the rope went taut, juddering slightly as it took the strain. The Range Rover stayed put, its tyres melted to the tarmac, and McLean was convinced the rope was going to snap. Then it slowly slid backwards, smears of sticky black rubber leaving lines on the ground as it was pulled away. Another explosion and a tongue of flame spat out, as if something in the building were trying to stop it leaving. Paintwork singed and the windscreen cracked, but inch by inch, then foot by foot, the car was pulled back from the fire.

McLean waited until it was well clear of the flames before approaching. He was fairly certain it was the Range Rover he thought it was, although the way the paint had blistered made it hard to be sure even what colour it was.

'I'd keep well back if I were you.' The chief fire officer stopped McLean in his tracks. 'Thing's leaking petrol. Could go up any time. Too hot to touch, too.'

Now that he'd mentioned it, McLean could smell the fuel and feel the heat. 'Should be safe enough there. Pull your men back.' He looked around for the brave man who'd attached the rope in the first place. 'And thanks. You'd've been well within your rights to tell me to piss off, asking you to do that.'

The chief fire officer grinned, slapped McLean on the

back. 'Nah. You asked nicely. Now let's get back a ways and let this thing burn itself out.'

His Alfa was parked nearby, the conflagration reflected in its windscreen and headlights. Too close for comfort now he'd seen what had happened to the Range Rover. McLean was walking towards it when an unseen hand picked him up, its fingers as hot as the sun. It threw him forward as if he were no heavier than a straw doll, then slammed him hard into the ground. One hand trapped in his pocket, he struggled to breathe, rolled over to see a huge mess of flame and smoke claw its way up into the night sky. In his confusion it looked like some terrifying beast, reaching out with flaming hands to grab him. There was a noise like a jet plane taking off right beside him, a horrible crunching of metal, smashing of glass. Then the gentle patter as a thousand thousand shards of shrapnel rained down on the heat-softened earth.

He curled up on the ground like a frightened child as the sounds slowly filtered back through his fractured hearing. The blast furnace intensity of the blaze settled down into a more natural roar as the fire slowly consumed the remains of the hospital. Finally, when the last of the glass had finished falling from the sky, he rolled over and looked up on a scene that could have been a war zone.

A group of firemen were huddled in the lee of a fire engine, sheltered from the blast that had melted its tyres and welded it to the tarmac. Further away from what was left of the building, the Range Rover stood like some dark totem, steaming gently in the glow. Other firemen were stirring, picking themselves up from where the explosion had thrown them, or rolling on to their backs and groaning at the sky. As McLean looked around, he couldn't see anyone not moving, nor were there screams of agony. He hoped against reason that no one had been badly injured. There was no such hope for the hospital.

Its frontage was gone, the rock pulverized by the explosion or collapsed in on itself. Flames still ripped through the mess, urged on by their success so far in devouring all they touched. It wasn't natural, that fire. Or was it just his head swimming?

Slowly, arms and legs complaining all the while, he picked himself up, trying not to sway as his balance came back in random waves. His hand was still clasped around his key fob, and without thinking McLean pushed the unlock button.

Nothing happened. When he turned around he could see why.

The heavy stone door lintel, still carved with the Weatherly family crest, lay across the Alfa's ruined roof. It had smashed in the windscreen, crumpled the bonnet and broken the suspension so that the wheels leaned out at an uncomfortable angle. The Alfa stared at him through broken eyes, dead and reproachful. A faithful hound to the last, he'd barely had it six months.

'Looks like you're going to need a new car.'

McLean turned slowly to face the chief fire officer. That he had come up to see what had happened was a good sign. It suggested there were no serious injuries or fatalities requiring his attention.

'Reckon I'll get a tank. That's the second one's had something dropped on it from a height.'

'Just as well you weren't in it, really.'

'Just as well,' McLean echoed, and a horrible certainty settled on him. He wasn't really thinking straight, could feel the shock dulling his senses. He shook his head to try to clear it as he set off in the direction of the still-smoking Range Rover, all too aware that to do so was to come closer to those unnatural flames.

'Where the fuck do you think you're going?' The chief fire officer bustled up behind him, catching hold of McLean just as he was reaching out to open the back. The smell of fuel was everywhere, hot metal pinging and clicking as it cooled.

'I need to open this.' McLean turned the back of his hand to the car, judging whether to touch it would burn. It was cooler than it looked, so he chanced grabbing the handle. Nothing happened.

'Told you it was locked, didn't I?'

'I need to get it open. Can we break the window?'

The chief fire officer looked at him like he was mad, shook his head, then pulled a small pry-bar out of his belt. 'I've got a better idea.' He jammed the bar under the back door and wiggled it around a bit. Inside, something cracked and the lock popped. McLean pulled up the door and peered inside. It was dark at first, shadow cast by the raging inferno beyond. It didn't take long for his eyes to adjust, and then the chief fire officer shone a torch inside as well.

'Bloody hell!'

The Range Rover had a large boot, lined with expensive pile carpet like the rest of the car. It had been covered up with black plastic bin liners in an attempt to keep it clean. On top of them, a shovel covered in mud very much the same colour and texture as that found just around the side of the building sat on top of a neatly folded Army-issue body bag. McLean shoved a hand into his pocket and brought out his phone. The screen had a crack in it, but still lit up. A name, a number. A horrible cold sensation in the pit of his gut.

'No one touches this until forensics get here.' He scanned around the area, searching for a squad car. There was nothing, and no time. 'And I need a vehicle. Now.'

58

As a little boy, McLean had always wanted to ride in a fire engine with the sirens blaring and the blue lights flashing. Sat between a couple of tired and sweaty firemen, both eyeing him with a mixture of animosity and wary fear, it wasn't quite as romantic as he'd imagined. They made good time back to the city, aided by the late hour. Soon, however, the limitations of such a large vehicle became apparent as they navigated the ever-narrowing streets of Sciennes. Eventually McLean leaned forward and tapped the driver on the shoulder.

'Just drop me here. I'll walk.'

'You sure, sir?' He could see the relief in the man's eyes.

'Sure. It's not far. Probably quicker on foot and we wouldn't want to panic anyone, aye?'

McLean jumped down from the warmth of the cab into the cold night, his feet slipping slightly on the icy pavement. He didn't wait for the fire engine to back up and head home, took himself as fast as he could to his destination.

Ten years earlier, Grumpy Bob had shared a small but pleasant detached house in Colinton with Mrs Bob. One too many late nights, or maybe just being married to someone like Bob Laird for a quarter of a century, had proved too much for Muriel, and she'd finally told him to leave. After they'd sold up and split the proceeds, Grumpy Bob could have afforded something much better than his tiny one-bedroomed flat in the heart of the student city, but it was close enough to the station and an easy walk to all his favourite pubs. He didn't spend much time there anyway. Did most of his sleeping on the job.

The front door to the tenement was open, stopped from fully locking by the expert positioning of a half-brick. It brought back bittersweet memories. McLean climbed the stairs silently, ears straining for any sound that might have been out of place. He wasn't sure why he was here, really. Unless he was ready to embrace the madness.

Quiet music played through the front door to Grumpy Bob's flat. That was never a good sign; he only played music when he was in a melancholy mood, and that usually meant whisky had been imbibed. McLean knocked on the door, then listened for any sign of movement within. Nothing but the music, warbling away.

He'd known Grumpy Bob going on fifteen years now, maybe more. Many were the times the old sergeant had ended up sleeping in McLean's spare room, too drunk or too tired or just not wanting to go home to Muriel. When the divorce had come through, he'd spent six weeks in there before finally getting his own place. McLean hadn't minded, but he had discovered something about Grumpy Bob's musical taste, or lack of it. He liked country and western, and a bit of the more accessible classics, particularly if they were reduced to short snippets. Sometimes he'd be caught whistling something incredibly bland from the charts, but mostly he liked to read his paper in silence. The music distorting its way through the door was like nothing McLean would ever have suspected Grumpy Bob of listening to. It was avant-garde, asynchronous, experimental. If he was being honest, it was shit.

He knocked again, all too aware of how loud the knocking sounded in the night-time hallway. 'You in there, Bob?' Loud enough to be heard, hopefully not enough to wake the neighbours.

Still no response, and now the music changed, growing noisier and angrier. The wrongness of it all was like a slap in the face. McLean took a step back, feeling the railings press against him. Then he lifted up his leg and kicked the door as hard as he could.

It flew open with a crash that would surely have woken everyone in the street. McLean didn't care. He scanned the hallway, expecting a bleary-eyed detective sergeant to come rushing from the bedroom in his stripy pyjamas. Instead, his eyes focused on the electrical socket beneath the coat rack. A cable had been plugged in, and it snaked across the narrow hall until it disappeared under the bathroom door.

'Bob. You in there?' McLean heard the music rise and it seemed like it wasn't music any more, but the wailing of a million tortured souls. He reached down and pulled out the plug from its socket at the same time as a startled shout echoed from the bathroom, followed by a loud 'Fuck!' and a splash.

Water cascaded under the door, seeping through the floorboards on its way down to the flat below. After a few seconds McLean heard the sounds of something large scrambling out of the bath, then a towel-wrapped and flabby Grumpy Bob appeared. He held an elderly cassette tape machine in one hand, water dripping from the plastic speaker covers. The cable looped out of the back of it, down to the floor and back up to the plug still in McLean's hand.

'Tony? What the fuck?' Grumpy Bob stared at the machine. 'How did this get in here? I've not listened to it in years.'

McLean tried not to smile as the relief flooded through him. 'Never mind that, Bob. When was the last time you actually took a bath?'

DC Gregg's nondescript ex-council semi was not far from Grumpy Bob's flat, which was just as well as neither of them had a car. McLean tried to call her as they walked, but his phone's cracked screen made it impossible to use. Just that name and number reappearing every time he switched it on. Grumpy Bob had left his own phone behind, which was pretty much par for the course. He spent most of the ten-minute walk muttering about baths and idiots and not being in his right mind. As soon as they arrived at Gregg's front door, McLean was glad he'd not been able to make contact.

'Smell that?'

'Gas, aye. And lots of it.'

'Got to get the main turned off.' No question as to where the gas leak would be; there were far too many coincidences already for that. 'Go see if you can wake someone up. Get on to the gas company.'

Grumpy Bob headed off along the street, putting a

sensible distance between Gregg's house and any spark from someone turning on their light. McLean watched him go, then headed round the back, looking for a way in.

He found a small window open just a crack. Twenty seconds with a pen and it was wide enough to clamber in. He paused only to let his ears adjust to the new silence before easing open the door on to a narrow hallway. The smell of gas was overpowering in here, making his head swim, his eyes water.

Upstairs was worse, as if that were possible. He found the master bedroom, two humps under a duvet, stepped quietly over to the bedside, crouched down beside the sleeping form of his newest detective constable. She slept on her side, covers pulled up around her, head scrunched into a large, soft pillow.

'Constable Gregg. Sandy.' His voice sounded odd, coarse and low. His throat tickled, forcing out a cough.

'You have to wake up now.' Louder this time, and the constable scrunched up her face.

'Come on, Sandy.' This time McLean shook her. She rolled on to her back, opened her eyes.

'Jesus, fuck!' She sat bolt upright, revealing rather more than he needed to see. Her hand shot out for the bedside light but McLean grabbed her wrist.

'It's me. Tony McLean. You can't turn on the light.'

Gregg relaxed slightly, pulled her hand away from his grip. He let go, stepping back as she pulled the covers around herself.

'What . . . ?' She sniffed. 'Gas?'

'Don't turn anything on. Got to get out of here.'

Gregg clambered out of bed. Naked as the coming

dawn. She grabbed a dressing gown, wrapping it around herself as she hurried to her husband's side.

'Barry.' She prodded him. 'C'mon, Barry. Wake up.'

Nothing. 'Shit.' She went to the window. Pushed it wide open. Fresh air tumbled in, but it was still hard to breathe for the gas.

'Upstairs windows. Not alarmed.'

McLean understood. He went into the front room and opened the window. The street was busier now; three squad cars and a van bearing the logo of one of the gas companies. Of Grumpy Bob there was no sign, which either meant he'd found some tea or he was organizing a quiet evacuation. Back in the master bedroom, Gregg was still kneeling beside her husband. She looked up, tears of panic in her eyes.

'Won't wake up.'

McLean didn't waste any time, just pulled the man up over his shoulder, the way they'd taught him all those years ago in fire training.

'Out.'

Walking downstairs was like sinking into foetid water. The air thickened with gas as they went, and Barry grew heavier with each step. At the bottom, Gregg headed for the front door.

'Alarmed?' McLean managed to ask. Gregg turned and stared at him until the implications clicked together.

'How'd you get in?'

'Loo.'

She nodded, hurried past. McLean staggered to follow. It seemed the easiest thing in the world just to sink to the ground and fall asleep. Barry was a heavy weight about his shoulders, but he was also an obligation. A life threatened for no good reason but spite.

By the time he reached the window, Gregg was already outside. Faces swam in and out of his vision as McLean passed the comatose Barry out. Hands grabbed at him, voices saying something about urgency? A need to get moving before something. Some time? He couldn't really be sure, even as he realized he was outside, gulping down breaths of fresh air. Then the hands were all around him, pulling him away, forcing tired legs to walk, run. Car engines roared, wheels spinning as they backed up the road, anxious to get away from something, though he couldn't immediately remember what. A noise. Was that Grumpy Bob shouting at him? Something about the time, a central heating boiler, a gas main stuck, a leak.

For the second time that night McLean felt himself hit by the massive, body-shaped fist of an explosion. The hard tarmac pavement rushed up to welcome him, and as the wind was driven from his lungs he couldn't help thinking there'd be the devil to pay.

59

'What the fuck are you doing here?'

Dawn had painted the sky pink and grey by the time McLean made it out of the hospital. His suit was ruined, his face and hands cut and bruised, but he was alive. DC Gregg's husband was expected to make a full recovery, too, which was more than could be said for their two goldfish. For some reason Gregg seemed to be more upset about their demise than the loss of her house. McLean had thoughts of home and soaking in a long, hot bath, perhaps getting a bit of sleep before going in to the station around noon. What he hadn't expected was to be accosted outside the hospital reception area by Detective Superintendent Duguid.

'And a very good morning to you too, sir.' McLean thought he was in a bit of a sorry state, but it was nothing compared to Duguid. Someone had set about his face with a crowbar, or at least it looked that way. His eyes were black and puffy, nose clearly broken. The bandage around his head suggested that he had received some medical attention. That and the sling supporting one arm. The other hand held a lighted cigarette, smoke coiling upwards in little jagged whirls. He was shaking, though for once not because of barely controlled rage.

'Christ. What happened to you?'

Duguid eyed McLean with his usual suspicion, made worse by the swelling around his face. 'Could ask the same of you.'

'Been a bit of a rough night.'

'Way I heard it you were hobnobbing with that Saifre woman. Not rich enough you have to go chasing that kind of tail?'

McLean almost laughed. 'Sometimes, sir, you get it so spectacularly wrong it's funny.'

'Do I look like I'm fucking laughing?'

'No. You look like you've been in a car crash.'

Duguid scowled, or something close to a scowl. 'Not far off. Fucking car-jackers boxed me in. Two Transits. Bottom of the London Road. Half a dozen of the foreign bastards.'

'And you tried to fight them off?'

'They were going to steal my fucking car.' Duguid took a long drag from his cigarette, hand shaking so much the ash tumbled to the icy ground. McLean wondered if it was just a coincidence that his boss had been attacked on the same night that half of CID seemed to have been targeted. He didn't really believe in coincidences. Not any more.

'So what happened to you, then?' Duguid flicked his used dog-end into a nearby bush. 'Come to blows with your new girlfriend already?'

McLean almost told him then exactly what he thought about Mrs Saifre and exactly who he was coming to the conclusion she was. Almost. He was tired and hurt and his brain wasn't working properly, otherwise his sense of

439

self-preservation would have stopped him even thinking about offering up such a ludicrous idea.

'I was out at Rosskettle Hospital. There was a fire, then an explosion. DC MacBride's still in there.' He flicked his head back at the hospital as if Duguid wouldn't know what he was referring to. 'I got off lighter than him. Better than DC Gregg, too. She's going to be looking for a new house.'

Duguid's face dropped as McLean listed the night's disasters. He skipped the bit about Grumpy Bob's bath; no need to confuse matters. Still slightly addled from his beating, or maybe just not caring enough, Duguid didn't ask what the two of them had been doing in Gregg's street at four in the morning.

'Jesus, when you poke the hornet's nest you poke it good, aye?' The detective superintendent pinched the bridge of his nose, then winced as he remembered it was broken.

'You think this is all my fault?'

'Isn't it always, McLean? When you get down to it?' Duguid stared at him, his piggy little eyes made even more accusing by his swollen face. 'You just don't know when to stop. It can be useful sometimes, but fuck me, it's irritating too.'

'You wanted justice. For Weatherly's girls.'

'Aye, I did at that. And two fingers to the high heidyins as wanted it all covered up nice and quiet. Fat lot of good it did me, too.' Duguid limped back towards the hospital door, turned stiffly before going back inside as if to say something else. Then just shook his head one more time and was gone.

*

The taxi dropped him at the bottom of the drive. McLean thought it a bit odd that the driver didn't seem inclined to take him to the front door, but it wasn't far to walk. He paid his fare and then watched as the car disappeared around the corner in a cold haze of exhaust. He was dog-tired, felt filthy, and his suit needed to go in the bin. Shoes too, probably. Still, the day had dawned cloudless for the first time in days, a weak sun just starting to paint the tops of the taller buildings gold. He was still alive, despite it all, and that had to be a good thing.

He noticed the first cat sitting on the wall that ran along the front of the property, separating his garden from the street. Not that unusual perhaps; there were plenty of cats around here; some feral, some loved and fed and watered. He even recognized some of the regulars, but not this one.

The next cat sat in the middle of the driveway, staring at him in that way cats do. This was more puzzling. As far as he knew, Mrs McCutcheon's cat had taken less than a week to establish herself as owner of this particular patch of the city, and few others dared venture into her territory. Yet this one was sitting as calm as you like. It didn't even run off as he walked past it.

There was another cat by the front door, and two more on the lawn. They all stared at him like Stepford wives, heads swivelling silently as he slowed. Looking up he saw more in the trees. It was midwinter, never a time for much birdsong, but the silence hanging over the garden was ominous. And yet instead of fear, he felt only an odd comfort in the feline army surrounding him. He laughed out loud at the thought: a feline army. Standing guard around his home and protecting him from the evil that had almost certainly been trying to get in.

Mrs McCutcheon's cat was sitting in the middle of the kitchen table. It, she, looked at him warily, then went back to cleaning herself. He reached out, scratched her behind the ears until she started to purr.

'Looks like I owe you,' he said, then turned to peer back out the door. 'I just hope they don't all want to be fed.'

60

Bathed, shaved, wearing clean clothes and having drunk enough coffee to wake the dead, McLean locked up the house and walked back down to the street, half an eye out for the cats that still watched him from all around. It wasn't far to where he was going, and Shanks's pony was pretty much the only option he had right now.

The sun had climbed about as far into the southern sky as it was going to manage at this time of year. It was weak against a thin blue sky, but it lit the snow-capped Pentlands and Blackford Hill, Salisbury Crags and Arthur's Seat. The cold air did its best to be fresh, not filled with the normal city fug. It was sweet to his lungs anyway, so long abused with gas and fire and brimstone.

It wasn't a long walk to the house. The Rolls-Royce stood by the stone steps leading up to the front door. This was wide open, heat tumbling out of the hallway like an escaping animal. McLean knocked on the door jamb, poked his head in.

'Anyone home?'

No one answered, so he stepped inside. He tried to remember his previous visit, walked across to the door he thought led into the living room.

'Tony. What a pleasant surprise.'

She emerged from the shadows at the far end of the hallway. As the light played across her face she appeared first old and haggard, her hair streaked with grey. Then the image shifted and he saw the same perfectly presented woman he'd taken out to an expensive restaurant just a dozen or so hours earlier.

'Mrs Saifre.'

'Oh, I do wish you'd call me Jane Louise. All my friends do.'

'We all wish for things we can't have. Karl about?'

'Karl?' Mrs Saifre seemed momentarily confused. 'Oh, Karl. No, he left.'

'Left? You sacked him?'

'Something like that, yes.'

'Have you heard about Rosskettle?'

'I have, yes. Terrible news. John Brooks came round first thing. No one was hurt, I'm told.'

John, not Detective Chief Inspector. McLean wondered if his boss knew what he'd got himself into.

'Your Range Rover was there, at the scene.'

'My . . . ?' Mrs Saifre clutched a theatrical hand to her breast. Then let out a little laugh. 'And you think . . . Oh, my, Tony. They told me you had an imagination.'

'I don't think anything, Mrs Saifre. I gather the facts first, then try to make sense of them. It's not always as straightforward as you might imagine. So perhaps you could explain why your Range Rover was parked up at Rosskettle just before it burned down? And why it had a muddy shovel and a body bag in the back?'

Mrs Saifre smiled, but there was no mirth in it. Rather it was the smile of a predator knowing it's going to feed soon, and well. 'We left the Range Rover yesterday morning because it broke down. I was there to see how your forensic friends were getting on. Had to wait almost an hour for the Rolls to come and pick me up. One of the reasons why Karl's no longer in my employ.'

'And the body bag?'

'That you'd have to ask Karl. The cars were his responsibility.'

'That would be Karl who you just sacked. And I don't suppose you've any idea where he is right now.'

'He lived here, in the servants' quarters. No idea where he went.' Mrs Saifre wandered across the hall to a sideboard. Several crystal decanters sat on a silver tray and she took her time un-stoppering one after the other, sniffing the contents before finally pouring a large measure of something amber and expensive into a glass.

'Dram?' she asked.

'Thanks, but I'm on duty.'

'Really? After the night you just had? I'd have thought they'd give you a little time off.' Mrs Saifre took a drink, leaned back against the sideboard.

'What are you going to do with the hospital site now?'

'Goodness me, am I under interrogation?' She pushed away from the sideboard and walked slowly across the room towards him, hips swaying provocatively. Without thinking, McLean slid his hand into his pocket, felt the thin slip of card tingling under his fingertips. Emma's postcard, he'd picked it up off the kitchen table just before leaving. His anchor to reality. Or at least a kind of reality.

'What are you suggesting? That I ordered Karl to bury Andrew out there at his favourite spot?'

'It's a possibility.'

445

'It's ridiculous, and you know it.'

'Well, we have your car and forensics will prove Weatherly's body was in the back of it. There's only your word you knew nothing about that.'

'Am I being arrested? Will you put me in handcuffs, Tony?' Glass in one hand, Mrs Saifre put her arms out, wrists together in mock submission. She gave up when it became clear he wasn't going to play. Slumped down into the nearby sofa.

'Look, I've no idea what my staff get up to half of the time. Andrew was my business partner, yes. But I work mostly out of the US these days. This is the first time I've been back in Edinburgh in almost a decade. If you want to know what's happening to the hospital site or where Karl might have gone after I sacked him, then you really need to talk to Jennifer. She was Andrew's mistress, after all.'

'You do know that Miss Denton is in hospital, don't you? She had a stroke. Not expected to regain consciousness.'

'Oh dear. Poor thing. I rather liked her.' Mrs Saifre put down her whisky glass and stood up again, stretching like a cat. She had a smell about her, an allure that even McLean couldn't deny. She was exquisitely made up, and yet somehow managed to appear tousled and vulnerable. She fixed him with hungry eyes, stepped closer than was really necessary.

'What did you really come here to see me about, Tony?' She reached out and took his right hand. His left was still in the pocket of his jacket, the thin slip of card between two fingers.

'I know who you are. What you are.'

'You do?' Mrs Saifre raised her hand to her lips, taking his with it. She kissed the back of his fingers ever so lightly, warmth spreading right through him with each slow touch. When she released it, his arm took far longer to sink back down to his side than gravity would have liked.

'Yes. I do.' McLean stood his ground as she reached up and stroked his cheek with the backs of her nails. The small animal deep inside him was screaming run, hide, get away. Only the thin card between his fingers gave him the strength to stay put.

'Then you're either very brave,' Mrs Saifre said. 'Or else very stupid.'

'Can I be both?'

She laughed, and far away a forest burned to the ground. 'This! This is why I like you, Tony!' She spun away like a little girl, pirouetting around the table before coming back to a standstill, close again.

'We should be together, you and I. We could do such great things.'

'Like driving a man to murder his children? What did you have on him? The bodies out at the hospital? Were you going to tell the world about his terrible secret?'

'I don't know what you're talking about.' Mrs Saifre pouted, and McLean knew she was lying.

'I don't think you meant for us to recover the Range Rover. That was your mistake. It was supposed to be destroyed in the fire. Convenient, too, that Karl should disappear. Did you arrange that like you arranged to have the other buildings razed, all evidence of your complicity

447

carted off site and destroyed? Everything pointing neatly back to Weatherly.'

Mrs Saifre stepped close again, and McLean finally saw the dance she was doing. She took his free hand again, her touch uncomfortably warm. 'You've got me all wrong, Tony. I helped Andrew, I really did. Made him what he was. I had nothing to do with his downfall. How could I?'

'Don't worry. I can't prove anything. Not trying to trick a confession out of you.' McLean extracted his hand from her grasp. 'And anyway, you'd just buy your way out of any trouble. You've got the money, the influence. I can't beat that.'

'Then come with me.' This time Mrs Saifre's eyes seemed to light up with excitement. 'With me at your side you could be anything. Chief Constable? First Minister? How about the first President of an independent Scotland?'

And there it was. The offer. The temptation. McLean studied Mrs Saifre's face, looking for any sign that she was joking. She was so hard to read, so unpredictable. That, of course, was her nature. This might have been some elaborate joke, but something told him it was true. If he said yes, if he surrendered to her will, then she would make it all happen. He could have fame and power and a beautiful woman at his side, in his bed. But more, he could use that fame and power to do good works. Others had, in her name, in the past. They were precious few in number, but they had existed.

The card in his pocket felt like it was vibrating between his finger and thumb as he stared into those black, bottomless eyes. So easy to lose yourself in them, so inviting to dive into that warm pit of sensual pleasure and carelessness.

Then he remembered another pair of eyes. Cold, dead, terrified and mad. Andrew Weatherly had stopped being useful to this creature, and look what had happened to him.

'Is that what you promised Weatherly? And all he had to do was give you his soul?'

'A soul's such an overrated thing. You'll hardly miss it when it's gone.' Mrs Saifre reached out to touch his face again. Slowly, gently, she pulled him towards her as she stretched her neck upwards for a kiss. McLean could fool himself and say he'd let her get that close on purpose. Truth was she had sneaked in under his guard. He was trapped, helpless as he watched those lips part, red as burning coals. Her glistening tongue darted over sparkling white, pointed teeth, moistening them with saliva that would burn whatever it touched. Her grip was insistent, bending him down towards her as she let out a low, hissing 'yes'.

But his hand still gripped the postcard. He could feel the shiny side with its picture of ruins and flowers, and there the other side, the words Emma had written to him. The little row of Xs.

'No. I don't think so.' He pulled away, surprised at how easy it was to do. Mrs Saifre stared at him, stunned, her hand motionless, still holding the air where his chin had been.

'Why?' she asked eventually.

'I'm already spoken for.' McLean let go of the

449

postcard, took his hand out of his pocket and straightened his coat. 'Goodbye, Mrs Saifre. I want you to leave now. Go back to wherever it was you came from. And don't ever threaten my friends again.'

He left her there, staring at him in bewilderment. Outside, the thin sun warmed his face as McLean closed his eyes and took a deep breath. Sweet air filled his lungs. He stood for a moment, just enjoying the fact that he was alive. Then he shoved his hands back in his pockets, dipped his head against the chill and headed off home.

'Seems there were some big old oil tanks in the basement, fed the boilers for the central heating. Five of the buggers. Must've been ancient; you can't have anything like that these days. A couple thousand litres in the bottom of each, turned to gas with the heat.'

Rossketle Hospital didn't look all that good in the cold light of day. There were a couple of places where the walls made it up to the second floor, but not many. Mostly it was a pile of rubble, steaming in the morning sun. Deep underground the fires were still burning, apparently.

'Not going to get much in the way of evidence out of there.' McLean stood alongside the chief fire officer, a good distance away from the mess. Two days had passed since the fire and explosions, but one of the fire engines was still there, its wheels stuck to the tarmac by the heat. From this side it looked almost normal, but he'd been around the other side earlier and knew just how hot things must have been.

'Not going to get much of anything. Clean-up's gonnae cost a bob or two and all.'

'Aye, well I'm sure that'll be taken care of.'

'By the cooncil, no doubt.' The chief fire officer spat at the ground as if the injustice tasted foul in his mouth.

McLean shook his head. 'Polluter pays. This belongs to Weatherly Asset Management. They've plenty of money. Them or their insurance company. Then I guess someone'll build houses on the site.'

'That'll be something to see them try. That hole goes doon a long way. And there's mine workings and all manner of shite underneath. All smouldering away. Might keep burning for years.' The chief fire officer spat again. 'Still, the hoosies'll be warm, aye?'

McLean took an involuntary step back as one of the walls collapsed in on itself with a cascade of sparks and a low rumble he felt in the pit of his stomach. They were more than far enough away to be safe, but the memory of the fire and explosions was still fresh. Andrew Weatherly had opened up a gaping maw here, its gullet leading straight to hell, and the creature that was Mrs Saifre had crawled out. Together they had woven something terrible, and now it was fraying at the edges. At least that was the irrational explanation; a rational one was still a work in progress.

He turned away from the scene, saw the wreck of his car off a ways. He wondered if he could get someone to cart the lump of stone back to his house as a memento. Perhaps put it in the middle of the lawn for the cats to sun themselves on. He'd not had the car long, but he felt a strange nostalgia for it. Time to go looking for something else.

'I'm not an old-age pensioner, sir. Can manage by myself.'

She batted away the hand that he'd held out to steady her, but the way DS Ritchie hobbled down the corridor, pausing every ten short paces or so to cough, gave the lie to her claim. McLean indulged her though, taking the time needed for her to leave the hospital under her own steam. She'd been to hell and back, after all. It was the least he could do.

'MacBride was going to tag along too, but he's had to go and have his stitches out. Going to have quite a scar once it's all healed.'

Ritchie gave him a withering stare. 'I don't need your help or his, sir. I've got this.'

Considering how close she'd come to dying, McLean wasn't about to argue. Or point out his role in her recovery. He wasn't really sure whether the drink of holy water he'd given her had done anything. It could have been the antivirals, after all.

They made it outside, and Ritchie stood a little straighter as the sun played on her face. She looked horribly thin, her hair lank and greasy, her eyes sunk deep in their sockets. Rest was what the doctor had ordered, but McLean couldn't help thinking plenty of wholesome food was in order as well. Perhaps he could take her to Chez Innes, except that he'd have to take the whole team then, and probably DC Gregg's husband as well. And that would be an expensive outing indeed.

'Where's the car?' Ritchie asked after a while, looking in the direction of the car park.

'Last I heard it had been towed to a scrappy in Loanhead.'

Ritchie frowned at him. 'You crashed it? But you only just got it.'

'I didn't crash it. It got flattened by a falling door lintel.' McLean waved over the taxi that had been waiting for him, running up a horrendous bill on the meter all the while. Ritchie looked at him in puzzlement, then her face broke into a grin.

'I'm not joking.' McLean opened the door. She let herself be helped into her seat, then he climbed in after her, gave the taxi driver the address. All the while Ritchie was smiling, which suited her much better than the frown.

'It's really broken?' she asked after a while.

'Squashed flat. Lucky I wasn't inside it at the time.'

'You'll get another one, though? I liked that car.'

McLean assured her that he would be getting another car, even though he had no idea when he'd have time to look for one.

'She went after us all, didn't she?' Ritchie said as the taxi eased itself into the traffic headed towards the city centre.

'Reckon so. Grumpy Bob, Stuart, even Sandy Gregg – and she's hardly been on the team a month.' McLean had a sudden mental image of DC Gregg holding her own with Mrs Saifre at the hospital. 'Stood up to her, though.'

'Heard old Dagwood got it in the neck too.'

'Car-jacked. Idiot would've been fine if he hadn't tried to fight back. Shook him up that bad he's talking about early retirement.'

'Bloody hell. And Christmas just been.' Ritchie coughed a little in her excitement at the news, but it was nothing like the lung shredding of before.

'Don't get too excited. He's named Brooks as his successor.'

'Can he do that?'

'Probably not, but I can't see them promoting anyone else.'

'That means there'll be a chief inspector post going, though.' Ritchie looked at him with a sly twinkle in her eye. McLean held up his hands in protest.

'Not me. Bad enough having to deal with you lot on a daily basis.'

'True. You never struck me as the ambitious type.' Ritchie leaned back against the headrest, closed her eyes. 'Still, if they give it to Spence then there's an inspector post open. Interesting.'

McLean watched her as she fell asleep, head lolling in time to the movement of the car. She wouldn't get Spence's DI post. Not because she didn't deserve it, and neither because he'd rather not lose her as a sergeant. He knew it was going to take her months to get over the mysterious illness that had laid her low. That alone would keep her out of the running for promotion any time soon. But more than that, she had long ago taken sides, chosen to work with him. Sad, but true, that would hold her back far more than anything else she ever did with her career.

'We ever going to find out who killed him?'

William 'Billbo' Beaumont might have fallen through the safety net, but his old regiment were doing their best to make it up to him with a decent funeral. The Old Kirk at Penicuik had been packed with uniforms singing old favourite hymns with gusto, and a perfectly turned-out honour guard had carried the coffin to the waiting hearse, its final destination a plot in a military graveyard alongside the remains of some of his former platoon members. Outside the kirk, McLean and Grumpy Bob stood to one side, not wanting to get in the way of the soldiers. Standing in the lee of the old stone building kept them out of the worst of the wind, too.

'It was the fall that killed him, Bob.' McLean shuffled his feet against the cold seeping in through his shoes. 'But I know what you mean. Know who it was, too.'

'Weatherly again?' Grumpy Bob shook his head. 'Don't you think you're pinning just a bit too much on him?'

'Oh, I know I can't prove it, Bob. And there's bugger all could be done about it even if I could. But he did it. Well, he set out to do it, like he'd done maybe half a dozen of the bodies we found out there. One every few years.'

'And the other bodies? Some of them go back centuries.'

'That's the point though, isn't it? Weatherly wasn't the first. Just the most recent. He made a deal and it brought him his fortune. But our man Billbo here mucked it all up. Escaped before he could be sacrificed. That's when it all went wrong.'

Grumpy Bob let out a low whistle. 'A deal with the devil.'

'The devil? Maybe. I don't know.' McLean shivered, though that might have been from the cold. A fresh north-easterly wind was bringing arctic air in from Scandinavia. It had little respect for things like clothes and skin. He remembered his last meeting with Mrs Saifre, the temptations she'd put in his way, the subtle power of her seduction. The things that had corrupted Weatherly so completely were of no interest to him; the influence, the wealth, the excess. But she'd played him differently, a dance that suggested he might be able to control her, use her to more noble ends. And he'd been tempted, he had to admit it.

'Poor sod was just in the wrong place at the wrong time, then.' Grumpy Bob nodded in the direction of the hearse as it pulled away from the kerb, vapour spiralling from the exhaust like playful ghosts in the frigid air.

'Could be, Bob. It usually is.' McLean watched as Lieutenant Colonel Bottomley helped Gordon Johnson into a waiting car, then climbed in beside him. It pulled away from the kerb in slow pursuit of the hearse, and for a moment he saw the ex-soldier clearly, sitting ramrod-straight, chin up. Gordy had been convinced the dark angels were coming for him, that his friend Billbo had gone to his rescue and ended up being the one taken. A selfless, heroic act to break the cycle of evil.

'Either that, or he was exactly where he was supposed to be.'

He'd grown accustomed to the cats filling his garden and prowling the streets around the house. They never came in, apart from Mrs McCutcheon's cat, of course. She was even more full of herself if that was possible, preening around the house with her tail up, sitting in the middle of the kitchen table as if she were the lady of the manor, sleeping curled up at the end of his bed.

McLean had tried leaving some food out for his new-found glaring of cats, but by and large they disdained his offers. Neither would they approach him for a scratch behind the ears. They were just there, watching – and, he couldn't help thinking, protecting him.

They didn't stop the postman, he was pleased to see.

And the takeaway delivery service seemed unaffected. He'd not seen or heard from Mrs Saifre since their interrupted kiss a couple of weeks earlier, though. As the cold, bright February sun had given way to waves of March rain, melting the snow and ice, turning the ground to mud, he worried that they might leave, but still the cats maintained their vigil. It was oddly comforting. He'd never really thought of himself as an animal person, certainly not a great cat lover. He'd taken Mrs McCutcheon's cat in out of a sense of responsibility, and she had repaid him time and time again.

Only this time she'd let him down, it would seem. She was nowhere to be seen, and there in the middle of the kitchen table, propped up against the pepper grinder, was a slim brown A4 envelope. McLean dumped his handful of case notes and bag of curry down on a chair with a sigh, picked up the envelope and slipped it open.

Inside, a half-dozen photographs were held together with a paper clip, a torn-off strip of paper wedged in at the top of the pile with a single handwritten word.

Thanks.

He leafed through the photographs, seeing first an image of Mrs Saifre climbing into her Rolls-Royce outside the house that had once belonged to Gavin Spenser. Another photograph showed the car leaving, a third it pulling up beside a private jet on an airfield somewhere. Two more photographs were Mrs Saifre climbing aboard and the plane taking off; not hard to work out the narrative he was being shown. And then the final image. The gates to the house, closed as they had been when he'd walked over there after the night everything had almost gone to hell. Only this time there was a big sign attached to one of the gateposts, the logo of one of the city's more exclusive solicitors and the words For Sale in big blue letters.

'Gone,' McLean said to the empty kitchen. 'But I don't suppose for ever.'

He left the photographs on the table, went to the front door and scooped up the day's post. It was mostly junk, still a couple of catalogues for his grandmother, and one small tatty postcard. He knew even before reading it who it had come from. Emma always chose pictures of ancient ruins, and she managed to find places even he had never heard of. This one came from somewhere in Montenegro, an old monastery perched on a clifftop over sweeping Mediterranean views. It looked like it had probably been printed in Communist times and had been battered about during its journey to Scotland. He flipped it over to read the words.

Getting there slowly. Two sad souls from this place. They cried when they left, like losing old friends. Heading eastwards. It gets harder each time. Missing you. E.

There were four large Xs under the E, and nothing else. McLean took the pile of post back to the kitchen, dumped the junk straight in the recycling bin. He went to the fridge and found himself a beer, then scooped his rice and curry out on to a plate, leaving enough of both for Mrs McCutcheon's cat when she deigned to make an appearance. Finally he shuffled the photographs back into the envelope, then propped the postcard against the pepper grinder so that he could see Emma's words to him while he ate.

Acknowledgements

Much has happened in the time between writing *The Hangman's Song* and this book. For one thing, the many separate police regions in Scotland have all been merged into one – the inspirationally named Police Scotland. My stories may have the occasional thing that goes bump in the night in them, but they are set in a reasonable facsimile of the here and now, and that needs to be reflected in the way Tony McLean's job has changed.

I am hugely indebted to Kaye Norman, who voluntarily condensed down the mountains of documentation on the change into something I could understand. David Erskine has been of invaluable help too, and to both of them I offer a heartfelt thanks.

Which is not to say that the Police Scotland in my books is a perfect example of how the real Police Scotland works. These are stories – fiction – and I have frequently changed things to suit the needs of the book. That's my excuse when I get something wrong, and I'm sticking to it.

Of course, none of this would have happened without my agent, the indefatigable Juliet Mushens. Or without the great team at Penguin: Alex, Bea, Katya, Tim, Charlotte and all the rest. A big thank you to you all, and to my early-draft readers, Heather Bain, Keir Allen and my brother, Duncan.

And to Barbara, thanks for being there.

The **Sunday Times** bestsellin

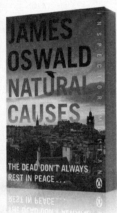

*'His writing is in a class above
most in this genre'*

DAILY EXPRESS

nspector **McLean** series

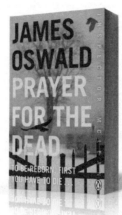

'Oswald is among the leaders in the new
batch of excellent Scottish crime writers'

DAILY MAIL

He just wanted a decent book to read ...

Not too much to ask, is it? It was in 1935 when Allen Lane, Managing Director of Bodley Head Publishers, stood on a platform at Exeter railway station looking for something good to read on his journey back to London. His choice was limited to popular magazines and poor-quality paperbacks – the same choice faced every day by the vast majority of readers, few of whom could afford hardbacks. Lane's disappointment and subsequent anger at the range of books generally available led him to found a company – and change the world.

'We believed in the existence in this country of a vast reading public for intelligent books at a low price, and staked everything on it'
Sir Allen Lane, 1902–1970, founder of Penguin Books

The quality paperback had arrived – and not just in bookshops. Lane was adamant that his Penguins should appear in chain stores and tobacconists, and should cost no more than a packet of cigarettes.

Reading habits (and cigarette prices) have changed since 1935, but Penguin still believes in publishing the best books for everybody to enjoy. We still believe that good design costs no more than bad design, and we still believe that quality books published passionately and responsibly make the world a better place.

So wherever you see the little bird – whether it's on a piece of prize-winning literary fiction or a celebrity autobiography, political tour de force or historical masterpiece, a serial-killer thriller, reference book, world classic or a piece of pure escapism – you can bet that it represents the very best that the genre has to offer.

Whatever you like to read – trust Penguin.